CONSPIRATORS' KINGDOM

Elyse Thomson

Two Laurels Press

Content Warnings

For my readers who prefer not to read the content warnings, please feel free to skip this section and dive right in.

For my readers who would prefer a list of content warnings before proceeding, I've provided what I hope to be a fairly substantive list below.

Content Warnings: death, violence, blood and gore, maiming, forced marriage, torture, kidnapping, swearing, alcoholism, sexism, classism, consensual on-page sex.

Glossary

<u>Royal Titles in the Empire of Mages</u>

Emperor/Empress: Supreme rulers of the Empire. Addressed as Your Majesty.

<u>Noble Titles in the Empire of Mages in Descending Order of Power:</u>

Magister: Male governor of an imperial province. Addressed as Your Grace. Plural = Magistri

Magistra: Female governor of an imperial province. Addressed as Your Grace. Plural = Magistrae

Dominus: Son of a magister. Addressed as Your Resplendence. Plural = Domini

Domina: Daughter of a magister. Addressed as Your Resplendence. Plural = Dominae

Illustrus: Landowning nobleman with a significant estate and/or distinguished military service. Plural = Illustri

Illustra: Wife of an illustrus. Rarely, a landowning noblewoman with a significant estate and/or distinguished military service. Plural = Illustrae

Nobilissimus: Son of an illustrus or a minor nobleman with a small estate. Plural = Nobilissimi

Nobilissima: Daughter of an illustrus or wife of a nobilissimus. Rarely, a minor noblewoman with a small estate. Plural = Nobilissimae

<u>Governmental Titles in the Empire of Mages in Descending Order of Influence:</u>

Praetor: The head of the imperial bureaucracy. Answers to the imperial family directly. Directs all administrative officials in the Empire.

Logothete: Minister in charge of a large administrative department (Taxes, Public Works, etc), answers to the praetor directly.

Asekretis: Middling minister assigned to tasks or specific projects by a logothete. Answers to a logothete directly.

Notarios: Lowest ranked bureaucrat, assigned humble tasks by an asekretis. Answers to an asekretis directly.

<u>Military Titles in the Empire of Mages:</u>

Strategos: Top general of the Empire's military forces. Answers to the imperial family directly.

Admiral: Top officer of the Empire's naval forces. Answers to the strategos directly.

<u>Slang in the Empire of Mages:</u>

Elementalist: Elemental magic elitists who discriminate against those without elemental magical gifts (control of fire, water, earth, wind, lightning, darkness or light). They believe theirs is the superior form of magic.

Menial: A mage without an elemental magical gift.

Feral: A derogatory term for beast mages.

<u>Royal and Noble titles in Maat:</u>

King/Queen: Supreme ruler of Maat. Addressed as Your Eternal Serenity. Their primary spouse holds the title of King/Queen and is addressed as Your Most Just.

Royal Consort: Other spouses of the king/queen. Addressed as Your Most Treasured.

Prince/Princess: Child of the previous king/queen, or children of the current king/queen. Addressed as Your Tranquility.

Prince/Princess Consort: Spouse of a prince/princess. Addressed as Your Harmoniousness.

Nomarch: Governor of a nome (province). Addressed as Your Most Fair.

Hatya: Landowning noble of Maat. Addressed as Your Candor.

Governmental and Administrative Titles in Maat:

Vizier: Top governmental official in Maat, answering to the king/queen of Maat.

Overseer: The top governmental or military official in charge of a large department (Tribute, Royal Guards, Border Defence, etc). Answer directly to the vizier. Or the title of an administrator in charge of an important position in a noble household or nome (soldiers, construction, etc).

Minister: A governmental official working directly under the overseer, in charge of a sub-department or large task. Answers directly to the overseer.

First Scribe: The top non-noble official of a nome, answers to the nomarch directly.

Scribe: Of lesser status than a minister, and assigned to a wide array of administrative tasks. Answers directly to a minister or first scribe.

LETHE, THE EMPIRE OF MAGES

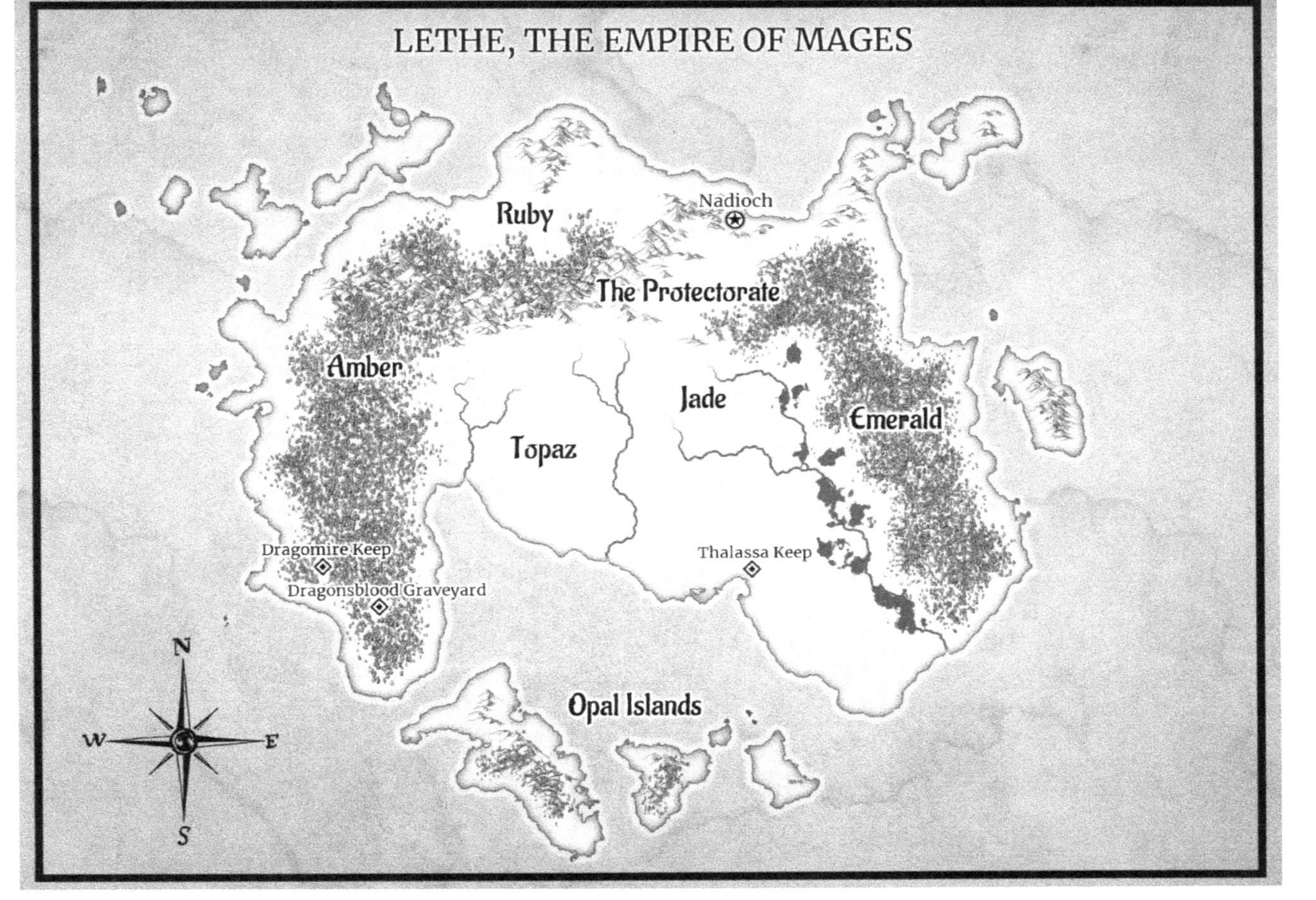

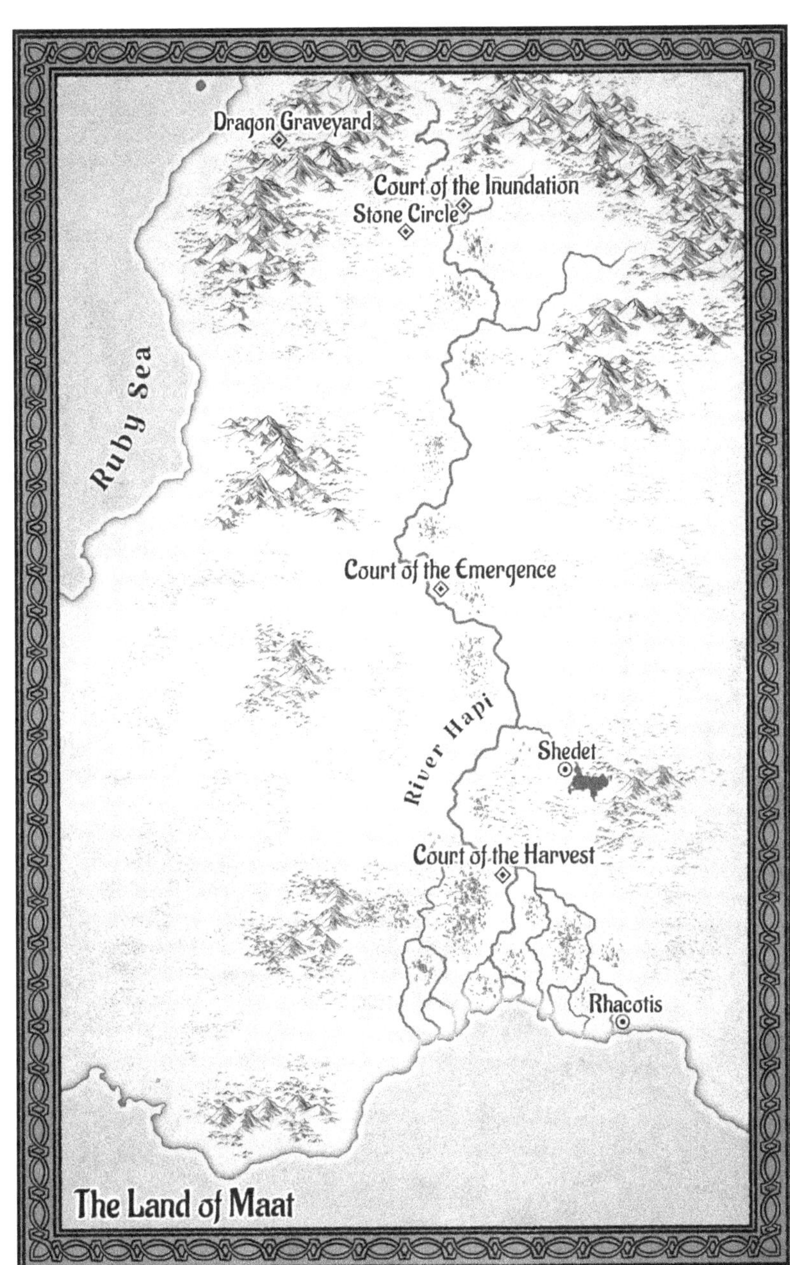

Dragon Graveyard
Court of the Inundation
Stone Circle
Ruby Sea
Court of the Emergence
River Hapi
Shedet
Court of the Harvest
Rhacotis
The Land of Maat

To Sophia,
For all the emotional damage this one caused...
you're welcome.

Chapter 1

Taisiya would have preferred to chew a mouthful of glass shards than to grovel on her knees. After all, grovelling was the purview of wretched supplicants and the powerless. Unfortunately, she found herself among their number through no fault of her own. The actions of her traitor father had landed her family in this unenviable position.

"My offer stands," Vasilisa, her attendant and confidant whispered with a grin, her grey eyes sparkling with mischief.

"Unfortunately, Empress Selene is more useful alive," Taisiya replied, her voice hushed.

In the halls of this palace, nestled deep in the heart of Lethe, the Empire of Mages, even the shadows had ears. Thankfully, the mage at Taisiya's side was adept at both detecting and disposing of spies.

"If you say so." Vasilisa tucked a curl of her pale blonde hair back into its proper place.

A grey-robed servant led the way to the empress' receiving chamber, their steps whisper-soft on the polished marble. The floor mosaics depicted serene flora and fauna, while the tapestries hanging on the walls were equally insipid. When she was at last presented to Empress Selene, Taisiya fixed a pleasant, practised smile on her face. Although they shared the same short stature and amethyst eyes, the empress' dark hair was swept off her face in elaborate braids, her flowing red gown heavily embroidered with gold thread, as jewels the size of her fist dangled from her neck. Next to her, Taisiya, in her modest lavender gown and simple jewellery, looked the pauper. That the empress was her half-sister, and the one who had slain their father, only added to the bitter hatred roiling Taisiya's gut.

"Illustra Taisiya Spark, Your Majesty," the servant announced, bowing deeply.

The new family name grated like sharp nails across an open wound. It was as much an insult as the demotion in title had been. Once, she'd been Domina Taisiya Amethyst, daughter of Magister Grigori Amethyst, the man who had governed the wealthy Amethyst Province. She had been one of the highest-ranking noblewomen in Lethe, descended from kings. Now, she was no one, above only a lowly nobilissima in rank.

Vasilisa and Taisiya curtsied low, hiding blackened hearts behind excellent manners.

"Copper, is it? Have a seat and get on with it." The empress gestured to the cushioned, opulently carved chair opposite her with a careless wave.

'Copper' was the demeaning nickname the empress had used for her while Taisiya had been under the influence of a foul ritual. One her father had used in a treasonous bid to rule free from imperial control. Taisiya prayed for the calmness and self-control not to murder her half-sister. Even after a year, the empress had not bothered to remember her name, preferring instead to refer to her by the colour of her hair.

Taisiya's eyes swept the room, taking in the cacophony of busy, intricate designs slathered over every surface, all in imperial red. Only accents of gold, silver and dark wood broke up the overwhelming hue. She sat opposite the patricidal bitch, Vasilisa standing behind her. Vasilisa tapped her shoulder ever so slightly, but only once. There was someone hidden in the room.

"I'm here to petition on behalf of our family," Taisiya began.

The empress snorted with derision, tossing her book on the ornate table between them.

"Our family? The only good thing our mutual relative ever did for me was die. Try again."

Taisiya tensed. If anyone was so foolish as to touch her in this instant, they would regret it. Unseen, electricity danced across her skin—her mage gift of lightning.

How could she forget that this woman was no ordinary noble? With her mage gift, Selene could create poisons at will, and kill with a touch or breath. She was only a year removed from the unwashed poisons merchant she'd been before marrying the emperor. Many a gossip told tales that the empress despised anyone who pleaded and begged, respecting only those who showed no fear at the prospect of sampling her favourite toxins.

A gamble, then.

"Shall I be frank, Your Majesty?"

"Please. I have better things to do today."

Yes, Taisiya supposed she did. The empress' elaborate coiffure was askew, her lip paint slightly smudged and the book she'd been pretending to read had been upside-down. The emperor, infamously infatuated with his commoner wife, must be hiding somewhere nearby, no doubt in a state of undress. It would explain the indecorous lack of guards or servants in the room. If rumours were to be believed, the royal couple were trying—unsuccessfully—for an heir, an almost impossible feat given that only a poison mage child could survive to term due to the empress' poison magic. Given the rarity of such a conception, it was a near certainty they would be adopting the heir to the throne, a situation Taisiya was depending upon. She would need to consider her words carefully. Unlike his wife, the emperor was no fool and had played the game of politics since he'd been old enough to speak.

"In case you've forgotten, my siblings and I were Father's victims, stripped of our magic and no more than living dolls while under the influence of that foul ritual. As I see it, the only mercy you've extended to us was sparing our now miserable lives. You took everything from us, including our reputations. All of my sisters' suitors have fled, and we are treated as pariahs. I've come because I expect you to take responsibility for the situation you've left us in."

They'd been evicted from their ancestral home, their father's name and image erased from every monument and text, their former titles stripped from them and given to another. Still the taint of treachery clung to them, leaving them part of the nobility, but welcome nowhere. As long as anyone thought the new, volatile empress disfavoured them, they would be treated like a disease, and her family's ambitions would remain fanciful dreams.

"I gave you new noble titles, a modest property, and plenty of coin to last you. Everything else is for you to figure out." The empress shrugged.

Taisiya narrowed her eyes.

"Do not think that the fate of my sisters and I has gone unnoticed by the nobility. That the crown treats innocent victims of traitors as collateral is a dangerous precedent to set. Knowledge of that dark ritual is now trickling through society. Who would dare come forward, were it to be used again, if they know that the fate of a pariah awaits them? If even the empress' kin are but an afterthought, what of those with less lofty relations? If you cannot be persuaded to act with decency, then at least have the foresight to act in self-interest."

The empress scowled but seemed to consider her words. Taisiya's gambit had succeeded. It appeared the rumours about Selene's temperament were true—she preferred hostile, simple truth to fawning flattery.

"What do you want?"

"For my sisters to find matches worthy of their former statuses, specifically among His Majesty's cousins."

"You want us to be one big, cosy, intermarried family? Angling to put your spawn on my throne, dearest sister?"

Taisiya raised a brow. It made good sense for the adopted heir to be a niece or nephew, and there was nothing outwardly sinister about wanting to give the empress a few to choose from. If Taisiya had the ear of the heir in question, that was all for the better.

"Anything less implies you wish to punish us, or that you've deemed us unworthy."

The empress tapped her bejewelled finger against the gleaming wooden arm of her chair as she frowned.

"The lot of you are more trouble than you're worth."

"Be that as it may, we are kin. Our futures will be determined by your favour."

The empress sighed dramatically.

"Gods below, fine." Then she smirked. "But have the praetor make a list these of worthy male creatures for you. I hear it's a hobby of his."

"Then I won't take up any more of your time, Your Majesty." Taisiya stood.

To have the ear of Praetor Nicephorus, Lethe's loftiest bureaucrat, was an unexpected boon she would not allow to go to waste. Though the task of matchmaker was beneath him, Taisiya would not question her good fortune this day. The empress waved her out, forgotten already. Taisiya didn't bother curtsying and left the way she came in. Once in the hall, Vasilisa chuckled softly.

"Your father would be proud."

"Thank you." Taisiya gave her a wicked grin in return.

What the neophyte empress didn't know, what no one outside the surviving women of her family understood, was that Taisiya and her sisters were as much traitors as their late father. Though she was related by blood, Empress Selene hadn't been raised by Grigori Amethyst. She and everyone else had failed to fully appreciate his cunning and vision. With careful scheming, they would take back their ancestral lands from the grasping talons of the empire.

"You need only one plan for success—" Vasilisa began.

"You need a multitude for failure," Taisiya finished.

Dead or not, Grigori Amethyst lived on.

Chapter 2

The provocations had begun piling up as of late. Mereruka reflected on this as yet another avenue supposedly closed to him. He took the rough papyrus note between his deep teal fingers and tore it, slowly, so that the messenger could understand his displeasure. His narrowed, pale yellow eyes met the widening dark brown of the bearer of the bad news. When the rending of the very last fibre ceased ringing in the silent room, the messenger cringed.

"Inform our Eternal Serenity the king that his message has been received and that I will cede my consort to him. Be sure to wish my brother the appropriate congratulations for acquiring yet another concubine."

The royal messenger swallowed and bowed.

"W-would the prince like to write these words himself, or-"

Mereruka snarled, knocking over his chair as he stood, the beaded braids in his long violet hair snapping to and fro with the violent movement.

"I'll excuse myself," the messenger squeaked before he turned tail and ran.

"*Tsk. Tsk. Such a temper.*"

Mereruka raised a brow at the grey tabby cat that slunk around the corner to enter the room.

"Are we alone, Bas?"

The cat turned to smoke before his eyes, shooting up and reforming as a young, dark-haired man with triangular ears, a long tail and a perpetual smirk.

"As alone as any two people can be," Bas replied.

Mereruka nodded towards the open door. Bas reached out a russet-brown hand and pressed the jewel by the doorway. A current of magic slid the heavy stone entrance shut. With only a small window, the room should have been dark, but the lofty ceiling was spelled to replicate the daytime sky. The light above radiated down on the decorative walls, glinting off the jewels embedded in scenes of waterfowl hiding amidst lush greenery and fish swimming through sparkling waters. A neat stack of papyrus scrolls sat by his desk in a rack, waiting for his attention, while many more were perched on racks against the far wall. Mereruka righted his chair, one inlaid with gems and made of precious wood—a rare commodity in arid Maat.

Bas grabbed the nearest chair and sat down with the indolent grace of youth. He trained his bright hazel green eyes on Mereruka, his ears twitching atop his head in anticipation as his sleek tail waved back and forth. Mereruka couldn't resist the temptation to tease him. He sighed.

"You used to be so cute as a kitten. What happened?"

Bas' face heated with embarrassment.

"Shut up, you old geezer."

"I still remember when you used to play with the rushes until you fell asleep."

Bas hissed a warning.

"You and your stupid memories! When are you going to tell me about the plan?"

"I always knew where you were, with that little gold bell necklace. How you pranced when you first got it, all puffed up with pride."

With a sudden burst of speed, Bas leapt over the desk between them, his claws out, ready to sink them into the fae. Mereruka swept to his feet, grabbed Bas' wrists and used his momentum to throw him onto the cool stone floor with a dull thud.

"Better luck next decade, Bas. You'll need to rein in your temper if you're going to be my right hand."

Bas winced but accepted Mereruka's outstretched hand. Chastised, the shapeshifter trudged back to his chair.

"Well? Why isn't The Prince of Dreams angry that his latest fiancée got snatched up by the king?"

It was a moniker he hadn't chosen for himself, but he wholeheartedly embraced it. He was exceptionally gifted with magic, a keen mind, and a reputation for fairness in his bargains. Mereruka made the dreams of others come true, for a price, and desire was a very lucrative business. He'd needed the connections it gave him. Khety refused to give Mereruka any political or governmental role outside ruling the nome of Rhacotis, unlike the rest of his siblings.

"Because Hemetre and I made a deal: ten years of her life in exchange for marrying the king."

"Really?" Bas tilted his head.

Mereruka nodded sagely as he sat back in his chair.

"You'll find that people desire most what they think someone else possesses exclusively. Hemetre was incensed at being passed over as a concubine several years ago. His Eternal Serenity fears my growing influence and was bound to mistake my engagement to Hemetre as a move to grow my political clout, so he took it, and her, from me. The messenger will no doubt tell tales of my fury, which will delight my eldest brother. Bargain concluded."

"Why bother? Haven't you lost face?"

Mereruka shrugged.

"But what of the king?"

"Isn't he just strutting about, crowing over taking your third fiancée out from under you? He even makes you tithe what you gain from your personal bargains. No one else is subject to that kind of indignity," Bas said.

"Yes, and in the process, proclaiming loudly that he fears my power. Every indignity is more proof of his growing tyranny. Every action he takes to stymy me makes the nobles grow restless, worrying that it'll be their daughters, their bargained gains, their wealth he'll take next. After all, if he's willing to do it to his youngest brother, a man fifth in the line of succession from the throne, who else will he deem a threat? One day soon, he'll go too far, even for the servile nobles of Maat. On that day, I'll be ready to strike him down and take what is mine. If I'm lucky, I'll have their applause when I do it."

Bas nodded and then scowled.

"Sometimes I think you fae are born loving your schemes and bargains more than your own flesh and blood."

Mereruka laughed. The shapeshifter wasn't far off the mark; not for the royal family of Maat, at least. He had six siblings and would happily discard them all for the chance to rule.

"Never fear a temporary loss of face, Bas. Provided you live, there will always be another chance to regain it. We play the long game. In another century, this slight will be long forgotten."

Especially if regaining face included disposing of those who had done the humiliating, as Mereruka so hoped.

Bas' ears twitched as he sat up with attention. In a moment he was smoke, and the next a juvenile cat was prowling about. The bell to his room chimed. Another messenger? Mereruka waved his hand, opening the door with a thread of magic.

The messenger that darkened his doorway wore the colours of the palace and the garb of a soldier. He was not attended by any of Mereruka's staff. Whatever this was, it boded ill.

"Prince Mereruka, I bring orders from His Eternal Serenity the King."

The messenger marched forward and placed a scroll before him, sealed with the king's own cartouche. Then he stood, back straight, waiting.

"Was there something else?" Mereruka raised a violet brow.

"You'll know when you read the letter."

Bas hissed at the soldier, whose eyes flicked over the cat before dismissing him. So few fae expected shifters in their animal forms to be part of a noble household. Foolish, but useful. But for a mere soldier to order a prince about... it made his skin crawl. Mereruka kept a bored look on his face as he unfurled the scroll. As he read it, he was glad that his teal colouring, unlike the many shades of clay that shapeshifters and witches were born with, allowed him to disguise the fact that all the blood had just drained from his face. In his hands were orders to make permanent ties with a land everyone—in the whole of Oblivion—had avoided for thousands of years. Apparently, the king had decided to rectify the slights of stealing his previous fiancées by ordering him to find a new one... among the inhabitants of the Cursed Continent.

"This is a joke in very poor taste, even for His Eternal Serenity," Mereruka said as he placed the scroll on his desk.

Bas leapt up onto the desk and perused the letter as he pretended to clean his paw.

"I assure you, the king is quite serious. An envoy arrived a few days ago, requesting diplomatic and trade relations. A ship is already provisioned. You're to act in the king's stead."

In that moment, everything Mereruka had ever built, schemed and secretly shed blood over crumbled around him. What did it matter that he'd accrued hundreds of extra years of life through meticulous bargaining if he was doomed to spend what remained of it far from Maat? What use were his connections, his carefully curated allies, his army of spies and soldiers, if none of them had warned him of, or were capable of saving him from, this fate? Mereruka eyed the soldier and considered his limited options. Killing the messenger was the obvious ploy, but if he'd barged his way into Mereruka's palace, there was no doubt a small army awaiting such a response. Open conflict with the royal guard, while unprepared? Suicide. Mereruka had been outplayed. He could only hope he would have the chance to repay the favour.

"Is this one of those chances? Because it looks a lot like a death sentence," Bas drawled, using mind-speak to question Mereruka without the soldier knowing.

Bas was not wrong. It seemed the inhabitants of the Cursed Continent were not content to keep their curses and doom to themselves. Their arrival in Maat had gone unnoticed by Mereruka's spies, and Khety had seized the opportunity they represented too swiftly for the prince to counter. His hands curled into fists as he stood. For now, he had no choice but to submit.

"Lead the way, then."

As he followed the soldier through the open, columned halls of his palace, Mereruka swore that if he returned from this voyage alive, he would no longer be content with waiting another century to take the throne for himself. May the forgotten gods have mercy on the king of Maat, for Mereruka would have none.

CHAPTER 3

"Are there vermin in the house?"

"No, Domina." Vasilisa only used Taisiya's former title when she was certain no one would overhear it.

Taisiya rolled her shoulders, tension dissipating. If Vasilisa's recognisance were to be trusted, a shadow mage spy answering to the Praetor Nicephorus had been watching them from the shadows. One day, Taisiya would allow Vasilisa to track down the spy and dispose of him, but not until it was safe to do so.

It was a pity there were so many things she needed to be patient for. And grateful for.

It was a small mercy that Taisiya hadn't yet been reduced to enduring the month-long carriage ride back to the estate of the newly appointed Magistra Zoe Jade, their sponsor and the empress' bosom ally. A teleportation mage had seen them to the entrance of the compound, once the seat of another traitorous magister before he too had been slaughtered by the crown. Taisiya's father hadn't been alone in his ambitions. Two other magistri, Sapphire and Diamond, had joined the conspiracy, their daughters used as fodder for the ritual. Those daughters had been similarly discarded by the crown once their traitor fathers and brothers had been killed. The former Sapphire and Diamond women lived in equally reduced circumstances on the grounds, while Magistra Zoe Jade had been gifted control of the former Sapphire Province and the responsibility for seeing to the welfare of the traitors' families.

Not that she'd done much.

Taisiya hated this place, a constant reminder of failure and death. Thalassa Keep was a hideous fortress of imposing grey stone, ringed with a murky moat of dubious liquid, made malodorous in the summer heat. Taisiya and her family lived in one of the cottages to the East. She and Vasilisa approached it, their leather shoes crunching the gravely, tree-lined, path.

"The spies haven't been by for months. The praetor was quick to give up his suspicions."

"We're all the better for it. Imagine if he knew…" Taisiya replied.

"Tizzy-tiger? Is that you?"

Milena, her youngest sister, opened the window of the cottage and leapt from the sill. Her unbound, auburn hair framed her pale, freckled face and a cheerful smile. Lavender eyes sparkled with mischief as she raced, completely unladylike, and jumped on top of Taisiya for a hug. Taisiya caught her and crushed her in a tight embrace. Milena had volunteered to be the first to lend her power to their father for the ritual but had paid for it dearly, left in a comatose state until he'd died and her magic and soul had been returned to her. She'd recovered with remarkable speed. Father had ensured she was cared for both day and night so that her body wouldn't suffer unduly. If only he'd been as thorough in all his plans.

"So? Has the first plan gone well?" Milena asked.

"Very. Let's go inside and I'll tell you all about it," Taisiya replied.

"Domina, if you'll excuse me." Vasilisa curtsied.

Taisiya nodded. Her closest friend preferred to wander the void when she could. Vasilisa smiled and slipped into a shadow in the blink of an eye, gone from this world into another.

Taisiya pushed open the door, as servants only came in the mornings to clean and drop off food. Walking into the atrium, she sat down at the thick, scarred, wooden table as Milena gathered their other sisters. A kettle hissed one room over. She ran a finger along the largest trough in the table's surface, holding back a grimace as she surveyed the surroundings. Every item was more than two decades out of fashion, and every piece of furniture showed signs of mending or wear—castoffs from Magistra Jade's servants, no doubt. While the magistra's keep was ugly outside, Taisiya had walked its halls. Only the finest of decorations, fresh flowers on every spare surface, and toadying servants in every hallway, all due to the immense natural wealth and overflowing coffers of the newly-minted Jade Province. But in Taisiya's humble cottage, there were no mosaics here, no rich tapestries, only simplistic, painted scenes on a few key walls, and all faded and chipping at the edges.

Yet the real treasures of the Jade Province sat before her. Milena hopped into her seat, agile as a cat, Daria poured the tea and settled into her seat without a sound and Sonya tossed back a strand of her hair. All fair-skinned redheads with purple-hued eyes, just like Father. And just like Father, they were natural-born schemers.

Daria posed in her seat so stiffly that the family swore they could use her posture to judge the straightness of a line. It lent her an air of imposing formality. No matter their reduced circumstances, not a single burgundy strand on her head was ever out of place, and her faded purple gown had nary a crinkle.

Milena was happy to discard formalities for comfort, her legs tucked under her, always fidgeting with her skirts, preferring instead the short tunics that allowed her freedom of movement. In another life, Milena might have commanded her own army, damn the opinions of lesser men.

Sonya, with shining rose-gold hair, never let an opportunity pass to put herself in the best possible light and strike a captivating pose. Even now her beauty and charm radiated, a woman meant to be a princess in a legend of old, making even the simplest gown appear fit for court.

Though they differed in temperament, they were all of them Magister Grigori's children, and equally dedicated to his grand plan. Taisiya loved them fiercely, and she would do everything in her power to see to their happiness and wellbeing. It was her duty, after all.

Taisiya cleared her throat and laid out her scheming.

"The bitch has agreed to introduce us to the emperor's cousins, and the praetor has assured me that a suitable occasion to showcase us favourably has already been planned. In only a week's time, several groups of foreigners will be arriving on our shores to commence diplomatic relations. The magistri, their heirs and a great many other nobles will be invited to attend. I've been assured the royal couple will introduce us personally to prospective husbands. I have a preliminary list with me, drawn up by the praetor himself."

Taisiya pulled a small, folded piece of paper from the pocket of her gown and smoothed it out on the table. Daria took it first and perused it with her usual icy affectation. Satisfied, she nodded curtly and placed it before Sonya.

"They're adequately close to the emperor in terms of bloodline," Daria pronounced.

Sonya hemmed and hawed over the list. She could ferret gossip out of even the most tight-lipped of servants and had acted as their window into the outside world since their banishment from society.

"Two must be struck from the list. One is a gambler and the other beats his mistress."

Taisiya nodded, grabbed a pen and ink and did just that. Milena sighed, grabbed the paper and looked over the names.

"No one on here sounds like any fun."

"Here we go." Sonya rolled her eyes.

"Wouldn't it be fun to live on a ship and kill pirates with a bolt of lightning?"

Taisiya held back her own sigh. Milena had set her sights on Admiral Zephyros, a wind mage. The eldest son of Magister Opal, Dominus Zephyros Opal rarely made landfall long enough to do more than resupply before he escaped his familial duties and was back at sea. Unless Zephyros were commanded by the emperor himself, the admiral was unlikely to ever sit still long enough to consider marriage. He and Milena had met briefly when they were children, and again when he'd brought troops to the door of their ancestral keep to evict them. Despite the grim circumstances, Milena had only praise for the handsome admiral. She was determined to have him. Taisiya feared she would never be able to dissuade her.

"It wouldn't be the worst idea to have a military man in the family. And Father always spoke of the importance of having a bolt hole or two," Daria said, ever the peacekeeper.

Daria was right, of course. If the continent ever became inhospitable, the Opal islands, with their penchant for grudging tolerance of imperial norms and customs, would be a safe haven for their family. And a man with a navy under his command would be a fine prize to garner for their greater plans. But could a man so close to the imperial family really be trusted?

"I suspect the admiral will be present at the delegation, given the emperor will need his insight on the feasibility of overseas trade routes with the foreigners," Taisiya added cautiously.

Milena's eyes sparkled. She stuck her tongue out at Sonya.

"If you want him, then you'll have to ask the strategos to force the introduction," Sonya pointed out.

The mood in the little cottage immediately dimmed. The strategos, Lethe's top military commander, had rendered their thirteen-year-old brother unidentifiable with his mace when Dimitri and Father had tried to escape the imperial dungeons before their executions. Dimitri, wicked and pitiless though he'd been, had been their younger brother nonetheless. Only the family crest on Dimitri's ring had allowed Taisiya to confirm their younger brother's identity after his brutal death. There had been so much gore. Taisiya swallowed back bile at the memory.

"We're all going to have to do distasteful things to see this through. If we let that deter us, we're not fit to be Father's children," Taisiya said into the silence. "Having to manipulate and flatter our enemies is a small price to pay in comparison to what Dimitri suffered."

Sonya, chastised, nodded.

"What about Theodore?" Sonya asked.

Theodore, their older brother, was absent, working as he did in the imperial bureaucracy. He was innocent, knowing nothing of his sisters' treachery. Theodore was the only one among Grigori's children who was kind and sweet to a fault. He was no more capable of deception or cruelty than he was of growing a second head. As such, he was to be protected through ignorance.

"Theo should marry for love. Father sent him to be part of the bureaucracy for good reason. I think it best he remains innocent," Taisiya said.

Daria and Milena nodded.

"To the Amethyst line." Daria held up her chipped teacup.

"To the Amethyst line." Milena and Sonya did the same.

"If you are going to honour our family, then at least use our real name, not the one that bastard emperor forced upon us when he killed your grandfather."

The four of them turned to see their mother, the former Magistra Oxsana Amethyst, standing by the balustrade on the second floor. Draped in her mourning robes, she descended the cracked steps of their little cottage with the same regal grace and dignity that she would have down the grand, polished staircase of their former home. Taisiya's eyes widened at the sight.

Upon learning of her husband's demise, Magistra Oxsana had salvaged as many family records, artefacts and wealth as she could before the imperial army had come to pillage it all. Even now, it lay hidden in secret caches, ready and waiting to see the light of day.

When the magistra had told the invading soldiers that the servants had made off with much in the night, they hadn't bothered to think that it might have been on her orders. Oxsana had held her head high until they'd been settled elsewhere, but as the months dragged on, she'd become a recluse, with nothing to sustain her but grief. She'd all but haunted the second floor of their cottage, either refusing to leave her bedroom or spending her days running her fingers over the few meagre belongings packed away in the storage rooms above.

As she approached their little table, her amber eyes sparked with light and cunning for the first time since Taisiya had woken screaming from the return of her soul and her magical gift. Not a hair on her mama's greying blonde head was out of place, her posture perfect from a lifetime of practice. A small part of Taisiya's tattered heart was mended by the sight. Though she'd stepped into the role with grim determination, Taisiya hadn't felt ready to lead their family so soon after her father's death. Now she wouldn't have to do it alone.

"Mama," Taisiya breathed.

Oxsana grinned in her ruthless way and poured herself a small cup of tea before she sat down and raised her cup.

"To the Dragonsblood line," she proclaimed.

Their grandfather's name. The name of every king and queen of their former homeland, stretching back into the days of myth and legend. A homeland Taisiya and her sisters would one day reclaim from the empire, transforming it from a lowly province back into a kingdom once more, just as their father had spent his life trying to do. The same as any properly-raised Dragonsblood would.

After all, they were born to rule.

"To the Dragonsblood line," Taisiya replied, grinning with her little act of sedition.

CHAPTER 4

If his orders hadn't made the king's intent clear, Mereruka's quarters on the ship certainly did. Trapped in a cramped, dim, iron-barred brig, he was sandwiched between crates and jugs of supplies, his legs bent as he sat crouched, unable to properly stand. Had the bars been crafted from any other material, he'd have made short work of his prison and the people sent to keep him there. As it was, even the nearness of the poisonous metal weakened him. Imported from abroad, such cages were reserved for the worst of fae criminals in Maat—the only time the use of the cursed metal didn't warrant an immediate death sentence. It was a pity he had so few allies on board. For this insult alone, he could have had the heads of every fae on the ship presented to him on a platter.

Certain that his jailors planned to throw him overboard a few days into the journey, it was to his surprise that his execution had not been forthcoming. Though Mereruka lived, a week of shitting and pissing in a pot his jailors refused to empty and no access to a bath had him longing for the ocean depths and freedom from his own skin.

Bas had climbed aboard in the form of a much-welcomed cat, remaining thus to elude suspicion. Keeping the noblemen company as they discussed Mereruka's fate, he reported back regularly. Bas slipped into the hold, fitting through the bars of Mereruka's prison with enviable ease. Mereruka's pointed ears twitched as he strained to listen to the sounds of any crew who might be nearby, but only he and Bas were in this gods-forsaken section of the ship.

"It doesn't look good," Bas said as he twined himself between Mereruka's legs.

"I'm not surprised. Any chance you can unlock the cell?"

"No. It's witch magic, and the trade minister is hiding the key in a pocket realm."

Mereruka cursed. Witch and fae magic didn't play well together, and neither did their races. In person, they could feel the grating, incompatible wrongness of each other's magic like an irritant against their very skin.

Unfortunately, only a witch or an object of their making would be able to undo the spells that locked the cell. Few fae could ever stand to study witch magic, and fewer still understood it well enough to counter their magic entirely. Where fae magic flowed like a living river or tangled like the roots of a tree, witch magic was bound, corralled and contorted into shapes and patterns that made no bloody sense to him. That the trade minister kept the key hidden in a realm of his own making could be a good sign—he must suspect someone aboard might sympathise with Mereruka's plight.

"And what of my doomed bachelorhood?"

It wasn't as though he wished to remain unmarried forever. He simply wished to marry a woman who would make a good partner for his schemes, and whose standing in Maat would benefit him. If she liked the idea of his brother's head on a pike, that would be an added bonus. He was unlikely to find a woman with any of those traits on the Cursed Continent.

"Do you want the good or bad news?"

"Both."

"They won't let you leave the ship until you swear an oath to take a bride from the Cursed Continent before the return trip. If you fail to wed before they set sail, they're to strand you there."

So Khety meant to completely erase his influence, if not through his marriage to a complete outsider, then through his banishment. He supposed he could refuse to leave the ship entirely—a revolting prospect given his current conditions—but they might very well decide to starve him into compliance.

"Go on."

"*They intend to demand the hand of a princess.*"

"Are there any such women in that place?" He had a hard time imagining any sort of governmental structure on the Cursed Continent, despite the reports Bas had made that an emperor and empress reigned there. A vaguely amusing notion, to be sure. An empire of what—mud, sticks and misery?

"*There are not.*"

Gods below, it wasn't a diplomatic mission so much as an attempt to inspire armed conflict with him as the cause. Insulting one's barbarous hosts was unlikely to go well, especially if rumours of magic not working within the bounds of the continent proved true.

"Do we have any allies on board?"

"*None that dare to be open about it.*"

A budding spy he may be, but Bas was no mind reader. A pity.

"I hope you have some good news."

"*They intend to let you pick the woman once the first request is refused.*"

If he survived their refusal. Hopefully they weren't all flea-bitten cannibals.

"I suppose I should be grateful for that small mercy."

Bas was uncharacteristically silent, looking away. Where was his usual sarcastic quip? Surely his adopted son hadn't left his adolescence behind quite yet. Mereruka reached out and turned Bas' fuzzy head to face his own. He narrowed his pale yellow eyes as Bas refused to meet them.

"What?" Mereruka demanded.

"Well...It seems they call themselves mages. No one knows what that means exactly, but the trade minister was present when their first envoys arrived and he said they felt...witchy."

"Gods below," he croaked.

To have witch magic crawling over his skin for the duration of the mission would be bad enough, but for a lifetime? Intolerable.

"Pray they don't think to force a vow of lifelong bonding or prohibit divorce."

Were he in Khety's place, it's what he would do. A shiver of revulsion ran down Mereruka's spine. At least if she were some kind of a witch, she would be dead within a few centuries, stymying his plans all the while. He could always wed an elderly woman, but if they forced a vow to share their lives, he would lose his own life when she died long before him, or be required to share his bargained years just to keep her alive by his side. Neither was acceptable to him. Only the Eternal Serenity could officially take multiple spouses. He'd have to become king for that reason alone. At least if he were forced to take a witch as his wife, not one of Maat's nobles would question why he sought to kill his brother. Mereruka suppressed the hysterical laugh bubbling up inside him.

"You should just find the most barbaric woman on the continent and unleash her on the court," Bas hissed as he paced.

Mereruka whipped his head to face Bas. Ideas turned over in his mind. Yes, perhaps he was thinking of this all wrong. If Khety thought to punish him with a cursed, barbarian bride, one with magic that felt like insects skittering across one's skin, there was no reason the rest of the court shouldn't also suffer along with him. Surely, the Cursed Continent had an abundance of bloodthirsty women willing to step over the corpses of his foes for the chance to become queen.

Mereruka laughed.

"Perhaps I will. But I have no need of a coarse barbarian. What I need is a shrewd villainess." He could only hope there were plenty where he was going.

"*That... doesn't sound wise. I take it back!*" Bas pleaded, his small paws on Mereruka's leg.

"Wise is no longer an option. We must be bold, Bas. When we arrive, I'll have a job for you to do."

Bas cursed, but nodded nonetheless. Mereruka could hardly wait to choose his future bride.

CHAPTER 5

Taisiya sipped sweet wine from a crystal glass as silk skirts whirled past her in time to a lively tune. The last time she'd danced in this hall she'd been a living puppet, unable to do more than record her surroundings without emotion or agency, such was the effect of the foul ritual. Now that she was here again, it came alive—the enchanted lights floating above, the scents of perfume and sweat, the polite laughs and vicious politicking. The hideously overwhelming amount of imperial red. A sense of triumph bubbled up from the pit of her stomach. The coin they'd spent on sumptuous silk gowns, bold jewellery and gems twinkling in their hair had been worth it. For the first time in a year, they looked like dominae again.

The empress had come through. Taisiya and her siblings had been seated next to the empress' table, and now Sonya and Daria danced in the arms of men introduced to them by the royal couple. Both were cousins of the emperor, had sizable estates, and assisted in governing the Ruby Province. They also shared the emperor's features: average height, black hair, warm, terracotta skin and general good looks. If the expressions of their partners were any indication, her sisters were charming the men into proposals between graceful twirls. It was to be expected, since Daria and Sonya had been in close conversations with their mother. Oxsana knew more about the eligible men of Lethe than even the praetor's spies.

Only Milena remained unpaired.

"Oh! There he is! Let's catch him before he slips away."

Milena's smile was predatory as she pointed out Dominus Zephyros Opal. He stood next to the strategos, a beast mage with tanned skin, exceptional height, incredible brawn and crowned with bullish horns nestled in short, dark hair. Suppressing the sick dread and anger, Taisiya turned her attention to the admiral. He wasn't especially tall, but he was unquestionably handsome with short, curly, blue-black hair, dark eyes and light brown skin, tanned from his many days in the sun.

"Keep an eye on him," Taisiya replied.

She scanned the crowd for the royal couple and spotted the empress not far from the towering Illustra Iliana, a tawny-skinned, blonde metals mage married to the strategos. She was also the empress' closest friend and confidante. She was reportedly much more approachable than the empress, but all who had tried to get to Selene through her friend had tasted the empress' favourite poisons. Iliana had recently been assigned the duties of governing the Protectorate, formerly the Diamond Province, the seat of the imperial palace and its territories. That the former blacksmith was woefully underqualified for such a role was painfully obvious. At least it was to everyone but the empress.

"Follow me."

Taisiya and her sister wove through the crowd on the periphery of the dance. When they stood before the empress and illustra, Taisiya and Milena curtsied low.

"Empress, Illustra, greetings," Taisiya said.

The empress groaned.

"Gods, who do I have to be polite to now?"

"Selene! It's hardly a chore," the blonde illustra reproached the empress.

"Empress, I am Illustra Milena Spark. I wish to be introduced to Dominus Zephyros Opal," Milena replied.

"Oh, you're *that* Milena!"

"You're correct, Your Majesty. Though you certainly did a thorough job of dragging my name through the mud while you used it." Milena's smile was a touch too sharp to be sweet.

The empress was taken aback by the comment and studied Milena with a critical eye.

Taisiya's lightning trickled along her fingers, sparking Milena. If only she could curse at her youngest sister. It had been their father's ill-considered idea to force Selene to imitate Milena, all to delay suspicion that he had used the foul ritual to siphon magic from his daughters. A gamble he'd made and lost. Milena had woken from her coma to a weakened body and a reputation in complete tatters, forced to listen to all the outrageous stories about their father's murderess while Selene had paraded about using Milena's name. Taisiya had been able to force promises from Milena that she wouldn't try to physically harm the empress, but it had been a hard-fought argument. Perhaps Milena wanted to marry into the Opal family so that she could move to an island where she'd never need to see the empress again.

"We look nothing alike. I wonder why anyone actually believed that lie," the empress said as she picked at an imaginary piece of fluff on her gold-embroidered sleeve.

The unfortunate truth was that the two looked very much like sisters. Though Milena was taller with a fuller figure and had a distinctly reddish hue to her brown hair, there was no mistaking the similarity. Even their impulsiveness was eerily alike. At least Milena could claim that she was the more beautiful of the two.

"It is a mystery to me as well, Your Majesty," Milena replied as she flicked an errant strand of hair from her face and raised her chin.

"Zephyros, did you say? He's just there speaking to my husband, Marduk. Let's head that way, hmm?" The illustra interrupted their posturing and steered the empress away with a touch more force than was strictly necessary.

Milena's smile turned satisfied at the sight. Taisiya elbowed her in the side and tugged her along.

"I shouldn't have to be nice to that whore's get," Milena hissed.

"You shouldn't, but you must, for now," Taisiya whispered.

When they approached the beast and wind mages, the empress made the proper introductions. Zephyros took her sister's hand and kissed it. Taisiya was happy to note a slight blush across his cheeks.

"It's good to see you've recovered. I am sorry that our previous meeting was-"

Milena waved her hand nonchalantly.

"You didn't have our former home looted because you wished to." She turned an acidic expression on the empress. "I believe that was under your husband's orders, was it not, Empress? Thankfully, Lethe is full of good and decent men like Dominus Zephyros Opal, who was kind enough to ensure Mama and I were allowed to dress before we were taken from the premises."

The empress nearly choked on her wine. Both the strategos and his wife blanched. Zephyros looked at Milena and then the exits of the hall, like he might have to plead for her safety and make a quick getaway. Taisiya would wring her neck, the little heathen. Had Milena gotten into some strange potion? How could she smooth this over?

Milena turned back to Zephyros, all sweetness and cheer.

"That's all past now, isn't it? Though I suppose if you wish to make it up to me, you can take me on an adventure! I have always wanted to sink a pirate ship with a bolt of lightning," Milena said with a charming smile as she led the shocked but intrigued wind mage away from their small group without so much as a backward glance.

The empress howled with laughter, wiping tears from her eyes. Taisiya nearly collapsed with relief. This was one of the few times she was glad of the empress' unpredictable humours. As she watched Zephyros and Milena's retreating forms, she could see her sister captivating the infamously flighty dominus. Perhaps two of her siblings would marry for love after all.

"Well, who do you plan to sink your claws into?" the empress asked Taisiya with an air of amused tolerance.

Men were, at best, a vexatious desire that, when she'd been tempted to indulge, only led to deep, abiding disappointment. It would be best to marry some doddering old man with only a few years left, if only so she could go about her business as a respectable widow. She'd yet to identify the most elderly of eligible bachelors, but it wouldn't be long until she found the perfect husbandly placeholder.

"No one. Not until all my sisters are happily and contently married," Taisiya replied.

"Wasn't there one more of you? The... spineless one? Theodore?" the empress mused.

The strategos pinched the bridge of his nose while Iliana shook her head, at a loss for her friend's behaviour.

A fire burned in Taisiya's gut, her posture stiffening at the insult. The empress was lucky Milena had not been present to hear it, or she'd be no more than a gory, blackened splotch on the gleaming marble floors. Taisiya was tempted to do likewise, but only after Vasilisa let the hungry inhabitants of the void at her first.

No one insulted her darling Theodore.

"Empress, may I have a word?"

"Eh? Yes, fine-"

Taisiya pulled the empress from her spot to somewhere without prying eyes and ears, while the poison mage spluttered her shock at the rough handling. Taisiya's glare at the strategos and his wife convinced them to back off. She dragged Selene behind a colonnade and rounded on her.

"Say whatever you like about me and my sisters, but *do not dare* to insult my brother," Taisiya warned.

"Oh? Is that a sore spot, *Copper*?" the empress taunted her with a grin. "Do you really not know?"

"Know what? Theodore is a coward, plain and simple. He was too afraid to lift a finger to help the lot of you when you were lifeless nothings under the ritual," she huffed.

"Then you really don't know..." Taisiya's laugh was bitter and hollow.

The empress' expression made her confusion plain. Taisiya snarled and cornered her.

"Theodore is the kindest, best man in the whole of Lethe, and the one you owe your life to. Your whore mother spelled and deceived my father, and returned to the estate with you, believing that presenting proof of her crime would win her the position of mistress, never mind that father never took a mistress in his whole life!" The empress raised her finger to make a point, but Taisiya slapped her hand down and continued. "Theodore was a child and excited by the prospect of another sister, but when he heard that your mother would be put to death, he grabbed all the gold and valuables he could carry and warned that filthy bitch to run for her life. He gave you your mother's life and enough coin to see you both well for a few decades at least. So the bravery and goodness of *my* brother is the only reason *you're* standing in front of me. Don't you *ever* speak ill of him again. If you do, I won't hesitate to cut that ungrateful tongue from your mouth!"

Taisiya got her pounding heart and ragged breath under control as the empress looked at her with an inscrutable expression. Horror washed over her. Gods below, she'd done it now. All the admonishments she'd given Milena, only to erupt in spectacular fashion herself. She'd ruined everything. After a moment, the empress spoke.

"It's been a long time since someone dared speak to me that way."

"Then you've surrounded yourself with sycophants, Your Majesty," Taisiya replied.

If she were going to lose everything else, she might as well keep her sharp tongue. She regretted the threat of violence only a little. No one had the right to speak of Theodore that way. No one.

To her surprise, the empress didn't seem at all put off by her angry outburst. Quite the opposite.

"Gods below, I know! Horrid, smiling liars, the lot of them!" She chewed on her lip for a moment, sizing Taisiya up. Then she grabbed Taisiya's hand and pulled her back into the hall, towards the tense illustra and strategos. "Come. You say you're not hunting for a husband just yet? Then I have a job for you. How would you feel about being my newest ambassador?"

CHAPTER 6

Mereruka felt the spell lying in wait, readying itself to sink its claws deep into his soul. Though he detested swearing word-as-bond spells, this one could have been worse. His jailors, the king's wretched pawns, were crueller than they were cunning. He repeated the distasteful words with a sneer on his face while he kept his mind on the thought of bathing for the first time in a week.

"I, Prince Mereruka of the Land of Maat, swear to uphold the king's orders and take as my bride a woman born on the Cursed Continent. I will not return to my homeland until this task is done."

The spell struck, piercing him through and settling into his very bones. The trade minister smirked and unlocked the cell door, a thick leather glove shielding his skin from the poisonous iron. Mereruka stepped from the cramped cell as the door swung open, careful not to brush up against the bars. He couldn't afford to let it destroy the glamour he habitually cloaked himself in. Stretching, his back ached in protest as he revelled in the new freedom.

He supposed he should be grateful at least that the royal bloodline was prohibited from swearing oaths of loyalty to one another, else Mereruka's schemes would have been stymied before they began.

Mereruka followed the minister to the top deck of the ship and shielded his eyes against the harsh light of day. Though his eyes watered, in the distance, he could make out the land and buildings of the Cursed

Continent, all outlined in a hazy blue. He breathed deeply. The fresh air was a blessing to his abused senses.

"Am I to play a part in this farce?" Mereruka asked.

Was he to be the sacrificial victim, or was he meant to smile and make nice with the people of the continent?

"You're to be the king's representative, the lead ambassador."

The one who was ostensibly in charge, and therefore responsible for all the diplomatic obstacles they'd plotted to place in his path. Mereruka closed his eyes, luxuriating in the sea air. Like this, he could almost imagine that he was near his home in the main trading port of Maat. Rhacotis. Gods, he hoped he'd see it again.

"Good," Mereruka said.

Time to ensure that future.

He seized the trade minister's head between his hands and snapped his neck. The other representatives gasped in shock. He released the body from his grip, and it flopped to the deck with a satisfying thud. Mereruka fished the prison key from the pocket of the corpse's kilt, tore the official ring from its hand and tossed the body overboard. Turning to the stunned faces of the men and women aboard the ship, Mereruka smiled. Ministers of the king's court, especially the bevvy of scribes before him, rarely had experience with such violence. Luckily, the soldiers were below deck.

"He insulted His Eternal Serenity's lead representative," he said by way of explanation. What else could a week's miserable imprisonment in an iron cage really be? At least the rest were wise enough not to protest. Mereruka turned to a young man whose light green skin had gone ashen. "You were his subordinate, were you not?"

He nodded, edging away.

Mereruka's strides ate up the distance between them. Taking the man's hand, he placed the ring within it.

"You've been promoted to the position of trade minister. Try not to repeat your predecessor's errors. Now, where is my bath?"

Taisiya's first ambassadorial experience was not at all what she'd expected. In fact, the role of ambassador wasn't what she'd envisioned after the dressing-down she'd given the empress. As it turned out, Selene had simply become sick of the lists the praetor had drawn up for her of qualified candidates who kowtowed to her but did little else. Taisiya had won the post by dint of having been raised with so-called 'frilly, noble etiquette' and being unafraid to speak her mind in the poison mage's presence. Whether or not the assignment was the empress' strange version of punishment was anyone's guess. With Selene, one couldn't be certain of these things.

"That's what you get for putting a blacksmith and a soldier in charge of foreign relations," Vasilisa snickered in her ear.

"Quite," Taisiya replied as she strode through the festive halls of the palace with a contingent of foreigners following at a distance.

The first to arrive had been a group of women in plain, heavy fashions and furs who claimed to be the High Council of the Witchlands of Maetzer. They'd seized Taisiya by the neck and spelled their language into her head and vice versa with a beam of light that left her with a short-lived migraine. They'd repeated it once more on both Illustra Iliana and Illustrus Strategos Marduk. Taisiya had been grateful that her first instinct had not been to strike out with a bolt of lightning.

Neither of the illustri had known when the group would arrive, nor had they prepared gifts or inquired ahead of time what kinds of accommodations the witches would find appropriate. Taisiya had been forced to step in to prevent the women from levelling curses at the lot of them. Iliana, as she insisted on being called, had thanked her profusely for entertaining the women and touring them around Nadioch. Why the inept couple had been placed in charge of the matter was beyond her. The empress obviously had no real notion of what a good diplomat needed in order to have things running smoothly.

Taisiya had sent Vasilisa off with a message to the praetor to provide her with information regarding all of the other foreigners invited to Lethe. If she got lucky, she'd have time to read over the missives Vasilisa had returned with before the next group needed to be presented to the royal couple.

As the sun reached its zenith, Taisiya curtsied before the thrones of the empress and emperor. Vasilisa stood behind her and curtsied lower.

"Emperor Belisarius, Empress Selene, I present to you the High Council of the Witchlands of Maetzer, answering your calls for diplomatic relations."

The women bowed and faced the empress. Taisiya stepped aside. The eldest marched forward and spoke in the language of the empire with only a slight accent.

"Greetings, Empress Selene. We wish you and your treasured consort many happy days, and thank you for sending your esteemed sister to see to our welcoming."

"Greetings, High Councillor. I am pleased you have come to Lethe. I have long been curious about the world outside our empire. But Emperor Belisarius is not a consort, he rules alongside me."

"Surely you jest, Empress. Men are fit for battle and caregiving, but their temperaments are ill-suited for overseeing a vast and complex territory."

"I assure you, High Councillor, we have not found that to be the case at all." Belisarius took Selene's bejewelled hand in his own, a dark brow raised. "In fact, a great many men are employed in the governing of Lethe."

The witches hissed heated comments amongst themselves before turning their outrage at the empress.

"You allow men to make important decisions? Violent, stupid *men*?!" one of the younger witches asked with near-comical alarm.

"I knew it! The stench of patriarchy has fouled this land. Now we know why it has always been called the Cursed Continent!" A woman with a proud bearing jutted out her chin as she sneered at the emperor, her half-shaved head exhibiting battle scars.

The eldest amongst them quieted their angry denunciations and turned to the empress, face and voice grave.

"The Witchlands of Maetzer do not make allies of patriarchal lands. You may contact us if your Empire of Mages reaches the proper state of enlightenment on these matters, but not a moment sooner."

The witches turned their backs on the crowd and formed a circle with their hands. A strange static crackled in the air as they chanted. Some members of the court began swatting at themselves, screaming at the prickly sensation of bugs crawling over their skin. Taisiya suppressed a shiver as an unpleasant tingle scuttled down her spine. Before anyone could counteract the strange magic, the group disappeared. The royal couple and nobles in attendance burst into animated conversation at the dramatic exit.

"Well, so much for that," Vasilisa said. "Who's the next to arrive?"

Taisiya sighed wearily and pulled a minuscule scroll from the pocket of her robe.

"Noblewomen don't sigh," Vasilisa chided her with a grin.

Taisiya wanted very badly to stick out her tongue at her closest friend. Given their location, she settled for a frown.

The document she unfurled had obviously been scrawled in a hurry, the script barely legible. A headache bloomed behind her eyes. There was only one other group who had agreed to travel to Lethe. Thank the gods for that. But as she continued to read the cramped missive, her stomach knotted at the dire information. Did the empress have a death wish? Who in the hells had been in charge of contacting the foreigners?

"Fae from the Land of Maat."

CHAPTER 7

"You know what to do."

"*This is still a bad idea.*"

Mereruka raised his brow at Bas.

"*Fine. But when you're so sick of her witch magic crawling all over you that you'd rather jump off a cliff, I plan to remind you I told you so.*"

"Duly noted."

Mereruka stepped from the lodgings of the late trade minister, freshly washed, groomed, richly dressed, and most importantly, smelling of excellent perfumes. Bas struck out to act as his spy. Their ship had finally reached the harbour of the Cursed Continent and the ship was close enough to the berth for the shifter to make landfall with ease. Mereruka had to admit that when he envisioned what this dreaded place might be he hadn't imagined...this.

They had sailed into a bay shaped like a crescent moon and had headed towards the largest berth. From there, a wide, straight street drew the eye upward. In the hazy distance, imposing mountains acted as the spokes of a diadem with a walled, gleaming palace the crowning jewel. The docks were bustling, full of the so-called mages, some who appeared as witches might, some like shapeshifters, jostling for space and selling their catch. Buyers haggled over prices as pickpockets plied their trade. Sturdy wooden and stone buildings of varying quality lined the cobbled streets. Though their manner of dress and language were foreign, the city appeared as any prosperous port might. The sight gave him hope that he might not, in fact, be marrying a barbarian and that the refined comforts of home might be on hand.

As their ship settled into place and the anchors let down, Mereruka gathered the diplomatic party before him.

"Remember that while we are here, we are acting as symbols of Maat. Our actions will directly affect the prestige of King Khety. If any of you act in a way which disgraces His Eternal Serenity or myself as his direct representative, I shall take great offence. I hope I do not need to remind you what happens to those who anger a prince."

Silence and darting eyes met his announcement. He'd hoped the next obstacles would make themselves plain, but he was not so lucky. The former toadies of the trade minister remained tight-lipped, their grudges simmering. So be it.

"Before we disembark, I demand that each of you swear a simple oath. You will swear upon your names that you will not leave this continent without your Prince Mereruka."

Mereruka watched as his enemies separated themselves from the innocents. While many were simply puzzled by his demand, a few—the plotters—kept their faces carefully neutral. They knew he'd caught onto one of their schemes. Each of them swore their oaths, cutting off at the knees Khety's chance to abandon him here.

That problem taken care of, he readied himself to descend from the ship. Before a rude plank could be placed on their vessel, one of the crew drew up the water of the harbour and turned it into a flight of steps. The mages sharing the pier looked upon their party and fled. He supposed he and his fellow fae, in all their many, riotous colours, would look strange to a people who had never beheld anything more exotic than the dull, clay-like colours displayed by other mages.

As his party reached the cobblestones, a number of carriages were waiting, their riders arrayed before them in their finery. Mereruka, standing at the apex of the group, could feel the weight of a thousand stares as the inhabitants of the Cursed Continent openly gaped. He stifled a sigh. Three approached him—two women and a man of uncommon brawn and height, crowned with bullish horns. Ah good—a shapeshifter. Mereruka recoiled as the man stepped forward, adorned with steel and carrying a sword of the same wretched metal.

One of the soldiers among the fae stepped forward, kitted in scale-like mail, curved sword of enhanced bronze in hand. Mereruka held out his palm to send the soldier back. No need to turn this into a bloodbath. If fae were unknown to these people, they might not know the threat and insult they'd given. Mereruka looked at the man and shook his head. He looked to the two women, one blonde and the other a redhead. The blonde looked uncertain, but the redhead had a serious, unflappable air about her. Pointing to her, he signalled her to step forward. Whatever she said to the man, he backed off warily, taking his cursed iron with him. The redhead approached.

Mereruka pressed three fingers to his lips in the hopes these strange peoples understood the sign asking permission to share language. She made no move or expression to show that she understood. Cursed Continent indeed.

"It seems they're ignorant of the language spell. If they make to attack, use barriers only," Mereruka said to the soldier at his side.

"Yes, Your Tranquility."

He turned to the woman and hoped she wasn't hiding knives on her person. Gathering the spell in his mind, he reached out to pull her head closer. She blinked in surprise. It must look as though he were leaning in for a kiss. If only. Her bright hair was soft and her bottom lip was plump. Mereruka had only a moment to realise that her magic wasn't repellent to him before her lips parted in shock and the spell struck, exchanging languages between them with a strand of white light. Locked in position until the spell filled his head to bursting with knowledge, he was pleased to see that no one had made to attack. Spell completed, he stepped back, his head pounding. The woman, already possessing a light complexion, turned a shade paler as she stumbled back. To his surprise, another woman leapt from the redhead's shadow and steadied her, her grey eyes assessing his party.

"Can you stand?" the grey-eyed woman asked.

"Yes, it's just a headache," the redhead replied, immediately contradicting her words by swaying on her feet.

"I apologize for the unpleasantness. Allow me to share this language with the others."

He turned without waiting for a reply, his people ready, and he gathered the spell on his tongue once more. Gods, how he hated this part. This time, the strands of light radiated out from his mouth to each fae before him. As if his skull were being cleaved in two once more, he comforted himself knowing the pain would disappear soon enough. Mentally shaking himself as his head cleared, Mereruka turned back to the welcoming party, such that it was.

In Rhacotis, the whole city would turn out for his arrival. Here, there were only a measly few carriages and a harbour full of slack-jawed barbarians.

"My name is Prince Mereruka of the Land of Maat. I am acting as lead ambassador in place of our king for the duration of our stay."

"I am called Illustra Taisiya Spark of Lethe, the Empire of Mages. I have been appointed as an ambassador by the Empress Selene. If you will follow me, I will escort you to the carriages so that we may show you your lodgings at the imperial palace."

Mereruka sent out tendrils of his magic in the direction of her gesture, but they recoiled. More iron. He wasn't getting anywhere near those death traps, promises of cushy lodgings or not. When he didn't move to follow her, she stopped, brow raised in query.

"I apologise, have I caused offence?"

"Is this your first time meeting a member of the fae race?"

"It is, Prince Mereruka."

Unsurprising, given the welcome.

"We find iron both toxic and repellent. Your man over there carries it on his person to greet us. It is considered exceedingly hostile."

She tilted her head and curtsied.

"If you will give me a moment, I will rectify that, Prince Mereruka. We meant no offence."

She turned and spoke to the horned man. His eyes widened and he turned to an armoured, winged man beside him. Unbuckling his sword belt and stripping out of his breastplate and greaves, he handed it all to the man beside him with orders that didn't carry on the breeze. The blonde woman turned to the carriages and blanched. A quick conversation between the blonde, the man, his soldier and the ambassador took place. The soldier nodded and opened feathered wings before taking off into the sky towards the palace. Odd. It seemed the ones that appeared to be shapeshifters were not, in fact, of that race. Taisiya turned from the two and approached him once more.

"Our carriages have many iron fittings and are not suitable to convey you to the palace. We will have palanquins brought immediately."

He almost sighed with relief. No more iron surprises—for now. Best to impress upon these mages what the fae could do—all the wondrous, beautiful, magical things—and all the terrible power they would bring to bear if insulted.

"No need, Ambassador. We brought appropriate conveyance with us." Mereruka turned to his new trade minister. "Bring the barge up from the hold, and summon something impressive to pull it."

Chapter 8

Taisiya did her best not to let her expression show how shocking the fae appeared. It was as if a mad artist had simply chosen every conceivable colour besides the usual ones to paint them with. She hid her reaction to the impressive fae magic as well. Wherever they could, they used it instead of manual labour.

A doorway was spelled into the side of their ship and a pink-coloured fae man hopped through in order to pull out a long, thin, floating barge with four seats facing one another, all festooned in bright, beautiful patterns and images. Except there was no explanation for how the ship was not taking on water, nor how the barge had fit in the hold, and certainly not at that angle, or how it remained weightless. As it was brought closer, gold and jewels winked along its side.

All the while, a pale green man the prince had called 'Trade Minister' drew a circle on the pier with glowing runes and called out a few commands. Two horses with enormous, pale blue wings on their backs leapt from the circle and allowed themselves to be tethered to the floating barge. Another impossibility. The mask of polite calm she'd been trained her whole life to portray was going to crack after a day like she'd had, and it wasn't even half over.

When she glanced back at the illustri, she was ready to scream. Though Marduk at least had the sense to do a passing job hiding his reaction, Iliana's eyes sparkled with awe and shock. At least she had the sense to cover her open-mouthed astonishment with a hand.

Bloody amateurs.

"Would you prefer to fly to the palace or walk along the streets?" the prince asked her.

His skin was a deep teal, and his long, violet hair, partially braided, reached to the small of his back. Pointed ears were pierced with gold and his chest bare except for the collar made of precious, brightly coloured stones and gold that came down over his pectorals. A jewelled belt secured a short kilt of bright white, embroidered and pleated at the front. An open, long-sleeved robe made of a gauzy material, also highly decorated, revealed more than it concealed. On his feet were jewelled sandals, glittering up at her from below. His eyes, the colour of citrine, sparkled with humour. How irksome. Especially given she thought he'd been leaning in for a kiss earlier.

His compatriots were dressed similarly, though less splendidly. The women wore tight, revealing, heavily embroidered dresses in the same bright white fabric, though their serious, business-like manner brought bureaucrats to mind rather than mistresses or wives.

This prince obviously meant to impress them with his showy magic. Taisiya didn't want to give him the reaction he sought. Especially not with that knowing grin on his face.

"It's entirely up to you, Prince Mereruka. The sky would allow us to avoid any foot traffic, but it will make it difficult to show you particular landmarks."

"The streets, then," the prince said.

"Will the rest of your party be joining us?" Taisiya looked at the barge tellingly.

Would the four seats become forty between blinks?

"They will summon their own steeds and travel behind us," Mereruka replied.

Oh but of course—more flying land mammals conjured from the ether. How silly of her not to assume as much. The scream trapped in her throat edged ever closer to her lips.

He held out his hand. As she placed hers in his, she nodded to Vasilisa. For now, it seemed their new visitors were not a threat. The darkness mage sank back into the shadow at Taisiya's feet.

"Where does she go?" he asked.

"The void. I could ask her to give you a tour, but it's not for the faint of heart," she said, hoping to goad him into foolish bravado.

A trip through the void would quickly rip away any sense of superiority the fae might have. Though the illustri had obviously telegraphed awe at magics these people considered routine, and injured the dignity of Lethe in the process, she hoped she would be able to shore it up before this whole affair was over. The last thing she wanted was for another nation to see Lethe as weak, ripe for the picking—or its highest placed nobles as easily impressed rubes. Especially not one ruled by the fae, a race known even in isolated Lethe as easily angered and immensely powerful.

"Interesting," he replied.

Damn. Not so easily tricked, then.

"Allow me to introduce you to my fellow ambassadors."

He placed her hand upon his forearm and they walked to where Iliana and Marduk stood.

"This is Illustrus Marduk, strategos of Lethe's armies and administrator of the Protectorate. His wife, Illustra Iliana, administrator of the Protectorate. Illustri, this is Prince Mereruka of the Land of Maat."

"We are honoured by your arrival, Prince Mereruka." Marduk bowed his head.

Taisiya glared at Iliana when she didn't extend the same courtesies. An ashen, bloodless pall marred her tawny complexion. Was she frightened by their appearances? No, it wasn't fear. She looked ill. What in the hells had happened? Just a moment ago, she was the picture of health.

"Please forgive the illustra. It seems she's feeling ill," Taisiya said.

The prince's eyes had narrowed, his lips pressed thin as he suppressed some unpleasantness, but with more success than Iliana.

"Is the illustra a witch?" the prince inquired with a grimace.

"No, she is a metals mage," the strategos replied, looking between the prince and his wife with growing concern as Iliana began trembling and clutching her stomach.

Without any more warning, Iliana threw up.

All over Taisiya's dress—and the prince.

Stunned, Taisiya didn't know what to do. No—she knew what she *wanted* to do, but violence and curses wouldn't fix this. Neither would summarily executing the strategos and his incompetent wife.

"I-I'm so s-sorry," Iliana stuttered.

"It's understandable, Illustra. Rest assured, I feel the same way about you." The prince's smile was made with a clenched jaw. "Though you claim not to be a witch, it seems you share the same physical aversion to the fae that they're known for." He turned to Taisiya. "Perhaps it would be best if you were the one to escort our group to the palace."

"Yes, it seems that would be for the best." Taisiya turned to the strategos. "Please return to the palace without us. I'm sure we'll be along shortly."

She hoped.

Thankfully, the beast mage didn't need to be told twice. He hurried Iliana off into one of the carriages and was on his way. Unfortunately, that still left Taisiya in a soiled dress dealing with an insulted delegation of fae whose prince had been vomited upon. She cursed her rotten luck. Just more evidence this role was one of Selene's punishments.

"Perhaps it would be best not to travel along the streets, Prince Mere-ruka."

She could just imagine the stench if the fae affected most mages the same way they had the illustra. Not exactly the welcome she'd planned, and it would all be on Taisiya's head. She couldn't let this go wrong, not when her family was so precariously toeing their way back into the good graces of the imperial court. Not when her sisters' futures were on the line. She could not fail them.

"I had the same thought." He eyed her soiled dress. "We brought many gifts for the empress, dresses among them. I'm sure she wouldn't miss one, if you'd like to change. I'll be doing so myself."

Taisiya's eyes widened, surprised by his kindness. She'd expected retribution, not comradery.

"I would be grateful for that, Prince Mereruka. Though I'm sorry it was necessary at all." She curtseyed.

He took her hand and placed it on his arm. As he patted it, he grinned.

"No need to apologise. We were concerned all mages would have the same aversion. I consider myself lucky to have found one that does not."

Though his tone was light, there was something in his eyes that spoke of some deeper meaning. Instantly on alert, she tried to parse it out as he led her back to his vessel. A staircase of water sprouted to give her access. One of the women, her skin robin's egg blue and her hair made of rippling water, led her to a small door. When she opened it, Taisiya had to suppress a gasp. The interior was far larger than the ship could have possibly allowed. The well-appointed cabin was impossibly large, with a ceiling painted like the sky and somehow radiating the same light. As Taisiya gawked, the woman returned with two men in tow who carried an intricately carved chest and a bowl of clean water with soap. The fae woman quickly shooed them away.

"The prince requested that this be given to you, Ambassador." She opened the chest to reveal a heavily embroidered white gown in a slightly looser, less revealing style than the ones worn by the other fae women. Beside it lay a pair of slippers dripping with jewels. "Is this acceptable?" she asked.

"Yes, more than acceptable," Taisiya replied.

The woman opened a drawer nearby.

"He also asks that you select appropriate footwear for his presentation to the emperor and empress."

Taisiya stepped over and perused the many jewelled sandals and slippers before her. She chose a pair that covered the toes. No one worth their salt appeared at court with their bare feet showing, sandals being the fashion of commoners and rural, provincial nobles.

"Do you need assistance to remove your dress, Ambassador?"

Vasilisa took that moment to step from a shadow. The fae woman leapt back with a squeak of panic.

"She does not. Does this gown require special knowledge to don?" Vasilisa asked as she pointed to the chest.

"No, it shouldn't." She shook her head, waves rippling about her face. "I'll bring these to the prince."

The blue fae woman wasted no time in leaving. When the door was shut, Taisiya looked at Vasilisa with a raised brow.

"You know that was funny." Vasilisa smiled.

Taisiya grinned.

"It was a little. Do you plan to do that a lot with our fae guests?" Taisiya asked as she and Vasilisa began shedding the soiled dress and robes and scrubbing Taisiya's feet.

Vasilisa shrugged.

"I'll stop when they start treating mages like potential threats. Right now, they look down their noses at us."

Taisiya nodded.

"The illustra certainly hasn't made my job any easier in that regard. Acting like some star-struck child one moment and then-"

"Puking all over the foreigners in the next? Yes, though I imagine that will bring her down a peg or two at court." Vasilisa snickered.

"Do you feel ill in their presence?" Taisiya asked.

Vasilisa shook her head.

"No, and neither did the strategos, going by his expression."

"Let's hope that the illustra is an outlier."

"So, how many dresses and shoes should I have prepared?" Vasilisa asked with a knowing smile.

Taisiya returned it. Being prepared for the worst was second nature.

"Triple what we have prepared. When you can, inform my sisters and their attendants as well. And secure the exclusive services of every expert laundress. I imagine that before the fae leave our shores, such professionals will be highly prized, and I want their services secured and their contracts written up before their value increases. We can make extra coin by letting other nobles buy out their contracts."

Taisiya turned around in the new gown. It was surprisingly airy, as if an inopportune gust of wind would carry it away, flowing along her curves like water. She might order a few to be made for the hot, humid summers of Nadioch.

"Well, how ridiculous do I look?" Taisiya asked.

"Not as bad as I feared. With the right jewellery, it could be quite fetching. Is it comfortable?"

"Quite. Should I champion it as a new fashion trend? I'm sure our guests would be happy to have a new market for their textiles."

As the words slipped from her lips, Taisiya paused. She'd been thinking of this all wrong.

Now that she was a few moments removed from the illustra's initial blunder, Taisiya realised what a gift it had been. Using Iliana's constitution as a stepping stone, she could reposition herself for her rise in society. If she could secure exclusive trade with the magically gifted foreigners, she could enrich herself socially as well as monetarily. Maybe she wouldn't even need to wed a wealthy old man to recoup her family's former fortune. Taisiya grinned. Prince Mereruka didn't yet know it, but he'd gotten himself tangled up in her net.

Vasilisa was about to reply, but looked to the door and sank into the shadows. The knock came moments later.

"Ambassador? His Tranquility the Prince awaits you on the barge."

CHAPTER 9

Never one to let a good crisis go to waste, Mereruka couldn't help but feel a little proud of his manoeuvring. When Taisiya stepped from the ship wearing the fae wedding gown he'd provided her, he savoured the chance to revel in the grim glances his enemies shot each other. Whether the ambassador was one of many mages free from a witch-like aversion to fae magic, it was impossible to tell. If she proved to be a rarity, he couldn't afford to let this lucky coincidence go to waste. She didn't know that in accepting his gifts and wearing them proudly, or by selecting attire for him, she'd as much as told his fellow fae that they were courting. He would be sure to gift her with jewellery and more gowns in the coming days so that she continued to serve his purposes. Whether he would need to manoeuvre her into becoming his bride or someone more suitable for the role appeared was yet to be seen, but this gambit at least allowed him time and room to breathe.

"Is there anything else I should be aware of before we reach the palace? I wouldn't want to cause further offence."

Taisiya's face gave nothing away, but her white-knuckle grip on the arms of her chair conveyed her discomfort at sailing through the sky. They'd levelled off seamlessly and proceeded at a stately pace, the creatures that pulled them along not bound by natural laws concerning momentum during flight. The barge was spelled to keep its occupants within its confines and the whipping winds to pass around them, allowing for pleasant conversation. The others had all summoned their own creatures and were flying at a respectful distance.

"I would not advise tempting my fellow fae into a deal. We will uphold our end of the bargain, but to the fae, wording is everything. If a bargain can be interpreted differently, we have the inclination to do so in the way that benefits us the most."

He couldn't very well have her making a bargain with one of his enemies that would prevent her from marrying him, after all. Though giving her such a warning might make luring her into a trap more difficult, if he needed to do so. Her shrewd, amethyst-coloured eyes searched his face.

"Just your countrymen, then? Not yourself? Then shall you and I make a deal, Prince Mereruka?"

He couldn't help his grin at her moxie. Thank the forgotten gods, she'd willingly put herself in his snare.

"What did you have in mind, Ambassador?"

"I wish to be the sole person in charge of trade between Maat and Lethe. Am I correct in my assumption that you are the one who can make that happen?"

It was wealth she desired? How pedestrian.

"You are." He nodded. "But what are you willing to give me in return?"

"The same exclusivity, naturally."

"No," he replied.

What need did he have of wealth? He probably had enough to buy her empire out from under her. She raised a brow, the same attractively boisterous shade of copper as her hair.

"King Khety has grand plans for this trade mission. He wishes me to take a wife from your land in order to create permanent ties."

"And what requirements do you have for a wife?"

Her cautious question had him smiling again. He was beginning to like the ambassador. Bold, and yet not so bold as to make his little game too easy for him.

"If possible, one with a constitution like your own."

"Yes, I imagine you'd quickly run out of footwear otherwise."

Mereruka laughed. He was of a mind to demand the emperor and empress make her his bride. Did they have that power? Though if he wanted her in truth, it would be better to win her honestly. He couldn't have her aiming for his head while he aimed for Khety's. Yes, an honest courtship would be better, but not strictly necessary.

"I expect I'll be going barefoot before long if the illustra is a fair representative of mage-kind. But as for other qualities, she must be shrewd and well-versed in politicking. Maat's court is no place for a demure, doe-eyed girl with romantic notions."

"Suppose I agreed to find this woman for you, what then?"

Not jumping at the chance herself? He supposed he would just have to show off his wealth and charms then.

"If you are successful, then I will ensure all official trade goes through you and you alone."

"And if I am unsuccessful?"

Clever woman. If she was this discerning upon her first meeting with the fae, and with so little knowledge, what would she do when she learned more about them?

"Then you shall grant me whatever boon I ask of you instead. That is the same stipulation any agreement with a fae would entail. If you make a deal, be certain you can uphold your end of it. Fae have a habit of being punitive when their sense of fairness has been thwarted."

"Will you give me a few days to consider?"

"You may have all the time you desire..." he began. Relief made her smile. The trap had been set. "I won't seek out another mage with this offer, but neither will I hesitate to seal the deal with another if they take the initiative. How many others in Lethe do you suppose are as ambitious as you, Ambassador?"

He could see her weighing her desire against her prudence, her eyes faraway. Would she fall to temptation?

"Only time will tell," she replied with a slow grin.

Mereruka bit back a curse. He couldn't bait her into a hasty decision, at least for now. It made him want to ensnare her all the more. When he next met with Bas, he would have the shifter learn all he could about Ambassador Taisiya.

It didn't escape Taisiya's notice that Mereruka used his entrance into the palace to dazzle every possible spectator. There was nothing the least bit humble or sedate in his performance. He leapt from the barge and offered her his hand with a gallant grin, creating a staircase out of magic, making it appear as if she were walking on oversized petals. The rest of the fae landed on their fantastical beasts and dismounted with equal flare before the creatures vanished into smoke and lights.

The people of the palace had obviously been warned. Few dared get too close to the fae. She and the delegation approached the throne room, unmolested save by the eyes of curious onlookers. Mereruka kept Taisiya's hand tucked on his arm as they led the procession, a liberty she allowed. If she indeed agreed to find the prince a wife, it would be best that every mage in Lethe associated her with their strange and intriguing guests. The doors to the throne room were opened well in advance of their arrival. The iron fittings had been replaced with brass. At least the illustra wasn't entirely useless, then.

"Emperor Belisarius, Empress Selene, I present Prince Mereruka of the Land of Maat." Taisiya curtsied low as the prince bowed. She tried to pull away from him only to find he'd recaptured her hand and placed it back on his arm. Though not one to cause a scene, she let an unpleasant trickle of electricity singe his arm in warning. She was not his prop—he was hers. He flicked a curious glance her way and winked.

Taisiya noticed to her relief that neither the emperor nor the empress seemed to sicken in the presence of the fae. Marduk was present, but Iliana was not. The praetor and a number of the logothetes, his highest-ranked ministers, stood to the side. A few, the praetor included, appeared to be struggling. Most of the magistri and magistrae were present, along with a smattering of important or wealthy lower nobles. Not all appeared in good health, but a fair number did. It boded well for her plans. She had time to discuss his deal with her family.

"We welcome you to Lethe, the Empire of Mages, Prince Mereruka." Emperor Belisarius nodded.

"May this meeting be the beginning of many years of friendship between our lands. His Eternal Serenity, King Khety, hopes that we will forge ties between our peoples and has bestowed upon me the position of lead ambassador to see that it is done. To show our sincerity, we have come bearing gifts."

Taisiya did her best not to gawk at him. In truth, the whole delegation had come with nothing more than the clothes on their backs and the jewels on their persons, beautiful though they were. The emperor and empress seemed about to reply when a thick, heavy force pressed on her from all sides. A number of mages paled, holding back sudden nausea while others fled the chamber entirely.

The pressure disappeared, and in its place, innumerable chests and gifts appeared. Between where the prince stood and where the feet of the imperial couple touched the floor of their dais, all manner of treasure glittered. The remaining nobles gasped in shock.

Statues of golden, jewelled beasts posed between chests full to bursting with more precious stones than Taisiya had ever seen in her life. Fans made of impossibly beautiful feathers stood tall next to a number of life-sized marionettes clothed in sumptuous, foreign fashions fit for royalty. Racks made of glittering silver and decorated with the heads of animals showcased more jewelled slippers and sandals than Taisiya could count. Clay amphorae as tall as herself were decorated with figures enjoying what could only be the advertised contents—alcohol, spices, perfume.

Instead of focusing on the extravagant display, Taisiya scanned the room. Two-thirds of the mages had fled from the fae magic. The remaining third were busy eyeing up the prince like he was the last drop of water in a decade-long drought. Her throat tightened in dread.

The hungriest eyes belonged to the shadow mage logothete in charge of intelligence and internal diplomacy, Nobilissimus Procopius. It had been that hateful vermin who had spied on her family for months after her father's death, sniffing at her skirts for any whiff of conspiracy. It had been that spindly bastard who had prevented her family from properly grieving her father and brother's deaths. The Damnatio Memoriae meant there had been no official mourning period, no procession, no eulogy, no feast, and no gladiatorial combat to mark the occasion and proclaim her family's wealth. They couldn't even have the cold comfort of having portraits made or small shrines erected in their honour or wear the appropriate colours. Not for a man and a boy who no longer had names, who were traitors to the crown. They'd been treated like pariahs, unable to mourn or move on under the ever-watchful eye of that loathsome man. Only through subterfuge had they been able to locate her father and brother's unmarked graves in the dead of night and rebury them in secret in their ancestral plot. And if she recalled correctly, that rat of a man had a daughter just old enough to be wed.

She knew very well the greed she saw in his green eyes, had seen it many a time in the eyes of covetous noblemen who had hoped to wed her and her sisters while their family stood tall. She'd seen it again in the sharp-toothed smiles of wealthy, untitled merchants who had eyed her and her sisters in the wake of their family's fall from grace. Procopius and his spies had taken enough from her and her family. Taisiya wouldn't—couldn't—give him the opportunity Prince Mereruka had to offer, damn the consequences.

"Prince Mereruka?" she whispered.

"Yes, Ambassador?"

"Let's make that deal."

Chapter 10

Whether it had been the obscene display of wealth or the openly covetous looks of the mages that had sealed the deal, Mereruka wasn't certain. He suspected it was the latter. Either way, he'd secured himself a suitable wife. If Taisiya failed to find another one to his liking, he would demand her hand in marriage as his boon.

As he sat in a place of honour at the emperor's table, he watched her speaking to her sisters nearby, intrigued. Even among family, she didn't let her polite façade slip. And all that without the aid of glamour. His compatriots kept mostly to themselves at their own table, save for a few brave mages willing to test their aversion to fae magic in public. Observing the mages' dining customs as best he could, he was still at a bit of a loss. Arrayed before him was a small armoury's worth of utensils. Perhaps the chefs held a grudge against their employers, for everyone was expected to saw away at the too-large pieces of food.

"Prince Mereruka, please tell us of Maat." The empress interrupted his perusal.

"Well, it is a great deal hotter than Lethe. We live mostly along the great river, the Hapi, that runs the length of our land. My palace lies at the delta where the river meets the sea. King Khety spends his time between his three palace complexes. The first in the north during the Season of Inundation, the second in the central region during the Season of Emergence, and the third in the south during the Season of the Harvest. The people are mostly fae and shapeshifters."

Mereruka stopped when he spotted Raemka, the head scribe of the mission, approach the dais with a scroll in hand. Raemka, a fae with skin of mottled, pale blue and hair of bright green, was an ambitious man who'd likely volunteered to go on this mission with the aim of seeing Mereruka disgraced. Given Raemka's lack of connections in Maat's court and his slavish devotion to Khety, he would have to ensure Mereruka's political demise if he wanted to gain Khety's favour at long last. Mereruka shot him a warning glare that was pointedly ignored.

"Emperor, Empress, I hope you will not look too badly upon this lowly scribe Raemka for interrupting your banquet with talk of business."

"Please speak, Raemka," the emperor said, waving him on.

"His Eternal Serenity, King Khety, in his infinite wisdom, tasked me to aid Prince Mereruka in securing meaningful ties with your land. As such, he asked for this to be read while in your presence." Raemka untied and opened his papyrus scroll, clearing his throat, "Greetings from King Khety of the Land of Maat. I send to you my youngest brother, Prince Mereruka, to make ties with your people. It is my fondest wish that he take a wife, a princess, from amongst your people, so that our lands may be bound together. If this pleases you, we will greet a new Princess Consort of Maat upon his return. So speaks King Khety." Raemka bowed.

The empress' smile turned acidic.

"There are, as of yet, no princesses in Lethe. And I will not be promising my firstborn to any, well wishes or no."

"Raemka, you were made aware of this before we arrived. Do not trouble our hosts again," Mereruka commanded, his hands fisted on his thighs.

He couldn't kill the scribe just yet, but Raemka had made it to the top of Mereruka's short list. That they would attempt to cause trouble so soon after he'd dealt with the late trade minister made him deeply uneasy.

"Please accept my deepest apologies." Raemka bowed deeper and backed away to his seat, his scroll sealed and tucked under his arm once more.

The emperor placed a hand on his wife's and sized up Mereruka. A ripple of strange magic swept his fingertips. Glancing down, he was horrified to find the tattoos on his hand glowing and visible. Had the emperor just broken the glamour Mereruka kept himself perpetually cloaked in? Was it a warning that the people of this cursed continent feared no magic because their emperor could dispel it at will? Fear slithered down his spine. He could not afford to have his glamour broken in public. Mereruka quickly reasserted the glamour that hid the damning truth on his skin and bowed his head.

"Please accept my apologies as well. The king was perhaps a little overzealous in his desire to see me settled. While I look forward to marrying a mage woman, I would never demand that which is impossible or repellent. In fact, your ambassador has agreed to help find a suitable woman."

"Did she now?" the empress asked. She tapped her finger on the table as she eyed him up and down. "I suppose you're handsome enough, though I doubt that's what they'll be after, given your little show earlier. Choose whomever you wish so long as she is amenable, Prince Mereruka, but keep in mind, the women of Lethe are rarely who they seem."

Mereruka took her warning with a grain of salt, for the fae nobles were little better in that regard. Glamour was only the most conspicuous of methods to conceal one's intentions after all.

The rest of the evening played out much as he expected—stilted, careful conversation and cautious advances by nobles interested in securing Maat's fortunes. Luckily, the mages who might have been sick in the presence of the fae kept themselves removed, though some with more chagrin than others. When the music began, the emperor and empress led the gathering in a graceful dance. It wasn't one he was familiar with,

but he watched the steps with interest. Dancing was something he greatly enjoyed.

"Prince Mereruka, would you like to dance?"

Taisiya surprised him by appearing at his side. She still wore the fae
wedding dress, though she wore more suitable jewellery now. He liked
the way the gown flowed like liquid down her body, an opalescent sheen
catching the light. The ambassador possessed a petite, well-formed figure.

"I'm afraid I don't know the steps."

"I'll teach you. The steps are simple enough," she replied, pulling him
out onto the dance floor. She placed his hands and began walking him
through the steps in time to the tune. In a few minutes, he was good
enough to keep up without stepping on her toes.

"I noticed that you used me as your shield at dinner," she began.

Damn.

"I spoke only the truth."

"The truth is rarely harmless. Still, it's made my job a little easier.
Follow my lead. I'll introduce you to your first candidate."

Taisiya guided him in the steps of the dance and had them gracefully
turning until they reached the other side of the hall. Several mages scattered. He, too, felt the unpleasant crawl of their magic along his senses
and was glad of their departure. In their wake, a young woman with
deep, rich brown skin, black, elaborately coiffed hair and eyes of piercing
green stepped forward. She curtsied prettily in her sparkling, lime gown.
She had a determined set to her jaw and a dazzling smile. Taisiya had
obviously lived up to her end of the bargain.

"Prince Mereruka, I present Domina Chloe Emerald."

"It's a pleasure to meet you, Prince Mereruka."

He took her hand and kissed it.

"The pleasure is mine."

Taisiya watched with a satisfied smile as the ball began winding down. Daria was beaming up at her chosen suitor, and Sonya was laughing at something her man had said, holding court at the centre of a close circle of prominent nobles. It had been too long since she'd seen them so happy. Even Prince Mereruka appeared pleased with the domina on his arm. Satisfied, she decided to catch a cool night breeze. Stepping out of the ballroom and into the gardens, she was careful not to stray too far into the shadows. It was doubtful there were many dark places free of amorous couples taking advantage of the merriment.

She was enjoying the fresh air, the lingering scent of some spicy-scented blossom and the soft slide of worn paving stones beneath her feet when she heard a laugh she would recognize anywhere. Taisiya followed it to the source. What she came upon wasn't entirely a surprise, but shocking nonetheless.

"Milena."

Milena flushed a deep scarlet. Zephyros turned an even darker shade. Their clothes and hair were in comical disarray. It seemed she'd interrupted something already halfway through. Milena's legs were hooked around the wind mage's core while he held her up in his arms, her back against the bark of the tree they stood under. They froze as they turned their faces towards her.

"Taisiya," Milena replied, her tone prim.

"Zephyros," Taisiya said.

"Ah, hello Taisiya."

"So, when's the wedding?" she asked, her smile wide.

They had a conversation with their eyes Taisiya couldn't follow. Taisiya frowned. Affairs before marriage were common enough to be of no consequence, so long as precautions were taken. She was about to remark that she'd only been jesting about marriage when Zephyros spoke.

"You don't care about a fancy wedding, do you?" Zephyros asked Milena.

"No." Milena shook her head, a small grin on her face.

"So... next week?"

Taisiya's heart leapt. Her sister would marry for love after all. Milena turned to Taisiya and smirked.

"You heard my fiancé. Now shoo!"

Taisiya grinned, held up her hands and turned from the sound of giggles and the rustling of fabric. Magister Opal had long despaired of ever forcing Zephyros, or any of his sons, to act as proper heirs and govern the province. That duty fell to the youngest child, Charis Opal, the apple of her father's eye. When she entered the ballroom once more, she found Domina Opal in a close conversation with Magistra Mina Obsidian, her lover. Opal was short of stature, like Taisiya, with fair skin, blue-black hair and dark eyes with opalescent whites. Mina was taller with light brown skin, brown-black hair and amber eyes. She had also once been a close friend of Taisiya's.

"Good evening, Domina, Magistra." Taisiya curtsied.

Mina clucked her tongue.

"Don't do that, Taisiya. I'll never think of you as a mere Illustra."

"It's good to see you, Mina." Taisiya smiled.

"And you. I'm sorry I wasn't on the continent to support you after... everything."

Yes, after her father's death and their hasty eviction from their home, Taisiya had found just how fickle and few her friends really were. Not that she'd ever expected to have another noblewoman to have her back. Though not shocking, given the circumstances, it still stung. Mina, one of the few noblewomen Taisiya had ever felt comfortable not displaying a perfect persona for, had written her but never visited. In fairness, she'd been busy finally living freely and openly on the Opal islands with Charis, the domina at her side.

"Don't apologise. The empress has been quick to make up for lost time. In fact, I've come here to tell Charis some good news."

"Oh?" Charis asked, sipping a glass of wine.

"It seems we'll be in-laws soon. Zephyros has proposed to my youngest sister, Milena."

Charis nearly choked on her next sip.

"Gods below, what dark magic did she use to do it? Zeph has been as stubborn as a mule for as long as I've been alive."

"Oh, I don't think she used any magic, per se."

"They're in the garden, aren't they?" Mina asked, her dark brow raised.

Taisiya nodded. She and Mina looked to each other and spluttered out unladylike laughs. Charis caught on a moment later as heat suffused her cheeks. She muttered darkly about men and their pieces.

"Father will be over the moon. He'll be singing Milena's praises for a decade at least." Charis sighed and smiled. "Welcome to the family, Taisiya."

"It's an honour." Taisiya curtseyed.

Finally, after a year of grief and failure, things were going right.

Chapter 11

Mereruka listed from side to side, escorted to his assigned quarters in the palace by a sleepy-eyed beast mage in the early hours of the morning. He'd danced, conversed and drunk mage wine until he couldn't see straight. The Cursed Continent made a potent brew. Thankfully, a bed waited for him—one so stuffed with feathers it might take flight in the night.

"Is there anything you require for the evening, Prince Mereruka?"

"No, thank you."

The servant bowed and closed the door.

In the full light of day, the room was decorated more conservatively than he was used to, but richly appointed nonetheless. He'd stripped to almost nothing when a knock sounded at his door. Groaning, he trod over to open it. Without a servant to assist him—not that he would trust a single member of the delegation—he was forced to do so himself.

Taisiya gasped and looked away. A blush reddened her cheeks. She looked pretty when she was flushed pink.

"I wanted to make sure you knew about your appointments tomorrow," she choked out.

"Appointments?" He hadn't made any to his knowledge. Then again, his mind was fuzzy when it came to details.

"Yes, two more noblewomen would like to make your acquaintance," she said, flicking him furtive glances.

How diligent of her. He grinned.

"I'm to be spoiled for choice?"

"Yes, I..." She swallowed, her eyes devouring the sight of him before she caught herself.

Interesting. Was she pleased with the sight of his body? She had such trouble averting her curious stares.

"You...?" he teased her, leaning on the frame of the door, closer to her. He wondered if he shouldn't invite her inside, exhausted though he was. He could not afford to let a chance at seduction slip through his fumbling grasp.

She cleared her throat and stared very pointedly at his feet. Even the tips of her ears were pink now.

Pretty.

"I didn't want any of them to get too confident. A little competition should help speed things along."

"It's a good plan," he replied, reaching out a hand to touch her. "Would you-"

"Tomorrow at noon! Be dressed and ready by then," she interrupted, jumping back. "And don't answer your door in the nude again. It's not... it's not done in Lethe."

With that, she turned and fled down the corridor. A pity.

"I'm still wearing my shoes," he muttered.

It seemed the mages were a prudish lot. He'd have to cure his future wife of this affliction before they returned to his homeland. Shrugging, he turned back to his empty bed, collapsing into it with a sigh. When he closed his eyes, it wasn't Chloe's bright green eyes that he dreamt of, but distrustful amethyst ones, both shy and hungry.

He slept like the dead until he heard Bas' voice. The morning light struck him like a body blow. Head fragile, the prior evening's pleasant fuzziness had fled, the remnant a distasteful feeling on his tongue.

"You look awful. I hope it was worth it."

Mereruka groaned at Bas' reproach. The shifter stood over him in his two-legged form and grinned devilishly.

"Water," Mereruka croaked.

Bas rolled his eyes but proffered a glass nonetheless. Mereruka gulped it down.

"Stay away from the wine," he hissed as he rolled into a seated position.

Bas tossed him a set of clothes.

"Get dressed. If what the ambassador said yesterday is still true, we don't have much time before you'll need to be presentable."

"You were here? Last night?"

"Yeah, I was. I got to see—and smell—you in all your drunken glory. Did you drink a whole damn amphora of wine? No, I don't care. If the ambassador hadn't ogled you first, I'd have told you to apologise to her for swinging your dick around in front of her."

"Language, Bas," Mereruka warned.

"Manners, Dad," Bas replied in an unflattering imitation of his nagging voice.

"You called me Dad. You haven't called me that for an age." Mereruka smiled.

Though he'd as much as adopted Bas as a child, the shifter had refused to direct any sort of endearment his way since he'd hit his adolescence. Gone were the easy hugs and easier laughs. Used to be all he had to do was make a silly face and his adorable little boy would laugh for days. He had to settle for teasing now. Bas blushed and tossed a pillow at Mereruka.

"Shut up! Do you want to know what I learned or not?"

"I'm all ears," Mereruka groaned as he hauled himself out of the bed and headed to the bathing pool in the adjacent room, his head pounding. When he returned to Maat, he was going to have one just like it built in his home. Mage wine was too strong, but their baths were exquisite. Bas stood in the doorway and looked askance as he spoke.

"Mages don't live very long. Two hundred years at most. Their magic is limited. Most of them can only command a single element. Those who are able use magic often, but it's always in very small ways. When I got to the palace, I heard all about what happened here about a year ago. Apparently, three governors plotted with a secret prince to overthrow the current emperor. They all died, but their families were spared. There was a lot of talk about the ambassador. She's the daughter of one of the traitors, but because she's also half-sister of the empress, she was only excluded from society for a year. Oh, and you'll get a good laugh at this. Apparently, a lot of the mages who can't stand to be around fae think *you're* the cursed ones."

"If only they knew," Mereruka sighed as he emerged from the bath, refreshed. He dried, dressed and plaited his hair with a strand of magic. "I want you to find out as much as you can about the ambassador and a noblewoman called Domina Chloe Emerald. What are they known for? Are they politically savvy? Do they have a history of crossing people for gain? I'll do my best to feel them out, and both seem suitable, but I'd rather be certain."

"I take it you're not worried about your upcoming marriage anymore."

"I've secured myself a bride already, one that doesn't make me ill. I'm just deciding if the others she presents to me are better."

"I guess she made a deal with you." Bas made a face that left little doubt as to his disdain.

"She promised me a boon if she fails," Mereruka replied, choosing a flashy collar necklace, latticed ear caps, golden cuffs, jewelled rings and a thick gemstone belt for the day ahead.

"And you didn't explain that she would be the boon. That's twisted, you know that, right? Carrying women off as part of a bargain is considered archaic."

"Maybe, but it's also effective."

"And barbaric. You'll get what you deserve one of these days. This is why everyone thinks the fae are shifty bastards." Bas shook his head. "Alright, I'm off. Enchant the twine again. I passed by a room and the spell broke. Had to dodge a bunch of angry servants for the next hour. Stray cats aren't nearly as welcome here."

Mereruka thought over this latest bit of news as Bas transformed into a cat. His own broken glamour from the night before weighed heavily on his mind. He shuddered at the thought of having his whole body revealed. It was a spell that fae knew instinctively, almost from the moment of birth. Most fae walked around with some form of it, concealing anything from a crooked nose to a monstrous form. Breaking a glamour or seeing through it was not something the wise usually tried.

"Stay clear of the emperor. I think he might be a null," Mereruka said.

"That would explain the broken spell. Try to take your own advice for once. If the ministers see your bare skin, you can kiss your shot at being king goodbye. See you this evening?"

Mereruka nodded and spelled the twine tied around Bas' neck to hide him from any eyes not his own. The shifter strutted over to the balcony and leapt into the branches of the tree below. Just in time, too. A knock on the door signalled the end of his reprieve.

Chapter 12

Things were going wrong.

The first inkling was when one of the women didn't show up for her appointment with the prince. Taisiya had waited like a fool for the silly girl to arrive, only to be informed—by hastily scrawled letter—that she'd had a change of heart. It was a humiliation she wouldn't soon forgive.

As a result, Taisiya found herself showing Prince Mereruka around the imperial gardens herself instead of filling his schedule with more bride-candidate meetings. In the meantime, Vasilisa was busy trying to discover if the insult was meant to make Taisiya lose face, or if something else was at play. She had too much riding on this bargain to fail.

As it turned out, stewing in her frustration was a good distraction from her discomfort around the prince. Try as she might, she couldn't forget what she'd seen last night. Mercifully, the prince had been too drunk to remember it, if his cheerful demeanour today was any indication.

"And what is this ugly little patch?" Mereruka asked as they passed by several flower beds ringed by low, pretty wooden fences but populated by straggling malodourous plants.

"These are the empress' poison gardens. The emperor finally relented after she threatened to start a menagerie of venomous creatures. I believe he saw the wisdom in allowing a few creeping vines rather than contend with a variety of insects and snakes."

"Naturally, no palace is complete without a garden dedicated to murder," Mereruka quipped, his brow raised at some of the specimens on display.

"The empress is nothing if not unique. I don't think she can help it, being a poison mage," Taisiya replied.

"That's one word for it," Mereruka muttered. "Speaking of the empress, why is it that she said there are no princesses here? I've heard you're half-sisters. Doesn't that make you a princess of sorts?"

Taisiya's breath hitched. She hated that she was related to Selene, despite how much she required the poison mage's assistance. But that was a temporary affliction. Soon, she wouldn't need the bitch.

"It doesn't," she snapped, inviting no further inquiry.

"Have I hit a sore spot? Forgive me. I have some familiarity with complicated family dynamics."

Was he baiting her? She stopped her stride and glared up at him.

"What, precisely, have you heard?" she asked, pulling her hand from his arm.

"Was my fishing expedition too obvious? I thought I was being rather suave." He winked.

"It was, and you weren't." She crossed her arms.

His grin went from charming to wolfish. He circled her like he'd caught the scent of fresh blood.

"Like any other noble, I enjoy a choice bit of gossip. I hear you're the daughter of a traitor, but despite being his victim, you've been treated like his accomplice. All while the empress, though sharing the same traitorous father, is treated like a conquering heroine and a spoiled wife. I wonder if you'll really be able to introduce me to more than a handful of bride candidates given your recent, if undeserved, disgrace."

If that were all they were saying about her, it would be a miracle. No doubt he'd kept the more vicious rumours to himself. One day she would have the wealth and power to make them pay, but until that time came, she would have to bear the insults. She gritted her teeth.

"Well, it seems you know everything pertinent, doesn't it? But our deal stipulated I need only find one wife for you, not a multitude. Was Domina Emerald not to your liking?"

"I liked her well enough."

"Then don't get greedy, Prince Mereruka. In this, or anything else. Don't think that I didn't notice the scribe describing you as the king's youngest brother, or the distinct lack of fae attendants following you about, despite your status. If our empire's recent history is anything to go by, reaching for something that requires you to do it over the corpses of your siblings rarely goes well."

The prince rounded on her and grabbed her wrist.

"It would be unwise to say such things in the open, Ambassador. The fae have excellent hearing, as do mages, I'm told."

Taisiya searched his pale eyes and saw not just fury but also a sliver of fear. A kernel of doubt made her pause. In truth, she'd been trying to goad him into revealing something of his position in his own court. She feared he was greatly disliked among his people, as not a single fae was regularly serving him during his stay. In fact, most seemed to avoid him entirely. If he were a lazy, unloved courtier, he would make an unmotivated, potentially disastrous business contact. Conversely, he'd be an unwise choice of partner if outsized political aims put him at odds with his king. Curious, she pushed further.

"Am I sending your wife to her death?"

"Do you care?"

She stopped herself from replying that she did. Truthfully, so long as the woman he chose was no friend to her, what happened once they wed was not her concern. Especially if it meant making connections with someone as powerful as Magister Emerald, who was renowned for putting shrewd politicking over the happiness or health of his children.

It would bother her a little to send someone to their certain doom, but not nearly so much if it meant her family were better off for it. Taisiya knew where her ultimate loyalty lay.

"Not as much as I should." She lifted her chin, defiant.

The prince's laugh was dark. He placed her hand on his arm and pulled her along the gravel path. She'd touched a nerve. Interesting.

"Then what *do* you care about?"

"My half of our deal. You can't give me exclusive trading rights if you're dead or incompetent."

"You make it sound like incompetence is the worse outcome."

"For my purposes, it is."

He scowled.

"A suitably unfeeling reply for a woman who prefers to act like she has a heart of stone."

Anything less was liable to get one killed or disgraced.

"If you'd wanted someone to coddle you, you should've brought along your wet nurse."

Instead of being put off by her insult, the prince... laughed. He howled until he was clutching his sides, in fact. In spite of herself, she caught herself thinking that he was a handsome man. And as soon as it crossed her mind, she crushed that thought into a bloody pulp beneath her heel. Exactly where she crushed every stray thought of his toned, sculpted, naked form.

Damnit.

"Are you done?" She arched her brow.

"Matching wits with you? Gods, I hope not." His grin turned amorous as his eyes softened. He cupped her face with his hand and stroked her cheek with a thumb. Her traitorous heart leapt. "Be my lover, Taisiya."

She pulled her face away and glared.

"Don't be vulgar. I'm not about to sleep with a man I'm trying to marry off," Taisiya spat back, though heat crept up her neck.

"Are mages so prudish? Just think, you could... advertise my charms, after sampling them for yourself."

"I assure you, no prospective bride would wish to hear of it," Taisiya retorted.

"I'm not married yet," he tried gamely.

She rolled her eyes and prayed for patience. And disinterest.

"Semantics."

"You liked me well enough last night. Had trouble looking away, in fact."

Taisiya choked on a squeak of indignation. Blood rushed to her cheeks in earnest then.

"You're pretty when you blush, Taisiya."

"Keep talking, Prince Mereruka, and the next woman I present to you will be a widow with a long list of husbands who all tragically died shortly after their weddings."

He chuckled. In an instant, the womanizer was replaced by the gentleman. She was beginning to wonder just how many faces this man had, and more importantly, which one she needed to heed.

"I apologise. I rarely meet a woman who keeps me on my toes. What can I do to earn your forgiveness?"

Taisiya turned her attention to the path ahead and did her best to cool her heated cheeks. Gods, this man was giving her whiplash. She hated that he could affect her so.

"I wish to purchase a number of luxuries from you. No doubt many of the nobles are keen to get their hands on a taste of what now sits in the imperial treasury. I want them to grow accustomed to seeking me out for such things," Taisiya said.

Even now, seamstresses in the capital were being asked to create imitations of the dress she'd worn the night before. Overnight, facsimiles of fae jewellery, footwear and statuettes had popped up in the stores of the capital. The scooped necklines of the season were being remade into deep, plunging points, and the structured skirts were giving way to dresses that flowed over every curve, moving like liquid and teasing at the form beneath.

"The goods are yours. But I don't want to be compensated with gold. I want you to don the best Maat has to offer and to do it in front of the whole of Lethe's court."

She'd planned to do just that. What better way to advertise her rising social and fiscal capital than by wearing the goods she would soon exclusively provide? But were they of a mind on this issue, or did he have another motive?

"Why?"

The prince shrugged.

"It's good business and because it pleases me that you do so."

She supposed under the circumstances it was the best answer she could hope for. At least he wasn't a lazy fool when it came to business. Taisiya led them back towards the palace proper. The time for strolling was at an end.

"Come, it's time for you to meet the next bride candidate."

And gods help the woman if she, too, were a no-show.

CHAPTER 13

Mereruka supposed it'd been at least a few days since the malcontents among the fae had tried anything. Bas was too busy looking into the backgrounds of various noble ladies to spy on his enemies. In retrospect, it had been a poor use of his limited resources.

The enormous beast mage Strategos Marduk approached him with Djadty at his side, deep in conversation. He'd gone on alert as the red-ochre-skinned fae smiled his crocodile grin at him, his white hair and sharp blue eyes shining. Djadty was one of the king's many royal guards, though one of the least favoured, ostensibly in charge of the safety of the diplomatic mission. Mereruka was certain the only one Djadty meant to keep from real harm was himself. A quick glance at his other enemies—the scribe Raemka and the quiet treasury official Itu—with their amused glances, confirmed his suspicions.

"Prince Mereruka, your man Djadty tells me that you enjoy regular sparring. If it pleases you, you're welcome to join my men during our practice tomorrow morning. We'll take care to replace our steel with more appropriate metals."

He was about to politely decline when Domina Chloe Emerald's eyes sparkled with interest. She'd kept close to him since he'd met with another woman a few days past. Even now, her hand was tucked into the crook of his arm and every starry-eyed woman who approached was quickly glared into a hasty retreat.

"How splendid! I'm sure many at court are keen to see what you and your men are capable of, Prince Mereruka. If you'll allow it, I would be happy to organize such an event," Chloe said.

"I can't speak for the prince, but I assure you I would happily participate," Djadty added.

"I suppose such a thing could be arranged with a few of my men," Marduk said.

"Wonderful! Of course, we must defer to your preferences, Prince Mereruka." Domina Emerald smiled demurely.

With few polite options left to him that wouldn't have him looking like every kind of spoilsport, Mereruka gritted his teeth and smiled. He was beginning to worry that Chloe was not a suitable candidate after all, if she couldn't read the situation between him and the other fae by now.

"I look forward to seeing what Lethe has to offer."

"As do I. Strategos, if you like, you could have a look at our weapons. I think you'll find our metal a vast improvement to steel," Djadty said to Marduk.

Mereruka spent the rest of the evening stewing over what Djadty had planned. Would Djadty try to maim him during combat? No, that would be too easy, too obvious. Was it a distraction to keep him occupied while Raemka and Itu set some other scheme in motion?

He turned over possibilities in his mind but came to no obvious conclusions save one—tomorrow, he had to overcome whatever obstacle they placed in his way. When Bas returned that evening with information, he feared none of it would help him in the trial to come.

"So? Which lady do you want to hear about first?" Bas asked.

"Surprise me, but be brief. I need you to try to find out what Djadty has planned for tomorrow during a sparring event," Mereruka said.

Bas snorted.

"You don't need a spy to tell you that. Djadty only ever has one plan—kill it with the pointy end."

"If he were my only enemy on this mission, I would agree, but Raemka and Itu will have also had a hand in this."

Bas shrugged.

"Maybe the sword is poisoned? What are you really worried about? You made them swear not to leave the continent without you alive and well, right?"

"I...did." Mereruka paused as he recalled his exact words. "Shit."

No, he hadn't.

"What?"

"I might have forgotten to specify what condition I had to be in."

"Shit! How could you forget that?"

Gods, he didn't know. No, that was a lie. He knew full well he'd let himself get overconfident after he'd cowed them all by killing the trade minister. Too busy thinking about how they planned to force him to wed a barbarian or strand him, he hadn't considered that they might have the moxie to murder him outright. In Maat, no one with killing intent had ever been able to approach him, save perhaps his brothers. That the fae here treated him with disdain was not unexpected, given they followed Khety's every whim in hopes of advancement. But if they also had secretive orders to kill him if it looked like he might return? He'd erred to think Khety would always be so discreet with his hostility.

"Okay, okay." Bas began pacing. "Most of the delegation is neutral anyway. The trade minister is dead, and he was easily the worst of them. That leaves Djadty, Raemka and Itu, maybe one or two of their subordinates."

"If the blade is poisoned, I believe the empress could be of some assistance. She is well versed in such things," Mereruka said.

"He won't attack you with iron, since he can't touch it himself," Bas added.

"We hope." Mereruka shivered in revulsion at the mere memory of it. If Djadty had a shapeshifter in his bloodline, he might have inherited a tolerance for the poisonous metal while remaining fae in appearance. After all, the soldier was not well known for his magical prowess, just his physical one. "I suppose that leaves us with the final possibility—a cursed blade."

"I'd like to see the stupid look on his face when it doesn't work," Bas grinned.

Mereruka nodded. Thanks to the many counter-curses Mereruka hid beneath his glamour, it was nigh impossible for such a trick to work on him.

"All the same, secure the waters of the Hapi. Khety wouldn't have been able to send a voyage out without some on board."

Bas nodded.

There was a reason Maat was wealthy beyond measure, and it wasn't that its nobles never cheated on their taxes or that they had more gold than similarly wealthy kingdoms. No, it was the control of the Hapi River. Blessed by some forgotten god with a love of the fae, its waters could cure what no magic could—iron poisoning. Maat's royals were tasked with guarding it jealously and at any cost, no matter how cold-hearted or miserly the fae living outside Maat found that.

"Alright, tell me what you've learned today," Mereruka said.

"Mages prize elemental gifts above all and look down on the rest. Those without elemental magic are called menials. Or ferals, which I think refers to the ones that look like shapeshifters. I don't think they use the term to refer to shapeshifters in their animal forms who've gone mad, like we do. I don't even think they know what shapeshifters are." Bas shook his head at the absurdity of it all. "Domina Chloe Emerald is the second daughter of Magister Emerald and sister to Magistra Zoe Jade. Jade was once the apple of her father's eye until several months ago when it came to light that she didn't possess elemental magic. Since then, the magister's favour has shifted to Chloe, who has become one of the most desirable bachelorettes in Lethe, owing to her family's long history, wealth, and status as one of the most powerful families, barring the emperor's own. No known scandals."

So Taisiya had chosen a truly ambitious woman for him. She was taking that aspect of their deal seriously, though whether or not his wife had one of these elemental gifts meant next to nothing to him. No matter what magic she possessed, it would pale in comparison to all that even the youngest fae child could do.

"And the ambassador?"

"Illustra Taisiya Spark, third of five surviving siblings, all lightning elemental mages. Previously engaged to a son of the neighbouring governor. Mother, Illustra Oxsana Spark, currently a recluse in mourning. Theodore is the eldest child, a known pushover and a bureaucrat. Daria is next, a bit severe but expected to be engaged to one of the emperor's cousins. Sonya is younger, a social butterfly, also soon to be engaged to a cousin of the emperor. Milena is the youngest, unruly and engaged to Lethe's most prominent admiral. Not much else to tell that you don't already know through gossip and rumours. They kept mostly within their former lands, and their connections and wealth vanished a year ago."

It didn't tell him much of use. He wanted to curse.

"Alright, look in on Djadty and the others. Any warning of what's to come would be a great help."

"I want extra compensation for this. I'll be up all night at this rate," Bas complained.

Mereruka raised his violet brow.

"Shall I remind you how difficult you were to house-train as a kitten? How many priceless pieces of imported cedar furniture you clawed to ribbons?"

"No," Bas mumbled, chagrined.

"Then go. And be careful."

Bas rolled his eyes.

"I'm always careful."

He shifted and was gone a moment later. Mereruka had nothing to do but wait.

Dawn greeted Mereruka unexpectedly. He'd tried to stay awake the night before, but he'd fallen asleep waiting for Bas to return, his jewellery and clothes leaving creases in his skin and a kink in his lower back.

"Shit."

"Prince Mereruka? I've come to escort you to the training grounds."

A polite knocking on his door signalled the beginning of his ordeal. Without any information from Bas, he would need to keep a clear, level head.

Mereruka soon found himself standing in fae armour inspecting the soldiers who had volunteered to participate in the sparring. It was mutually agreed upon that only those who could tolerate fae presence should participate. Mages of all kinds were forced to excuse themselves, and in the end, only a few remained.

Domina Emerald had been overly modest about her plans, for arranged around the sparring ring were intricate, earthen stands, with green, gold and deep red banners looped around the colonnades, turning the whole of it into an arena. There were even servants carrying trays of food and pitchers of wine. It was quite the feat of engineering—social and structural. The emperor and empress had decided to attend, along with most of the fae and a number of highly placed nobles. Taisiya and her sisters were scattered throughout, while those who had an aversion to his kind were seated furthest from the centre of the action and the seats that held his people.

Chloe softened out the creases in her lively mint dress, one blending the styles of Maat and Lethe, and stood to announce the beginning of the event. Mereruka and the others expected to fight stood in the centre of the ring.

"I would like to thank our generous hosts, Emperor Belisarius and Empress Selene, for agreeing to allow this bit of sport, and for our new friends from Maat for humouring us by participating. So that nothing gets too out of hand, I'd like to ask that no magic be performed during the matches."

Mereruka smiled and bowed in acquiescence.

"Are there any other handicaps you would like to insist on?" Djadty asked.

"I don't believe so, unless Your Majesties have anything to add?"

The imperial couple waved them all on.

"Excellent!"

Djadty touched the rune hidden at the base of his skull. His second set of arms sprouted from his back. A few of the fae in attendance hissed while the mages were caught between morbid shock and confusion at the fae reaction. Mereruka kept his face neutral.

Under different circumstances, Mereruka might have pitied the soldier, a victim of high-born fae prejudice against the use of runes and tattoos. It was a foolish one at that, and borne from the snobbery that the bodies of royalty, nobles and those who associated with them must be free of the marks of mercenaries and low-born malefactors who had failed to master high magics. Djadty was one of the few such individuals allowed to walk the halls of the king's palaces so marked, and only because he was devoted to Khety.

Djadty flexed his four arms and tossed his swords between his hands.

"If this is to be a true competition, there should be a prize! Perhaps our Prince of Dreams will agree to grant a wish to the ultimate winner of the sparring matches."

What in the hells was this about? Was this the trap?

"And yet I am a participant. Who is to grant me a boon if I win?" Mereruka asked.

Djadty shrugged.

"Don't be stingy, Your Tranquility. Grant a mage of your choosing a wish instead. Maybe our generous hosts, or the lovely mage who put this event together? If, of course, it pleases the emperor and empress." Djadty bowed.

"It pleases us," the empress called down with a grin.

"How could I refuse?" Mereruka smiled at the hopeful look coming from Chloe.

It seemed Djadty was vying for the top spot on his list of troublesome people to do away with. So be it. If this were all he had planned for the day, then Mereruka simply needed to prevent the soldier from winning that boon.

CHAPTER 14

Maybe the witches were right. Men were violent, stupid creatures. Taisiya glanced over at Domina Chloe Emerald, preening from the cooing and congratulations on the exhibition she'd arranged. Perhaps a number of women were as well. Then again, Taisiya often found herself in the minority opinion when it came to making a spectacle of violence and bloodshed. Violence was sometimes necessary, but it should never be celebrated. It hadn't bothered her so much a few years ago, but after having to identify Dimitri amongst the gory remnants... she found the prospect of unnecessary carnage repellent.

Milena sat herself beside Taisiya and stared at the fae who had sprouted four arms.

"I bet getting a tailored tunic would be a nightmare with four arms."

Taisiya coughed to cover her spluttering laugh. Milena smiled, brighter than she had in many years. It was good to see her so happy.

"Where is your fiancé?"

"Doing big, swinging dick things." She pointed to Zephyros, who stood in the ring, sword in hand and joking with the strategos. "So, Vasilisa told me you made a deal with the prince. A wife for exclusive trade. Smart. Except you'll owe him big if you fail. Why didn't you tell us?"

Damn. She'd told Vasilisa to keep that part to herself.

"Don't get angry. Vasilisa is just being a good friend," Milena said.

"Does it look like I'll fail in that regard?" Taisiya nodded to Chloe. "Besides, I'm working on a list of alternatives." Alternatives that kept skipping out of scheduled meetings. Was Chloe or her father behind it? Vasilisa's spying hadn't turned up anything yet.

Milena raised a brow and whistled.

"So it's as good as done, then. Word is, whatever Chloe wants, daddy makes sure she gets. Suppose he needed to put all that fierce doting somewhere after he decided having a healer for a daughter was beyond the pale. Piece of shit move, if you ask me."

Magistra Zoe Jade had been thoroughly cut off from Magister Emerald, her father, after Zoe let it be known she was a healer looking for a skilled mentor. Such was blind devotion to elementalism among the elites of Lethe. It had left Taisiya and her family further isolated. Social pariahs like Magistra Jade rarely held popular parties or made good connections on behalf of their wards, especially when those wards were the disgraced daughters of a traitor.

"The problems of being a former favourite child," Taisiya shrugged. "I'm sure the mountain of gold the Jade Province brings in helps cushion the blow."

"She can wipe her tears with a new silk dress every day and never run out."

They watched the sparring for a moment, an uncomfortable silence between them. The matches were fast, brutal and decided in moments. The strategos advanced while Zephyros was eliminated. Taisiya released a pent-up breath. The admiral had escaped with only scrapes. If he were to be family soon, that meant he needed to be ruthlessly protected. Even if it had meant shoving a bolt of lightning into anyone whose blade might do real damage.

"What will you owe him if you fail?" Milena asked as she fisted the material of her dress, turning to face Taisiya.

"I don't know." Taisiya couldn't meet her stare, eyes locked on her own fistfuls of cloth.

Milena clicked her tongue.

"That was poorly done. It'll be hard to plan countermeasures without knowing that."

"I know, I know." Taisiya sighed. "But when he teleported in all that treasure, in full view of the court, I knew someone would propose the same deal if I hesitated. Nobilissimus Procopius, for one."

"Fucking rat," Milena cursed. "What if he asks for something horrible? Like your firstborn? Or your eyes? Or your life?"

"Those are just stories," Taisiya hedged, convincing no one.

Milena placed her hand on Taisiya's, forcing her to look up.

"I think we have to plan for those stories to be true. If it comes to it, we can always kill him. The trade is a good opportunity but not a necessary one." Milena looked Taisiya up and down, noting the foreign fashions she sported as well as the imitations in the crowd. "I think you should seriously consider that you, or part of you, will be what he demands, and have a steel blade handy if he does."

Be my lover, Taisiya.

A shiver ran down her spine at the memory. She squashed it.

"You might need one anyway," Milena continued, "if Chloe gets it in her mind to be jealous of the attention he pays you and the gifts he gives you."

Taisiya looked down at her hands and took Milena's in her own. She did her best to breathe slowly. She needed to think—to plan.

Chloe was likelier to say something cruel rather than act on it, and Magister Emerald was conservative to a fault, never making a move unnecessarily. Magister Emerald had also given her his nod of approval just the other day for making the introductions on Chloe's behalf, and his goodwill was infinitely more precious than his daughter's. They weren't a threat in this instance—failure was. The chance of Chloe deciding to give up her prize was small, but not impossible. So far, every woman she'd proposed as an alternate had been enthusiastic the first day and then begged off the next, regardless of whether or not she'd met with the prince.

At this point, it was no longer a coincidence. If Chloe or the magister were the culprit, then Taisiya needn't worry about the bargain—it was as good as done. However, if they had no part in it, that left two possibilities: an unknown player or Prince Mereruka himself. Neither made complete sense. An unknown player with an unknown motive who kept gaining access to the prince's schedule and the names of the women he was meeting felt like a stretch, especially since Chloe hadn't given up and no one had stepped in to rival her. But the prince sabotaging his own chances at any woman, save Chloe? When he hadn't had the chance to meet several of the candidates and he'd stated his desire to be wed? What was she missing?

She couldn't think for all the noise of the crowd. Milena pulled her hands from Taisiya's.

"You know, I take it back. We might not need to worry about the prince much longer."

"What?" Taisiya's head shot up.

Milena tipped her head to the ring.

"I think the strategos is going to kill him."

If Djadty had failed to defeat Marduk, Mereruka doubted he would be able to claim victory against the hulking, lethal beast mage. But Djadty hadn't failed because he lacked the skill—he'd failed on purpose. Mereruka was ashamed to admit to having trouble trying to parse the plot the soldier had cooked up. Until, of course, the swords were presented to him and the strategos. Mereruka felt the spell before he touched his blade, holding back his sneer. A berserker curse. If they'd thought to have him sent into a bloodthirsty rage in order to be killed by the beast mage in self-defence, it was a good plan, but one destined to fail. As far as weapons curses went, it was laughably predictable. Bas was going to be sorry he missed the foolish look on the soldier's face when the curse died against the hidden protections inked into Mereruka's skin.

He held up the blade and pretended to inspect it before smiling.

"Skilled though I am, I suspect I'll be granting a wish of yours shortly, Strategos."

When the mage didn't turn to face him, reply, or even move, Mereruka raised his brow at the young man who'd handed Marduk the fae sword. The sword-bearer's face paled, a small creature staring up at a predator.

"Strategos?" Mereruka asked.

Between one heartbeat and the next, Marduk raised his blade as if to cleave the young man's head from his body. Just as Marduk's sword came down, Mereruka tossed out a shoddy, split-second barrier to shield the man. A scream erupted from the crowd as the sword-bearer fled. Marduk rounded on Mereruka, his murderous intent plain. Mereruka squinted, focusing his magic on the rune at his brow for spell-sight, and caught the ugly shadow of a curse wrapping itself around the strategos. He'd been an overconfident fool once again. The plan had been to have the both of them berserker-cursed—to fight until every bone was cracked, every muscle slit, every tendon split and not a drop of blood remained inside their bodies.

They'd decided to bring a body back to Maat.

In the next moment, he was forced to focus his entire being on defending himself from the onslaught. He barely had a moment to breathe, let alone cast a spell. Even whatever shoddy barriers he could erect were sundered by the strategos' unbelievable strength. As he was inexorably pushed back, the noise from the crowd grew in intensity. He prayed someone would recognize the strategos' fury as unnatural.

As a dark streak zipped past the corner of Mereruka's eye, Marduk's next brutal swing disarmed him. Mereruka leapt back. It wouldn't be far enough. Marduk's reach would cleave him in two. He didn't even have the time to process that he'd just taken his last breath when Bas appeared before him, his hands desperately gripping the sword arm of the strategos, claws digging in deep.

"It's a berserker curse! The sword is cursed!" Bas screamed.

Marduk grappled wildly with Bas but quickly succeeded in throwing him off. Marduk's primal roar echoed in the ring as he advanced once more, his eyes wild. Mereruka cast a spell of immobility, but to his horror, it failed. Just as Marduk made to swing, he stopped, the light of sanity dawning in his dark eyes.

"Marduk! Drop the sword! Now!" the emperor commanded from the stands.

The strategos immediately obeyed. The cursed blade clattered as it hit the ground.

"I-what-I don't-" he stammered in his confusion.

"The blade was cursed," Mereruka said, his knees feeling weak. That weakness fled when he saw Bas, blood streaming from his temple. "Bas!" He scrambled over to him and inspected the wound. Gods below, not his son—*not his son!*

"I'm fine. Stop fussing," Bas said, his eyes faraway, his hands clenching and unclenching.

Mereruka ignored the words and cast a healing spell as tears threatened to choke him. The flesh knit together and blood stopped flowing. Not even a bruise would form. Mereruka released a shaky breath, his heart hammering wildly in his chest. Bas could have healed the wounds himself if he'd shifted between forms, but young shape shifters rarely had the presence of mind to do so. Or the training given to shape shifter soldiers. Mereruka cast a glamour over them both.

"Your magic always leaves a weird taste in my mouth," Bas complained, his voice hollow.

Mereruka slapped him. Bas gasped. Mereruka grasped him by the shoulders and shook him as his own body trembled, hands digging in as he clenched his teeth and swallowed down a helpless scream.

"You stupid boy! You could have been killed!" Mereruka roared.

Bas' eyes watered and his voice cracked.

"*You* could have died, you stupid old goat!"

Mereruka's heart clenched in his chest. He pulled Bas into a crushing hug.

"Don't ever scare me like that again," Mereruka hissed.

Bas' arms encircled him.

"S-stupid old goat."

"Dumb cat," Mereruka said as he petted Bas' head.

"My cover is blown," Bas whispered dejectedly.

"Only for now. If we make it back to the ship alive, I'll take care of it," Mereruka whispered.

Bas' arms fell away and Mereruka pulled back to see the anger in the shifter's hazel eyes. Good. It was better than the look of the lost.

"Djadty needs to die."

"He will," Mereruka assured him as he stood. He held out his hand and helped Bas to his feet, dispelling the glamour he'd cast to give them a moment of privacy.

"Prince Mereruka, please forgive me!"

Mereruka turned to see Marduk kneeling before him.

"Did you curse the blade, Strategos?"

"No, I did not," Marduk replied.

"Then you are not at fault. Find the one who gave you the blade, and we'll begin the investigation there."

Mereruka knew who would be found culpable. The only question was if he would be able to use this as a means to kill three birds with one stone, or if he would have to content himself with Djadty's death alone.

CHAPTER 15

"I don't believe we've been introduced."

Taisiya eyed the young man who had saved the prince. Red-brown skin, black-brown hair and bright hazel eyes accompanied triangular cat's ears atop his head and a matching tail in the same shade as his hair. When he extended his hand, his claws were retracted but obvious. He took her hand and kissed it perfunctorily.

"Bas."

"Illustra Taisiya Spark, Ambassador for Lethe, the Empire of Mages." He had obviously come along with the rest of the delegation from Maat, based on his clothes, but he was not fae, if his complexion and transformation in the ring were any indication. "You seem close with Prince Mereruka."

"Mmm," he replied.

His ears flattened on his head before flicking back up again. He refused to meet her gaze. How very feline of him. She pressed him further.

"So close, in fact, I'm having a hard time understanding why we were not introduced sooner. His concern for you was genuine. The kind one reserves for family or the closest of friends. Which would you consider yourself, Bas?"

"Bas. Come," Mereruka called as he stood in close conference with the strategos.

"Excuse me, Ambassador," Bas said with a noticeable measure of relief.

Taisiya nodded politely and watched the young man beat a hasty retreat. Most of the spectators had left the ring, escorted by mage soldiers when they were deemed unnecessary to the investigation. The royal couple, the fae delegation, the strategos, his men, and a few others remained. Taisiya had been asked to stay, as she was nominally responsible for the care of the fae delegation. It was a tenuous reason, especially when Nobilissimus Procopius, the logothete in charge of internal diplomacy and intelligence, was already present. Still, she was grateful. Better to see with her own eyes how this would be resolved than to be forced to beg for scraps of information later.

In the training grounds, fae and mages alike were brought before the prince and strategos to be questioned in the open. The mage who had presented the fae blade to Marduk swore he'd been given it by a fae servant. That fae servant pointed the finger at another, then another, and so it went until it seemed almost every fae servant had touched the blade. The prince looked as though he was losing patience. Taisiya shared the sentiment as the summer sun burned ever hotter overhead.

"Why in the hells are we chasing our tails? Just call on Alexandra," the empress said.

"Your Majesty, we don't know if she can tolerate the fae," the praetor cautioned.

Yes, the praetor would consider that a real obstacle, considering he was one of those mages himself. He had always been pale, but pushing himself to be in the presence of the fae had left him ashen, his green eyes all the brighter for the bruise-like circles underneath, his now bloodless lips perpetually thinned as he fought back nausea. That at least was a little treat for her eyes.

"If you can bear it for a short time, so can she," the emperor said. He looked around at the mages gathered. "Illustra Spark, I believe we can spare you in this matter. Please locate Magistra Amber and bring her here."

Damn. She looked to the slight grin on Procopius' face at her dismissal. Double-damn. He was eyeing up the prince.

"The magistra is usually in the library at this time," the praetor offered.

He would know, given he kept tabs on the dangerous silver-tongued mage at all times. And rightly so. Magistra Amber had the ability to command anyone with the capacity to listen to do whatever she ordered. There was no one better suited to interrogation in the whole of Lethe, and until recently, she'd been cloistered in the palace, a prisoner. Only the empress' favour had spared her the life of a chained, collared pet. She now held the title of magistra and ostensibly ruled over Taisiya's former lands. Or she would, if the crown ever saw fit to allow her to leave the capital.

Taisiya excused herself, curtsied and turned from the training grounds. Once she was out of sight of the others, Vasilisa stepped from her shadow and began walking beside her.

"Have you already heard about the cursed sword?" Taisiya asked.

"Yes. Father told me," Vasilisa said.

Her father, Viktor, was also a darkness mage and had been Grigori's closest friend and aide. Viktor had been ordered to leave Grigori's side before the magister entered the capital and to take care of his family if he failed to kill the emperor. Viktor had been a true and loyal friend, even after Taisiya's father had passed, and had taken a liking to Theodore, whom he now served. Like Vasilisa, he preferred to wander the void and watch the world from the shadows.

"Any new information about our flighty bride candidates?" Taisiya asked.

"Several received threats of blackmail recently, though the source is unknown."

"Shit."

"My thoughts exactly."

Taisiya sighed, exasperated. She needed to lure the cretin out into the open if she could.

"The domina hasn't received one of these threats?"

"If she has, then she does a good job of hiding it. Not that I've been able to breach her home's defences. The magister has recently paid a great deal of coin for protection curses against shadowy spies."

"Unsurprising, given the praetor uses them so liberally," Taisiya sneered.

Just because Taisiya would—and did—do the same didn't mean she couldn't hate him for it. She rarely lost sleep over her own hypocrisy.

"Would you like me to purchase one?" Vasilisa smiled.

Taisiya shook her head.

"When the time is right, I want that spy dead and buried in the void, as well as any foolish enough to come afterwards."

Vasilisa laughed.

"No body, no crime and no accusations, not unless they admit to spying on an innocent."

"Precisely." Taisiya grinned. "As for our blackmailer... I have an idea, but I'll need you to do the heavy lifting."

Vasilisa arched a pale brow.

"Do I get to kill someone?"

"Potentially," Taisiya said.

"Then it would be a delight."

"Illustra Spark, could I have a word?"

Magistra Jade approached, her sparkling green eyes brooking no denial. Vasilisa stepped aside as the dark-skinned beauty's long strides ate up the distance between them. Taisiya was neither overly fond of nor hostile to the newly minted Magistra Jade. She'd provided shelter, clothing and food to her and her remaining family, but little else, and she'd never shared the hostility with which some of the other nobles viewed her.

"Of course, Magistra. What might I assist you with?" Taisiya curtsied.

"You can warn my fool sister away from that prince, for one."

She would do no such thing.

"Domina Chloe is more than capable of deciding for herself if she wishes to pursue Prince Mereruka."

Zoe scoffed.

"Chloe is a starry-eyed girl desperate for the magister's approval. And anyone with eyes in their head can see that the prince is trouble. I'll not let my sister fall prey to him and then be taken away from everyone who actually cares about her. If you don't have the decency to warn her off him, then at the very least find someone else for him to set his sights on."

"Have you spoken to your sister yourself, Your Grace?"

Zoe narrowed her eyes.

"You think I haven't tried? You know exactly what my family is like, Taisiya," she hissed. "She won't listen to sense right now, not when Father's approval is on the line, and she might not listen until it's too late. Help me protect her."

Taisiya narrowed her eyes. If anyone here had the power to protect a domina, it was the magistra, not the disgraced daughter of a traitor, desperately clawing her way back into the good graces of the court. Not to mention, it was her family's future on the line if this matchmaking scheme fell through.

"I will do my utmost to introduce the prince to other suitable candidates, but I will not put myself in the middle of a fight between Your Grace and Magister Emerald."

"Very well, Taisiya. But be careful whose good graces you cultivate. My loyalty doesn't waver. Magister Emerald's changes whenever it suits him. Good day to you." Zoe swept by, head held high and nary a single glance backwards.

Taisiya sighed. Just what she'd needed—another complication. She wished she did not need to cultivate the support of a woman whose loyalty would always be to the empress. Better to have the magister's support for the day she and her family finally retook their kingdom. If only she had enough wealth and power not to concern herself with upsetting Zoe.

"We need more candidates," Taisiya groaned.

"Want me to see if I can find some especially desperate ones?"

"Yes, and keep them in reserve for now. We need to root out that blackmailer first before I expend all my other options."

As they approached the doors of the library, trepidation slowed her steps. The silver-tongued could be a fearsome enemy. While Magistra Alexandra Amber remained a creature of the crown, if she ever learned to wield her political power in the same way as her voice, Taisiya could kiss her generation's chances of reclaiming their homeland goodbye. Vasilisa's grey eyes softened. She placed a reassuring hand on Taisiya's shoulder.

"She's not strong enough yet."

Not strong enough to rip out the secrets Taisiya kept close to her heart, the ones her father had protected with the power of another silver-tongue, one so much stronger than the young magistra. Even now, she was protected, just as she and her sisters had been when they'd boldly lied under interrogation over a year ago.

"And I don't think she'll ever try anything." At Taisiya's confusion, Vasilisa only chuckled softly. "See for yourself and try not to get too upset."

Taisiya was only confused for a moment longer. When she came to collect Alexandra, she found her in deep conversation with Theodore, bright smiles on both their faces. Maps and ledgers pertaining to lands once owned by her family lay between the two on the angled desk.

A surge of pure rage flooded Taisiya. The gall, to pressure her brother into being the one to ease Alexandra's transition to ruling a territory he'd—they'd—called home! Of course, Theodore wouldn't hesitate to help—not her selfless, sweet, amiable brother. If the silver-tongued mage thought she would get away with using Theo so shamelessly, she'd find herself gutted by lightning, damn the consequences. Only Vasilisa's unwavering grip on her shoulder held her back.

"Stop and really *look*, Taisiya," she whispered.

"Look at what? That shameless bitch using my brother?" Taisiya hissed.

"If he weren't your brother, what would that look like?" Vasilisa nodded to the two seated beside each other, their chairs nearly touching.

Taisiya paused and stifled her anger as best she could. If he weren't Theodore, but some other man, what would she see? Their eyes, hers amber, his deep purple, were sparkling. Their laughter was genuine, if hushed. The magistra had a flush across her pale brown cheeks and she found frequent opportunities to touch his arm, to tuck a strand of her white hair behind her ear. Theodore, for his part, leaned towards her, his knee skimming her skirts, the occasional nervous hand snaking through his short auburn curls.

"Shit," Taisiya cursed.

"I think it's sweet. And smart. If he were the calculating type."

Which he wasn't. Theodore was truly smitten.

Damn. Damn. Damn it all to the deepest of hells!

Taisiya could hear the grin in Vasilisa's voice and scowled.

"She's too young for him," she protested mulishly.

"She's of legal age to wed, and knowing your brother, he won't make any moves until she does. Besides, a decade age gap is nothing. Maybe if it were four decades, but it's not."

Rationally, Vasilisa was right. Once mages physically became adults in their early twenties, it was difficult to spot the difference between them and any mage under the age of seventy, unless hard living or illness stripped them of their natural vitality. At least it was until you spoke with one. Then the years of experience tended to make clear the difference.

"I don't have to like it."

"No, but look at Theodore. Doesn't he look happy?"

He... did.

"You've always said he should marry for love."

Taisiya groaned. She did say that—often.

"Let's get this over with. I don't want to be hearing gossip about the investigation later, I want to be telling it."

Vasilisa released her grip. Taisiya moved to interrupt the two.

"Magistra Amber." Taisiya curtsied. "The emperor requests your presence. I've come to escort you to the training grounds."

Both Theodore and Alexandra jumped at the sound of her voice, so blind they'd been to the world around them.

Only Taisiya could hear the scream inside her head.

"Taisiya! I haven't seen you since you became ambassador. You look beautiful." Theodore rose from his seat and hugged her.

"Thank you, Theo. But what are you doing here?" Taisiya asked as politely as she could.

"The praetor asked for someone to teach Alex—Magistra Amber—about her new role. I've been showing her what I can whenever I have a moment to spare," Theodore said, blushing at the misstep of referring to the magistra so casually.

"That's very sweet of you Theo." She smiled. "Will you be attending this evening's ball?"

He shook his head.

"Likely not. The logothete has me working like a dog."

"Take care then. And remember that Milena is getting married in a few days. Family only." She kissed him on his cheek and turned her attention to the magistra, who had risen from her seat and smoothed the silk of her sunset orange dress while they spoke. "Shall we proceed, Magistra?"

Alexandra nodded. She looked shyly to Theodore.

"Thank you, Illustrus Spark. Please let me know when you next have the time to spare for me."

With a few more polite farewells, they were headed back to the sparring ring.

"My brother is a very kind man, Magistra," Taisiya said, her tone censorious.

"I agree," Alexandra replied, her posture stiffening.

"It would be a pity if someone were to break his heart." She eyed the silver-tongue tellingly. "On a completely unrelated note, were you aware that a bolt of lightning travels farther and faster than the sound of, say, a scream? No? Just a bit of trivia." Taisiya caught Vasilisa out of the corner of her eye, pursing her lips to keep from laughing. "As I said, the emperor requires your gifts in the sparring ring. There's been an incident with a cursed sword that we'd like to get to the bottom of."

CHAPTER 16

"Is this Magistra Amber a professional interrogator?" Mereruka asked the strategos.

"She is a silver-tongued mage, her commands are impossible to ignore. We'll have answers with only a few questions from her," Marduk replied.

Gods below, Mereruka thought. She could put all his schemes in jeopardy with only a few questions. She sounded like an enchantress, or a siren perhaps. Such creatures were not to be taken lightly and often found themselves in positions of extreme power or wretched servitude. If Mereruka played this right, he might be able to rid himself of his enemies entirely.

Djadty stood nearby, glaring at the fae servants who had already been questioned. It still amazed Mereruka that a man as blunt, unimaginative and lacking in magical ability as the soldier had managed to swap in cursed swords despite all the servants involved.

"How were you able to overcome the berserker curse, Strategos?" Mereruka asked. "It's an impressive feat."

He had his suspicions about the emperor, but hoped this would prove them definitively. He'd rarely failed at casting a spell in the past, but the powers of a null might explain it all.

"I don't believe I did, Prince Mereruka. I don't even recall picking up the blade."

A careful, unhelpful answer. Damn.

"I'm curious about the boy. Bas, was it? Not many fully-grown men can stop my swing, let alone an unarmed one." Marduk smiled at Bas, who stood by their side, having already given his account of hearing one of the fae with spell sight gasp the name of the curse before running into the ring.

"I'm a shapeshifter, Strategos. We're strong as a general rule. And I'm nearly an adult. I'm already forty-two."

Marduk gave a sharp intake of breath, his eyes widening.

"Forty-two? When do shapeshifters come of age?"

"Fifty for most, one hundred for others," Bas replied.

Marduk looked to Mereruka and again to Bas.

"Forgive me for being rude, but how long do shapeshifters and fae live, usually?"

Mereruka saw Bas' ears twitch and focused his own hearing. Two sets of steps had entered the ring. Taisiya had undoubtedly returned.

"Barring incurable illness or a violent death? Around six hundred years for shapeshifters and one thousand for the fae, give or take a few centuries," Mereruka answered, nonchalant.

It would no doubt come as a shock to the short-lived mages. Better they learn their place in the world than to believe themselves a blessed race. If he was to be tied to this land for a century or so, he'd be damned if they went and kicked hornets' nests across the seas out of a misplaced sense of superiority.

"Though some shapeshifters, like dragons, are special exceptions. They too live about as long as the fae," Mereruka added.

"Ah," Marduk replied, a frown creasing his brow.

"Alexandra! We have a job for you," the empress called and waved, interrupting the conversation between Mereruka and the strategos. "Prince Mereruka, I'd like to introduce Magistra Alexandra Amber."

"A pleasure, Your Grace." Mereruka inclined his head.

Eyes wide as she took him in, the magistra curtsied low.

"It is an honour to meet you, Prince Mereruka."

Introductions done, the magistra lifted her head and made her way to the empress while Taisiya remained by Mereruka's side, her polite, disinterested mask firmly in place.

"I'm happy to be of service, Your Majesty." Alexandra smiled.

The woman possessed pale brown skin, white hair and strikingly amber eyes. She looked younger than Taisiya, despite her taller stature. The mages gave her a wide berth. Mereruka turned to Taisiya, her polite, disinterested mask firmly in place.

"So, what questions do you want answered?" Alexandra asked.

She stopped before the group of those already questioned. It must be the first time she'd seen the fae. Her eyes were riveted on them. The mages paled.

"Ask the prince or strategos. They're in charge of this mess," the empress replied.

"Strategos?" Alexandra asked.

"Ask the mages if they knew the sword was cursed before I handled it."

Alexandra nodded. She looked around.

"I don't want to affect anyone else. Would you mind giving me some room?"

"Come, Prince Mereruka, Bas. It's best not to listen when she speaks," Taisiya said as she led them to the edges of the ring.

"Bas, cover your ears," Mereruka said.

"Did you know the sword was cursed before the strategos handled it?"

Mereruka felt the pull of her words, though they hadn't been directed towards him. He took a step closer to the voice. He wasn't alone. Most of those present had done so; some had even fallen to their knees. The emperor, empress and a few others standing next to them were the only exceptions. That sealed it. The emperor was a null, or whatever the mage equivalent was.

A chorus of 'no's' answered her query, including the fae servants. All their faces were rapt, trancelike, their bodies swaying to be nearer to her.

Alexandra turned to Mereruka and the strategos, waiting for instructions. Mereruka suppressed a shudder. It seemed silver-tongue was just another name for a siren. Good.

"We've spoken to all the servants who handled the sword. Perhaps it would be best to speak to those with more authority. Djadty..." Mereruka turned to the soldier and savoured the wariness in his sharp eyes. "Perhaps you can answer a question. You're in charge of the safety of this mission as well as the few soldiers and their weapons. Did you know the blade given to the strategos was cursed?"

"No, Prince Mereruka," Djadty answered.

"Magistra Amber, would you ask Djadty yourself?" Mereruka asked.

Just as Alexandra opened her mouth to speak, Djadty lunged at her, blade in hand. As everyone in the ring was in the process of rushing to her defence, a blinding light and searing heat lashed out from beside Mereruka. He hissed at the nearness, narrowly avoiding a burn. By the time Mereruka heard the crackling clap, Djadty had been tossed back from the young mage. Taisiya rushed to the silver-tongue's side, frantically looking her over for injuries.

Mereruka, along with everyone else in the ring, hurried over to the downed fae. He came to a stop and surveyed the damage. Djadty's body was smoking, the stench permeating the air. His eyes had exploded and his sword had turned molten, melding to one of his hands. There was no coming back from that. One of the fae delegation, a soldier, pressed his ear to Djadty's chest in vain. He stood and shook his head.

"He's dead, Prince Mereruka."

Unfortunately, he'd died without naming Raemka or Itu as his accomplices. It was a setback, but at least he was left with only two rats to contend with.

Mereruka turned to the strategos and bowed.

"My deepest apologies for bringing this criminal into your midst. I feel it is only appropriate to offer a favour as recompense."

"Peace between our peoples, Prince Mereruka. That is what I wish for," the strategos replied.

A wise request, for a man of war. And one easy enough to keep. Mereruka doubted many from Maat would wish to visit the Cursed Continent, let alone fight over it.

"As long as I live, I will do my utmost to uphold that," Mereruka replied. "And who should I reward for preventing the attempted murder of your mage? I confess I didn't catch sight of the one who struck Djadty."

"I believe that was Illustra Spark. There weren't any other lightning mages present," Marduk said, his face grim.

Mereruka turned to see Taisiya helping Alexandra to her feet. He was beginning to really hope she failed to uphold their bargain. He'd thought the mages uniformly weak, their magic unimpressive. He had been wrong. Djadty's spectacular demise had most of the fae looking at Taisiya with new, more deferential, eyes. Desire, covetous and dark, curled in his gut. He wanted a bride who would be respected in her own right—a villainess as capable of inspiring awe as she did fear. And the speed of her lightning strike was both awesome and fearful.

The empress approached Taisiya and slapped her on the back with a cackling laugh, startling the ambassador.

"Nice shot! I didn't know you had it in you."

Neither had Mereruka. What else would he discover in the coming days? He eyed Raemka and Itu and smiled. Only two to go.

CHAPTER 17

"Vasilisa, I need—"

The darkness mage leapt from Taisiya's shadow, surprising the empress and Alexandra both.

"I know," Vasilia whispered, her hand rubbing calming circles on Taisiya's back. She turned to the others gathered. "Please excuse us."

Vasilisa helped support Taisiya as they dashed from the training grounds, away from the eyes of others.

"I can't-"

"Here." Vasilisa pushed her towards a potted plant adding a splash of green to the sea of imperial red mosaics.

Taisiya lunged for the pot and expelled the contents of her stomach. Vasilisa whispered calming words in her ear as she stroked her sweat-slicked back.

"We're alone for now but not for much longer. You're doing better."

"How can you say that? I... I smelled him and then—gods below."

There was nothing left in her stomach. Dry heaves had her shuddering.

"Even the thought of striking out with a bolt had you losing your lunch before. You had perfect control this time. You even held it together long enough for us to get away from the crowd. You're improving."

"Father would've been so disappointed in me. After all he entrusted me with, I can't even—"

"Hush! You're exactly the same as you've always been, the same daughter he always loved. Now stand tall, Taisiya." Vasilisa helped her stand and tipped up her chin. "Chin up. You will overcome this."

Taisiya quelled the trembling in her hands and took a deep breath. Would she ever fully overcome what the terrible sight of her brother's mangled corpse had done to her nerves?

No, she couldn't let that kind of defeatism rule her. Maybe, one day, the sight of such things wouldn't bring her back to that moment. Until then, she had Vasilisa and her family to rely on.

"Yes... yes, thank you," Taisiya said.

"Now let's wash out your mouth. Your breath is atrocious."

Taisiya chuckled and wiped a few errant tears from her eyes.

"We're not alone," Vasilisa whispered. She looked to the potted plant and pushed it into a shadow, depositing it into the void, hidden from this world. Taisiya almost wanted to giggle at the absurdity but refrained, hysteria threatening her composure.

Alexandra, her skirts gripped in her hands, rushed towards them. When she was within a few steps, the silver-tongued mage stopped.

"Illustra Spark, I... thank you. You saved my life. I was too dazed to say it before."

"I did tell you that lightning was faster than a scream, didn't I?" Taisiya said, regaining her former control at least outwardly.

"But why? I thought you-"

Taisiya held up her hand to stop the younger mage.

"Theodore is smitten with you."

"Just because of that?" she asked, her eyes wide as a fawn's.

"Do you really, truly care for my brother?"

"Yes, more than anything. He's the only one who doesn't look at me like... like I'm a monster."

That sounded like her brother, his heart big enough to shelter every broken, lost soul the empire over. He brought goodness and kindness wherever he went. It was no wonder the orphan mage who inspired fear had found his warmth intoxicating.

"And what wouldn't you do for him?"

"I'd do anything for him."

"Be careful about making grand statements like that, Magistra," Taisiya hissed. At first, the young mage looked down, beaten. Then she raised her amber eyes, determination coming to the fore. "Good. That's a much better look. I think, in time, you'll find that we are a family that will do absolutely anything for each other. I hope you will prove yourself worthy of that."

"I hope so too, Illustra Spark."

Taisiya nodded.

"Excuse me, Magistra." Taisiya curtsied and turned on her heel. As she was walking away, she turned her head to the side. "And you may call me Taisiya."

"Thank you, Taisiya." Alexandra smiled.

When they were far enough away, Vasilisa chuckled low.

"You are your father's daughter."

Taisiya sighed. Theo had certainly chosen a challenging lover. It wouldn't be easy to ensure their happiness or safety. It would be even harder to free her from the palace.

"Theo adores her. Whether I like it or not, she was family the moment I discovered that."

"Will you help her?" Vasilisa asked.

"I'll have to. She's a magistra in name only right now. Until she's ruling in her own right, she's still a pet of the empress, just with a slightly longer leash. I won't allow Theo's future wife to be a prisoner inside this palace."

Vasilisa smiled and steered her to a small parlour decorated in blues and devoid of other occupants. Taisiya sat down on a stiff chair.

"I'll find some food and drink for you," Vasilisa said before ducking into the nearest shadow.

Faster than Taisiya would have thought possible, Vasilisa returned through the door with a rolling tray, full to bursting with teas and delicate foods.

"Where-"

"Took it from a servant. Chloe and the others are too busy gossiping to notice its absence."

Taisiya took the proffered cup of mint tea and sipped. Vasilisa pushed a small, hot bun towards her.

"I don't think I can."

"Eat. Before you turn into one of those silly ladies who faint from self-inflicted stupidity."

Taisiya took a bite, her stomach protesting.

"You might not have heard it, but the prince wanted to reward you with a favour," Vasilisa said.

For killing a man in cold blood. The bun turned to ash on her tongue. She swallowed past a hard lump in her throat. No, not for murder. For protecting Theo's heart. For protecting his happiness. Protecting her family. Taisiya let out a slow breath. As long as it was for family, there was no task too dark, too cruel or too unreasonable. She would swim in shark-infested filth for them if that's what it took.

"I'll have to think of something suitable."

Maybe an end to this sword hanging above her head? Zoe's anger might be a problem, but only if she outwardly stopped introducing bride candidates to the prince. It would mean leaving herself dangerously short of potential candidates, but if he married Chloe without too much delay, she might be able to placate Zoe while still garnering the support of Emerald.

"Shall I bring him here?" Vasilisa asked.

"Yes."

"Then finish your tea and eat your bun."

Vasilisa's hard smile left no room for refusal. Taisiya did as she was told. She was, after all, fortunate to have such a good friend.

"Is Domina Emerald to your liking, Prince Mereruka?" Taisiya asked.

Mereruka considered her for a long moment. Though she had her mask in place, she was ragged around the edges, blood drained from her face and her eyes rimmed by dark circles. Had Djaty's death shocked her?

"She fulfils my requirements."

But she wasn't who he really wanted to get his hands on.

"Then as the favour you mentioned bestowing upon me in the sparring ring, I request that you officially ask for her hand in marriage."

It was not how Mereruka had imagined this meeting would go, nor what he'd envisioned her asking of him. Bas shifted on his feet, standing behind Mereruka's chair, pretending to be his attendant. Mereruka knew she'd had trouble with bride candidates refusing to keep their appointments or pleading a change of heart after meeting with him. She must be feeling the weight of their deal pressing down on her. Could he agree to the favour he owed her, and also get her in the bargain?

Mereruka suspected someone in the mage court wanted to prevent his marriage to one of their women and was pressuring candidates to step aside. If he gave the malefactor enough time, would they get to Chloe as well? The domina was a perfectly ambitious woman who knew well how to navigate court life. Chloe was intelligent as well as attractive, but the more he got to know Taisiya, the more he saw her on the throne by his side. Where Chloe had a romantic heart and seemed overly eager to be in his good graces, there was a dark, sharp undercurrent to Taisiya. He couldn't picture Chloe stepping over his brother's fresh corpse, but he could picture Taisiya wielding a blade of lightning against Khety given the right incentives. It was that viciousness in her that called to the viciousness in him.

"Then in three days, when the ugly incident with Djadty has had time to settle, I will do just that. But since you've asked me to rush this proposal and the conclusion of our deal, know that if she refuses me, I will consider it a failure on your part."

"That's absurd. What kind of reward comes with a punishment?" Taisiya asked, her eyes narrowing.

"Oh? Do you have a list of other candidates?"

"I have a few to spare," she replied, her tone grudging.

There were still more? Gods, he'd never imagined his show of presenting the gifts would cause him so much trouble selecting his first choice of bride.

"Then if Chloe refuses me, and the other candidates haven't run off, I won't consider it a failure on your part. I believe that is more than fair."

"Fine, but only if you swear not to do anything to the women that might harm your chances of marrying them."

Did she suspect him to be behind the intimidation of the candidates? *Success*. She really had no idea who was pushing her further into his trap if she thought he had a hand in it. So long as the one responsible wasn't Chloe, Taisiya would be his. All he needed to do was let it slip he was close to offering marriage to Chloe and the malefactor would do his work for him.

"Then we have an agreement, Ambassador."

Taisiya nodded and stood.

"If you'll excuse me, I have a wedding to organise."

"No need to do so on my account. We have more than enough magic to put together something spectacular by Lethe's standards in a matter of hours."

Taisiya raised a copper brow.

"I had no intention of assisting you in that regard. It is for my sister, Milena."

"In that case, would you like my assi-"

Taisiya held up a hand to stop him.

"No, Prince Mereruka. Weddings for our household are small, private affairs. Family members only."

Her tone brooked no argument. It was one she used often with him. And it always had him wondering what she was hiding when she used it.

With that, she swept from the room, his presence forgotten. He looked up at Bas, standing beside his chair, and smiled.

"No," Bas said, frowning.

"Where's your curiosity?" Mereruka asked, grinning.

"Self-preservation killed it! I'd rather not die by lightning bolt."

"We're going to that wedding."

"Who's the adult here?" Bas muttered angrily.

But Mereruka was decided. It was time he discovered more about the woman who intrigued him most in Lethe.

CHAPTER 18

Taisiya wiped an errant tear from her eye as Milena and Zephyros swore their marriage vows in Theodore's small home in the capital. They were so very clearly in love. She wondered why Milena had never said anything about the dominus to their father.

"She looks beautiful," Charis sighed.

"Your father is looking at her with at least as much love as the groom," Taisiya replied.

Charis and Mina chuckled. Magister Opal had finally managed to see one of his sons settled. Zephyros wasn't Opal's heir, but as it stood, he was the only one likely to produce any grandchildren. She could see the magister dreaming about baby clothes and the names of tutors.

Aside from the immediate families and their partners, no one else had been invited to the wedding. The magister had managed to get his other sons to attend, though it had been a near thing. After the ceremony, alcohol and food was served. In the main atrium, the men moved the furniture to make way for dancing. Daria produced her violin, saved from the looters, and played merry tunes for everyone to dance to until the guests were too tired to do much more than hobble back to their own properties in the capital.

When everyone had left except Taisiya's family and the wedded couple, Milena plopped down beside Taisiya on the couch, her brow slicked with sweat.

"That was perfect," she beamed.

"Good. You deserved it." Taisiya wrapped her arm around Milena and tugged her close.

"So, are we going to do it or not?" Milena asked.

Taisiya raised her brows.

"Are you certain? We can wait a few years, when you know him better. When he's proven himself."

Milena shook her head.

"He's ready to really be one of us. Trust me."

Milena could be terribly impulsive when the mood hit her, but she was calm and confident about this. She knew the consequences if Zephyros proved false.

"Alright. I'll tell Mama. Vasilisa?"

Vasilisa stepped from a shadow.

"Congratulations, Milena." Vasilisa nodded.

"Thank you!"

"Vasilisa, we're going to the graveyard. Will you and your father retrieve the portal?"

"Of course." She grinned. "Hell of a wedding night you have planned."

"The bride gets what she wants." Taisiya smiled. "And have someone fetch Uncle Vadik. He should be there."

Vadik, born a beast mage, had spent his life pretending not to be related to their family. No one would have expected their grandfather, a king, to allow such a child to live, much less raise him in secret under the guise of being a household servant. But the Dragonsbloods were almost entirely a canny lot, and their grandfather's ploy had ensured that, even though he and all his other children and relatives died in the Great War, both Grigori and Vadik had survived to continue the family line. Even now, should Taisiya's branch of the family fall, Vadik's would continue.

Vasilisa nodded before she melted back into the void.

Taisiya took a deep breath. It would be her first time being in charge of the vows as the designated heir, and the one charged with carrying out the execution if Zephyros failed to swear or uphold them. She prayed Milena's instincts about her new husband were right.

"Does he know what we'll be doing tonight?"

"As much as he can know before it's done," Milena answered.

"Poor man. He's in for a rude awakening." Taisiya smiled.

Mereruka and Bas had been stuck hiding in the attic until the wedding wound down and the wind mage sons of Magister Opal had left, taking their witchy magic with them. Getting any closer would have tipped them off that a fae was nearby. Luckily, the newest addition to Taisiya's family wasn't one of those so afflicted.

Mereruka had spelled himself and Bas to remain hidden from sight from all except each other. The spell would last until the break of dawn. Mereruka hoped it would give them enough time to see why Taisiya had demanded privacy.

"This is ridiculous. It's a small wedding. She just didn't want outsiders joining in," Bas grouched.

"Let's go downstairs. If nothing happens in the next hour or so, I promise we can go back to the palace." Mereruka smiled.

He had spelled his rooms at the palace so that any who made to disturb him would remember him saying that he was resting after a bit too much mage wine. By this point, any fae in Lethe would understand, and he doubted his hosts would question it.

"Fine," Bas sighed.

They crept from the attic to the first floor where everyone was seated in the rearranged furniture and chatting amiably around the open-air atrium. It went on long enough that Mereruka was worried he might have to leave before his curiosity was sated. Then Vasilisa appeared from the shadows.

"We're ready. It will take two trips to take everyone with Father and me going through the void. Taisiya, Milena, Zephyros, will you join me?"

The three in question rose and linked hands. The darkness mage burst into inky black flames before pulling them into the shadows.

Mereruka wanted to curse as a second darkness mage, a tall, grim-looking man, appeared and took Taisiya's mother and two other sisters. Theodore was left waiting, humming a broken tune. Mereruka took his gold earring and shoved a tracing spell in it, his heart hammering all the while. He would lose all trace of Taisiya once her brother was taken into the void. His only hope was the weave the strands of the spell into his earring before Theodore's escort returned, all while hiding the aurora of his magic. Sweat trickled down his back. This was taking too long. He still needed to infuse it with enough magic to cover a vast distance. As the grim man returned, Mereruka's heart hammered in his chest. It was now or never. He slipped the earring into the pocket of Theodore's robe. A moment later, Theodore disappeared into what Mereruka could only assume was the void.

"Well, we can't follow them now," Bas said, obviously hoping Mereruka might be persuaded to give up.

"Once they return to this world, I should be able to teleport us to the location of my earring's twin. I told you it was worthwhile to pierce my ears," Mereruka crowed.

Bas groaned.

Mereruka pulled out the twin of the earring he had placed in Theodore's pocket and concentrated on the innate magic connecting the two. Wherever the void was, it was not in their world, Oblivion, but somewhere altogether different. A pocket realm, perhaps? In a few moments, he felt the tug of magic on the other end of the tether. He would never be able to teleport otherwise, such was the complexity of the spell.

"Success!"

"If I die, I'm going to curse you," Bas muttered.

"Come! And remember, we're-"

"Unseen, not unheard. I heard you the first twenty times."

Mereruka was too excited by the mystery to reproach his son. He drew a teleportation circle using strands of magic, like the bands of an aurora dancing and weaving around his and Bas' feet. Between one blink and the next, he and Bas were directly beside Theodore.

The night was cold, and wherever they'd landed was far from any sign of civilization. The canopy blocked all but a few twinkling stars and hints of moonlight from touching the soft forest floor. They were lucky the ground muffled their footsteps as they followed Theodore to a small clearing where a tree had recently fallen. Bathed in moonlight stood three enormous bones arranged as a lintel. The family stood before them and waited for Theodore to join them. Mereruka and Bas stood aside, unseen to any save each other.

Mereruka grinned knowingly at Bas, who did nothing but scowl.

Taisiya cleared her throat.

"What we're about to do cannot be undone. Zephyros Opal, are you willing to risk everything you have, everything you are, for Milena?"

"I am."

"Your family ruled the islands for many generations before the empire made you its vassals. What is your family's true name?"

The wind mage seemed surprised by such a question.

"Tempest," he answered.

"Then swear no vows except with your true name, Zephyros Tempest," Taisiya said before turning to Vasilisa, who stood beside the bones. "Keep watch. Anyone who finds this place dies."

"My pleasure. Have a safe journey."

"Journey?" Zephyros asked.

"Shhh, this is the best part," Milena said with a giggle.

Taisiya pulled a golden blade from the pocket of her robe and pricked her finger.

"Wimp!" Milena taunted.

"It doesn't need buckets of blood, Milena. Now hush," Taisiya replied with a wicked gleam in her eye.

Mereruka pulled Bas closer to the group so that they stood behind Theodore. He squinted at the bones. They were easily twice the height of a man but thin, and if he weren't mistaken, there were carvings etched along them. When Taisiya pressed her bloody finger to the bones, the carvings lit up, turning a macabre lintel into a fully-fledged portal. Instead of the opposite side of the clearing, the portal now showed the eerily lit interior of a cave. Zephyros gasped.

Mereruka had no idea the mages knew about such things. Old magic might be common amongst the elves, who had very little in the way of innate magics, but was seldom used by others. In magic-soaked Maat, old magic was all but extinct. This was his first time seeing such a thing. Even Bas had stopped scowling.

"Come," Taisiya commanded as she led the procession into the portal.

Mereruka and Bas entered just after Theodore and followed him along the path between stalagmites. The way was lit with pale blue lights floating at regular intervals. Dug into the walls were alcoves where the bones of the dead were laid to rest, words in the mage script carved above. When they entered an enormous cavern, the party stopped. Mereruka stifled a gasp. Bones, too big to be of any creature save a dragon, lay curled around the cavern, the soaring ribs acting like the markers of a henge. Its skull lay facing the small entrance through which he'd stepped, its toothy grin an effective threat. In the centre, half-buried in the cave floor, glittered a gem as large as a table.

The petrified heart.

The most coveted of magical jewels in the whole of Oblivion.

"What is this place?" Zephyros asked, his voice unsteady as he looked around in awe and terror.

"This is our ancestral graveyard. Every member of our family who died in a manner where remains could be collected is housed here. Zephyros Tempest, tonight you will swear your ultimate loyalty to our family, the Dragonsblood line. Are you prepared?" Taisiya said.

Bas gripped Mereruka's hand, shooting him wide-eyed glances as his nostrils flared and tail twitched. Dragons were in the habit of summarily executing any who stumbled on their graveyards, and for good reason. They believed the hearts of their ancestors held a part of the deceased's soul, and the widespread demand for the magical gems of near-limitless potential was insatiable.

Mereruka swallowed, praying his spell held long enough for them to retreat.

"Well, it's that or death, right?" Zephyros quipped.

"Yes," Taisiya replied.

The wind mage sobered. Mereruka held a finger to his lips and jerked his head in the direction of the exit. Bas nodded.

"I'm prepared."

"Milena, you taught him the steps?"

"I certainly did."

"Good. Then—oh! Uncle Vadik! You made it." Taisiya grinned.

Mereruka and Bas leapt out of the way of a beast mage, whose steps were so light that not even their acute hearing had caught the sound. He wasn't especially tall, but he was fearsome, and he was blocking the exit with his broad-shouldered frame.

Curling horns adorned his head while great leathery wings were tucked behind him, and a thick, scaled tail trailed, lifted just high enough off the ground not to drag. He had the same colouring as the rest of the family, but he was noticeably older than Oxsana, with swaths of grey at his temples and wrinkles at the corners of his eyes. From what Bas had told him, beast mages like this Vadik, born of the nobility, were regularly smothered at birth owing to the prejudices of the empire. That he was alive and so clearly welcome was a good sign Taisiya and her kin were not so blinded by such petty differences. He couldn't have his prospective bride treating his son with disdain, after all.

Then again, if this Vadik were part dragon, it was no wonder they treated him with deference. Not even the fae willingly tangled with dragons.

"Hi, Uncle Vadik." Milena smiled.

"Is that how you're greeting your uncle these days, Milena? Have you become a lady now that you've married?" he asked, his tone gruff.

Milena winked at her husband before running at the beast mage and leaping at him, arms outstretched. He caught her without missing a beat.

"There's my monkey." He grinned, showing off a few too many sharp teeth.

He put her down and let the small woman tow him over to her husband, who stared at Vadik wide-eyed.

"Uncle Vadik, this is my husband, Zephyros Tempest, Dominus of the Opal islands. Zephyros, this is my Uncle Vadik. He pretends not to be related, so if we all die for political reasons, then our bloodline will continue."

Mereruka paused in his escape, head swinging in the direction of the conversation. Bas tugged on his arm, but Mereruka refused to budge.

"Oh, the admiral? I didn't think you'd risk being so ambitious so soon," the beast mage said as he stroked his short beard in contemplation.

"It's a pleasure to meet you, Vadik." Zephyros bowed.

Vadik nodded.

"Be good to her. Vows or not, I'll tear you to pieces if you break her heart."

"Only if you get to him first," Sonya chimed in with a smile.

Zephyros began looking a little uncomfortable before Taisiya cleared her throat, bringing everyone's attention back to the centre of the room.

"The customary threats can happen after the ceremony. Milena, Zephyros, stand on the heart."

"Heart?" Zephyros sputtered, his eyes going wide at the glittering gem.

"It's a dragon's heart, Zeph." Milena grinned.

"Ah, of course," he said, clearly overwhelmed.

"Now, cross the heart," Taisiya said.

The two stood in the centre and walked a few steps to opposite ends of the gem. They turned, following the curve until they stood on opposite sides once more. Then, as the magic began to wake, they stepped back into the centre. Pressure began pressing down from all over. Mereruka could feel the weight in his very soul. More old magic. He stood, rapt with wonder.

Milena pulled a knife from her pocket and pricked Zephyros' finger.

"I, Milena Dragonsblood, vow to take into our clan Zephyros Tempest. From today until his last, I demand his ultimate loyalty."

The heart began glowing in response to her words, lighting the couple in its eerie glow. The magic swelled in the cavern, unlike any Mereruka had ever felt before. Something strange and wild and old slithered across senses he'd never known he'd possessed. Suddenly, he was no prince, no powerful fae with magic coursing through his veins. He was just an animal, skittering prey wandering the dark with something hungry at his back. Bas's claws dug into his palm.

"Your turn," Milena whispered.

Zephyros cleared his throat.

"I, Zephyros Tempest, vow my ultimate loyalty to Milena Dragonsblood and the Dragonsblood clan from this day until my last."

The wind mage pressed his pricked finger to the gem at his feet. The magic in the cavern coalesced in the centre and sank into Zephyros. He gasped and clutched his sides.

Mereruka marvelled at the ancient word-as-bond spell. Swearing upon the actual heart of one's ancestor hadn't been practised for tens of thousands of years. How had it survived here, on the cursed continent? How had the dragon's heart? There were no dragons in Lethe, so far as he knew.

"Zephyros Tempest, from this day forward you are both family and vassal. We will protect you with our lives as you will protect us with your own. From this day until your last, we will keep your secrets and you will keep ours. If this covenant is broken, you will accept punishment by the hand of the Dragonsblood heir," Taisiya said.

Zephyros turned to look at Vadik, who shook his head and nodded to Taisiya. Mereruka felt as shocked as Zephyros looked. The wicked gleam in Taisiya's eyes said it all. The heir to an ancient dragon? Mereruka had to have her.

"I understand." Zephyros bowed his head.

"Great! Now that that's done, who wants a drink?" Milena asked.

CHAPTER 19

"Were the letters sent?" Taisiya asked as she sipped her tea.

"Yes," Vasilisa answered.

"And the curses?"

"Have already been laid."

"Excellent." Taisiya smiled.

Taisiya had just set her trap for whoever it was that kept intimidating the bride candidates. Unbeknownst to any but Taisiya and Vasilisa, the women who received letters to introduce them to the prince were now under the protection of curses. Any who sought to interfere with the meetings would find themselves sticking out like a sore thumb. If Chloe refused the prince, Taisiya would have three more women as backup.

"Why a curse to make them glow? Why not one that causes intense pain?"

"Because if they're a shadow mage, as I suspect they are, they'll be unable to run and hide as they've been doing this whole time."

Vasilisa had discovered that the candidates were being blackmailed in truth, with threatening letters placed in the women's personal quarters and no witnesses to the act. Whoever had employed the blackmailer had been unable to—or uninterested in—threatening Chloe, though it hadn't stopped Magistra Jade from appealing to her sister. Thankfully, the outrageously expensive enchantments kept shadowy riffraff away from Chloe, and despite the domina's daily outings and her sister's pleas, no one had managed to threaten or dissuade her while she was outside her protections.

"And if the blackmailer can't run away…"

"Then I can catch and kill them once the glowing wears off." Vasilisa grinned.

"After they tell us the name of their paymaster. Then we can reassure the women that their sordid secrets are safe, and they can meet with the prince free from the fear of scandal," Taisiya said.

Taisiya couldn't afford any more interference. The prince would be asking Chloe to be his wife today. Taisiya was fighting to keep her anxiety at bay, her stomach twisted in knots. What if Zoe had convinced her sister to relent after all? Taisiya had run through the very last of the bride candidates. The mages were beginning to grow suspicious of the way the other fae treated the prince. Failure was not an option. Her whole future balanced on the edge of a knife. If the prince didn't find a fiancée, she would have to prepare herself to kill him and potentially start a war with the fae of Maat just to be free of whatever ominous boon Mereruka might demand.

Taisiya jumped at the sound of the knock on her door.

"Illustra Spark? Several letters have arrived for you."

While she was acting as ambassador, she'd been given rooms in the palace. One of the upsides of the suffocating nearness to the empress and every other villain in the capital was that the postal service was exceedingly quick.

"Please enter."

A grey-robed servant handed the post to Vasilisa, bowed, and exited the rooms.

"Responses from the women," Vasilisa observed, unsealing the letters and passing them to Taisiya.

Taisiya grimaced as she read, dread crawling up her spine.

"Our malefactor has been busy."

"Each turned it down?"

Taisiya nodded. She needed to keep down the rising bile. Her last and only hope was Domina Emerald.

"Hunt the bastard down. So long as they're capable of speaking, I don't care what shape they're in when you bring them to me," Taisiya ordered.

"You're too kind." Vasilisa smiled. "My whip-work has been getting rusty lately," she cooed as she slipped into a shadow behind the couch.

Once Taisiya was alone, nausea threatened in earnest. Deep breaths were doing nothing to calm her nerves or stomach. She paced. All three candidates she'd written to were women she'd met just the other day who had made their interest plain and who were rather desperate for a husband. For the meddler to be able to take action so swiftly was disturbing, especially with the bargain breathing down her neck like some feral beast.

"There's still Chloe," Taisiya said to herself.

"Illustra Spark? I'm sorry to disturb you again, but it seems I missed a letter."

Oh gods, please don't let it be from the domina.

Taisiya's hands began shaking. She kept her voice level.

"You may enter."

The same servant entered, a flustered blush on her face as she handed Taisiya the letter. She didn't dare look at the seal until the servant departed. The Emerald family crest stared back, mocking her.

"It could be good news. An invitation. *To the wedding.*"

And maybe the dead would rise.

With trembling hands and a cold sweat trickling down her spine, Taisiya unsealed the letter. Her eyes scanned it, but the words weren't registering in her mind. The pounding of her heart almost drowned out the agonized noise that flew out of her strangled throat. The letter fell from her bloodless fingers and drifted like a feather to the floor. Strange, that something so terrible hadn't been announced with the appropriate fanfare.

A sharp pain on her wrists brought her out of her racing thoughts. To her horror, glowing yellow runes had carved themselves into her skin.

"No, no, no, no." Taisiya stood, trying to rub them off to no avail.

Another knocking on her door. Her head whipped in that direction.

"Ambassador, I believe we have a deal to see through." Mereruka's muffled voice came to her from the hallway.

"I- I'm indisposed, Prince Mereruka. Please come back another time," Taisiya said as she ran through her mental list of escape routes.

Other than the main door, there was a set of servants' stairs in the servant's room just off the main bedroom. She raced for the door of the adjoining private parlour. She heard him chuckle as she tore open the door to flee the receiving room.

"Oh, I think not."

He opened the door as the fleeting hem of her skirts sailed through the door of the private parlour.

"You little-"

Taisiya refused to listen to another word, her focus entirely on getting into the cramped servants' stairwell. She made it as far as the main bedroom before he caught her in his arms and whirled her up and off her feet.

"No! Please! I can still find you a wife! Just give me another day!" Taisiya pleaded.

The prince laughed, his merriment chilling her.

"No, Taisiya, I think I'll be collecting on my boon now, as we promised."

He set her down and turned her to face him, his grip on her shoulders unshakable. This was it. She would have to kill him. The gathered lightning in her palms died under her skin.

"What have you done?" she gasped.

"Did you really think a fae deal would come without protections for the one who collects? We'd never get our end of the bargain if our debtors could kill us so easily." He frowned at her.

What would he demand? She tallied all the things she could live without—eyes, ears, fingers, arms, legs, the skin off her back, her health, her youth, her voice. She prayed he wouldn't ask for her life but took comfort in the fact that even without her, their family would go on. Her affairs were in order. They'd been in order since her father died. She swallowed down the bile that rose in her throat and tensed, bracing herself as she stared at his bare teal chest, refusing to meet his eyes.

Father, forgive me.

"What...what do you want?" she choked out.

He crooked a finger under her chin and tipped up her jaw, forcing her to look him in the eye.

"You promised me whatever boon I asked for. I'm demanding your hand," He smiled as she paled, visions of blood and agony painting her mind a blinding red, "in marriage." He finished.

"W-what?"

"You're to be my bride. I'm not to return to Maat without one. Since you couldn't find me one, you'll do nicely."

"I—but—" she stammered as his words sunk in.

Lethe was her home. Her destiny and that of her family was tied to this land. It was everything she knew. Everyone she loved was here. Everything she desired and schemed for was here. She couldn't leave it. He pressed his teal finger to her lips to silence her protest, his grin wolfish.

"If you want your family to attend, best inform them soon. The wedding is tonight. I'll have a number of appropriate dresses and accessories brought to you here within the hour. Choose whichever you like. Do you have any customs you'd like to see observed?"

In a daze, she answered.

"The—the groom should wear the family colours of the bride and vice versa."

"And what would those be, Taisiya?"

She really looked at him then, this prince of a foreign land. He wasn't the least bit upset by her failure. No, he looked as pleased as could be. Had she been played for a fool this whole time? Had this outcome always been his aim? His pale citrine eyes sparkled with mirth. Gods, how had she not foreseen this? She thought he would demand her death as the price of failure. He'd stolen her life instead. Her blood boiled.

"Purple," she hissed.

He leaned down to kiss her forehead while she stood rooted to the spot.

"Purple, then. The marks will fade when the marriage ceremony is complete. Until then, don't get any ideas, wife," he taunted her as he strolled from the room.

Taisiya cursed aloud the moment the door was shut, beating the pillow on the bed in impotent rage until the feathers erupted. Initial outburst dealt with, she calmed herself by pacing. She'd made many plans. She'd failed spectacularly. It was time to do what any Dragonsblood was expected to, and make new ones.

CHAPTER 20

"She's definitely going to try to kill you after the ceremony, if her family doesn't first," Bas drawled as he lay on Mereruka's bed, his arms crossed behind his head.

Mereruka chuckled. He was soaking in the bathing pool, relaxing after a very satisfying morning. The many fae of the delegation were busy expending vast amounts of magic festooning the palace with the appropriate decorations. All, of course, after the very flustered and queasy praetor had hastily agreed to allow the use of the space, if only to get Mereruka out of his presence.

"Maybe. I'll just have to convince her that being Queen of Maat is better than being a wealthy ambassador of the Cursed Continent."

"Do you really think she's the descendent of a dragon?" Bas asked.

"A very distant one, if she is. It's more likely her people found the graveyard and claimed a relationship once they discovered some of the heart's properties."

He hoped he was wrong though. Even a far-distant relative of a dragon was good lineage by Maat's exacting standards.

"You're going to have to make it up to her, this whole shady bargain business. Otherwise, she might just let you make her queen and then decide she doesn't need you."

Mereruka laughed.

"Maat would never accept a lone mage ruling a kingdom of fae and shifters."

"Just like they'd never accept a tattooed fae as their king?" Bas retorted.

"That's fair." Mereruka grimaced. Some traditions needed to die, and that was one of them. Thankfully, he knew who he had to kill to put it to bed for good. All in good time. "Enough lounging. Let's show these uncultured mages what a real royal wedding looks like."

The whole of the palace had been overrun by strange and awesome magics. Pillars had been replaced by moss-covered, breathing giants, rearing golden horses, curiously silent, rainbow-hued waterfalls and other fantastical creations. The walls themselves were splashed with vibrant new colours in swirling motifs. The ceilings radiated daylight. The floors had become a living, moving scene of a tranquil, decorative pond, complete with brightly coloured, swimming fish and the illusion of ripples wherever one stepped. Strange and fragrant florals had sprouted within the past hour, perfuming the halls. The very air seemed to sparkle with gold dust and various crushed jewels. The mages of Lethe were, almost to a man, captivated with childlike wonder or struck with terrible fear.

Taisiya considered the beautiful fae wedding decorations and the festive atmosphere to be no more than hideous deceit. What would become the main processional hallway had been repainted with lies, a story told in moving paintings of a courtship that had never taken place, of a gallant prince and a swooning redhead. She would kill him for that alone. Magister Emerald would never forgive her. If she ever returned, she would never live down the shame of being a husband-stealing would-be matchmaker.

There was no joy in her heart on her wedding day, only sick trepidation at what lay ahead. And fury.

Milena picked at the airy fabrics of the twenty teal wedding gowns arrayed on mannequins and crammed into their receiving parlour, each in that flowing, revealing style favoured by the fae women of Maat. Zephyros knocked on the door and entered.

"Did you bring it, Zeph?" Milena asked.

"Yes."

Taisiya sighed.

"Alright, sit down and grab a spoke each. Vasilisa hasn't returned yet."

Vasilisa was still busy hunting down a man who would hopefully divulge the name of his master. Taisiya wished to be rid of the bastard whose actions had forced her into this damned sham of a wedding. It was only a shame she hadn't been present to feed Mereruka to the void.

Zephyros pulled a large silver ring with a number of sharp spokes from his satchel. They sat down in an informal circle and grabbed one handle each. It was spelled to ensure only those touching it would hear the words they spoke. With Vasilisa gone, Taisiya couldn't be certain there wouldn't be any spies present.

"As you probably guessed, I was the boon he demanded," Taisiya began.

"Why didn't you kill him?" Milena asked.

"You mean aside from not wanting to start a war?" Zephyros asked.

"Aside from that, my magic is sealed so long as my intent is to harm him. I can't even pick up a knife. My fingers go numb and it slips from my hand every time I try. I can't do anything to harm him until the marriage ceremony is complete, or so he says," Taisiya answered.

"We're not restricted by that, though," Milena pointed out.

"Still a potential for war," Zephyros said.

"You're right. My options, as I see them, are these: first, he suffers an accident shortly after the wedding since we know they can die by lightning. Second, I bear with it until I establish myself in Maat, then kill him. Or, third, when we undoubtedly meet the king, I make a deal for my trade rights in return for turning Mereruka in as a traitor."

"He's a traitor?" Zephyros asked.

"I don't rightly know, but it doesn't really matter," Taisiya replied.

"Ah." Zephyros looked uncomfortable.

"Whatever you need, we'll help you, Taisiya. No one fucks with our family," Milena said. "I'm just glad you have an extra dose of lightning. You'll need it in Maat if this wedding is any indication of their real powers."

"Extra dose?" Zephyros asked.

"Oh, right. So much has happened lately," Milena said.

"You haven't told him?" Taisiya asked.

"Told me what?" Zephyros raised a quizzical brow.

"We were willing participants in father's ritual," Taisiya began. "He studied it more than the other magisters suspected, and rewrote it when I agreed to it to ensure, when he died, that I would receive my magic back as well as his. Before I die, we'll use the ritual again, and hand down this combined power to the next lightning mage heir. If I die unexpectedly, Daria is spelled as the next heir."

"So..."

"Yep! We're dirty traitors. Father just wanted our kingdom back, but now that it won't happen, we've decided to just take the empire one marriage and heir at a time." Milena smiled.

Zephyros sighed.

"Not so different from the islands, or at least, some of the islanders. Don't say anything to Charis. She really believes in the whole unity of Lethe nonsense."

"I knew you'd understand." Milena kissed his cheek.

"If you're serious about it, then the best place for an accident is on the open sea. I can convince the strategos to allow a vessel or two to provide an escort at least some of the way to Maat. A lightning bolt makes a good signal that you want to be brought back, and it isn't an uncommon occurrence at sea. The men who serve under me are loyal to me first and foremost. If I say the ship went down and you were the only survivor, they'll corroborate it," Zephyros said.

"Thank you, Zephyros." Taisiya breathed easy for the first time since she'd received Chloe's letter. She could still turn this horrible situation around.

Zephyros smiled, lighting up his handsome face.

"Well, we're family now, aren't we?"

Mereruka watched as Taisiya marched down the aisle like a defiant prisoner to their execution. She didn't look upon him as a bride looks upon her intended groom. The violent promise in her eyes left no room for the pretence of willingness. No, when Taisiya looked at him with her amethyst eyes, he could almost see her calculating just how long she needed to be wed to him before it was seemly to become a widow. It was the first time he began to doubt the genius of his scheme where she was concerned.

If nothing else, she was undoubtedly the best-dressed woman in the whole of Lethe, in a flowing teal gown that covered her skin in fabric but did nothing to hide every nuance of the form beneath. A spectacular crown in teal, purple and gold sat upon her head, birds' wings, lush lotus blooms and iridescent butterfly wing decorations framing her pretty face.

Despite his initial concerns, the majority of the ceremony went off without incident. His and Taisiya's hands were bound by a strip of glittering red silk as Raemka was forced to smile and recite all the well wishes and blessings. Unfortunately, the scribe had one last trick up his sleeve.

"King Khety of Maat has generously provided vows for the prince and new princess consort to recite. If you will repeat after me, Your Tranquility?" Raemka's smile turned predatory.

Mereruka debated how it would look to kill the officiant at his own wedding.

"I, Prince Mereruka of the Land of Maat, swear to bind my life to that of Princess Consort Taisiya Spark, so that I may spend all my days with her," Raemka recited.

Bloody hells! They meant to kill him by letting her short life drag him into an early grave. He looked at Taisiya, her brow rising as he stalled. Was she worth sharing all his extra bargained years with? She was vicious, witty, pretty and powerful, no doubt. But he'd have to collect centuries more, just so that they lived the normal length of a fae life together, to say nothing of the many extra centuries he'd planned on living. Suddenly, this whole marriage business was a lot more serious.

"Prince Mereruka? Would you like me to repeat the vow?" Raemka smiled.

He tried to object but found his mouth sealed. The hooks of the original word-as-bond spell he'd been forced to recite reared their ugly heads. Only now he recalled saying he would both obey the king's commands as well as take a wife. Tricky bastard. Mereruka swore to make Khety's death a slow one.

Damn. So be it. He hoped Taisiya really was the descendent of a dragon. She'd need the ferocity of one to survive the fae court in the long term.

"I, Prince Mereruka, of the Land of Maat, swear to bind my life to that of Princess Consort Taisiya Spark, so that I may spend all my days with her," Mereruka said.

He felt the bonds of the spell wrap around him.

"If you will, Princess Consort Taisiya?" Raemka said.

"I, Princess Consort Taisiya Spark of Lethe, the Empire of Mages, swear to bind my life to that of Prince Mereruka, so that I may spend all my days with him."

Mereruka waited for the spell to claim him, but felt nothing. In fact, the bonds dissipated. If the reactions of his fellow fae were any indication, none of them suspected a thing. But what had it been?

He looked into her stormy amethyst eyes and did his best not to laugh with triumph as the truth hit him.

Her true name was Taisiya Dragonsblood, and no vow as sacred as a life-binding could be sworn using a false one. The fae didn't know her true name, nor had they used spell sight to confirm his entrapment. Taisiya didn't know how fae vows were made, so he could use this as a means to ensure his own survival once the marks of their deal faded.

Mereruka revelled in his unparalleled victory.

The emperor and empress approached them from their position on the thrones, bedecked in red finery of every kind and a pair of truly monstrous crowns.

"I, Empress Selene," the empress said as she stood beside Taisiya and just a little behind her.

"And I, Emperor Belisarius," the emperor said as he took up a spot behind Mereruka, yet still visible to the gathered crowd.

"Give our blessings to this union," they said in unison and placed their hands over those of himself and Taisiya.

Mereruka hadn't expected this part of the ceremony, and so had failed to prepare for it. As the emperor's skin touched his own, Mereruka's glamour broke—everywhere on his body. The fae present gasped and hissed, and even Taisiya's eyes widened with shock. Mereruka's skin, covered in glowing yellow tattoos to enhance his magic many times over, to protect him from harm, marking him like the basest of mercenaries not fit to enter the home of any noble, had been revealed to friend and foe alike.

The number of people he needed to silence before he reached Maat had just increased exponentially.

"Fuck."

Chapter 21

Not one of the fae would speak with him or his newlywed wife. Mereruka's dishonour had tainted Taisiya in their eyes. Though the mages were puzzled over this behaviour, they were too polite to ask, or more concerned with all the things he and Taisiya would be supplying to Lethe in future to care overmuch.

The matriarch of his wife's clan approached him like a dark wraith in her midnight purple gown. Her amber eyes were like chips of ice, and not a strand of her silvery-blonde hair was out of place. She raked him with her glance and found him wanting.

"It's expected that the groom dance with his mother-in-law," she stated flatly.

"Then may I have this dance?"

Without another word, she extended her hand and he walked her onto the dance floor. A few steps into the awkward dance, she spoke.

"For a manipulative man, you're not very astute."

"I'm not sure I follow."

Her raised brow brought to mind a deeply disappointed tutor.

"I could have killed you the moment you touched my hand. We know how you tricked my daughter into marrying you. The only reason you're still alive is because I believe Lethe, as it stands, is too small for Taisiya's ambitions. Are you in a position to become king of Maat, Prince Mereruka?"

He felt a warning chill go down his spine. How could this woman know of his plans? Was she a mind-reader? Gods below, he didn't think they existed on the Cursed Continent.

"Illustra Oxsana, only an imprudent man would speak openly of such things," he hedged.

"Do not dissemble, Prince Mereruka. I can run you through with a bolt of lightning as well as my daughter can."

He hadn't known that. Gods, he really had underestimated his new family.

"I am fifth in line for the throne," he replied.

"Then you don't have that many obstacles."

"Mmm."

"Your marriage to Taisiya has given her the gift of a brand new playground where none of her precious family members need to be protected. That is a freedom she doesn't know yet to cherish. Prince Mereruka, I will tell you plainly—the only title worthy of my daughter is that of queen. When Taisiya realises that the Land of Maat is at her mercy, and not the other way around, I expect you to work to set her upon its throne, or get the hells out of her way."

"I...see."

"See that you do, or suffer the consequences. I am done dancing with you. Escort me to my daughter."

He did as she asked and was immediately set upon by Taisiya's sisters, each with her own brand of threat to lob his way. One swore to stick iron needles in his eyes. Another promised to drown him in a vat of perfume. The third simply smiled and recited all the areas where a man could be stabbed and survive long enough to spend his last hours in agony. As the night wore on, the threats became increasingly dire and florid in description. There was no magic to prevent any one of them from murdering him this very night, as they had all made crystal clear.

Mereruka soon found himself hiding at his own wedding. Gods below, what kind of family had he married into? Every single one of them had seen fit to threaten gory, detailed death between forced congratulations. He needed a drink but dared not seek one out. Bas, the little traitor, had smirked and told him to deal with the consequences of being an ass on his own.

When he looked up from his seat, he found another redhead staring at him with deep purple eyes. This time it was the brother, Theodore, the one known to be a pushover. His smile was genuine and warm when he approached. He reminded Mereruka of Bas when he was a sweet, smiling kitten. Except when he approached, Mereruka could feel the dread nearness of iron.

"Good evening, Prince Mereruka. We haven't really been properly introduced. I'm Illustrus Theodore Spark, Taisiya's older brother."

"Good evening, Illustrus Theodo-"

"Of course, we *would* have been properly introduced had you truly courted my sister instead of tricking her into marriage."

Gods below, even the sweet kitten wanted his blood! Theodore sat beside him with the same amiable smile on his face, except now, Mereruka saw the hot, angry edge to it. Was the iron on his person?

"Though, I suppose you've had a chance to get to know her over the past few weeks of your visit here. My family, well, the ones remaining, are all very much made in the same mould as Taisiya. I fear I am the only one made of softer stuff than my sisters. It has left me rich in friends, but lacking in raw power."

"I don't-"

Theodore held up his hand to stop him.

"You see, my father tried to teach me many things, but the one that really stuck was that if I found myself incapable of some vital task, I must find someone loyal who would gladly do it in my stead. Over the years,

I've taken that to heart. After my father passed, I was lucky enough to retain the services of his closest friend and aide, Viktor."

Mereruka jolted when a man emerged from the shadow to his side and placed a firm hand on his shoulder. He had pale skin, fair hair and sharp grey eyes. His smile was chilling. The grim man from the sister's wedding had made an appearance.

"Viktor is a darkness mage. Have you ever been through the void, Prince Mereruka?"

"I recall Taisiya saying it wasn't for the faint of heart."

Theodore laughed, a bright, jovial sound at odds with the implied threat.

"Viktor, he should see it for himself."

Before Mereruka could bolt, he was dragged into a darkness so profound it disoriented his every sense. There was no gravity, no light, no sound, nothing but the terrifying, vise-like grip on an arm he only vaguely knew was attached to his body. Hot pain lashed his midsection. A moment—an hour—passed, and he was once again seated where he'd been before. It took him some time as his senses returned to him. He touched his side and hissed in pain. Three thin claw marks had sliced his skin.

"That looks painful. I'm a bit clumsy myself, so I usually carry around a good salve. Here." Theodore pulled out a small tin from a pocket of his robe and set to pasting the aromatic salve on his wounds. "I have a good friend, a potion mage, who made this for me. It's not as good as seeing a healer, but it's as close as you can get."

Indeed, the wounds were already closing and the pain numbed.

"She made this for me as well." He opened a second tin to show Mereruka before closing it. It, too, was pleasantly aromatic. "Had I used this on your wounds, you would be dead now."

Mereruka felt the pit of his stomach drop. He itched to use magic but the darkness mage kept a grip on his shoulder in warning and the iron dulled all but his glamour. Would the brother follow through on the sisters' threats?

"I suppose that topic is a bit grim for a wedding. Speaking of, I have a gift." He pulled a thin gold sheet from the pocket of his robe. "I know you can speak our language, but are you also literate?"

"No, Illustrus Theodore. The translation spell is only good for speaking." Mereruka swallowed.

"Oh, then I'll read the words on this for you. It says 'If ever Prince Mereruka causes Taisiya to weep with sadness, Theodore will feel her sorrow.'"

"I'm not sure I understand."

"You see, this is a tablet something one of my friends, a curse mage, made for me. He assures me that curses written on gold cannot be broken except by the one who cast them. Have you ever seen a curse tablet before, Prince Mereruka? You see, you roll them up like so." Theodore carefully rolled the delicate gold sheet and produced an iron nail. Mereruka swallowed down bile. *Shit.* "I suppose carrying this near you is rude, but then, so is forcing someone to marry you," he muttered before continuing his explanation. "Now, all I need to do is pierce the rolled-up tablet." He proceeded to do so and looked to Mereruka. "Traditionally, it's buried, but it's not strictly necessary."

"Why curse yourself, Theodore?"

Why hadn't he cursed Mereruka instead? Was Taisiya's entire family mad?

"Well, if you make my sister cry, now I shall know. And if I know, then my friends and I will go on a vacation to the Land of Maat and comfort her. And if you've broken her heart, then perhaps my friends and I will bring her back to Lethe *as a widow.*"

Mereruka's throat dried up.

"Illustrus, I believe Magistra Amber is here for you," Viktor spoke, his voice deep and commanding.

Mereruka looked up and saw a young woman with white hair, amber eyes and pale brown skin approach them. The silver-tongued mage from a few days prior. He prayed she would take these two murderous men from him.

"Is this your new brother-in-law, Theo?" she asked.

She was in league with the red-haired demon spawn. Gods help him. Theodore stood, a smile on his face. Viktor pulled Mereruka up as well.

"It is. Magistra Amber, this is Prince Mereruka."

She looked him in the eyes.

"Kneel, Prince Mereruka."

His knees slammed down onto the mosaic. Her voice had been like that of a siren, and he yearned to obey. She tipped his chin up with her finger and raised a bright white brow. The look in her sunset eyes chilled him to the marrow.

"I, too, consider Theo and Taisiya to be dear friends. Pray that we never meet again." She turned to Theodore and grinned. "You promised to dance with me until my toes bleed. Come on."

"I haven't forgotten, Magistra." He turned back to Mereruka. "I suppose all this is to say, welcome to the family, Prince Mereruka."

When Mereruka was alone once more, he put his head in his hands. He thought he'd become inured to threats over the course of the day. He was wrong.

"Your family is terrifying," Mereruka said between steps.

"My family loves me. If you find that terrifying, it's because you're scum and they know it," Taisiya replied as she danced with her... husband.

Taisiya wasn't certain exactly what his hastily hidden tattoos meant, but it was obviously something which had earned him great disfavour amongst the fae. She wondered if his fellow delegates would even argue if she killed him at sea. As it stood, that seemed the wisest option. There was no sense in keeping a husband who was a pariah among his own people. He would only prove to be a hindrance to her ambitions.

"None of that matters now. Do you not realise the situation we're in? Once we return to Maat, my tattoos will become common knowledge. I've hidden them beneath my glamour my entire life for a reason."

"I don't see why that should mean anything to me," Taisiya sniffed.

"Nobles of Maat do not abide those with magic inked into their skin. They believe that only bloodstained mercenaries and lowlifes need such things. When we return, we will be disgraced."

Taisiya raised her brow.

"No, *you* will be disgraced. I have no such markings on me, not anymore."

She punctuated that fact by allowing a trickle of electricity to roll along her skin where he touched her. He gripped her tighter, his eyes narrowed.

"My disgrace belonged to you the moment we were wed," Mereruka replied.

"Then no one will be surprised when I divorce you." Taisiya smiled. At his raised brows, she continued. "Oh, I had my sisters enquire about your peoples' marriage customs before the wedding. I believe you said that wording was everything, no? And I don't recall you saying, at any time, just how long I was expected to remain your wife."

She shoved a jolt of electricity into his palm. He stiffened with the pain and grunted.

"It's good that you remembered that, wife. Do you recall, exactly, the vows we just swore?" he asked through clenched teeth.

Taisiya frowned. The wedding vows were just like those that mages swore, and they never prevented divorce if the couple were determined to end things.

"What of it?" Taisiya asked.

"Those vows were written by King Khety, a man who very much wants to see me dead, dishonoured, disgraced or destroyed, all so that I don't threaten his reign. Those vows bound us, our lives magically linked. There can be no divorce, and there can be no other spouses. Most importantly, if I die, you die."

Taisiya saw red. Gods below, all her plans had crumbled to dust, all because of another fae spell. She wanted to scream, but they were still in public. Taisiya settled for digging her nails into his hand.

"You slimy son of a whore!" she hissed. "Why on Oblivion would you swear that vow? Why would you let *me*?"

"The only reason I'm alive and free is that I swore to follow my brother's orders *and* take a bride. He expected any bride of your land to bring me so much disgrace that my political ambitions would never recover. Now that he's had his way, the last of the spell that bound my actions has fallen away."

Damn him! She'd just attached herself to a man whose motivations left him on the bad side of his king. How she wished she could kill this scheming bastard.

"Why didn't he just make you swear an oath to kill yourself?" she hissed, wishing his king had been bolder and finished him off before she'd ever seen his wretched face.

"A very helpful taboo. One you should be grateful for. Maat once had a king as cruel as he was paranoid, who made every blood relative swear an oath of loyalty and obedience to him. Then he ordered them to kill each other, plunging all of Maat into chaos. My ancestor, his queen, slew him and restored order. The royal bloodline of Maat was then prohibited from swearing oaths of loyalty to each other. Had my brother been free to demand it of me, your future would not look nearly as bright."

"Bright?! You've *ruined* my future!"

"Your options are few now, Taisiya, as are mine, but they're not necessarily bad ones."

"I fail to see how this situation is in any way ideal!" Taisiya retorted.

She didn't have to kill him to get even, did she? What was a little maiming in the grand scheme of things?

"Are your ambitions so small? What could you have amounted to in this empire? You are already a princess consort by my side, wealthier than even the empress."

She could have been... she could have been the Dragonsblood heir. She could have carried out her family's grand vision. She could have married some doddering old fool and lived the rest of her life as a wealthy, respectable widow. Now she had a title beyond her wildest hopes, but the victory tasted of ash.

"A title which has become sullied by your own admission!" she snarled.

"If that doesn't please you, would the title of queen be to your liking?" he asked.

Taisiya laughed contemptuously.

"You wish to make me a conspirator against your brother? The one who outwitted you at every turn? You think I wish to be branded a traitor twice over? I have only just managed to drag my family out of that particular mire, I'm not about to step into it once again!"

"My brother is not some all-knowing deity. He is mortal, the same as I, and I have outwitted him before. I was content to wait to take his crown, but he has forced my hand. Fight with me, Taisiya, and I will make you a queen so powerful, so wealthy, you'll pity your empress for her wretched lot. Not only will the mages beg your forgiveness for ostracizing you, they'll be fighting themselves for your favour."

Taisiya did like the sound of that, but she was much too jaded to take him at his word. Mereruka was not to be trusted.

"And what of this disgrace? How do you plan to rehabilitate your reputation?"

"As of now, only the fae here know of it, and the long sea voyage home is not without its perils."

Taisiya was quiet as she thought it over. If her life was tied to his, she couldn't risk his brother or anyone else killing him. Even if she divorced him, her life would always be at the mercy of his own. She also knew, given what little she understood of his magic, that it was unlikely she could keep him confined to Lethe. Much as it angered her, he was now her one and only option. If she were condemned to be the wife of this man, then he would damn well work to give her everything she'd ever dreamed of and more.

"If the queen's crown is anything like the one I wore today, it will need to be recast. I have my own ideas about what would look best."

He smiled, the look in his eyes wild with satisfaction.

"It will be my pleasure to place it on your head."

"No need, Mereruka, I plan to take it from her brow with my own two hands."

Gods pity the Land of Maat. Its king had made an enemy of Taisiya Dragonsblood, and she wouldn't be satisfied until she made everything he possessed her own.

Chapter 22

Mereruka was deeply relieved that she'd bought his blatant lie about their lives being irrevocably tied. Such bald lies were uncommon in Maat, for the simple reason that a certain subset of the fae had the magic of truth-tasting. Such individuals rarely made themselves known, and so it was always better to err on the side of vagueness or omission when it came to one's speech.

Taisiya's anger and ambition pleased him. He had been blessed in this cursed land to find one such as her. Now, his lie would prevent her family members from killing him before they left for his homeland.

The first bump in the road occurred moments after the wedding party came to a close. He and Taisiya were brought to his chambers by blushing servants. When the doors closed, Mereruka looked to Taisiya, whose icy fury was barely suppressed.

"What a fucking joke," she cursed as she kicked off her shoes and fell into one of the chairs in the sitting area, tossing her crown away as if it were infested with lice. "I hope you've had a good laugh at my expense, Mereruka, because it'll be the last. Now, sit."

"Are you sure you don't want me to make it up to you?" he asked, his eyes drifting towards the bed. He was more than confident he could pleasure her senseless if she let him.

Her cheeks flushed, but her eyes narrowed.

"I've never gelded a man with a blade of lightning before. How kind of you to offer to be the first."

Mereruka, perhaps unwisely, laughed. Sitting down across from her, he smiled.

"You're perfect."

"If that were true, you'd be honeymooning with Chloe," she retorted.

"She was too sweet for my purposes. I find I prefer a woman with lightning in her veins."

He reached across the table, his fingers caressing hers. Unimpressed by his flattery, she yanked her hand away from his touch with a scowl.

"I expect you to be entirely honest with me, without resorting to lies of omission. I refuse to work with you otherwise. Tell me who Bas is."

"He's my adoptive son and my right-hand in training. I prefer to keep his existence a secret so that he won't be targeted," Mereruka answered.

"And how many mistresses do you have?"

"None."

"Keep it that way. I refuse to be forced to compete with another woman for your loyalty." She propped up her chin with the heel of her palm, her elbow resting on the arm of her chair. She tapped the finger of her free hand on the other lacquered arm. "How many stand in my way once we get to Maat?"

"Discounting the ones here in Lethe?"

Taisiya nodded.

"Six, including the king."

"Does he have children? Heirs?"

"No, thankfully."

"Good. I refuse to kill children," she said as she sighed. "I expect you to tell me everything you know about your... siblings?" At his nod, she continued, "As well as any cultural differences that will make my transition to Maat's court easier. Do you have any allies?"

"A few, though none that are expected to be brazen about it."

"So we can't rely on anyone within the court to favour us?"

Mereruka shook his head.

"We won't need it. Khety wanted to lower my standing through my marriage to you, a supposedly cursed barbarian. You should know that everyone outside Lethe considers your lands cursed. We don't even force our worst criminals to set sail for your shores. Be that as it may, when I return with a woman such as yourself by my side, I expect that attitude will change quickly."

Taisiya seemed to mull that revelation over.

"Cursed how?"

"The land itself is poisonous, cannibalism is rife, any children born here will be weak and sickly, magic doesn't work here, the list goes on."

"It's not much different from what we believed about the peoples outside the empire, that you're all uncultured barbarians, too busy killing each other to be worth our time…"

"If I may-"

Mereruka was interrupted by the pained moans of another man and the thud of a body hitting the floor. Taisiya turned around, facing the noise.

"You brought me a gift." Her smile was sharp.

"A wedding gift, as it turns out. I'm sorry I wasn't there when you needed me," Vasilisa replied, her glare reserved for Mereruka alone. She held a badly wounded man by the hair, his blood staining the rug.

"It was my mess." Taisiya shook her head.

Vasilisa pursed her lips but seemed to give up her argument in his presence.

"I present you with the servant of our rat. Now squeak, shadow scum, before I get angry." Vasilisa prodded the man with a vicious yank on his hair.

The man yelped in pain.

"N-nobilissimus P-P-Procopius." He stuttered.

Mereruka watched as Taisiya froze. The hair on his arms lifted with the nearness of her electricity. He could see the duelling instincts in her, one to lash out in anger, the other calculating the deepest cut. She was beautiful when she was vicious. This was the villainess he needed.

"Shall I dispose of him... is it Princess, now?" Vasilisa asked.

Taisiya scoffed at the title.

"No... no, as satisfying as that would be, I think Procopius should properly, *publicly*, atone for blackmailing the daughters of the nobility." Taisiya walked over to the shadow mage and crouched in front of him. "I don't care what your name is. I don't care if you have a family. I don't really care if my friend decides she wants to watch you get torn apart by wild dogs. But I suspect you wish to live. Am I right?"

"Y-yes," he replied.

"Then you'll do as I say. Or Vasilisa will find you in whatever shadow you call home and feed you to the void, far from the shadow path, where I know your kind are as helpless as the rest of us." Taisiya turned from the man and looked at the blonde darkness mage, "Put him somewhere for safekeeping. We need to travel to the graveyard tonight."

Vasilisa's eyes widened with her obvious question. Taisiya shook her head.

"If you think it's a good idea." Vasilisa looked Mereruka over like he was some flea-bitten creature her master had dragged home with her.

"I don't, but it seems I have very few options left to me. Let my family know as well."

When the darkness mage disappeared with her prey, Taisiya turned to Mereruka.

"Summon Bas. If he truly is your family, then there is something I expect you both to do before we leave Lethe."

Mereruka suspected he knew exactly what she spoke of. It wasn't ideal, but he could hardly refuse without revealing his chicanery.

"He shouldn't be far. Would you like me to get the barge ready?"

"No. We'll travel through the void."

He'd really hoped he would never have to do that again. But then, wasn't marriage all about compromise?

"As you wish."

Taisiya hadn't expected to return to the graveyard so soon, not for any official reason. She suspected that whoever Sonya and Daria chose as their husbands would need to be thoroughly tested before they risked bringing them here. As for herself, she hadn't expected to wed for years yet, and certainly not to a foreign, would-be traitor with kingly ambitions. She also hadn't expected to need to give up her position as heir so quickly, but it couldn't be helped. The role belonged to someone who would remain within Lethe, their hand guiding the future of their family. Not for the first time, Taisiya felt ashamed to have been given her father's gifts and his trust. She carried a part of his soul with her, and now she would be betraying everything that mattered. She'd be abandoning her duty.

For their part, neither Bas nor Mereruka appeared to be as impressed as they ought upon entering the grand, underground chamber. It was a place of otherworldly wonder, bathed in faintly glowing lights and housing the bones of the greatest creature ever to rule Oblivion—a dragon. As spectacular as that was, it was the crystalized heart of the dragon that always held her in awe. Every one of the Dragonsblood line, without fail, heard its strange, beautiful resonance and were drawn to it like moths to the flame. This was the home of her heart. It needed to be protected at all costs. They all knew it, felt it down to their marrow. And now she would betray it.

"Do you both remember the steps I taught you?" Taisiya asked them.

They nodded. Taisiya sighed. She looked around at her family, all of them expressing varying shades of misgiving. At least Uncle Vadik wasn't here to see his niece's disgrace. What a disappointment she'd become.

"I won't pretend to be pleased about this state of affairs, but given I'll be leaving shortly, I felt it was for the best. Mereruka, Bas, what we're about to do cannot be undone. Are you ready to risk everything you hold dear for me?"

"Yes," Bas replied shyly.

"Yes, Taisiya," Mereruka said.

"Then come, and prove it," Taisiya said to Mereruka.

They stood atop the heart and made the appropriate steps. The resonance tingled her ears and grew louder as she recited the words of the ceremony. Their world was created by the essences of forgotten gods, and yet her heretical heart felt that this was the most sacred place on Oblivion. She hated the man who would take her from it.

"I, Taisiya Dragonsblood, vow to take into our clan Mereruka of Maat. From today until his last, I demand his ultimate loyalty."

She pricked his finger with a sharp blade. If she was a little rougher than she'd needed to be, he wasn't fool enough to protest. Thankfully, she didn't see any hesitation in his pale eyes.

"I, Mereruka of Maat, vow my ultimate loyalty to Taisiya Dragonsblood and the Dragonsblood clan from this day until my last."

He pressed his bloody finger to the dragon's heart as the resonance reached a fever pitch. He grunted as the vows made their mark on his soul.

"Mereruka of Maat, from this day forward you are both family and vassal. We will protect you with our lives as you will protect us with your own. From this day until your last, we will keep your secrets and you will keep ours. If this covenant is broken, you will accept death by the hand of the Dragonsblood heir," Taisiya said.

"You're lucky we share no common ancestor, wife, else I'd be committing a grave crime by swearing this oath to you," he whispered.

"And *you* are lucky I'm giving you this honour at all. If our lives weren't tied, my family would have torn you to pieces," she whispered back.

He smiled and stepped from the dragon's heart. Bas repeated the process without complaint. When it was done, she turned to her family.

"Since we're all gathered, I think it would be best to decide upon the new heir."

"Why?" Milena asked. "Because of him?" She pointed at Mereruka.

"Because my judgement is obviously flawed. I won't even be present to guide the family in a few days' time. The role of heir belongs to someone who won't fail as I have," Taisiya replied, though it killed her to lay her shortcomings out in the open.

"I would have made the same gamble, Taisiya," Sonya spoke first. "It was too good a chance to miss."

"As would I. Though, I might not have thought to ask for exclusive trade rights in the first place," Daria added and smiled.

"No one is going to take your place as heir, Taisiya, not while you live. You're a week's journey away. It takes at least that long to get from the capital to almost anywhere important in the empire without a teleportation mage. Besides, unless things change drastically, our plans for the next generation are already set," Milena said, her arms crossed.

"I'll send you letters regularly, and keep you up to date on everything that happens in Lethe." Theodore smiled.

No, they were supposed to despise her, as they ought. They were supposed to reprimand her for her recklessness and chide her for her foolishness. That might have been easier to bear than their stubborn warmth. Leaders who failed were supposed to be punished, not embraced. Tears threatened. Her mother stepped forward and took Taisiya's hands between her own.

"You should remain the heir, Taisiya. It's what Grigori wanted, and it's only fitting that the heir reaches for the greatest possible power." Oxsana's smile was a touch wicked. She pinched her cheek. "What better way to do that than to take a wealthy kingdom for yourself?"

Taisiya swallowed past the tightness in her throat. She didn't trust herself to speak. Nodding, she let herself be comforted by familial warmth. She didn't know if or when she would feel it again.

"Come. Tell me what you plan to do to that vermin, Nobilissimus Procopius," Oxsana said as she pulled Taisiya from the graveyard, Mereruka and Bas following quietly behind.

<h1 style="text-align:center">CHAPTER 23</h1>

"Blackmail?!"

Taisiya tilted her head. Praetor Nicephorus, Lethe's most powerful bureaucrat, slowly regained his composure in the wake of her indictment against one of his trusted logothetes.

"This is a serious accusation, Illustra-"

"Princess Consort, Praetor," Taisiya corrected him. "And I would not dare accuse one of your logothetes without sufficient proof. You see, as I began the task of introducing Prince Mereruka to prospective wives, I found that within only a day or so, each of them begged off. This became so common an occurrence that I suspected some kind of mischief. I had my servant, Vasilisa, a darkness mage, keep an eye on a number of women I'd arranged appointments for. Lo and behold, she discovered a shadow mage delivering several threatening notes to the very same noblewomen." Taisiya placed a few of those same notes, retrieved secretly from the women's homes, in front of the praetor. "Under questioning, that shadow mage named your logothete, Nobilissimus Procopius, as his taskmaster."

The praetor read some of the letters' contents, blushed, and pushed them aside. The secrets contained within were certain to discredit and embarrass the women they were meant for. Taisiya had copied the information within, and kept the ones that contained darker, more treacherous secrets for her own, Magister Emerald's among them. Who knew he'd seriously entertained the same treasonous plot as Taisiya's own father? Now, Taisiya knew it. At least it made sense why Chloe had been forced to reject Mereruka's proposal. She looked forward to using that juicy secret in future.

"I hope you will see fit to burn those letters, and never mention what you've learned in polite company," Taisiya said.

Nicephorus nodded.

"Would you be so kind as to bring this messenger to me, Princess Consort?"

"With pleasure, Praetor," Taisiya said. "Vasilisa?"

Vasilisa stepped from a tall shadow in the corner of the room, the prisoner in tow. He looked very much the worse for wear.

"Antonio?" Nicephorus paled before his shock turned to red-faced fury. "Who else conspired with you? You never do anything alone!"

"Please, Praetor, have mercy!"

"Answer me!"

"No one, I swear! Nobilissimus Procopius only wanted one man to send the letters!"

Nicephorus' fists were shaking with his rage. Taisiya noted them with curiosity, nothing more. He'd already purged his ranks once in the recent past. No doubt he'd begin wondering just how many under him were as loyal as they seemed. It was unfortunate she didn't have an ally in Procopius' ministry to champion at this time. Perhaps Theo or Alexandra would know someone.

The praetor marched over to his set of bell-pulls and yanked the one with a black rope. Nobilissimus Procopius, a shadow mage, emerged from the same shadow Vasilisa had a moment earlier. When he took in the scene laid out before him, he attempted to flee.

Vasilisa coated herself in inky darkness and leapt into the shadow after him. The shadow mage logothete was no match for a more powerful darkness mage; coated in her element, she was as strong as any beast mage. When she tore him back out into the light and brought him before the praetor, she slammed his head on his thick, wooden desk, dazing him. Taisiya did her best not to grin as blood dribbled from his nose. Served that rat right.

"Nobilissimus Procopius, you've been accused of using your position to blackmail the noblewomen of the empire. Do you have anything to say to these charges?" Nicephorus asked.

Procopius glared up at the praetor and then turned his hateful gaze at Taisiya. She raised a copper brow in question.

"Only that I find it distressing you would take the word of a traitor's daughter over your own logothete."

"Unlike Nobilissimus Procopius, Prince Mereruka and I won't hold your children accountable for the sins of their father," Taisiya said. "A mercy he extends to your daughter, though it seems you couldn't find it in yourself to do the same for me or mine." She stared at Procopius. "And make no mistake, my husband was quite angry when he discovered that a man of high office pursued a vendetta against him."

Taisiya's eyes flicked up to the praetor, whose concern only grew. Yes, now he understood it wasn't just about a few indelicate secrets of a handful of noblewomen, or a matchmaker thwarted in her feminine ambitions. Future diplomatic relations with a strange and powerful kingdom were at stake. It was the first time she'd been able to make use of her new situation, and the power was heady indeed.

"You will be questioned by Magistra Amber and then sentenced accordingly, Nobilissimus Procopius," Nicephorus said. He took a key from the pocket of his robe and opened a drawer. When he came before the desk, it was with two negation collars in hand. He placed them around the two men's necks and pulled another cord beside his desk. Two armed guards entered the room. "Escort these two shadow mages to the dungeons and call on Magistra Amber."

Once that business was sorted, Nicephorus sat back in his chair.

"I hope that you and your husband will be mollified by my actions."

"Perhaps, though there is something you could do for me which would encourage me to sway his heart."

"I'm listening." Nicephorus grimaced.

"My former home has gone a full year without its magistra in residence. The people of the Amber Province have been left without a manager or advocate. I would like for the magistra to take her rightful place as ruler and caretaker of its people. It is her duty, after all, and it isn't as though there are so few teleportation mages about that she can't reside there and still be of service when the palace calls, no?"

He looked a little green about the gills as he realised what that would mean. A silver-tongue mage freed from the palace's control. In charge of a province. Being wooed by Theodore. And he could not deny her if he wished to avoid trouble from abroad.

"I... shall see what can be done."

"See that you do, Praetor. I will hear about it if you don't," she said with a smile.

The look on his face was somewhere between surprise and unease. Had he just now seen her fangs? Well, it was too late for that. Her family was now related by marriage to an obscenely wealthy foreign prince, their re-entry into the upper echelons of society assured, and her brother was on his way to becoming the magister of their stolen lands. Now, unless Nicephorus wished to anger her, he would lose control of his silver-tongued mage. For as sure as the night followed the day, when Alexandra set foot in the Dragonsblood fortress, its former servants would return to teach her how to stand on her own two feet, and ensure she was never a prisoner of the empire again. It was, after all, Taisiya's duty to take care of her family.

Taisiya rose, and he did as well.

"If you'll excuse me? My husband is eager to return to Maat."

As she swept from the corridor, she was met by Magistra Jade, who slipped her a steel blade when she took her hand in greeting.

"I see now why you were reluctant to sabotage Chloe's chances. I'm not sorry she's safe, but I am sorry you had to take her place. Take care of yourself. I'll do better by your family. Good luck."

Palming the dagger, Taisiya sighed. At least in failing, she'd secured one potential ally. Alone again, she continued on her way.

"Vasilisa, hold onto this for now."

Her hand snuck out from the shadow of Taisiya's gown and sank back into the void. Better not to give the fae any warning if she needed to end their lives.

She was nearly to her escort when the empress herself stopped her. Selene fairly hissed at the bevvy of servants following her. As they made themselves scarce, the bitch held out a decorative vial of perfume.

"It didn't look like you were a willing bride, and I don't sell people off for fancy fucking trade goods. Use this, and you'll become a widow instantly. And if anyone asks, I didn't give it to you."

"My thanks, Your Majesty."

If only she *could* kill her husband, she now had a plethora of ways to end him. It really was a shame their lives were magically linked. But for better or worse, she was committed to his scheme. One day, she would have a crown of her own, be a pawn to no one, and beholden only to her own ambitions.

Selene nodded and strode off, leaving Taisiya to her fate.

"You look like you had fun."

"I suppose I did."

Mereruka admired his comely new wife. Though he'd been forced to sleep on a hard couch too small for his frame, he was glad to see the sacrifice had been well worth it. That morning, Taisiya had stopped looking at him with bone-deep contempt. She was fast to accept the things she couldn't change and had woken with a new scheme in mind, now that she could use him as a prop and the power of Maat as a cudgel.

They had agreed that in public, they would show a united, affectionate front. She had seen to it that her siblings were gifted with all the remaining gold, jewels and textiles meant to be her wedding presents so that they could openly flaunt their new status and connections within Lethe. They set sail with the gifts and trade goods of Lethe, as well as a list of imperial buyers and merchants eager to do business with Maat—a list as long as he was tall. Before the cursed continent had fully faded from view, they faced their first challenge.

Most of the fae simply ignored him—the cut direct. A few, like the treasury official Itu and Raemka the scribe, were blatant in their hostilities. Only moments after stepping outside their quarters, the ship in open waters, Taisiya and Mereruka were accosted. It said something of their enemies' overconfidence that they dared do so while Mereruka openly carried a bronze blade at his hip. A quick scan of the upper deck confirmed the soldiers were below decks. Excellent.

"A barbarian wife for a lowlife prince. Our Eternal Serenity was wise to see you deserved nothing more. I look forward to the day we return, and you're forced to renounce your ties to the throne. Then again, I imagine the mark of disinheritance won't bother your already marred hide," Raemka sneered at Mereruka.

"Perhaps, if you beg very sweetly, our king will find a place for you in his palace, scrubbing the floors," Itu said to Taisiya.

Mereruka was about to respond, but Taisiya placed a hand on his chest, starkly pale against the teal of his skin.

"If I recall, your name is Itu?" At his silence, she continued, "Perhaps, if you beg very sweetly, your new princess consort will find it in her heart to forgive you your insult."

"I am a hatya. I owe no apologies to those who associate with tattooed scum. You would do well to learn this before you arrive in Maat," Itu replied.

"Husband, did that sound like sweet begging to you?" she asked Mereruka, all innocence.

"It did not, wife. In fact, I'd say that sounded downright disrespectful," Mereruka answered, enjoying her game.

"It's a pity. What is the usual punishment for insulting royalty in Maat?"

"Death," Mereruka replied with a grin.

"Far be it for me to question the customs of my adopted home," Taisiya replied, stepping away from Mereruka. "May the forgotten gods pity you, Itu."

Before Itu could respond, she struck him with a bolt of lightning, the thunder echoing across the sea. Itu flew across the deck and flipped overboard. Mereruka charged Raemka and swung a fist into his gut. As the scribe doubled over, Mereruka seized his head in his hands and snapped his neck. His body fell to the deck. Mereruka kicked it away but didn't bother to throw it overboard. Yet.

Mereruka looked around at the horrified expressions of the fae.

"Trade Minister."

"Y-Yes, Prince Mereruka?" the man asked, swallowing.

"Assemble everyone on the deck before us. And let them know that any disrespect or tardiness will be met with swift punishment," Mereruka said as he fingered his as-yet-unused blade.

The trade minister fled below deck, his frantic calls to assemble audible. Mereruka turned to Taisiya and whispered.

"Well done."

"Have you bribed the crew sufficiently?"

"Yes, they swore an oath of silence in return for a modest sum. You'll find that many fae from the lower class fail to share the views of their supposed betters. And before you ask, they know they'll be paid only after we arrive safely in Maat," Mereruka answered.

"How many more do you expect to be a problem?" she asked, her expression tight.

"Not many," he answered. She looked like she might be ill. His concern began to grow. "Are you well?"

"I will be," she answered through clenched teeth. "Vasilisa, be prepared."

"Yes, Princess Consort," Vasilisa replied from the vicinity of Taisiya's shadow.

"Where is Bas?" Taisiya asked.

"Ensuring no one gets the idea to hide and bide their time," Mereruka replied.

Bas was busy scouring the decks, sniffing out any who might try to take cover in a pocket realm or cook up a spell against him. It was a task uniquely suited to a shapeshifter and their keen senses. Any such individuals would find themselves locked in the cramped iron cell that Mereruka had spent his initial voyage trapped inside.

It wasn't long before everyone, save the crew, was gathered on the deck before him.

"Kneel before your prince and princess consort," Mereruka commanded.

The few who had seen the deaths of Itu and Raemka were quick to do so. A few from below deck, who had noticed his corpse, did likewise. The rest hissed and spat at him. Soldiers fingered their weapons.

"Vasilisa, take your pick," Taisiya said.

A soldier with saffron-yellow skin and closely cropped blue hair was grabbed from behind and dragged into the shadow cast by the mast, screaming. The fae nearby leapt out of his way and shrieked in terror as Vasilisa, coated in her dark flames, slowly dragged him into the void.

Once his head was subsumed, only the scrabbling, scratching of his nails on the deck could be heard from him, and soon, that, too, disappeared.

Taisiya raised her voice.

"I believe my husband ordered you lot to bow."

Another soldier, this one with skin a cool grey tone, blue hair and a hateful glare, rushed towards her. She unleashed another bolt of lightning and he was tossed at the mast, breaking his spine with an audible crack from the force of the blow. Taisiya's expression turned ashen but her back remained stiff.

"Whichever fools wish to die, please separate yourselves from the intelligent ones by standing," Mereruka hissed.

All bowed, except for a single scribe, a woman with a proud bearing and a look of disgust on her face. The fae man beside her put a hand on her ankle and pleaded softly, but his hand was kicked aside.

"Only filthy dregs would ever deign to bow to a marked, sullied man and his degenerate wife. None of you deserve the noble blood you were born with! None of you deserves the title of hatya!"

Mereruka struck out with his own magic. She screamed and dissolved, dripping and shrinking until she coalesced into a solid form. He had turned her into a fish. As she flopped around on the deck, gasping, he approached her with a leisurely step. None of the other fae dared move, either to attack him or aid her. Being able to forcibly transform another was the kind of spell usually reserved for the most powerful of practitioners. It only succeeded if you could overwhelm your opponent's magic to a frightening degree. Thanks to his tattoos, few in Maat who eschewed the magical marks could ever match him—or counter his spell.

He pulled the enhanced bronze blade from his belt and hacked her nearly in half. While she was still in the process of dying, he scooped her up and tossed her overboard. He wiped his bloody blade and gore-slick hands on the clothes of the shaking scribe nearest him and then sheathed it. He stepped over to Raemka's body and heaved it overboard before rejoining Taisiya.

"I'm impressed by how many intelligent fae want to survive the trip back to Maat," Taisiya said aloud. "I thought we'd have to slaughter the lot of them."

Mereruka laughed. "As did I, wife." He looked around at the cowed noble ministers and smiled. "Now that we're all peaceably assembled, I would like to present you with a choice: vow never to communicate, in any way, with anyone, ever, regarding my tattoos, and I'll spare your lives."

"If not, my attendant will be happy to feed you to that which hungers in the void," Taisiya finished.

After that, the vows came quickly and without further incident.

CHAPTER 24

As soon as the door to their cabin was shut, Vasilisa was waiting, bucket in hand. Taisiya clenched it in her hands and threw up. Every time she relived the sickening crack of the soldier's spine or the horrifying sight of a woman disintegrating before her eyes, her stomach heaved.

"Are you ill, Taisiya?" Mereruka asked, shocked.

"She has an aversion to gore," Vasilisa answered him. "I hope you'll take that into account the next time you melt a woman in front of her."

Taisiya heaved.

"Why didn't you say anything? We discussed what would happen." Mereruka pinched the bridge of his nose.

Her stomach was empty and the dry heaves weren't coming this time. Progress. Vasilisa swapped her bucket with a pitcher of water. She rinsed her mouth as best she could and drank the small amount remaining. Vasilisa disappeared into the void to dispose of the evidence of her weakness.

"It needed to be done, and I was confident I could keep it down until I could be alone," Taisiya replied, her throat raw.

"That was foolish," Mereruka hissed. "I need to know these things about you before we make plans. You need to trust me, or we'll be ripped apart at court. It won't be so easy when we reach Maat."

"Trust you?" Taisiya scoffed, "I trust you want Maat's throne very badly, and that you're prepared to do whatever it takes to secure it. I'm willing to help because it means I will be queen. But so far as my personal problems are concerned, they're no business of yours."

"No busi—" Mereruka began, his finger raised as if to scold.

"Are you seasick, Princess Consort?" Bas asked as he entered the cabin, interrupting Mereruka. He produced a small flask and handed it to Taisiya. She drank, grateful for the fresh, herbal flavours replacing the taste of her own bile.

"Of a sort," Taisiya replied.

"The princess consort has an aversion to the sight of bloodshed. She's just explained she didn't trust me enough to say as much," Mereruka griped.

Bas shrugged.

"You were an ass about the marriage. I'm not surprised."

"Traitor," Mereruka grumbled.

"You're a good son, Bas," Taisiya smiled.

He blushed, looking uncomfortably at his feet. She supposed he was embarrassed to be called a son by the woman who had only just married his father.

"Um, you know, I'm older than you, Princess Consort," Bas confessed.

"You don't look a day over nineteen." Taisiya frowned.

"I'm forty-two. I'll be an adult when I'm fifty."

"Gods below, h-how long do shapeshifters live?" Taisiya asked, dreading the answer.

"Six hundred years, give or take a few centuries. But *he* mostly barters for years of life, so I expect I'll be around as long as he is." Bas smiled.

Taisiya turned wide eyes on Mereruka. Did her new husband expect to live longer than six centuries? What kind of world had she just entered? The ground beneath her feet shifted.

"I suppose now is as good a time as any to get these things out in the open," Mereruka said as he shepherded her to a bank of cushioned benches along the far, windowed wall.

She sat down beside him and tried to rein in her shock. Just how different were they, these foreigners? To live so long and never bat an eye at all those many years? Did they know mage lives ended so much sooner? Was she like a short-lived pet in their eyes?

"I am two-hundred and fifty-eight years old, and, provided we survive to take the throne of Maat, I expect to live until I'm a thousand. Longer, if I can accrue more years of life through my deals with others."

A thousand years! He was already well over the age when even the longest-lived mages expected to draw breath. She suppressed a hysterical laugh with sheer willpower. Taisiya had long expected to marry a wealthy, elderly nobleman, and a prince of over two hundred most definitely fit the bill.

"But—" Bas began, but Mereruka held up his hand to stop him.

"Mages don't live that long," Taisiya said, swallowing her astonishment.

"Not usually, no. But as my wife, you will share in my bartered years. If we succeed, I will make a deal with you so that we will share the same lifespan. There's no need to think too deeply on these things until after we have our crowns."

"I see," she said. What else could she really say to that? The sheer scale of her ignorance was beginning to daunt her. Best fix that, and fast. "Why don't you tell me all about your family? If we're going to be killing them, I should know my enemies."

"Alright, now recite them back to me," Mereruka said.

Taisiya, an eager pupil, had been taking in all the information she could about his family members and how to identify them at court. If she considered the fae she'd seen to be a strange, colourful lot, she needed to be prepared for his siblings. He watched with some pride as she replied.

"Nefertnesu, older sister, married to a neighbouring fae court at a young age. Heart has been removed, transforming her into a beautiful, powerful fae with mage-like features but no mercy or kindness. She can be convinced to renounce her claim to Maat's throne with a suitable bargain. Tall, light brown skin, turquoise eyes, black hair. Trust only that she will act in her own best interests."

"Good."

"But what do you really mean that her heart was removed?" Taisiya asked.

For him, her transformation had been the darkest point in his life. It was the day the only blood family he'd ever loved died. His rage and bitterness at the loss of her changed the trajectory of his life as he set his sights on Khety's head. Mereruka had tried to explain it as best he could, but without knowing a person both before and after that horrible transition, the true cost of it was hard to convey. Nefertnesu had been like a mother to him, even though she was only several decades older, her warmth and cheery smiles brightening his childhood. She had raised him, protected him, loved him, spoiled him. Now, a stranger inhabited her skin, a self-absorbed creature of careless, unfeeling cruelty. Nothing of the Nefertnesu he'd loved remained. In every way that mattered, she was dead, and Khety had killed her.

"Most fae look like me, or those on this mission. Colourful, strange to your eyes, sometimes more or less monstrous depending on their heritage or chance, but those are just appearances. You already know that our hearts are very much like your own. In order to attain ethereal beauty and tremendous magic, the cost is one's feeling heart, a part of your soul. Except that piece is everything that made you good or kind.

They feel no real love, no guilt, just an indescribable need for more, more of something they can never attain and they can no longer understand, and they never want to go back to who they were. If you ever meet a fae who looks like a mage with pointed ears, it would be best to run. Those are the ones who have bled out their feeling hearts."

They were lost souls, dangerous, vicious, cruel and grasping. Woe to any who knew them.

Her brows pinched in confusion. It was a subject he didn't wish to dwell on. Insatiable anger simmered in his heart, a wound that would never properly heal.

"If she visits, you'll see what I mean," Mereruka added. "Next."

"Itet and Inkaef. Twins. The only two siblings who share a father. Itet is an older sister, eccentric, violent, overseer of the eastern border. Short, muscular, bright green skin, black hair, blue eyes, horns and hooves."

And an absolute pain in his ass, but rarely in a threatening way, unless she roped you into a drinking contest.

"And Inkaef?" Mereruka asked.

"Inkaef, an older brother, quiet, browbeaten, Overseer of the King's Tribute, beloved by his sister but few besides. Short, green skin, black hair, orange eyes, horns and hooves," Taisiya answered.

His least objectionable, least dangerous, brother. Truly, he was the best of the bunch.

"Correct. Then?"

"Serfka, older brother, vizier, similar role to the praetor, but has more power. He's on good terms with Khety and is well-respected. Average height, blue skin, silver eyes, grey hair, has four arms. He has taken the mark of disinheritance, and so is ineligible to become king."

And it was fortunate he'd never coveted the throne for himself. He'd had centuries longer to make connections and become beloved by the people of Maat for his even-handedness. If Serfka had decided to be ambitious, he would've been truly difficult to unseat.

"Next."

"Radjedef, second-eldest brother, Overseer of the Royal Guard, also on good terms with Khety. Conservative, traditional, will dislike me on sight, quarrelsome. Scaled red skin, bald, yellow eyes, tall, two sets of horns."

Gods, he hoped to kill that meddling bastard one day. Radjedef was a constant thorn in his side, happy to overtly quarrel with him on Khety's say-so. Getting rid of Radjedef would be a long-overdue delight.

"And the king?"

"Khety, His Eternal Serenity, the eldest brother. Overthrew the previous queen, his and everyone else's mother, in order to become king. Has been demanding years of life from your bargains as his due in order to increase his lifespan. Refuses to have children lest they overthrow him in turn. Subsequently, his siblings are childless, so that they don't risk appearing ambitious. Tall, wiry, bright orange skin, white hair, blue eyes, winged arms, clawed hands, legs resembling those of a bird."

And the day Mereruka killed him would be the best of his life, no doubt. He had much to answer for.

"I'm impressed by your good memory."

Taisiya grinned.

"Six people is nothing. I was forced to memorize the names of every noble in Lethe," she remarked, then narrowed her eyes in concentration, "So the previous queen had a harem of men?"

"Yes, Mother was only a traditionalist when it suited her. She kept a harem, but refused to marry and share her power with a king." Mereruka smiled.

His mother had never been the warmest sort, but she'd been fair and wily and he'd always admired that about her. His mother had been an old woman of nine hundred when Khety killed her. Mereruka had his suspicions that she was about to throw tradition to the wind once more and choose Serfka as her heir, rather than the eldest. Sadly, any proof of such a thing had been destroyed along with her. That no one had batted an eye at a son murdering his own mother was a testament to the awesome power royalty held over Maat, as well as the colourful, bloody history that had always stained its throne. After all, his mother's hands were stained with the blood of aunts and uncles Mereruka had never met, and cousins that would never be.

"I suppose I should ask, given the descriptions of your siblings. Are your extra appendages hidden behind your glamour, as your tattoos are?" Taisiya asked.

Her question brought him back to the present.

"Would it bother you either way?"

"No, I'm simply curious," she answered.

"I have none, though I do possess something that might count in that regard. It's something both the current Queen Betrest, Khety's long-suffering wife, and I share. Living scalp hair," Mereruka answered.

"Like that woman with the water for hair?" Taisiya asked.

"No, ah… well, try not to scream. I'm told it can be unnerving," he said.

When his hair, whether in braids or hanging free began to rise up, seemingly on its own, he watched her grip the material of her dress and hold her breath, her eyes wide.

"It's less alive and sentient than it is a conductor for my magic, like an extra set of hands. I'll feel it if it's cut."

"O-oh," She replied.

"You can touch it. It won't hurt either of us."

Tentatively, she reached out. She held one of the violet strands in her hand and slid her fingers along it.

"It just feels like hair."

Mereruka laughed, startling her.

"Well, it is."

Taisiya scowled and put her hand in her lap.

"Normal hair doesn't move like that. Why would I assume it would feel the same?"

A fair question, but a knock on the door prevented him from answering. Bas strode through with a large bowl of hot food, a pitcher of steaming water, and a teetering tower of dishes.

"Are you showing her your freakish hair?" Bas asked, his brow raised.

"He was," Taisiya replied.

"No one wants to see you do unnatural things with your hair," Bas hissed. He mumbled something about childishness before setting the food before them.

"You used to love it when-" Mereruka began.

"When I was a toddler, yes. No one needs to know that. Moving on. I brought dinner if you're feeling up to it," Bas said to Taisiya.

Taisiya seemed about to protest, a hand on her stomach and the dark circles under her eyes prominent.

"I—"

"She is," Vasilisa replied sternly as she materialized in the dark corner. "As am I."

Bas's hair was standing up on end and his tail had grown three times in furry width when he slowly turned around to face the darkness mage.

"Stop doing that!" he hissed.

Vasilisa smiled.

"Why? It's so much fun when you yowl in surprise."

"Alright children, stop fighting and join us for dinner. Taisiya, Vasilisa, this will be good practice. Some of our etiquette will be different from what you're used to," Mereruka said, interrupting the fight before fists were involved.

When everyone found a spot at the bolted-down table, Mereruka poured the hot water into bowls and passed them about.

"The food has been prepared so that it can be eaten with our hands and shared amongst us. The bowls are for washing our hands." At Taisiya and Vasilisa's shared look of incredulity, he added, "I'll show you how it's done."

"That can't be... sanitary," Vasilisa opined.

"It is if you're not filthy and mind your manners."

Mereruka washed his hands and went to touch the food. The second his skin touched the serving bowl, a spell activated. Instead of a spell to keep the bowl and food heated, as he'd expected, the clay lining of the bowl exploded, revealing an inner core of metal. Iron. Instantly, wicked spikes flew out. Bas covered his face with an arm but cried out when several sank into him. Vasilisa dove, her arms stretched, trying to spare Taisiya, whose hands and shoulders flew up to protect her face. They screamed as sharp metal pierced flesh. Mereruka's shock slowed his counter-spell, made weak by the iron. The acid burn of metal drove into his flesh. He swore and cried out. Vasilisa was the first to act, launching herself at the weapon without a care for her injuries and tossing it into the nearest cupboard.

"Taisiya!" she cried.

"Your arms!" Taisiya gasped as she opened her eyes to the sight of Vasilisa's arms, stuck like a sadist's pin cushion.

"Fuck!" Bas cried as he pulled one from his midsection.

As those around him began speaking, Mereruka stiffened against a rising tide of agony. Broken glamour and tattoos on display were the least of his concerns. Everywhere the metal pierced him, fire poisoned his veins. His magic guttered out like a flame in the rain. He fell to the floor with a choked groan. Uncontrollable shudders and twitches wracked his body, digging the spikes deeper.

"Dad!" Bas leapt from his seat and began pulling the spikes from him as fast as he could.

"Are they poisoned?" Vasilisa asked.

"Iron poisoning!" Bas replied, looking him over and pulling the last of the stiletto-like blades from his body.

Still the agony raged on. It didn't matter that none of the deadly metal remained inside of him. It had pierced his flesh. He might as well have poured poison directly into his veins. This was not how he'd envisioned dying, by some low-class witch's trick, hiding the feel of iron beneath enchanted clay. It seemed Khety had left nothing to chance.

"Gods below, we're going to die," Taisiya said, her voice hollow.

"What are you talking about?" Vasilisa asked, panicked.

"T-the marriage vows. Our lives are bound. If he..." She trailed off, "What can be done?" she asked Bas.

"The waters of the Hapi can cure it. I hid some below deck, in a red amphora with a green stopper," Bas replied, already up and heading to the door.

"Stay here and keep him alive!" Vasilisa ordered before she dove into the nearest shadow.

A grey haze clouded his vision and the voices around him were growing indistinct. Only the fire that consumed him assured him he was still alive. Taisiya bent over him, her eyes swimming with concern.

"I have it, now what?" Vasilisa said in the distance.

"He needs to swallow some, and then his wounds need to be bathed in it," Bas replied.

Bas propped him up and held him steady as Vasilisa uncorked the amphora.

"Hold his mouth open, Taisiya."

She did so, prying open his nearly locked jaw. Vasilisa poured the water down his uncooperative throat. He managed to swallow a small mouthful.

"Now his wounds!" Bas ordered.

Bas pointed them out and Vasilisa poured. The agony lessened bit by bit—a miracle. There was a reason the waters of the Hapi were so prized. Even so, it wouldn't spare him what came next. His flesh had been pierced, not just touched. The fire in his veins was replaced by a sweltering heat, and the agony by bone-deep weakness.

"Will he be alright?" Taisiya asked.

"Eventually," Bas sighed.

Vasilisa put the nearly empty amphora down and began pulling out the needles from her arms and side.

"At least they didn't go deep," Vasilisa griped.

Once she was done, she helped Taisiya pull out hers. The last pinged as it hit the wooden table. Taisiya breathed a sigh of relief. It was all Mereruka could do to keep his eyes open as she turned to him with a grimace.

"If these are your dining customs, they can go to the deepest of hells."

Mereruka would have laughed if exhaustion hadn't claimed him first.

CHAPTER 25

"You should have told me," Vasilisa grouched.

Taisiya did her best not to feel too hurt by her friend's reproach. It was deserved, after all.

"I know," Taisiya replied. "It slipped my mind." It was a weak excuse, even to her ears. She'd been so ashamed of falling prey to yet another fae spell after being conned into this sham of a marriage, she hadn't had the courage to tell Vasilisa—or even her family—what a complete fool she'd been.

Taisiya pasted the healing ointment over Vasilisa's wounds. Several more jars just like it had been part of a thoughtful wedding gift from her brother, Theo. Vasilisa had already seen to Taisiya's wounds.

"I can't protect you if I don't know the risks involved," Vasilisa hissed.

"I know," she said, chastened.

She could see the darkness mage's blood boiling.

"If he'd dragged you to the grave, I—" Vasilisa stopped herself, rage still simmering.

She didn't have to say anything. Taisiya knew how she would have finished her sentence. If Taisiya had died because of Mereruka, Vasilisa would have lost the one person on Oblivion she treasured above all others, and with it, her tether. Without Taisiya, Vasilisa might abandon the world of her birth, walk into the nearest shadow, and never leave the void again.

"I'm sorry. I should have explained when I told you that I was going to take them to the graveyard."

Taisiya pasted over the last of Vasilisa's wounds and went to check on Bas. The cat shifter obligingly showed her his healed wounds. He'd disappeared into smoke and reformed himself as a young man, erasing all traces of the attack. An enviable ability.

"If it makes you feel any better, he didn't tell me about the vow either," Bas said as Taisiya spread the ointment on where his wounds once were, just to be safe.

"It doesn't," Vasilisa sniffed.

"You weren't at the wedding?" Taisiya asked.

"While everyone was there, I snuck back onto the ship to secure the waters."

Taisiya flicked her gaze to the man—the liability—she'd wed. He slept fitfully in a hammock, suffering a fever Bas had assured her would pass. Taisiya had never imagined the fae reaction to iron would be so strong or so quick. The knowledge comforted her. No sane fae army would ever dare march on Lethe with its many assorted steel weapons. Then again, she might as well be as vulnerable as her husband to the metal. Vasilisa would no doubt collect and take care of their recent haul of poisonous metal, now that they were about to enter enemy territory.

"It's strange. I thought you would say your marriage vows with your other name," Bas mused.

Taisiya thought back on it. She would have repeated the vows using her official name, Spark. They didn't speak of their true family name outside of the trusted few.

"I did, most certainly. As far as the empire is concerned, the last Dragonsblood was my grandfather," Taisiya said. "What would that matter?"

"Well, you would still be married, but I don't think the spell to bind your lives would have actually worked. Fae spells like that only work with a true name, the one you consider true. It's why some fae use a false name," Bas offered.

Suspicion and anger began curling in her gut. She did her best not to press too firmly on Bas's next non-existent wound.

"He told me we were bound. It's why I made you two officially my family," Taisiya said.

Had she been foolish yet again? Would these humiliations never cease? If their lives had not been tied, she could have killed him on their wedding night. There would have been no need to leave her home behind.

"Did you feel a spell latch onto you? Did you feel one when you first made your deal with him?" Bas asked.

While Bas remained innocent of her growing anger, Vasilisa did not. She positioned herself closer to Mereruka, an iron needle already in hand.

"I'm not sure," Taisiya replied. She sent a hard look Vasilisa's way and the darkness mage backed off grudgingly.

She hadn't felt a thing during the marriage ceremony aside from her anger, but when they'd officially struck their deal? There had been a faint something, but she'd been so anxious, she'd put it down to the risk she'd been taking.

"I'm sure he'll tell us when he wakes up," Bas said.

His faith in his father was admirable, but perhaps misplaced in this instance. Vasilisa rolled her eyes.

"I'm sure he'll lie through his fucking teeth when he wakes up," Vasilisa muttered.

"I heard that," Bas snapped back.

"Good! Then grow up! If you haven't learned what kind of man he is after forty years, you're probably too stupid to live out your next forty," Vasilisa retorted.

Bas jumped to his feet at the insult. Taisiya leapt to hers and placed herself between them, her arms out. Sparks of blue electricity arced across her palms, keeping them at a distance from each other.

"Stop it! Both of you! If you have the energy to fight, then direct it at our enemies. Bas, who gave you the bowl?"

"One of the scribes. He was helping in the kitchen, handing out food to everyone," he replied.

"And this wasn't odd to you? Do the scribes usually help in the kitchen?" Taisiya asked.

Her impression had been that, with the exception of the crew, the fae on board were all nobles of a sort—hatya, they called themselves. From what Mereruka had described, Maat was as stratified as Lethe, if not more so. So what was a nobleman doing in the cramped ship's kitchen?

"I... I don't think so. I've seen him bring Raemka food before, but I've never seen him in the kitchen itself," Bas answered.

"What does he look like?" Taisiya asked.

"Green skin, pink hair, dark eyes, about Vasilisa's height with an average build. I think his name is Pepi," Bas answered.

"Should I go retrieve the little bastard?" Vasilisa asked.

"No, not yet. We'll all stay in here for the night, as quietly as we can. Let him think he's won. If there's anyone else aboard this ship who wants us dead, or who conspired with him, I want them to out themselves," Taisiya replied.

Luckily, no one had left the room through the door since Bas had come in with dinner. Vasilisa hadn't been seen in the hold. If they were fortunate, no one had heard them through the thick wooden walls since their ordeal had begun. Hopefully, whoever else was in on the plot would come to check on them in the hours to come.

Vasilisa sighed.

"You take the first watch. You're terrible at staying awake," Vasilisa said to Taisiya.

"I'll take second," Bas offered.

Taisiya nodded. Tomorrow morning, they would answer violence with retribution.

"Has he spoken to anyone?" Taisiya asked.

"No, he's spent the morning pacing," Vasilisa answered. "How do you want to handle this?"

Taisiya did some pacing of her own. Mereruka had woken briefly on Bas' watch, but not since. She couldn't rely on him for advice, though she suspected that killing their enemy was the only path he would have advised. Taisiya grimaced.

"Gruesomely," she answered.

She walked over to Mereruka and pulled back the thin blanket covering him. The healing paste had closed his wounds, leaving red splotches where Bas had applied it. Without his glamour, Mereruka's golden-yellow glowing tattoos were almost pretty against his teal skin, though anywhere the iron had broken the glyph, the tattoo had disappeared. In all, she counted eleven wounds.

"Will he be able to redraw his tattoos over the wounds, Bas?" Taisiya asked.

"If he bathes in the Hapi when we return."

"Good." She said, then turned to Vasilisa, "Give me eleven of the projectiles."

"I could just drag him to the void," Vasilisa offered, concern evident.

"No. He's my husband and my vassal. I should be the one doling out the punishment," Taisiya said, her stomach in knots. "Bas, go ask for the scribes and soldiers to assemble on the deck. Don't tell them why, just that their princess consort has ordered it."

"Alright. When they're there, I'll come back to tell you." Bas nodded before he ducked out of the room.

"Do you really feel a sense of duty towards him? Even if he lied to you about the vow?" Vasilisa asked.

"If he lied, I'll use it to force concessions from him. Either way, he swore a true oath to me. He can't be disloyal to me, even if he tried. For now, that's enough to merit my protection," Taisiya answered.

"He doesn't deserve it," Vasilisa hissed.

"No, but I suspect he can be persuaded to earn it," Taisiya sighed. What a mess she'd walked into. "What do you think of Bas?"

"Despite his years, he's as childish as his appearance suggests," Vasilisa replied.

"You've certainly had fun taunting him."

"What else is he good for? He needs to start pulling his weight. That he thought nothing of a nobleman in the kitchens makes his inexperience plain." Vasilisa raised her brow as if asking Taisiya to contradict her. She wasn't wrong.

"Then you should teach him."

"You can't be serious!"

"I'm quite serious. Mereruka thinks he has potential. If that's true, I can think of no finer teacher than you."

Vasilisa bristled but kept her comments bottled up, her lips pressed together in a mulish line.

"I'll go keep an eye on Pepi," she muttered before she left the cabin for the void.

Taisiya walked over to where Mereruka hung in his hammock and took a strand of soft violet hair between her fingers. He'd brought nothing but anxiety and unwelcome change to her door since she'd met him.

"You're more trouble than you're worth."

Mereruka smiled and blinked open his pale eyes. Taisiya dropped the strand of hair as she gasped.

"I look forward to proving you wrong," he chuckled softly.

"How long have you been awake?" She frowned.

"Long enough to know I'll be awarding you a number of concessions to earn your trust."

"So our lives aren't entwined?"

Gods, wouldn't that be a welcome bit of news if it were true? That kind of vulnerability made her insides squirm.

"Not by fae magic." He winked.

She wanted to sag with relief. Still, one problem might be swept away, but another remained. Her eyes narrowed.

"Why should I let you live? You're entirely untrustworthy." Taisiya punctuated the threat by producing a thin strand of lightning that danced between her fingers. Mereruka winced at the bright, flickering light.

"Because you find me handsome? And a queen can always find uses for a handsome man," he grinned.

Taisiya felt a blush creep up her neck. She scowled.

"I don't make a habit of mounting heads on my wall, but I might make an exception for you."

Mereruka laughed. Taisiya raised her sparking hand higher in warning.

"Ah, mercy, wife, mercy. Name your wish, and I'll see that it's done."

"Then I want your honesty. There can be no trust between us without it. And I will not aid a man as ambitious as you without it."

Mereruka sighed.

"That's fair. I lied about the vow because I wanted to live after our wedding. Though, in truth, I believe I am only alive because your mother wants you to be Queen of Maat."

"She does?" Taisiya asked.

Mother had said it was a good opportunity to spread her wings, but she hadn't mentioned overthrowing the current king of Maat. Taisiya's heart warmed at the thought.

"She told me in no uncertain terms to either make you queen or get the hells out of your way." Mereruka smiled. "Your ambition and your cunning would be wasted in your homeland, Taisiya. There was no one there worthy of being your partner, and no challenge great enough for your talents."

"The flatterer returns," Taisiya scoffed.

"And yet none of it is untrue. I thought marrying a mage would be my downfall. Now I suspect it was my salvation."

Taisiya glared down at him. A lazy smile tugged up the corners of his dark teal lips. He looked exhausted, his eyes were hooded, dark circles beneath them. Even the glow of his tattoos appeared muted. As much as she wanted to berate him, as much as he deserved it and more, he might not be awake long enough to finish a conversation.

"Go back to sleep. We're going to have a lot of planning to do once you've recovered. In the meantime, I have business to take care of."

"Killing our assailant?"

"Yes," she answered, fighting her anxiety. It would be a long time before bloodshed was no longer necessary to achieve her aims. She needed to overcome this horrid sickness soon, or she might not have the mettle to do what was necessary when a situation called for action. That her first instinct was not to attack when faced with a threat shamed her.

"I'm sorry. Do you want to wait until I'm well? I know you dislike bloodshed, and they're not going anywhere."

She wished she could let him soothe her, shield her, but it would only make her weak. And give her enemies time to regroup.

"No. I don't want them lurking about." She paused, her eyes on the door, "Tell me, is there anywhere on a fae body that is more sensitive than a mage's?"

If she were going to pierce the man through with iron, she wanted it to hurt so badly that no one ever dared try it again. They couldn't afford for Mereruka to be brought this low for this long once they reached Maat.

Lightning was a fine tool, but perhaps not one suited to countering curses, or being transformed against her will, not if she couldn't anticipate when it would happen. Fear was the only thing that would keep her safe if Mereruka were indisposed.

"I don't really know, but our ears are quite sensitive, as a rule."

"Are they?" she asked.

She'd been curious about his ears for a while now. Every so often, they would twitch when he was emotional. Taisiya turned back to Mereruka and ran the tip of her finger along the outer edge of his pointed ear. He sucked in a breath, his eyes wide. His hungry stare had her gut clenching.

"You're lucky I'm weak as a kitten, wife," he purred.

Taisiya jerked her hand away. Stupid. So stupid. What had she been doing? She turned away so he couldn't see her blush. Sometimes, she wondered if he'd cast a fae spell on her. Knowing him, it wasn't beyond the bounds of possibility. Though if she asked, and he hadn't, she might never live down the embarrassment. Best not to think on it. This spark of desire was vexatious but temporary. She would overcome it soon enough—either when he did something irredeemable, or when he proved so lacklustre that he killed whatever fool fantasies her mind conjured.

"Go to sleep, Mereruka."

"Meri."

"Pardon?"

"Call me Meri," he mumbled.

"I-" Taisiya started, but stopped when she turned to find he'd already fallen asleep. She clicked her tongue in frustration, muttering. "Trouble."

Bas knocked before he entered, his expression grim.

"They're all gathered."

"Good. Guard Meri-Mereruka." She corrected herself, blushing. To her horror, Bas' ears twitch at the slip.

He nodded but didn't meet her eyes, his lips pressed together to hide a small smile.

Damn it! Blood! Guts! Gore! Think of anything but that damn fae man! she cursed to herself.

"I'll return when it's done." She fled the cabin and her shame, finding a place before the gathered delegation. It was time to be done with the malefactors aboard this ship once and for all.

CHAPTER 26

Taisiya breathed deeply once she was free of the cabin. The fresh sea air was cleansing after spending so long cooped up. The day was bright and clear, the wind refreshing and crisp, a slice of beauty and tranquillity before bloodshed soiled the day. Taisiya didn't bother with any preamble.

"Pepi, step forward," Taisiya called out.

A green man stepped forward, his dark eyes grim. He didn't bother to tuck his pink hair behind his ears as it swept over his handsome face.

"I know you tried to murder my husband. You've failed, and your punishment is death. Because I am a generous princess consort, I will give you two options: tell me the names of your accomplices and you will die quickly. Refuse, and you will die in the exact manner you had planned for the prince. What is your answer?"

Taisiya tossed the iron bowl onto the deck to the shrieks and gasps of those assembled. Any sympathy they had for the man died when they recognised the infernal device and felt the nearness of the deadly metal. Several hissed. Pepi's face remained impassive.

"Your husband killed my wife. I am already dead. Do what you will."

"She was the fool who refused to bow?" Taisiya sneered. "Then you've thrown your life away for nothing. If she'd loved you, she would've chosen to live with you, rather than die for her pride. Vasilisa, the blades."

Vasilisa stepped from the shadow of the mast, fae leaping out of her way and cringing at the feeling of the iron's naked nearness. Taisiya took the blades proffered by Vasilisa and nodded. Vasilisa coated herself in darkness and held the fae man still as Taisiya sank each of the eleven blades into him. By the end, his shrieks and thrashing had been reduced to guttural groans and the occasional spasm. His ears, chest, arms, legs—all were stuck through with iron. Sticky crimson blood coated Taisiya's hands and she fought her rising gorge. When it was done, Taisiya looked at her companion.

"Feed him to the void. The sea creatures have already grown fat."

Vasilisa dragged the man by his hair into the nearest shadow without a word.

Taisiya looked at the tear-stained faces of the fae gathered. Terror, deep and primal, looked back at her from behind their colourful eyes. Good. Only monsters could inspire true, paralysing terror. Now they knew precisely their fate if they tried to cross her.

"Tell any who will listen that Princess Consort Taisiya delights in the cries of any fae who dares harm her beloved husband."

Horrid spectacle done, she turned from the crowd and returned to the cabin. Once the door was closed, she slid to the floor, her knees gone weak. Bas already had a bucket ready. Though her gut roiled threateningly, she wasn't sick.

"Progress?" Vasilisa asked as she popped into the room, bloody iron spikes gathered in her hand.

Taisiya nodded. She looked down at her blood-slick hands. Even though she hadn't been sick, she didn't feel any pride. If this was progress, why did she feel so hollow?

When Mereruka woke in the night, his fever had finally broken, though his body was stiff and aching. Raising his arm to steady himself in the hammock, he was pleased to find the strength in his grip had mostly returned. So had his ability to cloak himself in glamour, for that matter. Thank the forgotten gods.

Biting back a groan, he worked his way out of the hammock and to his feet. In the darkened cabin only Bas and Vasilisa slept in their hammocks. Taisiya's was empty. A pang of worry lanced his chest. Mereruka stepped outside the cabin, his footsteps as silent as he could make them. Once on the deck, the chill sea breezes had him shivering.

"Mereruka?"

Taisiya stood at the railing, copper tendrils escaping her sleep-mussed braids. She looked so damn small, her eyes wide with concern and a large, thick shawl wrapped around her shoulders. She made her way to his side.

"How are you feeling?"

"Well enough." He smiled and leaned down to kiss her head. "What has you up in the night?"

Her expression closed up as she pulled the shawl tighter around herself.

"My weakness, perhaps. You don't need to—"

"Nonsense," he interrupted. "I need to stretch my legs. Tell me everything." Mereruka placed his arm around her shoulders and guided her along the deck.

She was silent for a time before she finally decided to speak. He took it as a good sign that she hadn't pulled away from him.

"I killed the man who gave Bas the device. He wouldn't speak the name of the person who gave him the device. He was seeking revenge for the death of his wife... I... I wasn't sick afterwards, despite what I did."

He tightened his grip on her in reassurance.

"I did what I had to do, as princess consort, as my duty demanded, to ensure my safety and yours, and yet... I feel I've crossed a line. Lightning kills instantly but iron... I'm not proud of what I've done. This doesn't feel like any kind of victory."

"Good," he said.

"Good?" she asked, scowling. Taisiya tried to pull away from him, but he held her still.

"Bloodthirstiness is barely acceptable in a mercenary. In a queen, it's disastrous," he answered. Her eyes softened for a moment before she pursed her lips.

"And yet, to become queen, I'll need to make corpses of your siblings."

"Not necessarily. Banishment, being forced to take the mark of disinheritance, being completely disgraced—all of these are options. Khety won't go without a fight, but the rest? If we work together, I suspect we can outmanoeuvre the lot of them," he offered.

He could see her slip on that carefully closed expression, but the tension went out of her posture. Mereruka relaxed as well.

"I would prefer to kill as few people as possible. If they're dead, they can't be useful," Taisiya said.

Mereruka nodded.

"Then we're of a mind on this. A few of my siblings are rather important in the running of Maat. If possible, I would prefer to corner them into taking a mark rather than see them dead. They can be replaced in their duties, of course, but it would make a transition unstable."

When she looked up at him, her eyes tightened with concern.

"If you're fatigued, we can discuss this tomorrow."

"Is that genuine worry I hear, wife?" he teased.

She pulled away from him.

"Just practising my acting skills."

Mereruka laughed. He pulled her tight again.

"I'm thrilled you're so dedicated. Shall I practice my part as well, as your smitten husband?"

She frowned.

"You can practice all you like without me."

"Don't be so cold. I'm The Prince of Dreams, and your wish is my command. If we are to maintain a united front, the people of Maat should believe I am head over heels for you. When we arrive in Maat, what will your first outrageous wish be?" he smiled.

"My trading rights."

Mereruka chuckled.

"And?"

"A divorce."

"Denied!"

"Some Prince of Dreams you are." She rolled her eyes, but the corners of her lips were turned up. Progress.

"You wound my pride. Go on, what else?"

"Wedding gifts so numerous and extravagant that even Queen Betrest will have reason to raise her brows. After all, I gave the first batch to my family."

"And?"

"And? Isn't that enough?" she asked, her brows raised.

"Remember, I'm a wealthy, besotted prince. Cultivate some greed so that I might show you my affection through indulging you."

She smirked.

"Then I want my own palace. And a lake filled with the waters of the Hapi."

"Better! What else?"

Taisiya laughed.

"Statues?"

"They'll need to be made of solid gold and jewels and dressed in the finest silks," Mereruka added.

"A floating barge?"

"It'll be as big as a house."

"Summoned beasts?"

"You'll have the biggest, the fiercest, the most beautiful, the sweetest, and a dozen of each."

By now he had her with a grin on her face, suppressing giggles and snorts. An answering smile took hold of him. He was glad he could have her like this too, not just ambition and plotting, but smiles and warmth. Maybe there could be more than a simple partnership between them. Maybe one day there could be love. She wiped a tear from her eye.

"I hope you have enough coin and magic for this charade. Else we'll be selling our crowns before we can wear them."

"No coinage in Maat. We deal in goods, spells, deals and favours. Wealth won't be the issue. I'll need to have a few tattoos re-inked, though, and perhaps add a few more for good measure."

"Bas told me that you'll need more treatment in order to remove the wounds the iron gave you."

"I will, but it won't be debilitating this time. What did you do with the iron, by the way?" He asked. He hadn't sensed its nearness in the cabin when he'd woken.

Her eyes darkened.

"I put some of it into our attacker. Publicly. Then I had Vasilisa put it away for safekeeping."

He tried not to grin. Gods below, there would be stories of her spread far and wide when they landed. His barbarian bride, fresh from the Cursed Continent, was cruel enough to stick a failed fae assassin full of iron. Maat would tremble in her wake.

"Carrying iron is punishable by death in Maat, so keep it stowed in the void, if you can. Fae can sense it from a distance unless it's hidden under non-fae enchantments, and it would be a foolish thing to get ourselves killed over. But if anything happens to me, use it well."

"I'll keep that in mind."

"See that you do." He leaned down and kissed her brow.

"You don't need to do that when no one is watching." She looked away.

"I did it because I'm proud of you. Maat will be too busy trying to figure out if it should fear you or fête you to realise we're aiming for its throne."

"If they know what's good for them, they'll do both," she said, her voice fierce.

The sound had his heart pounding in his chest. She could give a dragoness chills.

"You really are perfect," he murmured.

She blushed.

"Flatterer," she scoffed.

"I've been called worse." He grinned. "May I kiss you?"

Her eyes darted away as the blush spread to the tips of her ears. Why did tenderness embarrass her? It was the one chink in her armour, the one place he felt he could slip through her barbed defences. If he was careful and persistent, could he capture her heart along with her lips? He looked forward to finding out.

"It's hardly necessary."

"I disagree. If we're going to pull this off, we can hardly do so if you're too much of a coward to kiss me," he goaded her.

"I'm not a coward," she protested.

"Prove. It."

"I'll do it when I have to."

"Am I not to your liking, little mage?"

She rolled her eyes. It was the closest he'd gotten to an admission of attraction. Something eased in his heart, a fear that she might not find him pleasing.

"Are you fishing for compliments?" she asked sardonically.

"I'll make it easy. I'll even close my eyes." He slid his lids shut as he said it.

"I'll leave you standing there like the fool you are."

"You'll leave me here like the *coward* you are," he countered.

She groaned in frustration, but she did move. He heard the slide of fabric as her hand slid up his neck and pulled his head down. A quick peck on the lips was all she bestowed before she pulled away. He opened his eyes and frowned. What in the hells had *that* been? He'd had less chaste kisses as a young boy.

"Am I your mother or your husband?"

She fisted her hands and stomped her foot, a snarl tearing from her throat. He was surprised she hadn't seen fit to electrocute him in her pique. Or breathe flames.

"Then *you* do it!"

Tempting though the thought was, he wanted her curious, desperate... needy.

"No," he grinned.

"*No?!*"

"No. I won't kiss you until you ask sincerely." He hid his grin behind a bit of glamour and a serious tone.

"Acting precludes sincerity by its very nature." She crossed her arms and huffed, raising her brow in challenge.

Gods, but it was fun matching wits with her.

"Then I hope you're convincing enough to fool me."

If he'd tweaked her nose with a finger at that moment, she might have bitten it off. Fuming, she swept past him, muttering about pains in her ass, pulling her shawl closer as a particularly chill wind cut across the deck. He shivered as he lost the warmth of her nearness.

"Goodnight, Mereruka. I hope you freeze your balls off out here."

"Meri, Taisiya. Call me Meri," he said. No one as close to him as she was expected to be would call him anything but.

She turned her head and glared.

"Then, by all means, freeze your balls off, *Meri*."

He held back from voicing a teasing accusation about her solicitude for his nether regions. She likely wouldn't take it well. He smiled instead.

"Goodnight, Taisiya."

Chapter 27

"How will I know if fae magic is being used against me?" Taisiya asked.

"You'll taste it, for one," Bas replied.

Taisiya still jumped slightly at the sound of his voice, so crystal clear, as if he were speaking directly into both ears at once. She knew it was one of a shapeshifter's magics, his mind speak. It took some getting used to.

She petted his furry head as he sat under her chair on the deck of their ship. He'd transformed into a grey tabby cat that morning, explaining that Mereruka had spelled the fae aboard the ship to forget him during the night. It was a spell that had taken him two full days to construct. Now, Bas could reprise his role as an undetected spy.

In the distance, Maat loomed, a hazy outline wavering above the sea. The breezes, while cool, had lost any real chill while the sun seemed to burn hotter and brighter by the hour. She was beginning to understand the rationality of wearing the gauzy fae fashions while simultaneously doubting the sanity of their hairstyles, as they almost universally wore their hair down. Sweat trickled down her back even now, with all her copper locks piled atop her head. She was going to be a veritable puddle by the time they disembarked.

"Bas is right, taste is a giveaway for raw fae magic. But only if the spell is being used on you. If it's being used around you, or as a ward of some sort, I'm not certain you would know, unless you're adept at sensing magic. Did you notice anything at the wedding?" Mereruka asked.

Taisiya shook her head. Even surrounded by fae magic, she'd not sensed it. The very idea of sensing magic was a strange concept. So far as she knew, no mage had that ability. It didn't give her much confidence for protecting herself against magical mischief. Though at least that niggling worry that Mereruka had used magic on her was put to bed. It left her with other, more embarrassing, concerns, but she had bigger problems at present.

Bas hissed under her chair.

Speaking of mischief...

"Vasilisa," Taisiya warned.

"It's training."

She could hear the childish glee in the darkness mage's tone.

"It is not! Make her stop!" Bas whined.

Mereruka pinched the bridge of his nose.

"How old are you, Vasilisa?"

"Thirty-five," she answered primly from the shadows.

"And when do mages reach adulthood?"

"Physically or culturally?"

"Vasilisa..." Taisiya groaned.

"Both," Mereruka said.

"Twenty and thirty."

"Then you're old enough to stop acting like a child. Stop harassing Bas."

"Why don't you make me?" Vasilisa taunted.

Mereruka gathered a ball of harsh light in his hands, made copies of it and directed them to dance around the table and chairs, erasing and chasing shadows this way and that. Vasilisa swore and shrieked.

"I can keep this up all day," Mereruka warned.

Taisiya doubted that. He'd all but fallen into his seat on the deck this morning, exhausted from casting the memory spell. Still, she kept her counsel. Vasilisa appeared out of the shadow of the mast some distance away and stalked up to their group.

"Fine," Vasilisa sniped as she rolled her eyes. She thumped down in an empty chair and crossed her arms.

Bas crept out from under the chair and leapt into Mereruka's lap. Pulling a small collar from the pocket of his open robe, Mereruka secured it around Bas' neck.

"You actually put a collar on him?" Vasilisa snorted.

"It ensures he's treated especially well, and it's spelled with protective charms," Mereruka explained. When he grinned, it was a touch savage. "I've made one for you as well."

"Kinky," Vasilisa deadpanned.

Taisiya covered her mouth and held back a laugh. Mereruka rolled his eyes and placed an oversized gold wrist cuff on the table before Vasilisa. She picked it up, inspecting it as if it were an insect.

"It's not going to bite," Mereruka sighed. "You'll need to wear it to be identified as a member of my household. With that, you can purchase things in my name and come and go as you please on my properties and anywhere else I'm welcome. It will also protect you from a number of common curses and spells."

Vasilisa scowled but slipped her hand and wrist through the too-large loop. Just as she opened her mouth to complain about how it would only fall off, it shrank. Instead of the huge gold cuff it had been, it was now a delicate bracelet with a central stone of carved turquoise.

"I don't taste anything," Vasilisa said.

"Then I wove the enchantments correctly," Mereruka replied. With a twist of his wrist, he summoned a finely crafted, gleaming wooden box. He slid it before Taisiya and opened the lid with a flourish. "The first of many, I promise, but for now, this is your battle armour."

Taisiya held back a gasp. The collar was a masterpiece of multicoloured gems, strung together by gossamer-thin golden chains in a dozen neat rows. Bas hopped from Mereruka's lap as he stood and made his way behind her. Lifting the piece from its bed of silk, he placed it on her, clasping it behind her neck, his fingers trailing down the sides of her neck and shoulders as he spoke softly in her ear.

"Every gem is spelled. When you wear this, you'll have all the same protections that my tattoos give me."

Had the air lost its heat? She shivered, and not just from the change in temperature.

"Thank you."

He walked back to his seat and grinned.

"It will also prevent you from wilting in Maat's heat. The air around you will be made a comfortable temperature for you. Eventually, you'll need to adapt, but we can worry about that later. I can't have my princess consort arriving in a dishevelled state now, can I?"

Her posture was perfect, her hands folded in her lap and a serene, almost-smile on her lips, Taisiya was the picture of calmness. All the while, electricity danced underneath her skin, her only outlet. What couldn't fae magic do? If she weren't careful, she would lose her nerve.

"Do all fae wear spells like this?" she asked.

"Some do, others consider it a point of pride not to. Actively sustaining a number of spells is something we all learn to do, but not everyone has the capacity or inclination to keep them up for a long time, hence the enchantment of wearable objects."

"And yet you wear glamour constantly," Taisiya said.

"That's different. It's as natural as breathing. Well, except for altering our facial expressions. That can be difficult."

Appraising her, he swept his eyes over her from top to bottom. She wore her makeup in the fashion favoured in Maat, a little heavier around the eyes by Lethe's standards. Mereruka had done the same, with a thick swath of gold outlining his eyes. It made his violet lashes pop against the gold and emphasized the pale yellow of his eyes. It suited him in a way she feared it never would on her. He snapped his fingers.

"I knew I was forgetting something."

"What would that be?" Taisiya asked, nerves making her feel ill.

Since Lethe had become little more than a memory, she'd felt her confidence plummet. Taisiya had done her best to get accustomed to the fae customs Mereruka had been teaching her, learning the steps of popular dances, memorizing the names and appearances of his siblings, the titles of Maat's nobles, and going over their initial plans. He'd explained that Maat was a land of people who celebrated the beauty, sensuality and joy of living, and did so openly. Pleasure and affection were not meant to be hidden behind polite smiles, conservative dress or closed doors. It was also a land of wealth and plenty, where its citizens rarely went hungry, and where neither one's gender nor one's choice of bed partner was made an issue. Most importantly, the king or queen was expected to maintain order, justice and peace among its people. So long as the chaos of court intrigues stayed within the palace walls, the people couldn't care less about who ultimately wore the crown. But woe to any who let their royal squabbles undermine the stability of the kingdom.

As the shapes in the distance became more distinct, she felt her insides become jelly. Vasilisa must've been feeling the same unease, hence her prickly behaviour. Taisiya was only half-convinced she wasn't just some exotic pet to the long-lived, magically gifted fae. Despite her husband's reassurance that he would share his years, she still wasn't certain how she would find her place. Did she even want to live for centuries? Would doing so mean outliving every person she loved?

"Your hair," he said. "We wear it down. Vasilisa?"

"On it," Vasilisa said.

She disappeared into a shadow before returning with a brush. Pulling the pins from Taisiya's hair, she brushed out the braids. No noblewoman wore their hair fully down in Lethe anymore, not unless they were commoners or hopelessly out of fashion. Such a style was more for noblemen these days. Nevertheless, Vasilisa brushed Taisiya's hair until it was swept away from her face and fell in waves down her back, a few braids woven in to keep it neat. Mereruka nodded. Vasilisa quickly styled her own thick curls into a semblance of the same style.

"Good." He summoned another box and opened it for her perusal. Nestled inside was an ornate tiara decorated in lotus blooms, with strings of glittering beads falling down from the band. As he placed it on her head, she knew only dread. Gods, what had she gotten herself into? It shrank down to fit her precisely. More fae magic. "You'll have many tiaras like this. You'll need to wear them when we're out in public and when we attend important events."

"And what about you?" she asked, raising her brow at his unadorned head.

He snapped his fingers and a curious crown perched upon it. Delicately detailed golden wings framed his face and attached themselves to a jewel-encrusted golden circlet at his hairline. A second set of golden wings fanned out and swept back at the sides of his head.

"Is there a significance to the wings?" she wondered.

Mereruka shrugged.

"King Khety has long favoured the style, given he owns a pair. The princes all wear circlets decorated with them."

"And the princesses?"

"Itet rarely bothers due to the constant fighting at the borders, and Nefertnesu is queen of another court and so wears one befitting her adopted land. Only Khety and I are married, so there are no other princesses."

Taisiya nodded. With her nerves threatening to overtake her, sitting still was an impossibility. She rose and went to the railing. At least here she could dig her nails into the wood. At least like this she could close her eyes, breathe in the salty sea air, and imagine she was not leagues from home. But she could only keep her eyes closed for so long. The bluest waters she'd ever seen reflected an unnaturally bright sun. As the port came into view, structures shimmered in the humidity. Buildings painted in green, blues, golds, reds and more rose as if emerging from the sea, only a hair above the height of the water. Further out, homes and businesses were arrayed in a haphazard placement atop mounds, water lapping gently at the walls. Small boats sailed between homes and larger buildings. In the middle distance, a grand palace rose up, its high walls brightly painted with Mereruka's likeness. If she stared too long, she might begin to think the whole of it floated on the waves. Maybe with the help of magic, it did.

Mereruka walked to her side.

"Are you nervous?"

"Have I made it too obvious?"

"No, you're doing an admirable job of hiding it. But you always put on your disinterested mask when you wish to hide your thoughts," he answered.

Taisiya sighed. She disliked that he could read her so easily now. How soon before the whole of Maat could sense her unease? How soon before her weakness threatened her safety?

"It's just nerves and a bit of self-pity. It will pass." She gave the railing another squeeze, as if in abusing it she could force it to take away the tangled knot inside her.

"You're quick to accept me as your husband when it comes to practical matters, but not when it comes to your heart. We're in this together, Taisiya. There is no shame in coming to me with your anxieties."

"I won't let them affect our plans. What use is there in discussing them?" she dismissed him. She didn't want to give him more he could use against her.

"Some might argue that once a fear is named, it loses its power," he mused.

Taisiya dug her nails into her palms as the specks of people began forming into recognizable shapes. Bright, dull, pale, dark—the fae were a riot of colours from head to toe with no rhyme or reason. Only the shapeshifters that wove between them seemed to conform to any familiar rules in their appearances. Gods below, she was going to stick out like a sore thumb.

"Everything is different," Taisiya whispered. "It's overwhelming."

Mereruka covered her eyes with his hands.

"What is different? What worries you?"

"The people, their magic, the buildings, everything," she answered.

"Beneath the skin, their hearts and desires are the same as yours. Some lust for gold, others for renown, some only wish to outshine their acquaintances. Others toil, content with their lot and despise change, while a few travel the world, seeking adventure. Some care only for themselves, others just for their kin, and some wish to care for the whole of Oblivion. Some specialize in their magic, like the mages, others wish to learn every spell ever created, some are gifted, while others are content never to learn more than a few basic enchantments. Our buildings are much like your own; floors, walls, ceilings, windows, just made in different colours and proportions. It may appear strange to you now, but in a few years, Maat will become as ordinary to you as Lethe."

He began pulling his hands away. She grabbed his wrists and held them in place. She wanted him to let her pretend, just for a few more moments. Breathing deep, relaxing her shoulders, she felt the thrum of his pulse against her fingertips. Her anxieties receded, if only a little. He was right. They were not much different from mages. Their ambitions were stepping stones; she only needed to know where to place her feet in order to rise. Their desires were hers to manipulate for her gain, the same as she had in the empire.

But one doubt could not be beaten back.

"Am I... just a short-lived pet in your eyes? Useful for a time, but ultimately insignificant?"

She had to know the truth, even if she hated it. She could not allow this affection—these momentary lapses in good judgment—to keep growing. Especially if she were just some transitory trial he simply had to endure. She could live with that, but she needed to know, to regain her balance.

He pulled his hands away from her eyes and placed them on her shoulders. Slowly, he turned her to face him. Brows furrowed and lips pursed, he was the picture of displeasure.

"Are we married?"

She raised a brow.

"Yes."

"Did you agree to become a queen at my side?"

"I did."

"Are you an unapologetic political strategist?"

"I am."

"Do you desire the power to chart your own destiny?"

"I do."

"Haven't I often said you are perfect?"

"You... have." She swallowed. *No, no, not hope.* She could not afford to hope. He'd once said she had a heart of stone, but she was mortal the same as him. If she let him support her, let him help as she got her balance, he would have power over her. He would get past her walls.

"Then trust that there is nothing insignificant about you. I risked my head to ensure you were my bride. I tricked and trapped and lied, and then bound myself by unbreakable oaths in order to win you, Taisiya. You are my perfect—vicious—other half." His hand cupped her cheek, his thumb grazing her cheekbone as his eyes sparkled with delight. "You demanded my honesty. This is the truth—only a fool marries someone they consider a pet, and I like to think of us as more intelligent than that."

Her heart leapt as he grinned. "Now, look upon your future subjects. Let them see the woman I see; a proud, fearsome mage with lightning in her veins."

Taisiya turned to see the people of Maat, all gathered to welcome their prince home. She straightened her spine and kept a pleasant smile on her face as Mereruka waved. Their ship docked at the bustling port. Ecstatic cheering rippled through the crowd as his return was trumpeted. Mereruka created steps of pastel clouds for their descent from the ship. She placed her hand in his and looked up at him as lovingly as she could. It was time to put on a show not one of them would ever forget.

CHAPTER 28

It was good to be home.

The jubilant, shocked welcome of Rhacotis—his city—was all he needed to understand that few had expected him to return. Before he'd arrived on the shores of the Cursed Continent, neither had he. And now he'd done the unthinkable. Mereruka might as well have risen from the dead. As he helped Taisiya down the steps, he couldn't help his smile. He was home, alive, and he'd brought death back with him—and she was a beauty.

He hadn't realised how much he'd missed Rhacotis until he'd set foot on the pier. Home smelled like aromatic spices mixed with the sea. Home was the place they called his name like a benediction. Home was where the sun shone brightest, illuminating the smiles of his people.

His two most trusted retainers appeared, pushing through the crowd.

"Prince Mereruka! Thank the gods you've returned," Nofret said as she knelt at his feet, her green eyes shining with tears.

The first scribe's skin was plum, her hair sparkling like spun silver and her fingers forever darkened by ink. Nofret was nearly as tall as he, heavy-set and possessed of surprising physical strength. Once upon a time, she'd been a trusted official of his mother's. Now, she set her brilliant mind to making Rhacotis wealthy and prosperous beyond belief.

"It is good to see you alive and well, Prince Mereruka." Qar knelt beside Nofret.

Taller and broader than most, the brown-skinned hippo shapeshifter was barrel-chested and thick-necked. His braided black hair fell forward as he bent his head, the ears of a hippo flicking, and ivory tusks jutting out from his bottom jaw. Mereruka had confidently left the defence of the delta and his city in Qar's hands. Though the hippo shifter was easily stronger than any wild hippo, he was not nearly as bad-tempered.

"Nofret, Qar." Mereruka nodded. "Meet my wife and Maat's newest royal, Princess Consort Taisiya."

Taisiya gave the barest nod of her head as he presented her, copper waves of hair swaying in the breeze. In front of his people, this raucous crowd, she was the picture of serenity.

"Greetings, Princess Consort Taisiya," they said in unison.

"Taisiya, Nofret is my first scribe and Qar is my overseer of the soldiers, who defends my lands and keeps the peace in my territory. They are trusted members of my household."

"Greetings, Nofret, Qar. This is my attendant, Vasilisa. Treat her as an extension of me." Taisiya tipped her head to her companion.

Vasilisa curtseyed.

"I pride myself on serving the princess consort and ridding her life of vermin. If you require my assistance, simply call out. I have tasted your shadows and can now locate you with ease." She looked to Taisiya, who smiled. "If there is nothing further, I will take my leave."

Despite the harsh sunlight, Vasilisa burst into black flame and sank slowly into Taisiya's shadow, waving her black, clawed hand. Fae in the harbour who witnessed it yelped and leapt back. To their credit, Nofret and Qar didn't budge.

So his wife did know when to have a flair for the dramatic after all. He placed a hand over hers on his arm and squeezed. *Good girl.*

"If we're speaking of vermin, then you should prepare yourself, Prince Mereruka. In your absence, a swarm has brazenly taken up residence in your home—at the suggestion of King Khety," Nofret said.

Mereruka glamoured over his displeasure—barely. It took a moment before he could release the stiffness of his posture. Someone had invaded his home? His place of refuge? They would die—painfully. It was brazen indeed to take up residence in another man's home, king's permission or not.

"They have been draining your treasury, raising prices, and charging enormous tariffs on all incoming trade as well," Qar said. "The people of Rhacotis have been grumbling loudly of late."

The bastards were trying to ruin him and destabilize Rhacotis. Of course they would. Khety was always jealous of him, of his well-run nome, of his contented, wealthy subjects. Had it not been enough to send him off to certain death? Had it not been enough to send multiple assassins with him on a supposed doomed voyage? Now he must endure the insult of his place of sanctuary being defiled. His blood was beginning to boil. How bad would the damage be?

Taisiya's thumb stroked his arm. He caught a sly smile turning up the corners of her lips.

"Are they telling us that a band of ruffians have been sleeping in my new home, eating my food and dispensing with my wealth?" she asked.

What new game was this?

"Yes, dear wife, I believe they are."

"How does Maat usually treat those who steal from royalty?"

"With extreme prejudice, Princess Consort Taisiya," Qar replied, a savage grin on his face.

"Then take us to our home, so that I might demonstrate my skills for the people of Maat," Taisiya said.

Nofret and Qar cleared the way to a small barge, one decorated so finely that every onlooker knew it to be from his palace. As Nofret's magic propelled them along the channels, the people of Rhacotis showered them with welcomes and flower petals until they reached his home, a modest palace complex seated atop a stone outcropping. Qar leapt from the boat and held out his hand for Taisiya. She took it gracefully and waited for Mereruka to disembark before placing her hand on his as they made their way to the doors, the soaring, painted walls a welcome sight. Armed servants opened the first set of colossal doors and knelt.

"I heard that my home has been invaded. Where are the miscreants?" Mereruka asked.

"In the courtyard, Prince Mereruka."

"Take us there."

They passed through the smaller buildings for his soldiers, servants and scribes, through the administrative offices and training grounds and into the core of the complex. His rooms and Bas', his library, his personal vault, the heart of his home. This was the only place he dared let down his guard. Here, in the very centre of it all, he'd carved out a private slice of paradise where only those he trusted were allowed. An ornamental pool ringed by palm trees and a garden of sweet-smelling herbs and flowers basked in the sun of the courtyard. Here there was room to spar and play, to lounge and chat, to entertain and feast. And here, a group of shameless hatya, toadies of his eldest brother, violated his sanctuary. Dancers and musicians frolicked through his gardens, trampling greenery underfoot while the nobles gesticulated with their cups, sloshing wine and beer over the painted floors. Another floated in his pond, naked and chuckling while several fish lay speared through on the dry stone. It was all Mereruka could do to keep from shaking with rage.

"Husband, do these people displease you?" Taisiya asked.

"They do," he said, his voice tight.

Keep it together.

"Vasilisa, would you like to begin?"

Inky talons reached up from a shadow and sank into the ankles of a lounging hatya. His screams echoed pleasingly while his compatriots fell off their seats and scrambled away. As he was dragged into the void, another tried to grab hold of his flailing arms. Waist-deep in the shadows, there was no purchase against Vasilisa's insistent pull into the void. His grip slipped and the man's head was dragged under. The second he lost his balance, Taisiya stepped away and let loose a bolt of lightning. Dead. Another, who had watched it all in horror, was struck a second later as the first clap of thunder reverberated in the courtyard. Dead.

The man in his pool had, by now, tread through the hip-high water to the edge while the entertainers shrieked and cowered in the farthest corner of the courtyard. All the exits to his inner sanctum were bristling with blades. There was nowhere left to run. The naked fae prostrated himself at Mereruka's feet, black hair plastered to his saffron and amber back.

"Forgive me, Prince Mereruka! King Khety suggested that your territories were without leadership in your absence. We all thought you had died on the Cursed Continent."

Mereruka fisted his hands at his sides. The man before him was a stranger. He leaned down and yanked the man's hand forward, noting the name engraved in miniature on his golden ring. So, the nomarch of Shedet had sent his useless brat to interfere with Rhacotis? He would answer the insult with blood. Mereruka slapped the man's hand away as his eyes narrowed. The courtyard was silent.

"Did His Eternal Serenity tell you to take it upon yourself to replace me in my home?" Mereruka asked.

"Not in so many words, Your Tranquility," the man answered.

"So, on whose authority did you break into my residence and command my household? On whose authority did you steal from my treasury? On whose authority did you meddle with the affairs of Rhacotis?" Mereruka demanded.

"King Khety-"

"Did not explicitly give you permission to do these things, did he?" Mereruka hissed.

"N-no, Prince Mereruka."

"Husband, he has admitted his crimes. Let us make an example of those who dare steal from us and call my homeland cursed." Taisiya sidled up to him and placed a hand on his chest.

He had to get his temper in check. Word of what happened next would get back to Khety and the rest of the hatya. They needed the story to be as gruesome as it was entertaining.

"Do you have something in mind?" Mereruka asked.

"Take him out in full view of the neighbours. Turn him into a bird. If he can escape my lightning, then he may go free. If not, well, he will pay with his life," she suggested.

Mereruka was surprised that she would willingly witness the grisly process. It cooled his anger. The spectacle would ensure Rhacotis knew who was in charge once more and put any other scoundrels on notice. It would also demonstrate his power and hers. He kissed the palm of her hand and took a deep breath.

"An excellent suggestion. Qar, drag him out of my palace."

"With pleasure," Qar growled.

Qar pulled the man up by his hair and shoved him along.

"Please have mercy, Prince Mereruka!" the man begged.

"Weren't you listening? My wife will give you a chance at freedom if you can avoid being struck by her lightning. That is more mercy than a thief like you deserves!" Mereruka snarled.

Before long they arrived at the entrance. The servants opened the imposing stone barriers and Qar threw the man to the ground with all his considerable strength. As he crawled for the water lapping at the bottom of the front steps, Mereruka snared him in his magic. As the people of Rhacotis watched the man slowly melt, sweat trickled down Mereruka's spine. The nomarch's spawn possessed a fair bit of magic, fighting the transformation with tooth and claw. But being a hatya, he'd refused to augment his power with a single tattoo. Fool. It took longer than he would have liked, but that only added to the horror of the spectacle. Eventually, he dissolved the man and reformed him as a duck.

By now, passersby had stopped their boats in the canals while others crowded on the small islands of dry land to watch the grim process. Some cheered, others yelled epithets at the intruder-turned-fowl. The bird clumsily took to the sky to the outraged shrieks of those gathered.

"Are they watching?" Taisiya asked.

"They're riveted," Mereruka answered.

Taisiya stepped forward and formed a crackling spear of lightning as tall as herself in her hand. As the harsh incandescence burned his eyes, she appeared as nothing less than a proud demigoddess, lightning streaking through her copper locks as her dress billowed about her ankles. Fearsome and implacable, she was a sight to behold. The spectators shielded their eyes as she posed to throw her lightning like a javelin. With a theatrical flourish, Taisiya unleashed the bolt. In the distance, a dark, smoking shape plummeted into the waters below. Food for the fishes.

The eyes of his people turned from the sight of the execution towards Taisiya. She stood tall, a stern expression on her face. His heart swelled at the sight. Mereruka swept her up in his arms. She gasped, wrapping her hands around his neck as her eyes widened. Grinning like a fool, he called out to the crowd, his voice amplified by a spell.

"The city of Rhacotis has been restored by my wife, and Maat's newest royal, Princess Consort Taisiya!"

Cheers rang out as Mereruka swept back into his palace. Despite his smile and the delighted looks of his household, anger over the desecration of his home simmered beneath the surface. Taisiya placed a hand on his heart.

"Your real home is here. They can tarnish brick and mortar, but they haven't truly destroyed the heart of your home, not if you don't let them. Trust someone who knows a little about such things."

He was surprised by the unexpected kindness. Hope took root inside him. Stopping his stride, he bent his head to kiss the top of hers.

"Thank you," he whispered.

"You're welcome. Now, shall we assess the damage?" she asked.

"Prince Mereruka? Princess Consort Taisiya? If you'll follow me, I'll tell you what has happened since you left Maat," Nofret said, her tone grim.

Chapter 29

Held in Mereruka's arms, Taisiya fought back a blush. It wasn't the most seemly of ways to get from one part of his palace to the other. It was also far from dignified or discreet. Surely he would tire soon? But as they passed the outer complex, giving a show to all and sundry, he never once faltered. She'd never allowed herself to get this close to him for this long. His spicy perfume tickled her nose, his muscular chest was hard against hers and all she could think about was his taunt. He wanted her to initiate their kisses. *Be my lover.* Foolish, vexatious, temporary madness. She had more important things to do. Taisiya crooked her finger. Mereruka bent his head obligingly, allowing her to whisper in his ear.

"How much do you trust them?" She nodded at Nofret's retreating form.

She hadn't discussed with him just how many in his household knew what he was about. It was a thoughtless error on her part.

"She knows I want the throne. She doesn't know how far I'm willing to go to get it. Nofret has no love for Khety, though. My mother was one of Nofret's dear friends. You may tell her what you feel comfortable divulging. Qar is as loyal as they come and would welcome a bit of bloodshed either way. Otherwise, best keep these things to ourselves," he answered quietly.

Taisiya breathed a sigh of relief.

"Alright, you can put me down now," she said.

Mereruka's grin was wolfish. That boded ill for her composure.

"At least wait until we're somewhere more private. Give the staff something to gossip about," he said.

"You have no shame," Taisiya hissed.

He shrugged, rubbing her against his chest. She fought down a blush as her hand grazed his nipple.

"I only bother with it on special occasions." When he looked down at her, his citrine eyes glittered with mischief. "You're burdened by enough of it for both of us. As your adoring husband, I should show you how to live without it."

"You should quit while you're ahead, Meri," Taisiya threatened him in a sing-song voice. He laughed.

"No no, it's my duty to help you shed your shyness. It will only hold you back once we get to court. Luckily, I have the perfect training in mind."

She sank her nails into his chest. It was the only thing she could do with so many eyes on her. Smiling through the humiliation of her cheeks heating, she imagined the ways she would punish his temerity.

"What wicked thoughts have you turning pink, wife?" he purred in her ear.

"The kind that would leave you incapable of fathering children," she hissed.

He chuckled. Taisiya had managed to steel herself against most of what life had to offer. Why was she having such difficulty holding onto her detachment around this man? He would inevitably disappoint her, just like all the rest. The thought helped her regain some semblance of self-control. She would be rid of this obscene fascination with him soon enough.

"If only I were a truth-taster, just for a few hours. I would call you out on your obvious deflections."

"A truth-taster?" she asked.

"A special fae skill, one you're born with or not. The lies of others taste bitter on their tongues, while the truth is sweet and pleasing. Few make themselves known, but most that do eventually retire from society, exhausted by the constant bitterness. It's why, wherever you go, it's best to be vague or misleading when choosing your words, lest one of their number catch you out in a bald-faced lie."

Taisiya shivered. Gods, if she couldn't lie, she would have died by now, executed for treason. Being able to lie with a straight face was a skill all noble mages perfected. It appeared she had yet another skill to learn to make her way in Maat.

An imposing stone door barred their path. Mereruka put her down to open it with a touch of his hand on an outsized jewel.

"They were unable to open this door and the door to your office, so everything is as you left it," Nofret said, bowing as she ushered them inside.

"Thank the gods for small mercies," Mereruka sighed. "Come. Have a seat."

A truly palatial set of rooms greeted her. The ceiling might have resided in the clouds for its height. A raised, enormous bed with a gauzy canopy took up one section, another was a sitting area with some kind of game laid out and a few scrolls lying about, another was filled with strange objects on shelves and large wooden wardrobes inlaid with precious stones. Given what Mereruka had said about wood's rarity in Maat, they must be costly imports. Decorations and patterns in blue and gold covered every conceivable surface; the floors, the walls, the furniture. The ceiling was the true masterpiece of the room; a subtly swaying painting of the daytime sky, complete with the light of day, softer and kinder than that she'd just experienced outside, emanating from nowhere and everywhere at once. Taisiya kept her bored expression fixed as she let her eyes wander. She took a seat near the strange game and waited for the first scribe to describe what new challenges they faced.

"Is Qar already putting the affairs of Rhacotis in order?" Mereruka asked as he slid into the seat.

"Yes, Your Tranquility. I suspect he's eager to get trade moving along again. He did his best to delay the implementation of the new orders as long as he could," Nofret answered.

"Alright, tell me what has happened to my home and Maat since I left."

Taisiya could see him tense, waiting for the worst, and placed a hand atop his. She knew what it was to lose one's home, to have it invaded and violated, to feel as if your sense of safety and sanctuary would never return. She might never walk the halls of Dragomire Keep again, but she had discovered that home came with you, so long as your family were there. Maybe one day, she would feel that again here, in Maat.

"Once you left, King Khety suggested at court that you may be away for some time and that your palace and city would be left without proper oversight. At first, no one thought anything of this, but not a day after you had gone, he raised taxes on the hatyas and nomarchs to a punishing degree. Then a few days later, as the taxes began trickling into the palace, he demanded Oblivion's Tithe be tripled. He made announcements that any hatyas or nomarchs who couldn't pay their fair share could barter their territory, their daughters, or their years of life in lieu of goods and gold," Nofret said.

Mereruka cursed, taking his hand from hers to run it through his violet hair.

"What is Oblivion's Tithe?" Taisiya asked.

"Every year, the king demands a small token from every household in Maat. When the inundation begins, he sails north on the Hapi to the northernmost seasonal palace and dedicates it all to the forgotten gods in his name," Nofret answered.

"Why increase the tithe? He has already increased the taxes." Mereruka frowned.

Nofret shook her head.

"I've heard rumours that he was cursed for sending you, his own brother, to the Cursed Continent, and is hoping more offerings will sway the forgotten gods to remove it. Begging your pardon, Princess Consort."

Taisiya raised her brows and smiled slightly. She supposed it could be a fun new game, deciding to punish anyone she disliked whenever they called Lethe cursed. But as Nofret was an ally, there was no call for such treatment.

"No need. I was made aware of how Maat views my homeland. For now, I don't mind using that misconception to my advantage."

"As you wish, Your Harmoniousness." Nofret nodded.

"He's gone mad!" Mereruka thumped his hand on the armrest of his chair. "Is he trying to destabilize Maat?"

"If he is, he's doing a good job. I've heard, in whispers, that many of the nomarchs are selling the waters of the Hapi in order to pay the king." Nofret shook her head, grimacing. "The three you disposed of were lesser sons of the nomarch of Shedet. I believe they were encouraged by the favour your brother, Radjedef, shows their father. They drained a tenth of the treasury, half sent to their father, and the other half for their own amusement. They raised taxes on Rhacotis in order to pay their own taxes and tithes, and refused to allow traders to sell their goods unless they paid exorbitant bribes to do business in the port," Nofret said, her eyes weary.

Taisiya didn't know this nomarch of Shedet, but she did recognize the name of Mereruka's brother. Radjedef was the Overseer of the Royal Guard and a generally quarrelsome man.

"Is selling the waters of the Hapi a crime?" Taisiya asked. Nofret had referred to the act in such a horrified way that it made her wonder.

"One of the greatest. Only the royals of Maat have the authority to make deals using it. Since they are ultimately responsible for its protection as they are for Maat's, it's the same as stealing from the king himself," Nofret replied.

Taisiya tucked that useful bit of information away. It would be simple enough to frame their enemies for the crime of selling the waters.

"I have sold small amounts in the past to wealthy individuals and ally nations. Its importance cannot be overstated. According to our knowledge, only a handful of such places on all of Oblivion exist. Only Maat and one other land have ever allowed outsiders to benefit from it," Mereruka added.

So to Oblivion, as well as Maat, control of the waters of the Hapi was the greatest show of power and wealth a person could demonstrate. At least, it was to the fae race.

"And a nomarch?" Taisiya asked.

"An administrator of a territory, much like a magister or magistra in your empire. A nome is the same as your province," Mereruka said.

"The Cursed Continent is an empire?" Nofret asked, fascinated.

"Yes, Lethe, the Empire of Mages," Taisiya answered.

"The empress is her half-sister," Mereruka said as Nofret's eyes widened.

"May she rot in the deepest of hells." At Nofret's bewildered expression, Taisiya added, "She killed my beloved father and youngest brother."

"Ah, you need say no more, Princess Consort. Though it is a hard thing to lose a parent and sibling in that way, I'm heartened to know that the prince has found someone who might understand that kind of grief. I would be happy to dedicate a few curses her way, if it pleases you," Nofret said, her eyes earnest.

"Not at the moment, but perhaps in future," Taisiya replied, warmed by the offer.

Ashamed as she was to admit it, she knew that Khety had killed his own mother and sold Mereruka's sister off, yet she hadn't thought that both she and Mereruka shared the same kind of bitter hatred for a sibling.

Another kernel of sympathy flickered in her chest. There were too many of them in the past few days for her liking.

She wondered why none of Mereruka's other siblings despised the king for his actions. Though he'd told her that both Radjedef and Serfka, the vizier, were on good terms with King Khety, she would need to ask him if his other siblings might be made allies rather than obstacles.

Mereruka leaned down in his chair, resting his chin on steepled fingers, brows furrowed in concentration.

"A tenth of the treasury, you say?"

"Yes, Your Tranquility. Grain and gold as well as enchanted gemstones and objects."

"Gods below, what a monumental waste," Mereruka groaned, pinching his brow.

"Ah, perhaps quite literally. The nomarch of Shedet has begun construction of a palace. I believe that's where most of the grain went, to pay the workers," Nofret offered sheepishly.

"Fuck!" Mereruka snarled, leaping from his chair to pace like a restless predator. "I'll have his gods-damned head!"

A new palace? Taisiya grinned. Perhaps it was not a waste of funds after all. Luck was on her side.

"Husband, dearest?"

He turned to her with a raised brow, halting his furious pacing at the cunning in her tone.

"I have always wanted a palace of my own. We should thank the nomarch of Shedet for being so gracious as to begin its construction for me. It is, after all, funded through our treasury."

His eyes widened and a grin broke out on his handsome face. Kneeling before her, he took her hand and kissed it.

"My beautiful wife is so very astute."

"My handsome husband is so generous with his compliments. Of course, we should go to Shedet to oversee the construction..." Taisiya looked away coyly.

"What is it, my love? Don't be so modest. Tell your husband what you wish for." Eyes bright with anticipation, he tilted her chin back towards him with a finger.

"Is Shedet far from here?" she asked.

Nofret was up from her seat in a flash. She grabbed a scroll and unrolled it before Taisiya, displaying a colourful map of an enormous land. It appeared like an upside-down flower in bloom. The delta was a swath of green bordering the sea, shot through with small veins of blue, the Hapi. A thick blue stem, winding in some areas, was bordered by vibrant green. All besides was a rosy golden shade of sand. Towns of importance were indicated in a script wholly unknown to her.

"This is Rhacotis." Nofret pointed to a small bay. "Prince Mereruka controls this territory here." She ran her finger along a great green swath. "The nome of Shedet borders the northernmost edge of the prince's nome. Each nome is named after its principal city. Shedet is located here, at a natural oasis." She placed her finger on the only patch of blue and green outside the great river that bisected the Land of Maat. A thin blue line connected the oasis to the Hapi.

A plan began forming in Taisiya's mind.

"Do you think the nomarch might be persuaded to give me a wedding present? Perhaps a territory of my own? Maybe his own nome? I have always wanted a palace by a lake. And now that I know how important the Hapi is, I should like to have a lake filled with its waters. Shedet is the ideal place."

Mereruka grinned, a hungry look in his eyes. She swallowed. If they had been alone, Taisiya was certain he would have leaned in to capture her lips. As it was, the timbre of his voice left no question in her mind as to the bent of his thoughts.

"For you, Taisiya, anything."

Chapter 30

Mereruka's day had been a long one. After setting his palace to rights and assessing his losses, he'd put Taisiya's plan in motion, calling and provisioning a force of soldiers, bureaucrats and palace staff to be ready to move.

Back aching and feet sore, he was eager to finally have a chance to use his newest facility—the luxurious mage bath he'd commissioned, with a few upgrades. The architect had formed it with magic, and it was just now real enough to use. Never fully comfortable allowing others to get close enough to undress him, he had the little oasis to himself. A flick of the wrist, and his clothes, jewellery, shoes and crown were laid out on a side table, waiting for a servant to remove and care for them when he left. The waters were pleasantly cool and fragrant, just as he preferred. Stepping into the pool, he relaxed onto a sunken bench to allow the waters of the Hapi to fully heal his iron-induced scars, watching the enchanted lotus blooms float by. The only flaw was that his wine was just out of reach. Sending a tendril of magic into his hair, he pulled the glass towards him.

"Bas is right. That's going to take some getting used to," Taisiya sighed.

Mereruka's eyes widened at the sight of her in an airy, transparent wisp of a gown. Did she know that the room's light behind her, meant to mimic the fast-fading last rays of sunset, left next to nothing to the imagination? Keeping his expression neutral, he reached for the glass, now within easy reach of his fingers.

"I'm certain, with time, you'll adapt." He smiled.

She sat down at the edge of the pool, dipping her toes into the water and casting glances around the chamber. Her necklace was absent, the heat undoubtedly the reason for this fortuitous meeting. Hair swept up in a messy style, her gown clung to her, outlining her nipples. Sweat beaded above her plump lip and flattened a copper curl to her neck, trailing down between her breasts. Hunger coiled through him.

"You made a passable copy. It's a shame you didn't see my family's ancestral keep."

"Oh? Was it impressive?" he asked.

Whatever it looked like, it would have paled in comparison to the sight before him. She shook her head.

"More unconquerable than striking, and with a great many hidden passages and escape routes. Only a trusted few knew them all." She grinned.

Mereruka nearly choked on his wine. Were they still discussing architecture?

"Would you like to build one, a copy?" he asked.

"No, but I think it would be best if we add a few features to your own."

"Is that what you've been doing today? Assessing my defences?"

She nodded.

"I had Nofret show me your home and describe the household management. I also met with your bureaucrats, sorted the imperial gifts and was liberal with your treasury in the city, appeasing the people and paying for some goodwill. It will take some getting used to, paying for things in enchantments, raw materials and foodstuffs, rather than coin. Qar escorted me. I don't think I've seen so many nearly nude people in all my life. Though, given what Maat feels like without that charm, I've begun to understand why."

She was rambling. He could see a faint blush creep up her chest and neck. Her eyes weren't on him, but on the cool water below. Was she too shy to slip in, despite her need?

"Would you like to come in?"

"I'll... come back when you're done." She reluctantly pulled her feet from the pool.

He stood and waded over to her. Taisiya was still, her eyes running up and down his body before she turned away. His sneaky little wife liked the sight of him. Good. He grabbed her ankle and caressed her calf.

He had a theory. If he used scheming as an excuse, she might be moved to overcome her shyness where he was concerned. When her mind hit on a good plot, she forgot her timidity. Though he'd promised not to kiss her without her request, it didn't mean he couldn't try to seduce her in other ways.

"Nonsense. You're wilting. Join me and we'll discuss our plan for Shedet."

She looked between him and the door, a coward's retreat. He sweetened the pot.

"I'll look away while you enter."

"F-fine. Turn around."

He did just that. If only he could memorize the sound of her peeling off her sweat-slicked gown. It took all he had to hold back a groan as it slapped the floor. Gods below, she was finally naked and in his presence. *Don't fuck this up.* She slid into the pool and sighed. Wading away from her, he sat down on his bench opposite hers, hoping the rippling water and a few strategically placed flowers concealed his arousal. He had a sneaking suspicion the evidence of it would scare her off.

"Do you expect a great deal of resistance in Shedet?" Taisiya asked.

Her expression said she was caught between timidity and business. Mereruka smiled. He could play this game with her. He simply needed to coax her out.

"If the nomarch is intelligent, yes. But I don't believe he is. I'll have a solid fighting force accompany us nonetheless."

Taisiya paused to mull it over. Damn water was rippling too much to see her form beneath it.

"And if we sent a number of the soldiers ahead, disguised as commoners? Would that be noticed?" she asked.

Right, he needed to keep his wits about him. She would notice if he were distracted.

"What do you have in mind?" His curiosity was piqued.

"He'll know we're coming. We don't plan on making our trip there in secret, right?"

"Correct. Royalty in Maat always travels ostentatiously."

"Then we should send a force ahead of us, disguised to avoid suspicion, and have them placed to quell a military conflict before it has a chance to organize. It will also have the added benefit of making our approaching caravan appear peaceable."

He sipped his wine. It was a good plan. If the soldiers were discovered, he could easily excuse their presence as protectiveness over his new wife.

"We'll speak to Qar in the morning and organize the soldiers accordingly."

Her smile was dazzling.

"Do you think any of your siblings share your hatred for Khety? For killing your mother?"

Gods, if only. Mereruka shook his head.

"No. Our mother wasn't the warmest sort. Nefertnesu, being heartless, is entirely untrustworthy. As for the twins Itet and Inkaef, I don't believe they have any real love for Khety, but things are good for them with him in charge, and neither is fond of change. Serfka and Radjedef, as you know, would side with Khety."

She frowned. Disappointed?

"Ah, and under what pretext will we be seizing the nome?"

"Any pretext we like. In Maat, though the hatyas and professional classes have wealth and land, there is a vast chasm between them and royalty. If we didn't need to worry about Khety using this against us, we could simply slaughter the nomarch's whole family for the insult of his son's invasion of my palace. No one would bat an eye." Mereruka waved his hand. "Ah, except maybe Radjedef, since he and the nomarch of Shedet are friendly, both being military men. But I suspect our list of grievances against them will be more than adequate as a pretext. They invaded my home, stole from my treasury and harassed the people of my nome. Even Radjedef, hot-headed prick that he is, would have a hard time defending that. We will offer them their lives in exchange for their territory and settle them elsewhere in Maat. It's more than fair."

"And you don't believe we need to be cautious of their resentment?" she asked.

Mereruka shook his head, sipping his wine. Now that he had returned, any who acted against him and who possessed any sense would be running for the hills. It was how things should be.

"I think that's unwise. Fae live an inordinately long time. Either kill your enemies, or co-opt them. Why not install one as the first scribe of the nome and find prestigious but not especially powerful positions for the nomarch's family within Shedet's administration? We would keep them in our sights, and their knowledge of the nome could prove valuable. Any children unsuitable for administration could be married off to neutral parties without ties to real power," Taisiya suggested.

"Is that how you would have neutralized the threat of your own family?" he asked, curious.

Taisiya smirked.

"It only would have worked if they'd acted quickly, and only for a single generation. Any true Dragonsblood who visited the graveyard would know the second they stepped foot in there that the territory was theirs to rule and protect, that the heart's resonance was the marker of a hallowed home. How else could a family hold the same territory with the same conviction and purpose stretching back beyond written memory?"

Is that what the descendants of dragons felt when they found the graveyards of their kin? Perhaps she really did have a drop of monster's blood in her.

"Very well. We can be generous in this instance. It will deny Khety anything to foment trouble with, too."

Taisiya nodded. In the short silence that followed, her timidity returned. She swallowed and looked away from him.

"Go on. Tell me what bothers you," he said, hoping to coax her out.

"Will you just…"

"Yes?" he asked, enjoying the sight of her turning thoroughly pink.

"Just kiss me and get it over with?" She asked so quickly she blurred the words together. She hugged her chest, covering her breasts and refusing to look him in the eye. Tension held her still.

His first impulse was to do just that. He liked her vicious little mind, and he liked this shy side of her as well. The idea of taking the lead in the bedroom pleased him. But the phrase 'get it over with' poured cold water over any enthusiasm. In truth, he was a little affronted. That bit of pique held him back. Normally, he might have enjoyed luring her out of her shell, but her request rubbed him the wrong way.

"With such honeyed words, who could deny you?" he grumbled.

When she chanced to look up, she would see that he had not moved an inch from where he sat. Sipped his wine instead, in fact. Much as he wanted to see what there could be between them, he wanted no question as to whether or not she yearned for him in return. He liked her enough that her rejection would sting, and loathe as he was to admit it, he didn't want to go to bed licking that particular wound.

"So… you won't?"

"Hmm? Do you want to be kissed? Or do you want it to be *over with*? Which part were you sincerely asking for?" He raised his brow and leaned back.

"Oh..." Her eyes widened with surprise. She looked away guiltily. "Have I hurt your feelings?"

"Wouldn't yours be, if I treated such things with you as an embarrassing chore?" he retorted.

Her cheeks heated further, this time with anger. Her brows furrowed and her eyes turned stormy.

"Damn you! I'm doing my best!"

"Then your skills in this regard require a great deal more practice," he replied. "If you want a kiss, then come over here. I'm not going to force one on you."

Her anger had her marching three-quarters of the way over to him, her arm covering her breasts. The last few steps, though, seemed like they might be too far. Her thoughts were like vines, grabbing hold of her ankles. Thoughts written so plainly on her unguarded face. Fear. Shame. Uncertainty. Hardly the passion he wanted from her. Hurt, he decided to goad her.

"If you make it those next few steps, don't kiss me unless you intend to do so like a lover would," he said as his heart thundered in his chest.

Damn. So much for seducing her. Would she even bother to move now? He'd been a bit of a cad, letting his fear of her possible rejection spur him. Her face fell.

Gods, he'd messed this up. He'd suspected the mages were a bit of a prudish lot. Why had he pushed her so quickly? Was there a way to salvage this? She looked so vulnerable, defeated. *Shit.* He was going to have to give her a glimpse of his own vulnerability to make it right.

"I never want to feel like a chore to you, Taisiya," Mereruka murmured.

Whatever had moored her to the spot suddenly loosened. She stepped forward, erasing the distance between them and swallowed nervously. Leaning down, she kissed him, a soft brushing of her lips. He kissed her back, startling her with his ferocity. At her gasp, he slid his tongue along hers. Hands gripping his shoulders, she pulled him in instead of pushing him back. Her tongue began teasing his, and he stood, drawing her flush against him. He angled his head to kiss her deeper, earning him her moan of pleasure and the bite of her nails digging into his scalp. Hands pressed to her back, his fingers wandered up and down the length of it. Grabbing her shapely rear with one hand, he ground his hips against hers. Her jerk of surprise had her rubbing dangerously along his erection. Merciful gods, the friction was delicious. They pulled their lips apart, both breathing heavily.

He wanted to be inside her very badly.

"Do you want to see where this takes us, Taisiya?" he asked, his voice deepened with desire as he took a steadying breath.

To his surprise, she chuckled.

"As if the destination were a mystery?" she panted, her eyes locked on his lips.

He leaned down and kissed her tenderly, wringing another moan from her. When their lips parted a second time, she was trembling. Her eyes fixed on his mouth, her fingers holding him close—her desire was plain, but still she hesitated. What was it she feared? Had someone hurt her? The very thought made him murderous.

"Not... not yet. But... can we do this again?" she asked.

He groaned, pulling her hard against him, revelling in the soft, wet heat of her skin against his. His copper-haired wife was full of passion. She wanted him, he was certain, but something was holding her back. No matter, he could be patient, now that he knew what awaited him.

"You plan to tempt me sorely? It's cruel of you, but then again, I wanted a wicked woman for my wife." He looked into her amethyst eyes and kissed her. "We can do this anytime you like. In fact, I insist on it." And may the forgotten gods bless him with the self-control he would need in the days ahead.

"Oh... good." She smiled and then glanced down, a sharp inhalation the only clue that she felt his length against her. "Should I get out first, or would you...?"

"Go ahead. I'll be there shortly." He sighed.

"Will you turn around?"

"No," he said flatly.

"No?"

"No. I plan on enjoying the sight of your pert bottom as you run from the room."

He snapped his fingers, ensuring any towels were well out of reach. She flushed.

"That's not very gentlemanly."

"I'm gentlemanly when it counts," he purred, sneaking in a last taste of her lips. He squeezed her rear. She squeaked, pulling his hair in retaliation. He groaned, but couldn't help his grin.

"I won't be able to sleep," she mumbled.

He snorted.

"Neither will I."

She scowled, but there was no anger to it.

"It's too hot."

"The air under the bed canopy is spelled in the same way your necklace was."

"Oh, thank the gods. I'll, um, leave first." She hesitated as she pulled away.

He did his best not to hiss at the sight of her fully naked before him. She possessed beautiful curves and breasts big enough to fill his hands. Her nipples were a shade lighter than her kiss-darkened lips. What he wouldn't give to taste every inch of her.

She turned away quickly enough and tread through the water of the pool. Mereruka was pleased to note that he did, in fact, enjoy the view of her as she dashed away.

Chapter 31

"You look pleased," Vasilisa teased as she waggled her pale brows and sipped her drink.

"I suppose I am," Taisiya replied with a smile.

"So… I don't have to drag this one through the void as punishment for being a shit lover?" Vasilisa grinned.

Taisiya raised her brows. It had been their unspoken agreement that Vasilisa was free to torment as she pleased any man who ruined bed play for Taisiya—which was all of them. She'd had enough terrible, selfish lovers in her past to keep Vasilisa's more sadistic tendencies fulfilled. Taisiya was beginning to fear that there was something wrong with her rather than her partners. Everyone *else* seemed to enjoy themselves. Maybe with Mereruka, it would be different, but she wasn't ready yet for the potential disappointment.

"I don't know what you mean," Taisiya sniffed.

Vasilisa snickered.

Seated under the shade in the recently restored inner palace garden, they dined on sweet and savoury dishes as the morning sun inched towards its noontime brilliance. Mereruka had left early with Bas to survey the city, leaving her with a searing kiss and promises of gifts upon his return. A bevvy of servants had come moments later with Vasilisa at the helm to prepare her for the day ahead. Palace staff had seen to their every need and then retreated, allowing for privacy.

"And? What of the staff, bureaucrats and soldiers in our new home?"

Vasilisa leaned back in her seat, shrugging.

"Elated at their master's return, impressed by you if a little wary. No one is particularly discontented, though I've been hearing rumours and speculation about the king."

"As have I. Cursed for sending Meri to the Empire, squeezing his vassals for tax and religious tribute, generally destabilizing Maat…" Taisiya replied.

In theory, he was the perfect target. A king who brought strife and chaos to his people engendered his fair share of ill will. And in Maat, where the greatest purpose of royalty was to ensure peace, order and stability, the king's actions were especially unwise. But would it be enough? Many tyrants inspired as much fearful loyalty as hatred.

"Meri? Are you getting cute with him already? Gods save me." Vasilisa shivered in revulsion.

Gods below, she'd used his pet name without thought. Taisiya blushed and scowled, clearing her throat as she fumbled for a good excuse.

"Apparently it would appear odd if I referred to him otherwise."

"Uh-huh." Vasilisa rolled her eyes.

"It's for appearances. I can't afford to slip up," Taisiya insisted.

Vasilisa did not appear at all convinced.

"Just promise me you'll find someone else to gush to while you're in your honeymoon phase. I tolerated it in the past because your sisters bore the brunt, but I'm-"

"I know, I know. 'Profoundly uninterested in such dreck.'" Taisiya mimicked her dour tone.

It had been years since Taisiya had been struck by anything more than a passing fancy for a handsome but ultimately inadequate man. But Vasilisa was singularly uninterested in romance or lovers, so any discussion not revolving around jokes and teasing about those subjects had the poor woman looking longingly at the nearest shadow.

"Precisely." Vasilisa nodded. "It seems you've heard everything I have but for one. Apparently, the king's latest concubine is throwing her weight around, getting openly spoiled to the point that people are wondering if Queen Betrest will be replaced before long."

"Oh, she will. Just not by a concubine." Taisiya grinned as she sipped her drink.

"It sounded like she's a queen in name only. Betrest has the prestige and wealth of her position, and the respect of many, but little real power," Vasilisa added.

Vasilisa had been busy. She always knew where to lurk to get the best gossip, and no one loved to gossip more than palace staff.

"I suspect the king is the paranoid sort. He refuses to produce an heir lest they overthrow him, so I'm not surprised he hoards power for himself as well," Taisiya mused.

Taisiya had never heard of a monarch so fearful of being replaced that he refused to secure an orderly transition upon his passing. Though given how many years he'd taken from Mereruka, it would be centuries yet before Khety died of natural causes. All the more reason to ensure his expedient demise.

Vasilisa chewed thoughtfully on a fig.

"That's going to make him really fun to fuck with."

Perhaps rumours of a bastard or three might tip the king over the proverbial edge.

"I completely agree." Taisiya smiled. "How are you finding Maat?"

Vasilisa had left her father, her only family, behind in Lethe to come with Taisiya. As grateful as she was that her best friend had agreed to be by her side, Taisiya would send her home if the darkness mage no longer wished to remain. It would break her heart to do it, but Vasilisa deserved to be happy.

"Bloody hot without this bracelet. How do the women walk around with their hair down without this charm? I'm convinced it's glamour.

I've never wanted to shave my head more than the minute it took to shove the bracelet back on."

Taisiya had a good laugh at that. She'd dared to join Mereruka in the cool bath just to escape the heat, so she had an idea of how desperate Vasilisa had been. Taisiya stared down at the drink in her hands, bracing herself to offer her closest friend a way out of the life Taisiya herself had agreed to.

"I'm not leaving, you know," Vasilia told her. "I'll miss Father as much as you'll miss your family, but we can always invite them to Maat, and until then, we have each other. Now stop looking at me like you're worried I'll beg to return to Lethe."

"Is that what I looked like?" Taisiya asked, hiding her smile behind her cup as she willed joyful tears to abate.

Vasilisa rolled her eyes and then perked up.

"Your husband and the kitty have returned."

Moments later, Mereruka swaggered through the doorway to the courtyard, a familiar grey tabby close behind. Several unfamiliar faces craned their necks beyond the guards standing watch at the entryway. Mereruka took her hand and kissed it with mischief in his eyes. It appeared it was time to put on her best smile and act her heart out.

"Good day, beautiful wife. Are you ready to be spoiled?"

He pulled her up from her seat. She wrapped her arms around him, twirling a strand of his violet hair around her finger.

"Oh, silly man, I was born ready. The real question is, can you impress me?"

"It will be my pleasure to find out," he purred. "I've invited Maat's best artisans to our home. Would you like to see what they can do?"

Taisiya nodded. He led her from the courtyard to a grand receiving chamber where the artisans waited. The ceiling shone with the pleasingly realistic depiction of the current skies, brightening the room. The first to approach laid out a crude stool for her to sit upon. She looked to

Mereruka, wondering if it was some sort of insult. What kind of royalty sat on a rude stool in front of guests? When he smiled encouragingly, she relented, seating herself. The artisan began weaving a glowing aurora between his fingers. The stool was transformed into a plush seat decorated with gold, gleaming wood and precious stones. Palace servants brought a tall mirror before her. What she saw was nothing less than a throne, one that made the empress' look like much abused, second-hand furniture. She couldn't help her grin.

"This pleases me," she said imperiously.

Mereruka nodded.

"A few more, if you will. One for every kind of occasion," he said.

The artisan bowed deeply. With a flick of his wrist, the throne disappeared, its likeness appearing on a curious scroll held by the artisan's helper. He would repeat this process after every nod of her head or Mereruka's. And so it continued, each seat as comfortable and beautifully crafted as the first.

The cobbler was next, slipping on an unassuming, plain pair of sandals that he quickly transformed into shapes, forms and designs that couldn't possibly exist without magic holding them together. Their likenesses were also transferred to a helper's scroll.

"I want them all. In every colour," Taisiya said.

"Then you'll have them," Mereruka replied.

Vintners, brewers, bakers and chefs tempted her with their wares between the parade of cabinetmakers, glassblowers, potters, painters, sculptors, cosmeticians and perfumers. Long past the time when she was growing ill at the sheer amount of gold Mereruka must have spent on her, the jeweller, a shapeshifter woman who appeared to be some kind of arachnid, approached. Her sharp-toothed smile was far from reassuring, but the blindingly beautiful creations she presented in each of her four hands made Taisiya gasp with delight. Her underlings opened other boxes of such luxuries before her, their heads bowed.

"Behenu is the most gifted jeweller in all of Maat," Mereruka whispered.

If what she saw arrayed before her were any indication, then Mereruka was not praising the woman highly enough. She'd never seen such delicate jewellery before. Gold latticework as fine as spiders' silk, clear, perfectly cut gems that sparkled with the barest hint of light, rings so delicate and beautiful she feared they might break at her touch. But it was the necklaces which best showcased her talent, each one a marvel of intricate beading and master goldsmithing.

"I shall have everything here. Do you also make crowns?"

"Yes, Your Harmoniousness. I brought a few." Behenu snapped her finger and servants bearing ornate boxes appeared.

The lot of them were presented to Taisiya, one after another. Gold circlets deceptive in their simplicity. Tiaras made of solid gemstone. Several were in the style of her first crown, jewelled circlets with strands of spun gold dripping jewels down the length of her hair. Each and every one was stunning. Mereruka had not been boasting when he assured her that she would be a queen so rich it would put the empress to shame.

"All of them?" Mereruka grinned.

"All of them," Taisiya answered.

Behenu smiled.

"And you needn't wait to wear them, Your Harmoniousness, for they were handmade rather than through magical means, and as such don't require any weaving spells to settle into reality," the spider-woman reassured her before bowing and taking her leave.

The last to approach was the dressmaker. Her assistants placed an enormous, gauzy sack of fabric over her head. By now, Taisiya had grown accustomed to the plain forms the fae of Maat used to weave their illusions onto. The fae woman wove her spelled cloak into every colour possible, noting the ones Taisiya liked best. Colours done, she began reshaping the fabric into dresses ranging from impractical splendour to dazzling yet sensible to decadently indecent. Mereruka's eyes lit up at the racier frocks, and Taisiya nodded her assent, especially at those that had him nearly choking on his wine.

By the time the last artisan had left, the sun was setting and Taisiya was exhausted. She sat in the courtyard with Bas, Mereruka and Vasilisa, her new little family.

"Vasilisa, if I ever stop thinking that this kind of wasteful acquisitiveness is obscene, you may slap me," Taisiya said as swigged her wine, feeling bedraggled despite her finery.

"If you ever make me stand by your side to watch you do it again, I will slap you repeatedly," Vasilisa groaned as she arched her back.

"Just wait until tomorrow." Bas grinned, looking no worse for wear. The lucky little furball had lounged in a plush bed at Mereruka's feet brought especially for his comfort while servants tempted him with tasty treats. There was something to be said for the ease of a cat's life.

"*Tomorrow?!*" Taisiya and Vasilisa asked together, with equal alarm.

Mereruka nodded.

"The barge-maker will come tomorrow."

"Gods below, I'll need one just to store my new purchases. Have I impoverished us?" Taisiya asked grimly. They'd only just begun assessing the full extent of the damage to the treasury. Perhaps she should have been more circumspect.

Mereruka snorted.

"No. You only asked for what was presented. Had you demanded a hundred times more of everything you liked, it would have only momentarily dented our treasury. Though you have been profligate, you have not purchased nearly enough to make Queen Betrest blush."

Taisiya stared at him, horrified.

"Lethe must look like some insolvent backwater to you."

He shrugged.

"It looked young and mostly stable. Maat has existed in its present form for tens of thousands of years and we've long grown fat off our control of the Hapi." When he grinned, it was a touch savage, "Though now, should you visit Lethe, you will outshine all its inhabitants."

Hells, she could probably buy the bloody palace out from under the imperial swine. The nobles of Lethe would be begging to eat out of the palm of her hand.

"Speaking of, I'd like to send a fair number of gifts to my family and begin trade with the empire. When can a sea-going vessel be made ready?" Taisiya asked. The sooner her family prospered, the sooner they could wrap the empire around their fingers.

"Are you certain you wish to send it so soon?" Mereruka asked.

"Why wouldn't I?"

"Don't you want to see what your new nome will have to offer? Once the barge is completed, we'll be on our way to Shedet. Besides, where else are you going to put your palace's worth of new goods?"

"He has a point," Vasilisa said.

"And before the barge is ready, you'll need to approve the new scribes, soldiers and palace servants that need to be hired to oversee the running and security of Shedet," Bas pointed out.

Taisiya slumped in her seat. There was so much to be done. Then again, what had she expected? If she wanted to be queen, she was going to have to scheme and work harder than she ever had. Their enemies were no pushovers, and she wouldn't even be playing a game she'd begun herself. The first move had been Khety's. As she looked at those around her, Taisiya's resolve hardened. For her family, what wouldn't a Dragonsblood do?

Chapter 32

Mereruka had quickly learned that when his wife was working, he should either make himself useful or scarce. When he'd come into the office he'd set up for her personal use, he'd found her buried under rolls of papyrus, dictating letters, commanding a small army of servants and duplicating documents being read aloud into Lethe's script. At the mention of another appointment, he'd feared for his own health and had taken to commissioning her barge himself. Taisiya spent the morning exhausting herself with her many tasks. By the time the sun had reached its zenith, she had already chosen the staff for her soon-to-be palace. It was only then, once his business was complete, that he dared interrupt her.

"Perhaps a refreshing meal in the shade would rejuvenate you," he said as he kissed her cheek.

He offered his hand and she reluctantly put down her reed, wiping the traces of ink from her fingers on a towel provided by one of the servants. Though by now all the palace staff knew the mage language and she had several personal scribes, not a one knew how to write in her language. He would have to see to it that one of the scribes was trained to read and write the mage script.

"That does sound good." She sighed and took his proffered hand.

Just as he was leading her to the courtyard where a hearty meal had been laid out, Qar appeared, his expression grim and his hippo ears twitching angrily.

"Forgive me, Your Tranquility, but I couldn't stop her."

Her? Mereruka's sigh was drowned out by the booming echo of the doors of the inner palace being flung open with a powerful, hooved kick.

"Gods below, you're actually not dead!"

Mereruka raised a violet brow at his elder sister, Itet. Her blue and gold soldier's tunic complimented her shocked blue eyes. Black hair fell down her back in thick braids, the teeth and claws of fallen foes woven in as grim decoration, swinging with her strides and noisily knocking against each other. No crown sat upon her head, but in Maat she didn't need it. Itet's reputation preceded her. Oversized skein in her lime green hand, she took a swig. Full of alcohol, no doubt. As she raced forward, with no concern for personal space, she inspected him all over, her horns nearly impaling his chin.

"Shockingly, neither are you," Mereruka replied.

Her bawdy laugh was rich and unrestrained. She circled Taisiya with great interest.

"Princess Consort Taisiya, this is my sister, Itet," Mereruka said by way of introductions.

Taisiya sized her up, her mask firmly in place, standing still as a statue while his sister gawked.

"You look like a witch," Itet accused.

"Better a witch than a goat," Taisiya retorted, her eyes lingering tellingly on Itet's horns and hooves.

"Ooh! A feisty one! We should go drinking together." Itet smiled.

Mereruka stepped between them, narrowing his eyes at Itet.

"Don't agree to that. What she calls drinking, any sane man calls a death sport," Mereruka warned. When he'd been younger, Itet had often cajoled him into drinking with her. It had never once ended with anything other than his own misery. Taisiya would be lucky to walk away with a hangover if he let Itet have her way.

"Just because you can't hold your liquor..." Itet rolled her eyes. "Anyway, come meet my twin, Inkaef." Itet slipped around him and took

Taisiya's hand, propelling her towards Inkaef before Mereruka could snatch her back. She was lightning fast on her hooves when she wanted to be, no matter her level of inebriation.

Inkaef was busy trying to mollify Mereruka's guards in the outer palace. When he spotted Itet with Taisiya in tow, he cringed, running a lime green hand through black hair, amber eyes flat with resignation. If a beleaguered sigh could be embodied, Inkaef was it.

Mereruka followed closely, noting his brother's wide eyes as their trio approached him. Where Itet was muscular, Inkaef was soft. The life of a courtier was as perilous for one's head as it was for one's waistline. Where Itet was battle-hardened and bold as brass, her twin had survived through inoffensiveness, and they both dealt with their wilier political foes by drinking them under the table.

"Inky, look! He's not a revenant after all. You owe me a dozen horses!" Itet boasted.

Inkaef at least had the decency to look embarrassed by the wager.

"Mereruka." Inkaef nodded.

"Inkaef," Mereruka replied.

They'd long ago decided that they had so little in common, there was no point in making small talk neither would actually care for. Mereruka only wished he could have so cordial a non-relationship with his other brothers.

"What's your name?" Inkaef politely inquired.

"Taisiya," she replied.

"Pleased to meet you. I am Prince Inkaef. I assume you are my brother's wife?"

"I am."

"I apologise for Itet's... enthusiasm. When she heard rumours of Mereruka's return, she needed to see for herself," Inkaef explained.

"As you can see, I am alive and well," Mereruka said.

He folded his arms and gave Itet a hard stare. Inkaef, at least, could read between the lines and had the grace to know an unannounced visit was hardly polite. Itet, however, was never one to care for things such as decorum or manners. She studiously ignored Mereruka, swinging an arm around Taisiya's shoulders.

"In case you were wondering, I'm the only royal in Maat who has any fun. I don't usually bother with going to court, except Khety has insisted we join him once the inundation starts." Her aggrieved eye roll said it all. "Breaking skulls on the border is more my thing. When you get bored of fancy parties, I'll take you on a proper hunt. You can hunt, can't you?" Itet asked.

Taisiya looked Itet up and down, the wheels turning in her head. She smiled.

"Are you very fond of that bracelet?" Taisiya asked.

"Eh?" Itet peered at her wrist, confused. "Not really."

"Throw it up high, would you?" Taisiya said as she pulled away from their party.

Mereruka grinned as Itet threw it. She'd read his sister well. A small bolt of lightning shot out from her fingertip, shattering the bracelet and gaining the attention of all nearby as the crackling echoed out in the yard between inner and outer palaces. Itet's blue eyes were wide as she whooped with excitement.

"Does that answer your question?" Taisiya smiled politely.

"I have an idea. Divorce him, marry me." Itet pointed at Mereruka and then herself. "We could have so much fun!" She squealed with delight as Inkaef watched, shaking his head with a chagrined look.

Before Taisiya could answer, Mereruka stepped forward, reclaiming his wife's hand.

"She's not a shiny new toy for you to chew on, Itet. Now, trot along. I think you've had enough fun for today." Mereruka tilted his head to indicate the exit to his palace.

Itet stuck her tongue out.

"You're boring."

"And you're not yet drunk enough to be funny," Mereruka retorted.

"Too true," she sighed. "Alright, fine, we'll see you at court. Just so you know, Khety's been a real royal prick lately. His feathers got ruffled when rumours started flying about him being cursed for sending you away." Itet winked, nudging Mereruka with an elbow.

Mereruka sighed as Inkaef choked on a cough and looked around to see who might have heard his sister's incautious pun. That Khety had a set of hawk-like wings was well known.

"Your humour always did leave something to be desired," Mereruka replied.

"I think we've taken up more than enough of your time, wouldn't you say, Itet?" Inkaef did his best to physically steer Itet away.

"Until next time, Itet, Inkaef." Taisiya nodded her head.

As they walked away, Mereruka leaned down to whisper in her ear.

"Well played."

"Thank you. Itet does seem to be a handful," Taisiya remarked dryly.

Mereruka chuckled and led Taisiya back into the protected peaceful-ness of the inner palace.

"I think that's the kindest thing anyone could say of her, barbaric little imp that she is."

"Inkaef seems... fine."

Mereruka laughed loudly at that.

"Trust me, he's the least bothersome of all my brothers. If only they could all be so bland and inoffensive."

"But then, it wouldn't be half as satisfying when we crush them underfoot, would it?" Taisiya asked with a grin.

"No, it wouldn't." Mereruka smiled.

CHAPTER 33

When Mereruka had explained that the tethered boulders presented to her several days past would make her barge float effortlessly through the skies, Taisiya had worried for her new husband's sanity. She needn't have done so. The boulders had been valuable trade goods from a series of wandering, floating islands currently making their way south along Maat's desert border. Taisiya had worn her best, expressionless countenance as she once again recalibrated her idea of what was possible with only the minimum amount of internal screaming. She even managed to nod along as Mereruka told her that, based on their speed, he suspected the islands would remain neighbours of Maat for at least a century. At least the trade good would be certain to dazzle the people of the empire, just as it had her. Every day, yet more inexplicable magic made itself known, making her feel as lost as the day she'd first glimpsed Maat. Then again, she'd not been truly lost.

As the thought crossed her mind, another curious magic sent her heart pounding.

"Wife, you grow more beautiful by the day," Mereruka purred in her ear.

"And you more handsome," she answered, daring to stroke the edge of his pointed teal ear.

By now, their act was flawless. Servants and commoners tittered and giggled when they spied the two of them in the palace, or sighed wistfully as they sailed along the bustling, natural canals of Rhacotis in each other's arms. The story of the besotted prince and his mysterious bride had become so well known that none would doubt it. Vasilisa ensured they'd also heard tales of Taisiya's heartless cruelty and her willingness to kill any who wronged her husband. She was a woman feared, respected and envied.

At times, even Taisiya had begun to believe the rumours of their romance. Sometimes she would catch Mereruka in a rare unguarded moment, and the look in his eyes would make her toes curl. Their stolen kisses, in the few times they could be truly alone, had her convinced she might combust. Those kisses had her daydreaming more often than she would ever admit, and wondering if, finally, this time, with this man, what came after would be worth it. It never had in the past, but he was beginning to give her hope that the future would be different.

She was brought back to the present as he shivered at her touch, his eyes gone dark with desire. It took him a short time to compose himself, to loosen his fervent grip.

"The oasis of Shedet is in full view now. And Nofret has informed me that Maat's most renowned architect is currently vacationing in the area."

"How fortuitous. Shall we hire him to build my palace?"

"I've heard he is a difficult man with a mercurial disposition. Even in the face of royalty," Mereruka hedged.

"Then make the nomarch convince him in return for his life." Taisiya grinned. "I'm certain he'll be more motivated than the average man."

Mereruka nodded as he led her to the railing of the floating barge. It was being pulled by a team of ethereal creatures with glittering butterfly wings. Below, the enormous lake around which Shedet thrived was visible. Black earth swathed in lush green and dotted with homes, fields and properties ringed the bright blue. Beyond the influence of the life-giving waters, she could see the curious rose-gold-hued sand of the unforgiving desert, a colour she'd grown accustomed to as they'd sailed high above it on their journey here. Beyond the delta, Maat was a land of sharply contrasting extremes. Life flourished, but only up to a starkly delineated point, after which death reigned in the hot, dry, rocky sands.

The shadow of their barge passed over the nomarch's manse. In the distance, a great building project had only just broken ground. Soon, its builder would know the bitter taste of loss and regret. She had a reputation to uphold, after all. No one who harmed her family would be spared.

"What do you think of your nome, Taisiya?"

"It will do nicely," she replied.

Mereruka revelled in the flurry of panicked activity their arrival at the building site caused. When he disembarked with Taisiya at his side, both in their royal finery and attended by a hoard of servants as well as a scowling Qar, work stopped and workmen knelt with their heads bowed. Ensconced in a palanquin big enough to comfortably fit a dozen people, they were brought around the perimeter of the survey. A few workers disappeared into the ether, no doubt informing the nomarch. The overseers blanched at the sight of them. Did they know the source of their master's windfall? Or were they surprised that it was he, and not the nomarch's son, who had stepped off the opulent barge?

"What do you think of the project, Princess Consort?" Mereruka asked, knowing the workers could overhear them.

"It's... cosy." The description dripped with derision.

Mereruka might have chuckled, but he was strung as tight as a bow-string. Already, Henenu, the nomarch of Shedet, was being hurriedly carried on his palanquin towards them. When he stepped down from his conveyance, both Mereruka and Taisiya barely needed to look down. The nomarch was a man of uncommon height and brawn, more comfortable with an enchanted blade in his fuchsia hand than he was with reed and ink. Though his practised smile and his graceful kneeling might have fooled others, the wariness in his dark eyes betrayed his unease.

It struck Mereruka then that an uneasy man with martial prowess was not someone he wanted anywhere near his wife.

"Prince Mereruka, I'm flattered and humbled by your unexpected visit. I had heard rumours of your return, but I didn't believe them. Please, allow me to welcome you to Shedet and to entertain you in my home."

Taisiya clicked her tongue. Henenu flinched.

"Allow me to introduce Maat's newest princess consort and my wife, Princess Consort Taisiya, recently of Lethe, the Empire of Mages," Mereruka said.

Taisiya glared down her nose at the kneeling fae before them. Before Henenu could greet her, Taisiya spoke, her words like acid.

"I'm afraid we'll need to turn down your offer of hospitality. It would sour my disposition if I had to watch someone entertain us using our stolen wealth."

Henenu's eyes widened with terror and he prostrated himself before them.

"Please, Prince, Princess Consort, allow me to explain-"

Mereruka snarled, cutting off his excuses.

"The penalty for stealing from royalty is death, a fate your foolish son has already suffered." At the nomarch's flinch, it seemed he'd not heard of his son's untimely demise. "That I have not already severed your head for your gross insolence is a testament to my forbearance and my wife's generosity."

"No one has ever returned from the Cursed Continent, Your Tranquility! Everyone thought you had perished!" Henenu said, his panicked breaths disturbing the sand beneath his lips.

Thank the gods he'd not attacked. He hoped to sway them with words. For now.

"Did you just refer to my homeland as the 'Cursed Continent'?" Taisiya asked with venom in her tone.

"Forgive me, Your Harmoniousness!" Henenu gasped. "I meant no disrespect, I-"

"Enough! You have stolen from me, had the gall to make a monument dedicated to your crimes and now you dare to insult the princess consort! I shall have your head for this!" Mereruka roared.

None could fail to understand the situation now. Just as they'd planned, Taisiya played the part of appeasing wife. He trusted it would offer Henenu enough hope not to decide he had nothing left to lose. A warrior like the nomarch could kill several people in the blink of an eye. He was centuries older than Mereruka, and he'd spent very few of them idle. Qar's hand slid to the pommel of his sword.

"Dearest husband, calm yourself. I shall render justice on our behalf."

"He deserves no lenience!" Mereruka bellowed for effect.

"No, he does not," Taisiya said soothingly as she petted his chest.

Mereruka did his best not to shiver at her soft touch. He turned his focus on the quivering mess of the prostrated nomarch before him and the potential threats around him. By now, several of Henenu's sons and daughters had come to the building site and watched in horror. Several of Mereruka's men, disguised as labourers, kept close watch, lest they strike while their father grovelled. Each was a threat in their own right, most of them being near enough to Mereruka in age and many gifted in martial arts.

Taisiya descended from the palanquin with grace and poise, aided by the magic of their attendants. If she needed to use lightning, she couldn't be touching him. He had to remind himself that she wore as many protections as he, and that his overseer of the soldiers was nearly as fast as her lightning. But when her sandaled feet touched the ground, it took an effort of will to hold himself back. Any indication that Mereruka feared Henenu's reaction would make both Taisiya and himself appear weak.

It had seemed so simple when they'd planned the scenario. Now, faced with the reality, his confidence shrivelled. As she stepped closer to the hulking nomarch, his instincts screamed at him. If Henenu struck, he might hurt her, kill her. Why had that fact never crossed his mind before? Why had he agreed that she should be the one to punish Henenu? What good was flaunting her power if she died?

He scowled and crossed his arms to hide his wildly beating heart.

"Nomarch Henenu, do you deny your crimes?" Taisiya asked with admirable calm as bile crept up Mereruka's throat.

Gods, what if this foolish posturing got her killed? The very thought was like ice in his veins.

"I do not, Princess Consort. Please, show mercy."

Please, gods, let him surrender.

"Hmm." She tapped a finger to her lips. "I don't believe you've properly congratulated us on our marriage. In the Empire of Mages it is customary to give the newly wedded couple many gifts. Luckily for you, Henenu, you have something I want."

"Name it and it is yours, Your Harmoniousness," Henenu said, a sliver of hope in his voice.

Taisiya clapped her hands.

"Splendid! Then I shall have your nome. Our treasury has already financed the construction of a palace. Now, it will be made into one fit for a princess consort."

Henenu flinched, shocked into a moment of silence.

Mereruka held his breath as the nomarch tensed. He should trust in their plan, in her, in all the precautions they'd taken, but he could not beat back his dread.

"And what would you do with me, Your Harmoniousness?" Henenu asked haltingly.

"Perhaps, if you are very, very well-behaved, I shall allow you and your family to live in Shedet and work for my benefit."

The—now former—nomarch contemplated his reduced fortunes, his hands balled into white-knuckled fists. Mereruka scanned the gathered crowd. Everywhere he saw threats, all of them aimed at Taisiya. He nearly came out of his skin in the few heartbeats it took for Henenu to reply.

"Princess Consort, you are merciful and fair. Shedet is lucky to have you as its nomarch," Henenu murmured.

Luck had favoured them, for he did not make to lash out at Taisiya. Luck. He'd gambled her life. Just to settle a score with a man of little consequence. Shame scalded him, eased only by the knowledge that they had been victorious. Henenu had admitted his crimes and relinquished his rights to the nome in front of witnesses. Not even Henenu's ally and Mereruka's brother, Radjedef, would be able to save the former nomarch now.

Some of Henenu's sons and daughters gasped, others hung their heads in shame, but not one moved to attack.

"Yes, and so long as its people are obedient, they need never watch their kin be annihilated by a lightning strike," Taisiya whispered, just loud enough for Mereruka to hear.

She was assisted back into the confines of the palanquin, back within his protective embrace. Mereruka's gut ceased clenching in sick anticipation. Once at his side, the corners of her lips turned up in triumph. Mereruka eased his scowl and kept his attention divided between her and Henenu's frozen posture.

"I have dispensed justice, dearest husband. Is your anger appeased?" she asked.

He needed to calm his racing heart. They still had the last bit of their plan to enact.

"If you are happy, then I am pleased." He smiled, though he doubted it reached his eyes.

Taisiya nodded.

Mereruka scowled at Henenu and his children. At least in this, it was not an act.

"Henenu, your first task is to locate Maat's most renowned architect and convince him to build my wife's palace. I believe he is vacationing in the area. One of your children will show her people to your former home so that they can acquaint themselves with the administration of her nome. I trust you and your family will find accommodations elsewhere," Mereruka commanded.

"Yes, Your Tranquility. It will be done," Henenu replied, lifting himself from the ground on shaky knees and backing away with his head bowed.

And with that, Mereruka and Taisiya had doubled their territory without shedding a single drop of blood. It should have pleased him utterly, and yet he dreaded what this newfound fear might mean for their future schemes.

CHAPTER 34

She hadn't dreamt this nightmare in months.

Taisiya sat quietly in an overstuffed chair, embroidering the hem of a silk dress. Daria was similarly occupied, her back ramrod straight. Sonya's eyes glazed over as she turned the pages of a small book of etiquette. Only the rhythmic scuff of paper on paper punctured the horrid calm of the room.

Men with dour faces and swords at their hips watched over her and her sisters, their eyes piercing and distrustful. That dreadful grey fog held her captive, dulling her thoughts and dousing even a flicker of feeling. She knew her father was scheduled to be executed. She knew her young brother, Dimitri, would die alongside him. Yet she knew no fear, no desperation, no fierce need to save them from their fate. No. The palace servant had suggested she embroider, and so, like the soulless puppet she'd become, she'd complied. The Ritual had robbed her in the vilest way, not even leaving her with the sense to understand the profound loss.

The growing commotion echoing through the palace halls failed to rouse her. When the booming of thunder shook the delicate tea set arrayed before her and caused the dress to slide from her fingers, she merely picked it up and continued her task. As the screams of the maimed and dying rang out, she smoothed a wrinkle in the skirts.

Taisiya felt nothing—was nothing.

Until that changed.

Taisiya had once met a travelling wind mage, an eccentric map maker who claimed to have escaped an avalanche. He described the moment he'd known he might perish, and his mad flight to escape the death racing down from the mountain top.

When she was sane enough to think again, it would be his passionate description of raw, primal fear, anger and sick exhilaration that she compared her awakening to. In the moment the foul magic that bound her soul broke, something in Taisiya broke too.

To the alarm of their minders, Taisiya and her sisters howled and screamed, clawing at their throats and chests. Unfathomable agony tore her open and filled her to the brim, her tortured cries inadequate to the task of conveying it fully. Electricity, too powerful for her to handle, scorched her nerves. She writhed on the floor as thought and rage and fear and bone-deep sorrow returned to her. Cruellest of all was the return of love. For as it enveloped her, a sense of her father's protective arms around her whispered, ghost-like, across her heart and mind. And in a moment, that, too, was taken from her, replaced with the knowledge that he was dead and she would never know that love again.

In this nightmare, memory merged with dream, grief with hope, and she found herself chasing that last fragment of her father through the darkness. He was forever out of reach. His stern but affectionate expression slowly dissolved until she no longer remembered his face.

Except she usually woke up at this point.

As she chased the fading ghost of Grigori Amethyst, Taisiya realised her feet were throbbing in pain. Her sweat, mixed with blowing sand, grated against her skin. This was wrong. So wrong. Taisiya stopped herself, though the desperation to reach her father's welcoming embrace fizzed in her veins. She turned from the siren call of his love to shake herself awake.

When she opened her eyes, it was to a darkness as profound as that of her dreams. She blinked her eyes, hoping they might adjust to the weak light of the stars in the sky. Slowly, she made out her surroundings. Two dark figures walked ahead of her. She caught the familiar scent of Mereruka's perfume on the breeze.

"Meri?" she called out, uncertain and disoriented.

Was this just another dream?

"Fuck!"

The angry, hissing voice of a stranger had her heart tripping in her chest and her gut sinking to her knees.

"Meri!" she screamed.

Taisiya lunged for her husband as the dark form of the stranger rushed her. Hot, sharp agony stopped her in her tracks. As she gasped in pain, the stench of alcohol and sweat rolled off the stranger. She gripped the hilt of the dagger like a lifeline, nearly blacking out with the pain as he tried to yank the blade from her belly.

"Stubborn bitch!" he snarled.

Ah, gods, she needed to focus. Weakened though she was, she was a Dragonsblood. Lightning was in her blood. She called forth all her quickly dwindling reserves and struck her attacker. The arcing electricity flash-blinded her with its brilliance. It tossed the stranger away on a cry of pain, but wasn't nearly enough to kill him. Taisiya fell to her knees as the muted thunder rumbled across the open desert.

"Here! Here! I can smell blood!"

Taisiya thought she heard the sound of Bas' voice.

"He's running away!" Bas called.

"No, he's not," Vasilisa snarled.

A wet scream, cut in half, echoed out.

"Wake up! Wake up, Dad!" Bas howled.

"Just fucking slap him!" Vasilisa commanded.

Taisiya's head felt heavy as Vasilisa's sure hands probed her. If her friend hadn't propped her up in that moment, Taisiya might have fallen over. The only warm parts of her were the searing wound and the hot, sticky blood spilling from between her clenched fingers.

"Shit, shit, shit, shit," Vasilisa swore.

"Bas? What's going on?" Mereruka asked in a daze.

"She's bleeding out! Get over here and heal her!" Vasilisa shrieked.

"Taisiya? Taisiya!" Mereruka gasped. "The blade. It needs to come out!"

"If I take it out, she'll bleed to death in an instant!" Vasilisa shouted back.

"At the same time, then," Mereruka ordered. "Bas, hold her steady."

Arms encircled her from behind like a cage. Vasilisa pried her fingers from the hilt of the blade, her talisman, the only thing keeping her alive. Tears tracked down Taisiya's cheeks. Every movement was agony, every breath torture. *Please, gods, let this be another nightmare. Let me wake up.*

"I'm scared," Taisiya whispered.

"Be brave, love," Mereruka choked out. Magic, bright and colourful as an aurora, gathered and danced in his palms.

"Ready?" Vasilisa asked.

"Now!" Mereruka said.

Taisiya, mercifully, blacked out.

Taisiya's bloodless lips grimacing in agony. Copper hair a wild mess about her haggard face. Her amethyst eyes glistening with fear. A bronze blade glinting up at him from her gut, the accusation of his overconfidence spelled out in rivulets of her blood. The wet, sucking sound of the blade's removal from her flesh had nearly undone him. The sound alone would torment his every nightmare for decades. The sight of her before him as he wove his limited healing magic had imprinted itself behind his eyelids, a penance he would pay every time he closed his eyes. Mereruka cursed himself for not taking the time to have stronger healing magic inked into his skin. When he finally managed to close the wound, he nearly vomited. Hands trembling, he reached out for her. The panicked creature inside his chest needed the warm weight of her against him. He'd almost lost her.

Bas handed her over to him. Mereruka cradled her in his arms. He struggled for a shred of control. Helplessness was a potent, vicious thing in his breast. It reminded him of the loss of his sister, Nefertnesu, the woman who had all but raised him, and whose very soul had been ripped out of her. He'd borne her loss, even though it had changed him to his core. But this felt different. He didn't think he could bear the loss of Taisiya. He felt like he was one step from shattering, even though her heart beat steadily against him.

"What happened?" Mereruka asked.

"I couldn't sleep, so I was walking around the mansion. I smelled blood and found one of our guards with his throat slit, hidden in an alcove. I rushed to your room but the soldiers there had been hypnotized and said you'd both gone for a walk with the dead guard. I told Qar and grabbed Vasilisa and we scoured the desert around the manse, looking for you," Bas explained.

Vasilisa's eyes were haunted. She smoothed the hair off Taisiya's face over and over, as though in a trance. Mereruka felt an irrational sense of anger towards her. She was supposed to protect Taisiya with her life.

"And you? Where were you?" Mereruka growled at Vasilisa.

Trance broken, Vasilisa slowly raised her eyes to meet his. She looked at him with the eyes of a furious, wild beast.

"*Me*? Where was *I*?" she asked, her voice calm in the same way as the eye of a storm. In a blink, the storm was upon him, a snarl in her voice. "Where were *you*?! What in the hells were *you* doing?! What the fuck kind of all-powerful fae are you?! She almost died because you didn't protect her! If you were *anyone* else, I'd-"

"What?! What would you do, you useless, fucking wraith?!" Mereruka yelled.

Vasilisa shrieked, her body bursting into opaque, inky black flames. Black talons replaced her fingers and where her eyes might have been, crimson, glowing orbs stared at him with animalistic malice.

Good. He wanted her anger, and needed her to be the object of his.

"I'd drag you to the void-"

"And feed me to it?" Mereruka interrupted, goading her as he bared his own teeth.

"I'd rip you to shreds and devour whatever remained!" she howled.

"Enough! Enough!" Bas threw himself between them, his claws out as he pushed them apart. His eyes were wide with horror. "Both of you, stop!"

Mereruka blinked in surprise at the sharp pain of Bas's claws in his flesh. He hadn't noticed his own racing heart, or his shuddering, angry breaths. He clenched his teeth. This was wrong of him. Vasilisa had done no wrong. He wasn't mad at Vasilisa, not really. He was furious with himself. It was he who had failed his wife.

The black flames coating Vasilisa dissipated, though her rage remained.

"I stopped sleeping in Taisiya's shadow after she married *you*. You... you made an *oath*. *You* were supposed to protect her, too!"

Tears of shame burned his eyes.

"I'm sorry. I'm sorry," he whispered, clutching Taisiya closer.

"Let's... let's go somewhere safe. The barge is tethered near the manse," Bas hedged, his voice placating, trying to soothe their hopelessly frayed nerves.

Mereruka nodded. Vasilisa wiped away errant tears with the palm of her hand, smearing blood across her cheek.

"Who stabbed Taisiya?" Mereruka asked.

Vasilisa walked over to the body, kicking it before she crouched to inspect the face.

"One of the nomarch's brats," she announced.

Bas stepped over and tilted his head.

"The heir. *Former* heir," he corrected.

Mereruka stood, careful not to jostle the precious bundle in his arms. Gods, he'd almost lost her. His mind, his heart, the very marrow in his bones rebelled at the thought. Something hot and dark and wrathful pumped through his veins, giving him strength.

They would know her pain and her fear a hundred-fold. He would become the most malevolent being to ever walk the palace halls of Shedet. He would paint the walls in their blood and use their bones to build her a throne. He would reign as king of their suffering, offering up their tortured cries as music to his wife's ears.

"Grab the blade and the body. When I slaughter Henenu's entire line, I want everyone to know why."

CHAPTER 35

Mereruka refused to hide in the barge. The manse had better facilities to take care of Taisiya. Bas followed behind him while Vasilisa went ahead to get a pot of boiled water and rags to clean the blood off Taisiya. Guards were roused at the sight of him with Taisiya in his arms, spreading the word amongst his people as to what had happened. Mereruka sent a tendril of magic into his spell-sight tattoo as they neared the bedroom he and Taisiya had retired to. Aside from the expected comfort-related spells, malice coiled under the bed. A sleepwalking curse, meant to trap the dreamer while they followed the malefactor to their doom.

"Under the bed. There's a sleepwalking curse," Mereruka told Bas.

Bas shimmied under the bed and retrieved a small drop of amber with a glowing red pinprick in the centre. It was a foul curse indeed, and difficult to procure. How had the nomarch or his heir gotten their hands on it?

"I'll put it in a vault on the barge, for safekeeping. Should I tell Qar and Nofret what's happened?" Bas said.

Mereruka nodded and carefully laid Taisiya on the bed. In the light, she looked like a corpse, her breaths shallow while blood streaked her hair and soaked her nightgown. Vasilisa was there a moment later, tending Taisiya with gentle efficiency. Bas ran off to secure the curse and inform his closest aids of the assassination attempt.

"Vasilisa, I'm sorry. None of this was your fault."

She paused in her ministrations a moment before she continued, never turning her face from her task.

"You're not the only one who loves her."

His heart stuttered in his chest. This was just supposed to be a marriage of necessity to someone he knew was as much a schemer as he. But almost from the start, he'd found himself wanting more. He hadn't expected to love a wife, he'd only hoped he would like and respect the one he eventually married. But that was before her and her copper hair and wicked smiles and intriguing blushes. That was before she'd become his partner in conspiracy and ambition. Yes, he supposed he did love Taisiya. The realisation was both a blessing and a curse. An unexpected joy and a terrifying weakness his enemies were certain to exploit. He shook himself. There would be time for this later.

"She's my... tether. My reason to leave the void," Vasilisa continued.

"You need a reason to leave it?" he asked Vasilisa as he sat by Taisiya's head, coiling a copper tendril around his finger.

Vasilisa nodded, wringing bright red liquid from the rag and dipping it back into the bowl of clean water.

"Every darkness mage does. In the void, only part of me is a woman, the other is... not. There, I don't have to feel the way I do here. It's... easier. Simpler. Peaceful."

"Aside from the hungry things, you mean?"

Vasilisa smirked.

"Never known a place without pests."

Mereruka sighed. Neither had he. They shared a wan smile.

He was ashamed of how he'd treated Vasilisa. His own fear and misplaced anger were no excuse. Maybe he would find something the darkness mage liked and gift it to her. Taisiya would no doubt aid him. After all the thorniness of their relationship thus far, it was a relief to have made a truce with Vasilisa, however tenuous it was. He began to relax.

Then Vasilisa gasped.

"What...?" She stared at the place where Taisiya had been stabbed.

Mereruka's eyes latched onto the same horrifying sight. Where the skin had been rejoined—a blue-black oozing lump, like a caterpillar from the deepest hell. Dark, forking veins spread out, reaching towards her heart. Denial came first, crushed swiftly by terror.

"The blade! Get the blade!" Mereruka ordered.

Vasilisa disappeared and reappeared in a minute, blade in hand. Mereruka inspected it closely with his spell-sight. His blood turned to ice.

"It's been cursed with corruption." He choked on the words.

One of the foulest of curses. If one infected by it didn't die from it, they would arise as a veritable plague.

"Then heal her!" Vasilisa pleaded.

"I... I can't. This is beyond me," he stammered.

Just as it was beyond the skills of any healer in Maat.

"Then get someone who can!"

"Healing spells will only spread it faster. My magic can't fix this," he explained, his voice hollow.

What in the gods' unknowable names had Henenu been thinking when he acquired the blade? Such items were banned even from the royal armoury.

"What if... what if we cut it out? Would that work?" Vasilisa asked, desperate.

"What's this about cutting?" Bas asked as he re-entered the room, fresh gown in hand. At their stark looks, he sniffed the air. "Corruption." He gasped, gown forgotten on the floor as he rushed to Taisiya's side. "We need a light healer or dragon blood," he said, his voice tight.

"No one in Maat possesses the healing light," Mereruka said woodenly. He would know, given he had once entertained the notion of using the curse on his brother.

"Then where is the dragon blood?" Vasilisa asked.

"I don't... we don't have any," Bas admitted.

"Where can we get some?" Vasilisa insisted.

"From a dragon," Bas said.

Vasilisa grabbed the shifter's shoulder and shook him.

"Don't get cute! *Where?!*"

"There aren't any dragon shapeshifters in Maat, and the dragons that are here are feral!" Bas replied.

Mereruka heard the strangest of buzzing noises in his head, drowning out the frantic bickering of his son and his wife's friend. How easy it would be to slip into that place inside himself, to hide from the horrible fate which awaited his wife, to live in denial that yet another person he loved would be snatched from him as he remained wholly powerless.

Mereruka watched as a black tendril crept closer to Taisiya's heart. Fear and rage jolted him from his stupor. She wasn't dead yet. He was not wholly powerless. He must call upon his wrath, his hatred, his resolve. Taisiya would not die. He would not have another person he loved taken from him. Squeezing the hilt of the corruption-cursed blade, his mind raced. Was the nomarch wise enough to have the cure on hand along with the blade? As the saying went, those who live by the sword, die by the sword. Though Henenu had gotten lazy through Radjedef's favour, a man well-versed in battle was surely prepared to be struck by weapons just like those he owned. Or even by the very ones he owned.

"Rouse the rest of our soldiers. Bring Henenu and his family before me in chains. If there is any dragon blood close by, we must pray that it's in his possession. Tell Qar and Nofret that I want them protecting Taisiya."

Vasilisa and Bas stopped their squabbling in an instant. Vasilisa disappeared into a shadow while Bas relayed his orders. In minutes, the weary, dishevelled former nomarch and his family were thrown, bound and prostrate, before him. But they were minutes Taisiya did not have to spare. Mereruka stood before them in the receiving hall, not bothering to hide his rage. He picked up the blade from a nearby pedestal and shoved it in Henenu's face.

"You raised your children poorly, Henenu. Your son attacked my wife with this blade. Take a close look. Perhaps the curse is familiar to you," Mereruka hissed.

Henenu squinted at the blade before his eyes went wide with horror.

"I see that it is."

"Your Tranquility, please-"

Mereruka snarled and threw Henenu's head to the cold stone floor. He had no time for mewling and begging.

"You have no right to beg! You *will* die for this, Henenu! But you do have a choice." Mereruka's voice softened. He leaned down to whisper in the man's pointed ear. "If you tell me where the dragon blood is, your death will be painless and swift. If you refuse, it won't be either of those things, and I shall make you watch every member of your beloved family die slowly—tortuously—first."

Henenu was silent a moment, his eyes drifting back to the tear-stained faces of his wife and children before he looked back at Mereruka, re-signed.

"If I tell you, what of my family?"

Mereruka's heart stuttered with relief. The dragon blood was within reach. He kept the rage plain on his face.

"They will be exiled immediately, escorted to the desert border and ritually barred from ever stepping foot in Maat for the rest of their days. But if my wife dies, then I shall send them to her homeland, to her grieving family, with a sack of iron spikes and a letter detailing what became of her and at whose hands."

Henenu froze. Time for the killing blow. Mereruka looked at him with a ferocious grin on his face.

"And Henenu? My wife's family is vicious, calculating and have a special place in their hearts for her. I will have my answer now."

Henenu closed his eyes, resigned to his fate.

"It is stowed in a pocket realm. You will need my assistance not to set off the traps."

Mereruka nodded at the soldiers.

"Take him." He turned to Henenu. "And be swift. If I grow impatient, your family will suffer."

Every moment he was gone, Mereruka's anxiety grew. Taisiya didn't have long before the curse took her life or worse. When the soldiers escorting Henenu teleported back with the bastard and the small bottle of blood, Mereruka felt faint with relief. He held out his hand to receive the bottle from the soldier. A flash of movement caught his eye. A blade rushed towards him. Mereruka fell back as Bas shoved him, deflecting the blade with his claws and hands.

The bottle fell from the soldier's hand and was snatched before it hit the ground by the blade-wielder. She leapt away, bottle in hand, a triumphant grin on her face. Bas hissed, blood dripping from his wounds, refusing to move from his protective position in front of Mereruka. Vasilisa was absent. Mereruka prayed to the forgotten gods that she was circling in the shadows.

"Back off! Don't come near me! Release my family or I'll spill every drop of this blood!"

"Back away!" Mereruka ordered his soldiers.

"Nebet! You fool! You've doomed us all!" Henenu shouted.

"Listen to your father, Nebet. Do not test me," Mereruka replied, his voice calm in a way his heart was not. There was so little blood in that vial. He needed every drop to cure Taisiya. This woman was the only thing that stood between him and Taisiya's life.

"No! You listen to me. Do as I say, or your wife will die. I don't fear death, but if the rumours are to be believed, you fear losing your precious wife. What will you decide?" Nebet sneered.

Mereruka grabbed the corruption-cursed blade once again and walked towards her family, a dawning horror on Nebet's face.

"No! I will smash this bottle!"

Mereruka watched her expression as he passed the blade over the bowed heads of her family members. Tears formed in her eyes as it passed over the smallest head.

"Then smash it. I will ensure that you live long enough to watch this one die of corruption. Or maybe he won't die, Nebet. Maybe, he'll survive. Maybe I'll let you watch as I feed the rest of your family to what he becomes, knowing you were responsible for it, all because you destroyed the only thing that could cure him. What will *you* decide?" he asked.

Nebet backed away, inching closer to a shadow along the wall. Mereruka kept his expression blank as black talons crept towards Nebet, silent. She screamed in pain as those same talons severed the hand in which she held the bottle. Nebet fell to the floor while her hand, still clutching the bottle waved down at her from above.

"Time's up, bitch," Vasilisa hissed in her shadowy form.

Nebet crawled away, cradling the bleeding stump as Vasilisa advanced. The darkness mage grabbed a blade from the nearest soldier and ran the fae woman through. Henenu and his wife cried out.

"That's for hurting my kitty," she said as she pried the bottle from the fingers of Nebet's severed hand. "Are we done here?" Vasilisa asked Mereruka, inky black flames hiding her features and making her appear as if from a nightmare.

He nodded. Much as he wished to wipe them all from existence, Taisiya didn't condone the killing of children. Perhaps he was getting soft.

"Kill the adults. Exile the children," Mereruka commanded.

Mereruka dismissed Qar and Nofret from their vigil, instructing them to ensure that Henenu and his family did not survive the night. Then he raced to Taisiya's side.

"The two of you should hold her down. Dragon blood is as painful a cure as there exists," Mereruka said.

Bas grabbed her legs while Vasilisa held her arms. Mereruka summoned a wooden spoon and placed it between Taisiya's teeth. That done, he opened the bottle. When the first drop hit the black mass near Taisiya's gut, Mereruka braced, ready to hold down a flailing, insensate mage. He'd known the pain of dragon blood once before and would not soon forget.

Nothing.

Taisiya remained still as the blood dissolved the corruption before their eyes. Mereruka listened to Taisiya's weak heartbeat, shocked that anyone living could remain unconscious and still for such a thing.

The blood chased the corruption through Taisiya's skin, obliterating it. Soon, the black lines disappeared. The only evidence of the attack was her blood-encrusted gown. Mereruka took the spoon from between her teeth and dripped a few drops of blood into Taisiya's mouth for good measure.

"She doesn't smell like dragon kin," Bas said with wonder.

Mereruka gathered Taisiya in his arms, grateful that she lived. As he looked down at his wife, he began to wonder. Just what in the hells *was* a mage?

Chapter 36

Taisiya woke with a foul tang in her mouth and the haunted citrine eyes of her husband staring intently at her. He chased the servants from the room and returned to her side.

"Meri?" she croaked.

"You must be thirsty," he said, proffering a glass in an instant.

He helped her sit up and drink. The liquid was bliss on her throat, washing away the taste on her tongue. Her mind muddled, she simply leaned against him, head cushioned by his chest. In that moment she simply breathed him in, existed, warm and safe in his arms. She placed a hand over his heart, surprised to find it hammering. He wrapped his hand around hers and squeezed. As sleep faded and the waking world came into sharper focus, she noticed the distinct feel of bare skin grazing her bare nipple. Finding herself nude, Taisiya froze. She might have blushed, but for the memory of a blade sinking into her.

"What happened?"

Mereruka tensed, releasing a shaky breath.

"We were cursed the moment we fell asleep in this bed. We sleepwalked into the desert, where the former nomarch's heir planned to kill us. You woke first and he stabbed you. Bas and Vasilisa found and saved us. We removed the blade and you fainted. But when we returned, we discovered that the blade had also been cursed. Corruption is foul magic, illegal even for a royal to use, and incurable by normal fae magic. Only dragon blood or healing light can cure it. We were able to procure some."

Taisiya took a moment to absorb it all. The shock must be numbing her. She couldn't find it in her to feel fear or anger.

"I guess we're not dragons after all," she quipped.

Mereruka was on her in the blink of an eye, looming over her, her wrists captured in his hands. He pressed her down with the weight of his body as his violet hair curtained their faces. It was as if the whole world outside had disappeared and she was alone with a man coming undone.

"Don't... don't joke," he said, his voice tight.

He released her wrists without a fuss. Her thumbs stroking his high cheekbones, he leaned into her palm, seeking her comfort. She ran fingers through his silky violet strands, careful of his ears.

"You almost died," he whispered, tortured.

"I know," Taisiya replied.

She would never forget it. It took an effort of will to banish the thoughts from her mind.

"I forbid you from dying!" he growled.

Heart skipping a beat, she searched his desperate eyes. Warmth blossomed in her chest, unbidden. This was not the reaction one had for a mere co-conspirator. Could he truly care for her? She felt ashamed to admit that she wanted more than just his respect and the crown their combined efforts would bestow. She wanted his tender feelings, his love, his passion. Gods below, she was well and truly sunk now.

"Kiss me," she whispered.

He hesitated, eyes locked on her lips.

"I don't think I can be gentle right now." He swallowed.

"Then don't be gentle."

As soon as the words left her, his lips crushed hers. His tongue swept along hers, possessing her. She wrapped her arms around his neck, a hand gripping a fistful of his hair, as much a lifeline as a leash. But her husband seemed to have no intention of escape. His violet strands wrapped around her wrist, a silken shackle. When he pulled her close, not even a whisper of air separated them, their bodies melded so that she couldn't tell where he ended and she began. Only his kilt separated them as their legs tangled. Hand shaking as he gripped her, one slid down her waist. She moaned as he slanted his lips across hers, deepening his furious kiss.

This was what she'd always craved, this mindless passion.

"Gods, get a fucking room," Vasilisa taunted.

Vasilisa's voice was like a bucket of freezing water, dousing the flame building between them. It appeared she needed a word with her friend about timely entrances and the lack thereof.

Mereruka reluctantly pulled his lips from hers, his tongue sweeping across her bottom lip. Taisiya shivered as his eyes, darkened by lust, continued to stare at her lips, as if he were staring at some great prize. When he turned his face to speak, Taisiya ducked her head against his neck, the better to hide her blush.

"We're *in* a room, Vasilisa. *Our* room," he grated between ragged breaths.

"Then get a different one. She needs to recover," Vasilisa retorted.

Mereruka sighed and muttered a prayer. Taisiya's lips curled up at the corners. His hair unravelled from her wrist and she grudgingly released her hold on it. Gone were his haunted eyes. Glamour? Or had he truly recovered? As he pulled away, he took his solid warmth with him. She missed it already. It must have been obvious. When he went to stand, he pulled the thin sheet up over her and winked.

"Cock-block," he grouched at Vasilisa.

"Go bitch to someone who cares."

Mereruka chuckled.

"And go take a bath. You reek."

Mereruka waved with a rude gesture before he disappeared into the adjacent bathing room. Vasilisa returned the gesture with a grin before she turned to Taisiya. The moment Mereruka was gone, Vasilisa launched herself at Taisiya.

"You scared me half to death," Vasilisa whispered.

Taisiya petted Vasilisa's wild blonde curls as the darkness mage shook in her arms. Her grip tightened as memories assailed her. *Breathe*, she reminded herself. The blade was no longer in her gut. The agony was a memory. She was whole. She was safe.

"You saved me. I'm still here. Thank you, Vasilisa," Taisiya murmured.

Vasilisa pulled away, turning her head to hide the evidence of a traitorous tear. She would not—could not—die, not like that, leaving her friend behind. Not knowing what she knew, aware of where her friend would go, never to return. She'd sworn long ago to drag her back into the light and keep her there, and Taisiya would be damned before she broke that vow.

"Don't cry, or I'll be forced to stuff you full of sweets and call you Va-va."

Vasilisa scowled.

"Gods forbid. You're not cute enough for that to work anymore."

Taisiya chuckled. Vasilisa managed a small grin. Voices drifted from the bathroom. Mereruka and Bas. She recognised the sound, but couldn't make out the words.

"It was a joint effort," Vasilisa sighed. "Even the kitty. If he hadn't found the body, we might not have…"

Taisiya took Vasilisa's hand and squeezed. Their eyes spoke the words they dared not utter. Taisiya was alive, and she wasn't going anywhere Vasilisa could not follow. Vasilisa released a shaky breath and nodded, squeezing her hand before she chased away the shadows in her grey eyes.

"Anyway, I'll help you get dressed and fed."

Taisiya nodded.

"What's become of the nomarch's family?" she asked.

Vasilisa flinched, a flicker of darkness creeping up her spine, there one moment and gone in a blink. She was quiet for a moment as she pulled a simple dress from a nearby wardrobe.

"We all agreed that mercy wasn't an option. Not for the adults. They're dead now. The children have been exiled."

"Good." Taisiya fisted her hands as she looked down at her belly. There was no evidence of the violence, save for the fear trickling down her spine. A new horror for her to revisit in the dead of night when her defences were down. She released her breath slowly. She would overcome it. A Dragonsblood could overcome anything, save death itself. "Any dissent as a result?"

Vasilisa helped her into the dress and began brushing her hair. The gentle tug on her scalp soothed her. This assassination attempt would no doubt be one of many. She had to have her wits about her.

"Not after Mereruka put your bloody dress and the cursed blade on display at the execution. The lesser nobles complained that they didn't want the bodies to be buried anywhere near the traditional burial grounds."

Taisiya raised her brow.

"The curse is that terrible?"

"The kitty explained that in Maat, it's on the same level as using iron, if not worse. They take a dim view of things they're incapable of curing with their own magic. In better news, that famous architect heard about what happened and demanded to be the one to build your palace. He swore to make it curse-proof. Naturally, we accepted."

"Naturally," Taisiya replied. "I suppose we return to Rhacotis soon?"

At the very least, her suffering had not been in vain. A curse-proof palace was quite the boon, especially when she didn't have glamour to hide all manner of protections inked into her skin. Perhaps she should start having them stitched into all of her clothing?

"I'm afraid not," Mereruka said as he re-entered the bedroom, still dripping from his bath. She followed one such droplet with her eyes. A tendril of dark violet lay plastered against his chest, outlining his pectorals, his taught abdomen. The strand ended at his hip bone, and there the droplet rolled down his muscular thigh. She hadn't seen him fully nude in broad daylight, and hadn't had the moxie to stare overlong. Now that she did, she noticed the distinct lack of hair anywhere but on his head. It made certain things appear...prominent. Oblivious to her heated gaze, he dried his hair with a towel. It was the only part of him covered by one. Taisiya reluctantly tore her gaze away from the alluring sight.

"Ew," Vasilisa said flatly, turning away. "At least put on your weird damn skirt."

"I swear I told him to," Bas grumbled.

Taisiya blushed, realizing she hadn't even noticed the shifter as he'd exited the bathroom.

Mereruka chuckled.

Vasilisa flicked her ear when Taisiya tried to turn her head to get another peek at her husband.

"S-so, we won't be returning to Rhacotis?" Taisiya asked.

"No. Bas just informed me that the inundation has officially begun. Khety will commence the journey to the Court of the Inundation, the northernmost palace, and we've been *invited*..." He said the word with disdain. "To join the court for the season, along with the rest of my siblings, so that he might celebrate our union."

Taisiya's nails bit into her palm. No doubt the season would end with either them dead, or Khety. By the look in Meri's eyes, he thought so too.

Vasilisa snorted.

"So that he might take our measurements for our coffins, more like," Bas said.

"Precisely," Mereruka added with a grim smile.

"No rest for the wicked, I suppose," Taisiya sighed.

Her first weeks in Maat were shaping up to be hectic indeed.

CHAPTER 37

They had decided to meet the king and his court at the Court of the Emergence, located in the centre of Maat, overlooking the winding Hapi. A sprawling, city-like group of buildings competing in size and splendour rose up on the banks of the Hapi, the entrance like the mouth of a cave of wonders. The wealth of Maat fairly radiated from the rooftops. It gleamed from within as well. Painted murals moved and danced, making the floors and walls a bright and dizzying simulacrum of stylized life. Statues of former kings and queens, posing triumphant over enemies, or glaring their disapproval of all who would come after, lined the sky-high halls. Even lowly soldiers and scribes dressed as well, if not better, than many a noble in Lethe.

Shapeshifters were conspicuous in their absence, for everyone Taisiya saw was entirely fae, or at least appeared so with skin a veritable rainbow of colours. Some had horns, others wings or tails, a few even appeared more like living flowers than men or women. And yet none appeared as beast mages might. Mereruka had explained that Khety thought shapeshifters beneath full-blooded fae. Not even shifter servants or officials were allowed in his presence, including those attached to Mereruka's household. Qar had been forced to stay aboard the barge, tethered outside the palace walls. Courtiers roamed the halls and the many lush gardens, participating in games, banter and professional lounging. But these were no layabouts, their eyes hunting for new victims to crush beneath their feet. Their curious stares were like hot needles as Taisiya passed, her hand on Mereruka's arm. She studiously ignored them. A princess consort need never take notice of a mere hatya. Still, the last time she'd felt so notable, she'd been branded the child of a traitor and all but chased from the halls of power. She could only pray her second such attempt would prove more successful.

Whispers reached her, wondering aloud if this was truly Prince Mereruka and not some glamoured imposter, or if he'd returned as a revenant, or if the woman at his side was a powerful, evil sorceress, puppeteering him. He never deigned to make eye contact, inviting no practised flattery or introductions. She was grateful for that at least.

As they approached the royal receiving room, the decorations changed—strange animals, statues and gold, everywhere the glint of gold. Every few paces, another gilded, painted statue of the king, a wall scene featuring his image, his every honourable action and victory immortalized in all visible mediums. Though she couldn't read the text, the moving images told the stories unambiguously. Beside the towering depictions of Khety stood the much smaller, though no less detailed, images of his siblings. Taisiya had worried that it would be difficult to remember the names and faces of Mereruka's family. She was happy to discover it had been a baseless one. By the time they were but a long hallway away from their destination, she was confident she could identify each of them. She recognised Mereruka in the family scenes and had taken to trying to spot his image. It was better than dwelling on her fears.

"Nervous?" Mereruka asked.

"Yes."

"Good. It would be unwise to relax at court. Or look at all impressed. Expect this to be a whirlwind of introductions and insults. Give as good as you get. And remember-"

"Never tell an outright lie. I recall," Taisiya responded.

The courtly manners Mereruka had been teaching her were seared into her brain. It really was a shame that she couldn't lie, as she was used to. She was so good at it, after all. Though she supposed if she could, that would simply mean having to keep all her lies straight. A headache she didn't need, as she had plenty of legitimate concerns already.

Mereruka nodded, pleased.

Nerves of a different kind jumped about in her gut. But she could be brave. She'd survived a stabbing, and what she had to say couldn't be more painful than that.

"Would you like to make a deal?" Taisiya asked.

His ears twitched.

"I'm listening."

"If we survive this evening-"

"*When* we do," Mereruka interrupted, his tone stern.

I forbid you from dying. Her heart skipped a beat.

"Then promise me an evening, just us, no one else, somewhere safe."

He halted abruptly, his brows drawn with guilt and worry for her.

"I swear to be a better protector to you. I won't allow my carelessness to put you in harm's way again."

Taisiya shook her head. Ah, gods, she was making a mess of it. She could plot the downfall of her enemies without issue, so why was she always so hopelessly tongue-tied when it came to intimate matters?

"That's... that's not what I meant," she said, her eyes darting away from his face.

"Oh...? Oh!" he said, her meaning dawning on him. His grin turned sly. "We have a deal, my beautiful wife." He kissed her hand as she fought a blush. "Do you remember that I told you about fae magic having a taste?"

She blinked, confused by the change of topic.

"Yes, vaguely."

"None of my siblings possess magic that tastes like a common, recognizable food or drink. Except Khety."

"Of course he does," Taisiya replied flatly.

"Word to the wise, never eat a date in his presence."

"And you? What does your magic taste like?" Taisiya asked. She supposed he must have healed her that night, but she thankfully recalled little of the aftermath.

He shrugged.

"Bas tells me it tastes like a combination of sour fruit and medicinal tea."

That accounted for the terrible taste on her tongue the next morning. Taisiya couldn't help her look of disgust.

"That's repulsive."

Mereruka grinned.

"Imagine the fortitude of fae magic instructors."

Taisiya laughed. It was just as well. The doors to the receiving chamber opened of their own accord and they were ushered inside on a hush of quickly dying conversations.

It was time to meet the man she planned to dethrone.

The moment Mereruka entered with his wife on his arm, Itet spotted them, dragging Inkaef along like a ragdoll. She held a goblet of sloshing liquid as big as her horned head. Dread gripped him. Mereruka steered them away and through the throngs.

"Are we running from Itet?" Taisiya asked, amused.

"Sparing ourselves from her rapier wit. If you thought she was a handful in Rhacotis, you don't want to know what she's like when she genuinely believes she's funny." And by the size of her cup, she'd drunk enough to believe herself the epitome of comedy.

With some careful, graceful footwork, they managed to lose Itet in the crowded throne room. Entertainers plied their trade for groups of chatting, drinking nobles while others gesticulated wildly, intent on fierce debates. Each time Mereruka passed with Taisiya on his arm, he did his best to pretend he couldn't see their avid interest, though it was not always possible to avoid. Here in the Court of the Emergence, Khety ruled. These were his allies, not Mereruka's. They'd long known their king had no love for his youngest brother, and were not above cunning tricks with him as their victim in order to curry the king's esteem.

Just as another pompous ass-kisser thought to be the first to halt their strides, Taisiya redirected him, squeezing his arm. The fewer people they had to endure today, the better. He lifted her hand to his lips in thanks.

Itet and Inkaef weren't powerful enough to pose real problems to his plans. The vizier and the overseer of the royal guard? They were another matter. From this point forward, the real tests would begin. The whirlwind continued as his next sibling was upon them.

"You made a right mess of Shedet, Mereruka."

This was someone they could not so easily side-step.

"Good evening to you, Serfka." Mereruka grinned.

Serfka crossed both sets of his pale blue arms and glared, his silver eyes level with Mereruka's. Pleased to know he hadn't misread the vizier, Mereruka held his ground. Serfka cared not at all for the deceased monarch, only for the bureaucratic mess his death had left behind.

"In any case, Shedet made a mess of Rhacotis first," Mereruka said.

Serfka released a frustrated sigh, pushing a strand of grey hair from his face. In the centre of his forehead, the mark of disinheritance marred his skin. It was the only mark a royal might bear without social consequence, taken as it was to demonstrate the complete absence of ruling ambitions. Being the vizier, Serfka had felt it safest to take the mark rather than court the king's suspicion. A coward's choice, to be sure, but at least it made Mereruka's goals that much more attainable.

Serfka's look of resignation said it all. Angry though he was, the Vizier was not unreasonable. If he knew what had happened to Rhacotis in Mereruka's absence, and what had happened when he'd sought recompense for it in Shedet, Serfka knew he had no real reason to denigrate his little brother's actions. The vizier was nothing if not well-informed.

"I'm relieved you're not truly dead, Meri, and that all the wild rumours are just that." He smiled, a genuine, weary quirk of his blue lips.

"As am I. Though I believe Inkaef is less pleased. It seems he made a bet against my good health and will be short a dozen horses as a result," Mereruka said.

Serfka chuckled. The brotherly affection had been short-lived. He quickly straightened his posture and nodded officiously.

"You had best get Shedet's affairs in good order soon, or I'll make it my business to audit it."

"I will keep that in mind, now that I'm its nomarch," Taisiya replied, dragging Serfka's attention down to her.

"You?" Serfka asked, as if seeing her for the first time.

"Me. It's my wedding present... to myself," Taisiya said as smugly as possible.

"Apologies for the late introductions, Serfka. This is my wife, Princess Consort Taisiya, Nomarch of Shedet, recently of Lethe, the Empire of Mages. I had hoped the crown upon her head might have clued you in," Mereruka added.

Serfka's greatest pride was in having Maat so well run that its king rarely had to lift a finger. Any threat to the peaceful, good governance of Maat was a threat Serfka dealt with using the same zeal Itet saved for drinking and her sanctioned brawls at the borders. It also meant Serfka had a certain tunnel vision when he was preoccupied with dragging Maat's affairs back in order. Serfka appeared mortified by the oversight.

"Prince Serfka, Vizier of King Khety. I apologise for my rudeness in overlooking you, Your Harmoniousness." Serfka took Taisiya's hand and kissed it by way of introduction.

"A man who knows how to apologise? You must be quite popular." Taisiya grinned.

Serfka returned her practised smile with one of his own.

"If you have any need of administrators for your nome, you need only ask," Serfka offered.

"We are blessed with many capable minds." Mereruka politely declined his offer. Though Serfka was not an enemy, he had no desire to give him, and potentially Khety, an opening to interfere. There were enough spies trying to infiltrate his ranks already.

Serfka nodded.

"Come. I'm sure His Eternal Serenity is eager to see you," Serfka said as he looked over his shoulder and motioned them to follow.

He led the way through the throngs of courtiers, politely brushing them off with consummate skill. Mereruka kept Taisiya close and followed in his brother's wake, eager to escape the attentions of the other nobles. Meeting the entirety of his family would be more than enough to deal with for one night.

Alas, the night was not over.

Before they could reach Khety, Radjedef intercepted them. Garbed in an ornamental military tunic, the overseer of the royal guard shouldered his way into view and stood bodily in their way, his beefy arms crossed and a smirk on his face. Mereruka steeled himself to deal with his second-least favourite brother. Taisiya tensed beside him, no doubt picking up on the open hostility in Radjedef's reptilian gaze.

"Is that a new whore, brother? Not afraid Khety will steal her from you like the last one?" Radjedef grinned, leering at Taisiya with his bright yellow eyes.

"Radjedef!" Serfka shouted despairingly, horrified by the insults.

"Husband, is this unpleasant red snake of a man your brother?" Taisiya looked Radjedef up and down, curling her lip as she might at the sight of a pile of steaming offal.

"This is Prince Radjedef, Overseer of the Royal Guards. No one is more ashamed of—or bewildered by—our shared parentage than I," Mereruka answered. "Would you like to be introduced to him, my love?"

"I'll pass." Taisiya raised her chin and looked down her nose at Radjedef. A feat, given his looming height.

A little thrill of victory warmed him as Radjedef's scowl darkened. Narrowing his eyes, Radjedef barred their path as the trio attempted to pass him by, his red, scaled, outstretched arm nearly touching Mereruka's chest.

"Ah, ah. No, you will not. State your name, witch, or I'll see you're escorted deep into the desert."

Taisiya's nails bit into Mereruka's arm.

"Radjedef, you're being outrageously rude! You know perfectly well-" Serfka began.

"I know nothing of the sort, *Vizier*. Best leave His Eternal Serenity's safety to one who knows best, hmm? Or do you presume to intrude upon my office?" Radjedef interrupted, his trap plain.

Serfka reluctantly backed down. The vizier had been in the right. Radjedef would have known the names and backgrounds of anyone invited into Khety's presence. But Radjedef had always been prone to throwing his weight around, swaggering about with the importance of his position. It was all a very badly disguised act to hide his crippling sense of inferiority when compared to the highly competent, well-respected vizier. Being a mediocre second son had taken a psychic toll on the hot-headed Radjedef, stuck as he was between the older, powerful king and the younger, popular vizier.

Mereruka felt the warning hum of Taisiya's electric currents under her skin. Though the mask she wore spoke of bored disinterest, her anger was at a fever pitch. Radjedef waited with a leer on his face for Taisiya to answer his threat.

"I am Princess Consort Taisiya, Nomarch of Shedet and the wife of Prince Mereruka. I would tell you to ask the last miscreant who tried to escort me into the desert what happened, but you can't. His blood and that of his family water my fields, and their corpses feed the scavengers," Taisiya replied, her voice as sharp as a blade.

So.

Fucking.

Proud.

If Mereruka could have asked her to marry him all over again, he would have.

Radjedef's fury was a sight to behold. Mereruka regretted the absence of a painter in that moment. He would have loved to capture the image for all time. Radjedef's pointed, red ears twitched openly with no hair to hide them, and he looked ready to skewer Taisiya with the four horns atop his head. It was no wonder—the late nomarch of Shedet had long enjoyed Radjedef's favour. That open favour had more than likely emboldened Henenu and his children to act against Rhacotis. It wouldn't shock Mereruka if Radjedef had also supplied the late nomarch with the dangerous, cursed objects he and Taisiya had been subjected to. If he could have linked Radjedef to the corruption-cursed blade, Mereruka would have counted it a great victory in his campaign for the throne. He would have to content himself with the sight of two prominent veins standing out in bold relief against his brother's temple.

"Henenu is a great man, he-"

"*Was*, brother. *Was*. He is dead, along with his murderous, thieving children," Mereruka interrupted him, a smile of vicious, naked delight on his lips. "Now if you'll excuse us, we're here to greet King Khety."

Chapter 38

"Serfka! You've found my wayward brother. Come, Mereruka, let me see you and your little wife." Khety beckoned them forward with a smile.

Serfka bowed and backed away, melting into the crowd with practised ease. When the sea of nobles and entertainers parted, Taisiya and Mereruka stepped forward and knelt.

Taisiya did her best to keep her expression as neutral and bored as possible. Khety's statues, sculptures and murals had failed to capture the predatory menace with which he held himself. Given the dignified depictions, she'd expected someone less intimidating.

Khety reclined gracefully upon his throne, his sky-blue eyes intensely focused. With skin the bright, saturated orange of a sunrise and his long hair a blinding white, the ornate golden kilt and accessories only made him more dazzling. He rolled his shoulders, dismissing the woman kneading them. Arms resembling the brown feathered wings of a hawk sprouted from him, yet at the juncture, hands with wicked talons bid the crowds to part. Jewelled, golden cuffs circled his thin ankles, his clawed, bird-like feet and lower legs making fashionable sandals impossible. Khety looked like he might take flight at any moment—and then hunt her down like prey. Despite his smile and welcoming words, Taisiya knew a predator when she saw one. Khety wanted them dead.

It was a good thing she planned to kill him first.

"King Khety, Your Eternal Serenity, I have returned from my voyage having secured trade and permanent ties to Lethe, the Empire of Mages.

They are eager to become our friends and have sent us tokens of their sincerity," Mereruka said.

Taisiya felt a familiar pressure as Mereruka summoned the treasure. In an instant, the many varied gifts of Lethe were laid out before the king. The sartorial finery of the empire was displayed—shining silks, embroidered robes, delicate lace, gleaming leather, luxurious furs, some crafted into complete outfits, others sent as neat, perfectly folded piles of raw material. Beside that were the amphorae of wine, beer and spirits, along with containers of the best quality grains. Plant cuttings and seeds were next to the perfumes and jewellery, and scattered throughout were beautifully crafted wooden objects inlaid with precious stone, for Mereruka had made mention that his land, lacking in an abundance of trees, prized such things. All in all, it was equal, if not superior to, the gifts bestowed upon Lethe by Maat. Taisiya would not have allowed anything less.

Khety stood, his taloned feet clicking audibly on the marble floors in the silent room, and picked his way through the veritable hoard of goods with a dismissive expression.

"Raise your head, Princess Consort," the king commanded.

Taisiya obeyed. Khety took her chin between his fingers and inspected her, turning her face side to side, noting her distinctly rounded ears with barely disguised repulsion.

"Mereruka, introduce us."

"This is my wife, Princess Consort Taisiya, Nomarch of Shedet, recently of Lethe, the Empire of Mages."

"Is it true that your land is cursed, Princess Consort?" Khety asked, releasing her chin.

Well, at least he hadn't led with a complaint about her carving out a piece of territory for herself. Or by calling her a witch.

"If it is, then we find it no great impediment, Your Eternal Serenity," Taisiya answered.

She could see what he was doing, trying to diminish her in front of the court, and by extension, Mereruka. She wouldn't let him win this game.

"And yet your people are incapable of doing more than a single spell each," he said, his tone one of pity.

Whispers raced through the court. Khety had been well-informed. Perhaps she and Mereruka should have sailed into Maat on a ghost ship instead. Fear and fury coiled in her gut. She couldn't allow her homeland to appear weak in their eyes, for her sake, and for that of her family. Her magic had inspired enough fear in the fae aboard the ship. She would need to paint the proper picture for those in attendance now.

"And yet we have needed nothing more than this to create a wealthy, unified empire," Taisiya replied. "In Lethe, we do not pity a bolt of lightning, or the raging fire it sparks. Neither do we pity the waves that sink a ship, nor the gale-force winds that drive them. Perhaps it is different in Maat." She smiled brightly. "I wouldn't know, I have only been in your lovely kingdom for a few weeks."

She could have heard a pin drop in the breathless silence gripping the chamber. Even the music had ground to a halt. Khety's stare was measuring. Then, suddenly, he laughed. The jovial sound cut the tension in the room in an instant.

"Brother, your bride has sharp wits and a sharper tongue! She'll do well in Maat. Welcome to my land, little Princess Consort, and enjoy the banquet." He nodded. Though his lips were curved in a smile, his eyes were like chips of ice.

She'd won this game, but his expression promised retribution.

As if those gathered finally dared to breathe again, the conversations and entertainment resumed. Servants hastily carried away the many gifts and entertainers struck up a lively tune. Mereruka stood tall with her and claimed her hand, avoiding the gossips and well-wishers by pulling her into a dance. Thankfully, it was one to which they'd practised the steps.

"That was dangerous," he whispered.

"It was necessary. We cannot appear weak," Taisiya replied.

"I wasn't castigating you. You played that well." Mereruka grinned.

Taisiya allowed herself a small smile.

"He didn't seem... *thrilled* by your return." She chose her words carefully.

"Would you be pleased by an ambitious man circling your court? Or by an ambitious couple allied with a feared, unknown empire?"

Taisiya shook her head.

"I'm looking forward to ruffling his feathers," she said.

"As am I," Mereruka added.

"Why didn't Queen Betrest greet us?" Taisiya asked.

She hadn't seen the queen near where the king had been seated, nor among the faces of the banquet guests. If her depictions were to be believed, she would be hard to miss.

"Over the decades the queen has become... ornamental at best. It wouldn't be a surprise if she preferred the company of her friends over her husband's at events like these. Especially since the king is otherwise engaged." Mereruka nodded his head to Khety.

As they danced, the king lounged on his throne, petted and fawned over by a beautiful fae woman with pale yellow skin and hair that resembled pink peach blossoms. She was dressed almost as finely as Khety himself. Certainly as well as Taisiya. If she'd been wearing a crown, as Taisiya and Mereruka did, it wouldn't have been a stretch to assume she was the queen.

"The king flaunts his mistresses so openly? With his wife presumably in attendance?"

"Khety's lovers all have the official status of royal concubines and are bound to him as though wed. I had heard she was his newest favourite. Hemetre was engaged to me before I was sent to Lethe." At Taisiya's frown, he explained, "She wanted to be Khety's concubine, but he wouldn't give her the time of day. I made a deal with her. His petulant jealousy was easy enough to manipulate. He snatched her away from me within a matter of weeks, all as I'd expected. Now she's Her Most Treasured, the Royal Consort Hemetre, and I am ten years richer."

Taisiya watched as the beauty Hemetre poured the king more wine and whispered softly in his ear as he sipped it. Khety listened, enraptured. Taisiya pitied the queen, wherever she was. If Betrest kept out of their way when they took the throne, Taisiya had a mind to reward the woman for suffering such a lacklustre spouse.

"I've spotted Betrest. Do you wish to greet her?" Mereruka asked.

"Yes. I'd like to take her measure," Taisiya answered.

She needed to know if the queen would pose as many problems as her husband, or, indeed, if she were capable of posing a challenge. When Mereruka pushed them through the throngs, it was to find the queen holding court in miniature. She was unmistakable in her crown; with skin that glittered like gold and deep green hair braided with gleaming jewels, Betrest radiated dignity and sophisticated poise. Instead of flatterers and entertainers, those surrounding her were engaged in a lively debate. Serfka, the Vizier, was here, listening as the queen gave her opinion on some matter of state. Why the cunning Khety preferred the fawning attentions of Hemetre to Betrest's obvious charms was beyond her.

Their arrival was met with the queen's polite smile. Her violet eyes betrayed nothing.

"Queen Betrest, I present my wife, Princess Consort Taisiya." Mereruka bowed.

"Greetings, Prince Mereruka, Princess Consort Taisiya. Have you come to join us in our discussion of the Ruby Sea canal project?"

Taisiya shook her head.

"Primarily to make your acquaintance, Queen Betrest," Taisiya replied.

"How sweet of you. I don't suppose you've yet had a chance to acquaint yourself with the royal projects. Perhaps your husband will see fit to inspire a passion for Maat's intellectual affairs as well as he indulges your passions for its physical riches."

So that was the game she wanted to play? Establish the pecking order before taking her true measure? Sympathy abandoned, Taisiya's expression never slipped. She could appreciate a well-crafted, cutting remark when she heard one. It didn't mean she would take it lying down. No, she believed in hitting where it hurt most and then pouring salt in the wound. Queen though she may be, the king afforded her little value or power, so here she stood, discussing projects she had no power to administer or decide upon. If a hierarchy needed to be established, Taisiya would climb over Betrest's metaphorically skewered corpse to rise above her.

"I'm certain being the nomarch of Shedet will give me the perfect opportunity to learn about my new homeland." She looked up to Mereruka with adoration. "Maat really is such a wondrous place. I find myself infinitely blessed to live here, administer a territory, and have married such an attentive, indulgent husband."

When Taisiya looked to Betrest, she could see the merest tightening at the corners of the queen's eyes. Taisiya beamed. Betrest, at least, was cunning enough to spot her fangs. Let her stew on that for a time, and think twice about lobbing the first insult.

"My head will grow fat with your praise, my love." Mereruka hid his smirk behind her hand as he kissed it. He turned to Betrest. "It is good to see you so engaged in your discussions of the *king's* many projects. We won't distract you any longer. As always, it has been an honour, Your Most Just."

Mereruka bowed and Taisiya followed his lead.

Betrest nodded, her purple eyes flinty with stifled anger.

"Good evening to you Prince Mereruka, Princess Consort Taisiya."

When they left, the queen's companions started up their conversations once more, though they were less animated with the cloud of Betrest's indignation hanging over them. Mereruka's eyes were full of mischief as they stepped back onto the dance floor.

"You placed that dagger so elegantly, wife. I'm completely smitten."

"And you, husband, twisted it so gracefully. I find myself quite charmed."

As Mereruka led her in another dance, Taisiya couldn't help thinking that she had, in fact, married exactly the kind of man most suited to her. She could hardly wait to start plotting in earnest their rise to the throne of Maat.

Chapter 39

After a night of tense introductions, the sun peeked over the horizon, painting all of Maat in its warm orange glow. Golds, blues and greens glittered in the early morning, the cool of night already burned away. As the Court of Emergence slept off a night of revelry, Mereruka reclined comfortably on the deck of his floating barge, picking at a light breakfast and grateful he'd not been tempted to drink too heavily. Taisiya sat across from him, already resplendent in a gown that hid none of her sensuous curves from his sight. If he was very lucky, he would have the chance to remove it from her later.

Vasilisa, hiding in a shadow nearby, was ready to warn them of any who might overhear their discussions. Bas sat alert beneath Mereruka's chair in feline form, ready to do the same. Now that Taisiya had taken the measure of his siblings, he wanted to hear her thoughts before making any plans to bring their downfall.

"Who shall we crush first?" she asked.

Mereruka smiled.

"I would most like to see Radjedef crushed underfoot, but the circumstances to do so have not yet materialised. If I can trace the corruption-cursed blade to him, then he will be exiled or executed."

Already, Nofret had people infiltrating Henenu's former ranks, gleaning whatever information they could about the blade and its provenance.

"That would be ideal..." Taisiya hedged, a playful look on her lips.

"But?"

"Vasilisa and I have an idea, but it hinges on some specifics we don't fully understand."

"Oh?"

"How is Oblivion's tribute collected, stored, moved and offered? How does Khety ensure the offerings are made in his name?" Taisiya asked.

She wanted to tamper with the offerings? Devious little villainess. It was a bold move.

"As Khety journeys north on the Hapi, one of the barges in his convoy is dedicated to collecting the tribute of the surrounding villages and stored aboard. Once they reach the northernmost palace, the Court of the Inundation, it is brought out to the designated spot on the edge of the fertile land and offered in prayer to the forgotten gods, whereupon it sinks into the ground. Khety is the only one allowed to speak the prayer and he also has the containers holding the offerings stamped with his cartouche." At Taisiya's questioning look, Mereruka explained. "A clay seal bearing his name. My cartouche is on the gem in Vasilisa's bracelet, to indicate that she belongs to my household."

Taisiya's grin was a touch wicked. Mereruka couldn't help his excitement. What cruel trickery had his sly wife conceived?

"And these seals, they're legible to Khety before he dedicates the offerings?"

"Yes."

"So what would happen if, say, all the seals bore someone else's name? Maybe Inkaef's?"

Mereruka howled with laughter.

"It would be quite the scandal. Given Khety's recent behaviour, I have no doubt Inkaef would be disinherited, maybe even exiled," Mereruka mused. "Seeing the browbeaten Inkaef try to usurp favour with the forgotten gods might bring Khety's paranoia to a fever pitch."

For so long, only Mereruka had borne the brunt of Khety's distrust. If he thought even the most loyal and placid of his siblings were out to get him, no doubt he would begin casting furtive looks on everyone around him. And a fearful king made unreasonable, chaotic choices that could be used against him.

"Would it be enough to potentially sway Itet to our side? She hardly seems interested in politics. With her beloved twin exiled by Khety, we could offer Inkaef amnesty if she renounces her claim," Taisiya added.

Itet would do anything for her twin. If this scheme worked, he could see eventually persuading her to agree to their terms, or at the very least, agreeing to stay out of their way. Itet had no special love for Khety and found politicking to be a great chore. And if Itet became enraged by a punishment given to her twin, so much the better. Should she aim for Khety's head, only one would be the victor, and Mereruka would place his bets on his eldest brother. Several potential outcomes could mean multiple siblings wiped off the playing board and potentially weakened.

"We may not be able to ally with Itet just yet, but she's as fae as I. If we offer her a good deal with her brother's fate on the line, she'll be sorely tempted to take it. And if she aims her axe at Khety, we only stand to benefit."

"Wonderful. Now, how is the tribute protected and how do we get around that?" Taisiya asked.

"There are guards and barriers of the highest quality. Inkaef holds the sole key that opens a portal through those barriers. He is no fool. He will have that key hidden in a pocket realm of his making."

Docile he may be, but careless? Not with his official duties.

"A pocket realm?" Taisiya asked.

"Fae have the ability to create spaces within reality. It takes a great deal of magic to create one and can only be sustained by regular sacrifice. And that sacrifice must be both living and unwilling. Wild animals are often captured for the purpose."

Mereruka didn't keep one very often. Most would expect him to, and it would be the first place desperate and determined people looked to find evidence against him or weaknesses to exploit. In truth, as convenient as pocket realms were, they were a needless, potentially dangerous complication.

"Often, but not always?"

Taisiya grimaced. Mereruka shook his head.

"Eons ago, the fae of Gaia created an entire world of their own. Some of Maat's earliest histories speak of Wild Hunts conducted by enemy fae, collecting sacrifices to build and sustain their world. It is illegal in Maat to sacrifice a person for the sake of sustaining a pocket realm. But laws like that are only codified because some see fit to transgress them."

Taisiya shivered. It was the only reasonable response. Some said the souls of those sacrificed to keep a pocket realm alive felt the agony of being torn apart piece by piece until there was nothing left. It would have been a fitting way to deal with Khety, except one had to possess a great deal more magic than one's enemy in order to offer them up to the voracious spell. He decided to keep those macabre titbits to himself.

"So, find the pocket realm, get the key, slip through the barrier and replace the seals," Taisiya said.

"I'll need to disguise myself as Inkaef to get by the guards," Mereruka added.

"Will your glamour be up to the task?" Taisiya asked.

Mereruka sighed. If only it were that simple. Transforming one's face, and the features and expressions on it, was a level of skill he didn't possess. Thankfully, there were other ways to go about impersonating someone, for a time at least.

"I'll need a strand of his hair or a drop of his blood. My glamour could allow me to look similar to him, but the guards will know his face well enough to spot the difference. I'll need that piece of him to focus the spell."

"Where does Inkaef live?" Vasilisa asked from the shadows.

"Inside one of the royal apartments in the Court of Emergence, at present," Mereruka answered.

"I can get us that strand of hair, but I don't know how to locate a pocket realm," Vasilisa said.

"I can find it, if he keeps it nearby," Bas said, speaking directly to their minds.

"Is it safe for Bas to wander through the palace?" Taisiya asked.

"If he stays well away from Radjedef and Khety, yes. Khety has long banned shapeshifters at court, on pain of death, so no one would think a shifter would dare walk among them. He'll have my collar on, so they'll think he's my beloved pet and treat him well. It's more likely he'll have to dodge courtiers looking for an easy way to win my favour by returning him to me unharmed."

"I'll keep an eye on him. We'll retreat to the void if we need to," Vasilisa added.

"Look for his official cartouche as well. Better to have the real thing than to create a fake," Mereruka said.

"Hair, cartouche, pocket realm. Anything else?" Vasilisa asked.

"That should be all," Mereruka replied.

"Then come along, kitty. We'll travel the shadow path."

Mereruka could hear the glee in her voice. He pitied Bas already.

"Wait! No! You sadistic bitch!" Bas yowled, his claws digging grooves in the wood of the deck as Vasilisa dragged his feline body into the void. *"Dad! Taisiya! Help!"*

"Safe travels, Bas." Taisiya's smile was understanding but ultimately unmoved.

The sound of his curses ringing in their heads was gone the moment he sank completely into shadow. Mereruka suppressed his own shiver. He did not envy his son in the least.

"How, exactly, did you win her loyalty?" Mereruka asked.

Taisiya looked down, eyes on her hands folded in her lap and smiled sadly.

"After her mother died, Vasilisa refused to leave the void. I lured her back to our world by dangling her favourite sweets on the end of a fishing line, hovering just far enough above a shadow that she would have to come part way out to get them. The void may provide solace, but I hear it is distinctly lacking in baked goods."

"You... *fished* for her?" he snorted.

"I suppose I did." Her smile was irreverent.

The image was patently ridiculous. Mereruka laughed so hard he had to wipe tears from his eyes. Taisiya's eyes brightened.

"And you? How did you become Bas' father?"

"Essentially the same way. Bas was feral when I found him, living as a kitten rather than a little boy. When shapeshifters refuse to take their common form, the form that looks like you or I, they lose their reason and eventually the ability to shapeshift altogether, trapping them. Eventually they go mad. I lured him in with regular food and then promised him a whole roasted duck if he ate it using his hands. Eventually, he decided to stay rather than return to whatever hole he'd been living in."

Bas never spoke of his birth parents or family, if he even remembered them. He'd been such a scrawny, feisty little toddler. And for many years, he'd been the only person Mereruka would gladly call family. He might have saved Bas from becoming feral, but Bas had forced Mereruka to become a better person.

"I hadn't thought I would hear the word 'feral' again once I left Lethe." Taisiya wrinkled her nose in disgust.

"Imagine my surprise when I heard it referring to the mages who resemble shapeshifters, and not people stuck in the forms of unnaturally strong beasts, slowly going mad."

"Is that a common occurrence in Maat?"

Mereruka shrugged to hide his unease. He couldn't imagine his life without Bas, didn't want to think about what would have become of his son had he not seen the little boy behind the kitten's wary eyes.

"More common than I would like."

Taisiya reached a hand out to his and squeezed.

"I look forward to seeing what they can accomplish once they get over their dislike of one another," Taisiya said.

"Like we have?" Mereruka asked.

Taisiya rolled her eyes.

"Flirt," she accused.

"Tease," he retorted.

"Scoundrel."

"Villainess."

Taisiya smiled broadly.

"Now you're flattering me."

"I speak only the truth," he assured her.

"Calling what fae speak 'the truth' is like putting a bow on a pile of horse shit and calling it a gift."

Mereruka grinned. He did so love it when his wife was moved to profanity.

"Interestingly, in Maat there's a beetle-"

He trailed off as her gaze slipped over his shoulder. He turned his head. Nofret approached with a small papyrus scroll.

"Forgive the intrusion, Your Tranquility, Your Harmoniousness. Queen Nefertnesu of Keftu has sent you a message."

Mereruka accepted the scroll and read over the contents. *Damn*. He'd been hoping to avoid this. Apparently, news of his miraculous return and recent nuptials had travelled far and fast. He really did need to expand his spy network.

"It seems we've been invited to present ourselves to my sister, freshly arrived from Keftu," Mereruka said. "Remember what I told you of heartless fae?"

"That they will look like mages with pointed ears and that they are extremely powerful."

"And Nefertnesu is one of them. We will have to tread lightly."

It occurred to him then, when Taisiya didn't ask to see the letter for herself, that he was really going to have to begin teaching her the written script of Maat. That kind of ignorance could easily cause Taisiya to lose face, or worse, her life.

Mereruka nodded at Nofret, who took her leave.

"Did you have something in mind when it comes to Nefertnesu?" Taisiya asked.

"I do," he answered.

Nefertnesu had been sold off in marriage over a century ago to the land of Keftu. It wasn't an altogether strange or tragic fate for a princess. Except that the fae who ruled Keftu had, only two centuries earlier, been taken over by a man who insisted on his court bleeding out their feeling hearts, as he had done. It was a dreadful magical ritual that conferred power, but at great cost to one's very soul.

The worst had been that the political marriage hadn't been necessary. Khety's first foreign campaign hadn't been the resounding success he frequently portrayed it as. When the rival, restless fae court began eyeing Maat after it had been militarily weakened, Khety decided to strengthen ties with Keftu rather than risk a skirmish.

Itet was the oldest sister, but already plaiting her hair with souvenirs of her kills. Nefertnesu had been pretty, shy and sweet, easily browbeaten into being sold off. Easily bullied into undergoing that horrid rite of passage. Bitter anger still heated the blood in his veins, even after all this time. If only he'd been stronger, older, more powerful, Khety might not have been able to force her hand. If only he'd been able to do more than bow to his eldest brother's orders, he might still have the sister he loved by his side. Instead, all that was left was the foul revenant wearing her skin. It was the most senseless, cowardly offence Mereruka laid at his brother's feet—one Khety would pay for in blood.

The only silver lining was that, as a result of her marriage, Nefertnesu wasn't allowed unfettered access to the Hapi. And a fae as cold, ruthless and calculating as she had become would be eager to make a deal for access to more.

"And?" Taisiya asked, prodding him.

Mereruka shook himself from his morose thoughts.

"Nefertnesu's access to the Hapi is exceedingly limited by Khety. If we make a deal to supply more of it to her, in exchange for her renunciation of her rights to Maat's throne, she will likely agree."

"And if she doesn't agree?" Taisiya asked.

"Then we would be best served trying to find a way to kill her before she reveals my intentions to Khety," Mereruka answered.

He was counting on Nefertnesu being suitably miffed that Khety had essentially cut her off from any real access to the Hapi, and her desire to see him brought low as a result. As she was now, she could kill them all with an errant thought, such was the power of a heartless fae.

"Do you think she's impervious to lightning?" Taisiya asked.

"I would hope not, but heartless fae have access to magic even I can only dream of."

"I should wear my best armour then." Taisiya fingered her jewelled collar.

Mereruka nodded and stood, holding his hand out for Taisiya. It was best not to keep a fickle queen waiting. She slipped her pale hand in his and smiled.

The battle had begun.

Chapter 40

Nefertnesu's beauty was terrifying in its allure. How could anyone stand to be in the presence of such a creature, and not become slavishly devoted to the mere sight of her? It was a question Taisiya was beginning to ask herself. The queen smiled, her red-painted lips setting off the sparking turquoise of her kohl-rimmed eyes. She tossed a strand of glossy midnight hair over her shoulder, the waves cascading behind her flawless, light brown skin. Only her pointed ears marked her as fae, rather than the most beautiful of mages. As Nefertnesu sat back in her seat, Taisiya admired her perfect figure, accentuated by a gown with a tight, revealing bodice and a jewelled, tiered skirt. Whatever magic she wielded was as intoxicating as the sound of a silver-tongued mage's voice and twice as lovely. If only the earthy taste in her mouth would stop distracting her from her open-mouthed appreciation.

"Sister, you're being rude." Mereruka clenched his teeth as he said it.

"Am I?" Nefertnesu asked primly.

"My wife is not your plaything."

Taisiya was about to argue with Mereruka that Nefertnesu was not at fault and that he should keep quiet. Compared to Nefertnesu, her husband's very presence was grating. The queen sighed dramatically and rolled her eyes, and even that was enough to make Taisiya's heart flutter.

"Itet is right. You're boring."

When Taisiya blinked, the compulsion disappeared, along with the taste on her tongue. Nefertnesu was still blindingly attractive, but the need to worship at the altar of her beauty had gone. Taisiya scowled at the woman. *Fucking fae magic.*

Taisiya's surroundings came into sharper focus. When exactly had they arrived in this place? She suppressed a shiver. The private courtyard afforded to the queen was shaded by date trees and surrounded by gilded columns. Perfume and floral scents wafted on a breeze created by servants bearing oversized fans. The ornamental pond in the centre was filled with shimmering, languidly swimming fish and floating lotus blossoms. Altogether, it was much too cheery a scene given the violation that had just occurred.

"Greetings, Princess Consort Taisiya. You may wish to wipe the drool from your chin. Never fear, my beauty has left many in a state much less dignified than yours." She smiled winningly.

"Don't give her the satisfaction of checking for something which isn't there."

Nefertnesu laughed, the sound like tinkling bells. Was anything this woman did physically unattractive? Taisiya had never been insecure, but this woman was going to give her a complex.

"What is a mage, precisely?" Nefertnesu asked. "You look like a witch, but your magic doesn't hang about you like a rotting creature in the sun."

Taisiya could only surmise that tact had also been removed in the ritual that had stolen a part of the queen's soul.

"Most wield the natural elements."

"And?"

"And we have never needed to describe our race to outsiders."

"Yes, the Cursed Continent has hardly been a vacation destination for the rest of Oblivion." Nefertnesu leaned back in her seat, apparently satisfied with Taisiya's non-explanation.

"How do your children fare, sister?" Mereruka asked.

She lifted her shoulders in an elegant shrug.

"The eldest failed to survive the initiation. My husband will be wanting another in a few decades to replace him, selfish cretin. If I could have someone else ruin their body for me, I would. As for the younger ones, they're being raised somewhere out of sight, ugly little beasts that they are. Motherhood is such a burden. It will be a relief when I can stop pretending to care. By the by, if Maat has a soul weaver, send them to Keftu. The last competent one disappeared some decades ago and we had to kill the recent one after he botched a number of initiations."

"Good help is so hard to find," Taisiya said, the sarcasm entirely lost on the queen.

Taisiya kept her horror off her face by an effort of sheer will. She finally understood what Mereruka meant when he described what became of heartless fae. Nefertnesu was wholly unaffected by the loss of her child, merely inconvenienced by it. She'd known noblewomen disinterested in raising and having children, but none so cavalier about the death of their own. Taisiya's heart ached for the queen's surviving children.

"It certainly is! Make no mistake, people are only worth what they can do for you. Never forget that."

"I'll engrave your words on my heart, Queen Nefertnesu."

If she found any of these soul weavers, Taisiya would kill them herself.

The queen laughed again, the sound distinctly joyless.

"Your wife is charming, despite her physical shortcomings."

"The standards in Maat are somewhat different from those in Keftu," Mereruka said.

Nefertnesu shivered, her delicate features twisted with disgust.

"I try to forget that I was ever so weak and hideous. Are you certain you wish to remain so... defective, brother?"

Taisiya's heart stuttered at the very thought.

Mereruka cocked his head.

"And fall victim to a botched initiation?"

She waved her hand dismissively.

"I shall invite you to Keftu when we capture a new soul weaver. Now, shall we get down to business? You've never bothered entertaining me for longer than it takes to exchange greetings."

"We would like to make a deal," Taisiya began.

Nefertnesu's pointed ears twitched in unconcealed interest, giving her away despite her schooled expression. She turned to the nearest servant.

"Leave. All of you. Don't return until I seek you out." When the servants had done as she asked, she turned back to Taisiya and Mereruka, raising her chin. "Elaborate."

"Your stores of the waters of the Hapi are probably running dry after all this time. A few miserly drops every year is hardly befitting for a sister of the king of Maat. I wonder what the court of Keftu would look like if you only had more to boast of. Who knows, perhaps you could even make a supplicant of your husband," Mereruka began, a knowing smile on his face as he leaned back into his seat.

"What would you be willing to give us for more?" Taisiya asked, raising her brow.

"I would require much more than I am currently allotted," Nefertnesu said.

"Would an amphora as large as say, my wife, allotted once per year for the rest of your life, be enough to tempt you?" Mereruka asked.

"Ten amphorae. And they should be as stout as Inkaef," Nefertnesu countered.

"Two amphorae," Mereruka replied.

"Nine."

"Four."

"Seven."

"Six. Final offer," Mereruka said.

"This is acceptable. Name your price." Nefertnesu smiled.

"Give up your inheritance rights to the throne of Maat." Mereruka's tone was serious.

Nefertnesu's puzzlement was plain, then she broke into peals of laughter. She wiped tears from the corners of her eyes, never once smudging her make-up.

"That's it? You're a fool to think I cherished such a thing. The only good thing about Maat is the Hapi, and as you've just proven, there are ways to get that without having to rule it. I will renounce my rights. Are you certain you don't want anything else? I may feel my first pang of guilt since my initiation if you leave it at that."

"Naturally, that you never communicate about my motives or the waters I will be giving you."

"Naturally. I agree."

And that was that. But Taisiya couldn't help thinking of the queen's children, awaiting a terrible fate or a grisly death. Like it or not, they were her nieces or nephews, and a Dragonsblood protected their own. Mereruka was about to seal the deal when Taisiya placed her hand over his.

"And one of your children. Your favourite," Taisiya said.

Nefertnesu's expression was as vicious as it was exultant.

"If you weren't so plain, I might think you fae, Princess Consort. Consider the deal made. A lifetime of access to the waters for my rights to Maat and one child of mine, as well as my silence regarding your rather adorable ambitions."

Taisiya felt a sudden weight between them, one that sunk deep into her bones. Strange, that there was no taste on her tongue, just a simple, undeniable knowing. The deal had been struck.

"Though, once again, you've made fools of yourselves. I don't favour any of my children."

Nefertnesu's smile was as cold and beautiful as fresh snow.

Mereruka waited until they were walking down a deserted hallway before whispering to Taisiya.

"Why did you ask for a child of hers?"

"Several reasons," she answered cryptically.

"Such as?"

Taisiya surreptitiously glanced around before she replied in a hushed tone.

"A hostage for good behaviour. Though she may not favour them, I suspect if harm came to one at another's hand, it would make her lose face. In future, if we decide to expand, it would be good to have an ally ready-made to govern Keftu. Lastly, compassion. I can't imagine being raised by that creature."

Neither could he. Not after he'd been raised by the true Nefertnesu.

"All that ran through your head in the moments before she was going to agree?"

Taisiya nodded, refusing to meet his incredulous stare.

Mereruka bit back a grin. Sometimes she could be unexpectedly adorable. He'd purposely asked after the queen's children, hoping to demonstrate exactly what he meant by heartless fae. The change in her posture from merely formal to tense had been almost imperceptible, save that he knew her well enough to notice and he'd been watching. Taisiya had wanted to save those children from their fate the moment she knew what would become of them. Though he might have enjoyed teasing her for it, he settled for kissing her palm.

"My wife is so quick-witted."

He might have swept her up in a proper kiss when she blushed at his knowing tone, but a flash of yellow caught his eye. They were no longer alone, and he hadn't heard the interloper sneaking about.

"Who goes there?" Mereruka demanded.

Hemetre shyly tip-toed her way around a brightly coloured column, the look on her face tremulous.

"Your Tranquility, Your Harmoniousness." She bowed.

He could see her trembling as they approached, the peach blossoms of her hair rustling in a non-existent breeze.

"What are you doing, sneaking about, Your Most Treasured?" Mereruka asked.

"I... I'm trying to keep away from the heartless fae delegation roaming the halls. They... scare me. You never know when they'll be violent. His Eternal Serenity doesn't understand..."

Mereruka pinched the bridge of his nose. Hemetre, though having won the position of royal concubine and in possession of her own independent fortune, was not always the brightest in other matters. In the short time he'd known Hemetre, she'd mentioned her fear of the heartless fae. He supposed since she'd grown up in Keftu, she would know better than most what cruelties they were capable of. It was no wonder then why she'd come to Maat, where there were no fae so afflicted. Her green eyes pleaded for permission to escape. A single pang of pity lanced his heart. She'd made a good bargain with him and paid up without a fuss. He supposed he owed her some small token of aid.

"If you want to avoid them, then stay away from this group of buildings. Queen Nefertnesu herself is staying just down the way."

Hemetre squeaked in terror.

"I-if you'll please excuse me..."

"Go." Mereruka nodded.

She took off at a sprint, her flowing gown snapping to and fro as she disappeared around the corner.

"What in the hells does anyone see in that silly creature?" Taisiya asked.

She was pretty to be sure, but vapid and jealous, interested only in the acclaim her current position afforded her. No doubt she would soon rue the day she'd coveted Khety's attentions.

"I really couldn't tell you. Now, shall we retire to the barge and celebrate our success? I'm eager to be out of this pit of vipers."

Taisiya chuckled.

"It is a bit crowded, with us here. Let's give the rest of them some breathing room, for a time at least."

Chapter 41

After her meeting with Nefertnesu, Taisiya was grateful to retreat to the barge as the court roused from its party-weary sleep. Ships, both floating and sailing, began readying for the journey north to the Court of the Inundation. The fleet of ships floating below on the Hapi was impressive indeed. At the forefront, Khety's ship was unmistakable—twice as large as any others, the wood gleamed as brightly as the gold and gemstone accents, and smaller boats travelled back and forth from it to the banks on either side, doling out the king's largesse to the gathering crowds. The banks of the fast-swelling river were abuzz with activity and sightseers, crowding the shoreline, eager to witness their king's yearly procession and partake in his generosity. It had the energy of a beloved festival. One day, she and Meri would be on the prow of that ship, waving to excited crowds.

For now, she was grateful it was not her standing there, baking in the blinding noontime sun. Taisiya reached for the jewel that allowed her access to their cabin on the floating barge.

Mereruka's teal hands covered her eyes as he pulled her close, her back held snugly against his bare chest.

"I have a surprise for you," Mereruka purred in her ear.

"Oh?" Taisiya asked, suppressing a shiver as he nibbled on her earlobe.

"Close your eyes."

Taisiya complied. His hand fell from her face, instead leading her through the open door.

"Alright," he said.

When she opened them and looked about, everything appeared exactly as they'd left it that morning. The cabin, if it could be called that, was palatial in size and lavishly furnished, yet another unfathomable fae magic that allowed a space to be bigger on the inside than the outside could possibly allow. Her eyes darted about at ceilings spelled like the daytime sky, polished stone floors covered in beautiful rugs and walls painted in tranquil scenes of the deltas. But no flowers, jewels, sweets, or dresses were laid out—nothing. Except for a bucket, half-filled with water, a small fish swimming circles inside. Her smile disappeared.

"Has anyone ever explained to you what a surprise is?" Taisiya asked, scowling.

Mereruka chuckled.

"What? Is it a magical fish that grants wishes?" Taisiya asked, folding her arms as her scowl deepened.

He laughed and picked up the bucket, kissing her forehead.

"Don't be silly. Why would a fish grant wishes?"

"Why would a fish in a bucket constitute a surprise?" Taisiya retorted.

"It's a necessary ingredient. We made a deal, didn't we? If we survived meeting my family, you wanted an evening alone, somewhere safe. There is nowhere safer for us than a pocket realm of my making."

Suddenly, the pressure of Mereruka's magic felt like a terrible weight in her bones. He poured the contents of the bucket out before him where they hung, suspended, as the bright, aurora-like tendrils of his magic devoured the wriggling fish. The pressure was gone in an instant, leaving Mereruka smiling. He held out his hand, and Taisiya placed hers in his, unsure. Once again, nothing had visibly changed. Stepping backwards, he led her along with a smile. She expected him to bump into the wall, but instead, he began disappearing into it. Taisiya stopped mid-step.

"What—"

"Come, Taisiya. You won't regret it."

She looked from his citrine eyes to the wall that seemed to swallow him. What magic was this? Did pocket realms swallow their makers as well as their sacrifices?

"I would never hurt you."

For all his many tricks, she believed that. Swallowing her fear, she stepped forward, closing her eyes, half expecting to come face first with a solid surface. Mereruka pulled her through what felt like a thick, dry soup. She held her breath as she struggled past whatever barrier this was.

"You're through now," Mereruka said.

Taisiya opened her eyes and gasped.

"Where are we?"

The sky was dark and filled with twinkling stars, while cheery, glowing lights bathed the room in a warm glow. Perched on a cliffside, they were treated with a panoramic view of the Hapi, the moon above providing enough light to see the swaying palm trees in the gentle, fragrant breeze. Not a few paces away, a simply decorated room with only three walls and a gauzy fabric roof opened to invite them inside. A large, lush bed scattered with flower petals, a modest pool with perfumed waters and a table set for an intimate meal awaited them.

"A modest pocket realm. Does this please you?" he asked, sweeping his hands wide.

Taisiya nodded as she turned around, taking in her surroundings.

"It's hidden from anyone outside, and any who try to trespass will be at my mercy. So long as we're here, we're safe from prying eyes, ears and magic."

"It's beautiful."

"Not as beautiful as you."

Taisiya smiled. His flattery had returned full-force.

"So, it's just us?"

Mereruka nodded, pulling her close. If she didn't know better, she might think he was using the same nefarious magic as his sister, drawing her in like a moth to a flame. She wanted him badly enough to risk ruining the comradery they shared and the high esteem in which she held him. She placed her hands on his bare chest, delighted by the feel of him, her heart both fluttering with anticipation and yet calmed by the safety she found in his arms.

"Just us," he answered.

"Then, will you do something for me?"

"I hope to do many somethings for you." He grinned.

She chuckled, nerves nearly making her shake. This time it would be different. It had to be. And for that, she wanted of him what she'd never had the courage to ask of anyone else—his true self.

"I want to see you without your glamour."

His smile faltered.

"You... want to see my tattoos?"

Taisiya nodded. She'd liked what she'd seen of them, the soft, magical glow of them against his skin.

"They're a part of you and they're pretty."

Mereruka's brows pinched, his eyes searching hers for a falsehood he would not find. He rubbed his upper arm, looking askance as he fought some internal debate. For the first time, he appeared lost—vulnerable.

"You're certain?"

"Yes."

Mereruka released a shaky breath, dropping his glamour and exposing his glowing saffron tattoos for her perusal. Holding himself still, his expression was wary, as if expecting her rejection or disgust. Instead, she traced the designs with her fingers, savouring the taut muscles of his torso, lingering over those that had been re-inked. His hand in hers, Taisiya examined the designs at her leisure. Every finger had multiple spells, an intricate tapestry paid for with pain and patience. She circled him, parting the silky curtain of his violet hair, revealing the designs that snaked down the lean muscles of his wide back and disappeared beneath his kilt.

"Do you have them everywhere?" she asked.

"Almost. I'm not a *complete* masochist," he quipped.

She trailed her fingers across his back, revelling in the soft glide of skin on skin, and rounded him to stand toe to toe.

"Do I pass muster?" he asked, his tone joking but his eyes cautious.

"There was never any question that you would." She reached up to pull him in for a kiss.

He bent down, his kiss tentative and soft. That wouldn't do. She wanted his passion. She wanted to be lost in him. Taisiya ran a finger along his pointed ear, goading him. He shuddered and gripped her tight, kneading her rear, slanting his mouth across hers, claiming her tongue with his own. They stumbled onto the bed, a tangle of tongues and limbs, hands grasping, desperate to be closer.

"This will be easier without clothes," he panted.

"Then take them off."

"Your wish, my command."

With a snap of his fingers, their clothes disappeared. The heat of his bare skin against hers had her heart tripping in her chest. His erection ground into her hip and it was all she could do not to moan.

"Show-off."

"Always," he purred.

He nibbled on her ears as she dared to touch his, kissing down the length of her neck, nipping her in places she'd never known could be so sensitive. When his lips found her nipple and tugged, she cried out. As his clever fingers began tweaking the other, she gripped his head, biting back another undignified sound, unsure if she wanted to pull him away or press him closer. He chuckled against her breast, the coolness of his breath sending a shiver of pleasure down her spine. Violet strands circled her wrists, pulling her hands away as his eyes met hers.

"Stop holding back, Taisiya. I want to hear how good this is for you."

She could feel her face flaming with shame.

"It's embarrassing."

"Do you like what I'm doing?" he asked, tongue teasing her nipple.

"Y-yes."

"Then let me hear your little gasps and moans. There's no one here but us, and I like the sounds you make."

"But—"

"But nothing," he growled, grinding his erection against her, eliciting a sharp inhale. "That's better." Mereruka smiled, bending his head back to his task.

Her hands bound by his hair, he played with her nipples until even the barest hint of his breath was enough to make her moan.

"Meri, please, I need to touch you too."

"Trust me, if I let you go now, you'll be tearing out my hair." He winked, trailing kisses down her stomach, heading right for her aching core.

She stiffened, clenching her legs together. When he flicked his citrine eyes up at her, he must have seen her trepidation. He stopped, hair releasing her wrists in an instant.

"We don't have to do this, Taisiya. Would you like me to stop?"

"No! No... it's just..."

He waited patiently, threading his fingers through hers. Gods, why was this always so difficult for her? She was certain her face was beet red as she fought to say the words she dreaded speaking.

"I've never really enjoyed what comes after kissing."

The silence was palpable, as was his stillness. Taisiya couldn't meet his gaze, certain she'd ruined everything now. What husband would be happy with a wife who wasn't able to enjoy the act itself?

When he finally responded, his voice was deadly calm.

"Did your previous experiences bore you? Or did someone make it unpleasant for you?"

That wasn't the face of a disappointed man. No, it was the face of a man plotting murder most foul.

"Both? It was always uncomfortable but mercifully brief," she replied.

"Has Vasilisa already killed them?"

Taisiya shook her head. Dragged them through the void, most certainly, but killed? No.

"Good. I'll have the pleasure myself."

"You're being overdramatic."

"That's a matter of perspective. One I don't share." He brought her hand to his lips and kissed it. When he released a gusty sigh, his breath made her skin tingle. "Nothing we do together should be either of those things. If you dislike something, you need only say so and it will never happen again. If you say stop, I will stop."

"Oh," she said. He wasn't disappointed in her. He wanted things to be good between them. Taisiya blinked back tears as warmth blossomed in her chest, chasing away the dread. Now, all that remained was anxious need. "T-then don't stop."

He moved back up to meet her lips with his own, his slow kiss driving her mad. By the time he was again moving towards her breasts, she was a wild thing in his arms. He teased her oversensitive nipples, making her moan. She gripped the sheets between her fists as his kisses moved passed her navel.

"M-Meri?"

He stopped. "Trust me?"

She nodded. Whatever it was he was planning to do to her, he was convinced it would be pleasurable. He parted her thighs, kissing her from her knees down her inner thighs, his eyes flicking back to hers between every touch. When his lips finally met that hot, aching part of her, his tongue scalded her.

"F-fuck! Meri, what are you—"

But his tongue was on her again, wringing stunning pleasure from her as she cried out. As the pleasure built, all she could do was moan and writhe and pray it never stopped. But just before she reached the height of it, he stopped. She nearly wept. It was all Taisiya could do not to beg.

"Do you like that?"

She couldn't speak, simply nodded her head as she panted.

"I thought you might."

She couldn't even begrudge him his smug smile as he bent his head back down and continued his indecent assault. As his tongue tortured her in the most pleasurable, maddening way, he slipped a finger inside her, and then another, stroking her until she thought she might come apart. And then she did, screaming his name as he viciously wrung more pleasure from her body than he had any right to. She bucked against his tongue, her thighs gripping his head as she rode the ebbing waves of ecstasy.

Exhausted and shaky, she locked eyes with him.

"Gods, Meri..." she said, her voice nearly hoarse.

"Again," he growled, his eyes darkened by lust.

"What? I couldn't—"

And yet his clever tongue proved she could. Mereruka dragged her back up to the pinnacle in half the time, her heart nearly exploding from her chest. By the time he was finished with her, her throat was raw from screaming his name. It would be a miracle if she ever managed to unlock her fingers gripping the sheets when it felt like they were the only thing keeping her tethered to the world of the living. Given how her heart was racing, they might be. When he looked up at her from between her thighs, his grin was pure, wicked triumph. He pulled her close.

"I want you to ride me. Think you're up for it?"

She laughed.

"You've turned my bones to jelly, but I think I can manage."

Taisiya crawled atop him, her core aching. His length in her hand, she teased him back, noting where she touched him that made him groan. It was a heady thing, this power to make him mad for her touch. She could get drunk on it.

"Taisiya," he warned her, voice dark with need.

She smiled, arranging her deliciously limp body and guiding him into her, revelling in the feel of him sliding in, filling her. Gods, he was the perfect fit. Her hands braced on either side of his head, she bent to kiss him as she slid up and down the length of him. Their ragged breaths echoed out into the night between needy kisses that turned hotter the longer she rode him.

"Does this feel good?" he ground out between clenched teeth, his hands gripping her hips like a lifeline.

"Mmm."

He released a shaky breath as she angled her hips, his next stroke making her moan.

"Hold tight," he growled.

She wrapped her arms around his neck as his hands sized her hips and he drove himself deep. Taisiya gasped. She ran her tongue along the shell of his ear, his next thrust making her see stars. Snarled words incomprehensible, he was wild and unrestrained, as lost as she. Just when she didn't think she had the strength to continue, he ground the length of himself deeper and cried out her name in a guttural prayer.

They collapsed, gasping for breath. When her mind cleared from the fog of lust, she searched his face, tracing the designs there with the tip of her finger. His eyes were bright with adoration.

"You're so damn beautiful, Taisiya."

She beamed.

"Every woman knows post-coital compliments are meaningless."

His winded laughter echoed in the room.

"And what is the requisite waiting period?"

"I'll have to check my sources."

"You do that." He chuckled, pulling her close and stroking her hair.

She snuggled into his chest, unable to hide her smile. For the first time in her life, she could discard the fear that she was broken, unable to enjoy intimacy. Mereruka would never know the full extent of the gift he'd given her.

"I've decided we're staying here, like this, forever," Taisiya announced.

"King and queen of our own little paradise."

"Mmm."

She kissed his sweat-slicked chest as they lay in the afterglow.

"Discounting the snakes, of course," he said.

She pulled away, frantically searching.

"Where?"

Mereruka snickered until he couldn't hold back his howls of laughter. Taisiya scowled. He was an abominable trickster. She pinched him, continuing her assault until his laughter died down. He captured her wrists in his hands and grinned.

"Mercy, wife."

"Never."

"Taisiya?" he asked, his expression solemn.

"Yes?"

"You're so damn beautiful."

Her heart skipped a beat.

"Meri?"

"Yes?"

"I l-"

Before she could say the words filling her heart to bursting, he pulled her behind him, his muscles taught and his magic at the ready.

"What?"

"Someone has dared to enter," he hissed.

Taisiya waited with bated breath. Between one blink and the next, Bas appeared, disoriented. Mereruka sighed, releasing the tension that had his muscles coiled tight. He pulled the sheets up to cover himself as Taisiya pressed herself against his back. When this was over, she was going to have a very pointed discussion with Bas about boundaries.

"Dad?"

"Bas." Mereruka's growled reply mirrored her distinct displeasure at the intrusion.

"I-woah! Oh gods, I'm sorry!" Bas turned to face the wall, hands covering his eyes.

"It obviously couldn't wait, or you wouldn't have entered," Mereruka groaned.

"We managed to find the hair and the pocket realm Inkaef is carrying around. But something happened."

"What?" Taisiya asked, fear creeping up her spine. Vasilisa had not entered with Bas.

"Nefertnesu has been murdered."

Chapter 42

It took an effort of will to calm the twin cyclones of wrath and anger whipping through him. His perfect moment with Taisiya had barely lasted more than an afternoon. A scented bath, a sumptuous dinner, fine wine, presents and then another bout of leisurely lovemaking had been in the offing. Mereruka had been planning for this moment for weeks, labouring over every detail so that his shy, reticent wife would know how good it could be between them—so that she would crave his touch again and again.

Couldn't that heartless husk have waited one more day to get herself murdered?

Mereruka took a slow, deep breath, willing himself to set aside that bit of misplaced fury. He wasn't even angry at Nefertnesu, but it was easier to be angry over her death—the second one, so far as he was concerned—than to admit he'd held out the slimmest of hopes that her heart might one day be restored to her. But now she was gone for good, and the gods only knew what became of dead fae whose souls were split in life. He'd failed her for the very last time. There was nothing left of his sister to mourn or miss, and his tears had long run dry.

"We'll be out shortly," Mereruka replied to Bas' shocking pronouncement.

"But-"

"She's not going to be more or less dead if we take time to get dressed, Bas," Mereruka reminded him.

"Right. Sorry," Bas replied, and pulled himself out of the pocket realm.

If Mereruka used a tendril of magic to speed him on his way, Bas was at least wise enough not to complain.

Taisiya peeled herself away from him, robbing him of the feel of her breasts against his skin. Already hurrying to pull her clothes back on, he caught her wrist and held her still.

"Meri?"

"Take a moment. Step into the bath with me. We'll likely be called to court. We can't go there in our current state."

"Ah," she said, taking inventory of her mussed hair, sweat-slicked skin and rumpled clothes.

She allowed herself to be led into the scented bath and sat between his legs on the submerged bench. He summoned a brush and began running it through her hair, willing himself to be lost in the soft copper waves. In truth, he needed a moment to bask in her, to take comfort in her nearness and the knowledge that the woman he loved was alive and well and hadn't gone somewhere he couldn't follow.

"Meri?" she asked.

He sighed, pulling her close.

"I'm a fool."

"You're allowed to mourn her death."

Of course she knew exactly what plagued him.

"I mourned her death two centuries ago when the woman who raised me was forced to cut out her feeling heart."

"And yet a part of you still loved her, no matter how monstrous she'd become."

He rested his head on her shoulder.

"Yes."

She touched his arm, stroking it beneath the bathwater.

"I had a younger brother very much like her. He was a wicked, pitiless boy, but we loved him, even if he was never capable of truly loving us in return. We mourned his death all the same. Love doesn't have to be rational to be real."

Mereruka kissed her shoulder.

"I was convinced that if only I could convince her to repair her soul, hells, even if I could trap or trick her into doing it, I could make up for my failure. I thought I'd given up the boyish fantasy that one day, I would be able to save her. Apparently not. "

"Hope is a precious, cruel thing. It keeps us going when all else seems lost. But Meri?"

"Hmm?"

"So does vengeance."

He chuckled.

"I suppose you're right."

"I usually am."

"Then let us make ourselves presentable and begin plotting." He kissed her head and continued brushing her hair. His wife really was his perfect, vicious, other half.

"Do you think we'll be suspected of her murder?" Taisiya asked.

"No. Not in truth, but will Khety spin this to his advantage? Definitely. More likely, one among her own delegation killed her. The 'why' is the more important question. If Keftu wished to start a war with Maat by killing Nefertnesu, then they made a poor choice. Khety would never start a war over her. Maybe Keftu's king wanted to get some concession from Maat. Or, most likely, a rival for Nefertnesu's position killed her, away from the prying eyes of Keftu's court."

"What of our deal?"

"It's null and void." He shrugged.

"And her children?"

"Will likely follow her. Without Nefertnesu's power to protect them, and a new queen likely to take her place, their days are numbered. Keftu's court is like a pride of lions. When a new power takes over, traces of their rival are erased," Mereruka answered, his voice grim. Whoever his nieces and nephews were, he hoped they gave as good as they got. He finished adding a few braids to her hair and quickly ran the brush through his own tangled locks.

Taisiya stood and towelled off, retrieving her gown.

"Then we must move quickly," she said, her expression uncompromising. "Will you help me?"

"You want the children that badly?"

She nodded, a fire in her amethyst eyes.

"I don't want Keftu's current court lying in wait for ours to make a single misstep. If their king is anything like Nefertnesu, it will only be a matter of time before they decide they needn't wait for Maat's permission to take the waters of the Hapi. They must be eliminated. If we can make vassals of them, it would be ideal, but I would settle for having them as trustworthy allies. The children, with their hearts intact, will be crucial for that to happen."

Mereruka was inclined to agree with her. With enough well-placed whispers, he could potentially destroy Keftu by fanning the flames of internal division, so rife amongst ambitious, heartless fae. But the children would need to be secured and raised first. A power vacuum was only useful if he had a pawn of his own, ready and waiting to take advantage.

"Then we'd best get our hands on them," he said, finishing his ablutions.

Mereruka reasserted his glamour, erasing the sight of his tattoos. Taisiya frowned, disappointed. He kissed her head. Strange, wonderful woman.

"Ready?" he asked.

Taisiya took his hand and grinned.

"Always."

When he pulled her from the pocket realm, Bas and Vasilisa were waiting. Vasilisa looked them up and down, a knowing smirk on her face.

"So, are little ankle-biters forthcoming?"

Taisiya's scowl was matched by Mereruka's.

"Fine, fine." Vasilisa held up her hands in mock surrender. "The king's messenger has already come and gone."

"You've been summoned to court. You're the last to have seen Nefert-nesu alive," Bas explained as he proffered the scroll.

Mereruka perused it.

"I doubt that, given she's been murdered. Damn Khety and his posturing." Mereruka sighed. "Alright. We need to be properly dressed for this."

"Agreed," Taisiya answered as Vasilisa led her behind a screen, a new dress already in hand.

"And let me answer the questions. He'll try to pin this on us, and you're not as skilled in courtly speak," Mereruka added as Bas handed him a new kilt and belt.

"If I were he, I would do the same," Taisiya remarked. "Vasilisa, have the iron ready in the void. If we must, we'll kill them all at once."

"Yet there's four of us and five of them, discounting the queen," Vasilisa pointed out.

"I'll take Khety. Bas can handle the vizier," Mereruka said.

"I want Radjedef," Taisiya said.

"Then the green imp Itet is mine," Vasilisa said.

"And Inkaef?" Taisiya asked.

"He's more likely to run than fight, and you have excellent aim," Mereruka answered.

"Why can't we just do it this way?" Vasilisa asked.

"Because once spells start flying, our plans will quickly fall apart. We would be lucky if we all survived intact. I would rather finance this coup with our patience than our blood." Mereruka replied, fastening a new jewelled collar around his throat.

Under no circumstances would he slay Khety and the rest of his siblings unprepared, without a proper plan and backup in the form of his own soldiers. Not one of his siblings was a complete pushover, except for maybe Inkaef. And after Nefertnesu's death, he wasn't about to do anything too hasty. No doubt Radjedef had tightened security.

Bas handed him his winged crown. Taisiya picked from one of several and Vasilisa placed it on her head, arranging Taisiya's copper hair and adjusting her make-up. That done, Mereruka held out his hand to his wife. Bas took the form of a cat and Vasilisa sank into Taisiya's shadow.

Their journey to the throne room was unimpeded by the usual parade of courtiers. Instead, a long line of armed soldiers met them at every juncture, bowing deeply as they passed, yet casting them wary glances. A sombre, tense mood had settled on the palace. Not once in Maat's long history had the annual journey to the Court of the Inundation been halted, nor had Maat's monarch ever been forced to backtrack. When they entered through the enormous doors of the throne room, Khety sat with Betrest at his side, his expression cold. The rest of his siblings were awaiting them.

"You have a lot of nerve to make me wait, Mereruka," Khety began.

"I might apologise, but our sister is dead. Discovering the culprit and appeasing Keftu should take precedence over your grievances with my timing," Mereruka retorted, allowing his anger to show. It was no secret that he'd loved Nefertnesu the most.

Taisiya made a show of soothing him with a stroking of her hand on his arm. Hopefully, the rest of his siblings would think him on edge over her loss. Good. The best performances held a kernel of truth.

"Her servants say you were the last to meet with her," Khety accused, his implication clear.

"Did her servants also inform you that we were invited there? She wished to greet me and was curious about my wife. When we left, she was alive and in good health, and I'm happy to swear to that upon my name. I assume her travelling companions have been questioned?"

"It's being seen to," Khety replied.

Khety's eyes narrowed, no doubt frustrated that Mereruka had cut him off at the legs. To offer a vow of truth was as good as giving one, and everyone here knew it. It was also a vow Mereruka could give with a clear conscience, without fear that his other motives might be unveiled. In this instance, the truth, or a limited slice of it, would set him free.

"If you need someone to vouch for our timing, you need only ask your concubine," Mereruka added.

"Which one?" Khety asked, bored.

"Hemetre. We saw her just as we left Nefertnesu's rooms."

"We've already heard from Hemetre," Khety stated.

Khety eyed them, tapping a taloned finger against the arm of his throne, the click-click-click echoing in the empty hall. What fresh scheme was he concocting?

"I accept your statements on this matter as true. However, I am busy interrogating the delegation from Keftu. I want you to contact their king to explain the situation. You are, after all, The Prince of Dreams. If anyone is best suited to mollifying such a man, it would be you and your sharp-witted wife. Can I entrust this task to you, Mereruka? Or is this too much responsibility?"

Accept, and make himself the focus of a wily, cruel, foreign king. Refuse, and appear incompetent. Taisiya squeezed his arm, her gaze steady. If she was ready to play Khety's game, so was he.

"We would be honoured to act as Maat's representatives on this matter. I assume I will have full discretion in our dealings with Keftu?" Mereruka asked.

The clicking ceased. The silence as Khety's talon stopped mid-air was deafening. Khety's hand balled into a fist before he laid it to rest.

Had he hoped to set Mereruka to the task and then castigate him for invented failures?

Not today.

"You will, but I expect you to preserve Maat's dignity in this," Khety said.

"Always, Your Eternal Serenity," Mereruka replied.

"Then you may make use of my scryer to contact Keftu."

A spy to report on every word and gesture they made. Their every action would be picked over and analysed for a reason to attack them. Mereruka nodded and bowed. Taisiya followed suit. Khety waved them away.

"The rest of you may go. If we learn anything new, you will be summoned," Khety said, ending their meeting.

It behove Mereruka to resolve this situation with Keftu, before Khety elicited false confessions from the foreign delegation that would put Mereruka at a disadvantage. Thankfully, Keftu's king wanted what its late queen was greedy to secure—the waters of the Hapi. And Mereruka suspected he could buy off the king at a fraction of the cost.

"Mereruka, Taisiya, please, follow me. I'll show you to the scryer." Serfka hurried to join them.

They followed him through the airy, sombre halls of the Court of Emergence. That Mereruka hadn't been forced to shed his siblings' blood this day was a real success. Khety would have to try harder to destroy him. Merely throwing him at the non-existent mercies of Keftu's king wouldn't suffice. Now, it was time to meet the bastard who'd ordered his sister to be made into a monster and take the first step in ensuring his downfall.

CHAPTER 43

"It's a pity. She was an excellent queen."

They weren't the words one would usually associate with a husband who had just found out he'd become a widower. Nor was the boredom in his tone or affect. Taisiya did her best to school her features in the face of this heartless, beautiful creature. Seated in a throne of jagged, multi-hued gems, the king of Keftu was dazzling in his perfectly bronzed, sharp-eyed, sharp-jawed way, his voice as deep as the sea and twice as deadly. A veil of unnaturally still water, spelled to form a window into the foreign throne room, allowed them to speak. Taisiya was grateful that no one could use it to bodily walk through to the other side. Her skin crawled at the very idea of being in the man's physical presence.

"You have our heartfelt condolences," Mereruka said.

The king sneered and clicked his tongue.

"Have you forgotten to whom you speak? Sweet words are a waste of air. What will you offer me to make up for this disgraceful inconvenience?"

And there it was. His wife's death—a mere inconvenience.

"So that you might honour her memory, a statue of gold and gemstones made in her likeness." The king looked ready to complain when Mereruka added, "As tall as, say, the height of your throne room?"

Mollified, the king smiled.

"So you do understand our language, brat. What else?" he asked, reclining in his glittering throne.

"We would like to offer her weight in water, the Hapi's waters, to be precise. Surely, she would wish you to have it."

He tapped his finger lazily on the arm of his seat, a look of amused tolerance on his face.

"This is acceptable."

"If I may?" Taisiya asked.

"Speak." The king waved his hand indulgently.

"Nefertnesu's children may be considered obstacles to your future queen. We would like to offer to shelter and educate them, until, or if, you find you have need of them," Taisiya said.

His baffled expression gave way to laughter. Better for her to look the fool in his eyes than to allow those children to die. For all their sakes, it would be best not to have such a creature sitting on the throne of a neighbouring kingdom. Taisiya's heart pounded in her chest the longer he laughed. Fear that he might reject the offer or take offence held her immobile. When he was finally done, his smile was amused as he wiped tears from his eyes.

"So bloody sentimental. Gods, the lot of you are so pathetic. Fine, take the brats. It will save the cost of proper tombs were they to remain here. And on that subject, bury the late queen in Maat. No need to send the body back to Keftu."

Relief flooded her.

"As you wish." Mereruka bowed.

Taisiya followed her husband's lead.

"Make haste with the promised goods and send someone for the children. I've no intention of sparing my people for the task."

The king of Keftu lifted his chin at his own scryer, who quickly stopped the spell. All that was left before them was a plane of still water, suspended in the air. Khety's scryer fed the water back into a large amphora and bowed before taking his leave, no doubt to inform Khety of every word spoken.

They were alone.

"Knowing what they become, why would any sane fae consent to it?" Taisiya asked, chilled.

Mereruka shrugged.

"Some will do anything for the kind of power it promises. Are we so different?"

"We still have our hearts." Taisiya frowned.

"Is it wrong to choose evil if you no longer understand the difference? Or is it worse to choose evil in spite of knowing the difference?"

Taisiya's frown became a scowl. There was no evil in desiring power, only winners and losers. It was far better to strive for it than to be someone else's stepping stone.

"My husband, the philosopher."

Mereruka laughed.

"It's a question for the sages. I have no desire to see what lies on the other side of that wicked spell. Thankfully, the only fae capable of performing it, the soul weavers, are rare breeds, and apt to keep such knowledge to themselves. I imagine the only thing worse than being one of the heartless is having to live amongst them with your own heart intact."

Mereruka led her from the room, her hand tucked into his arm. She was infinitely lucky that arm was teal, rather than a more familiar shade. The thought of him becoming a monster like that turned her heart to ice.

"The soul weavers don't remove their own hearts?" Taisiya asked.

Mereruka shook his head.

"You can't remove something from someone else that you don't understand yourself. Or so I'm told."

As they walked out into the sunlight, Taisiya did her best to shake off the gloom.

"If we ever find such an individual, we should kill them. We can't allow such magic to be used in service of our enemies."

"Agreed. Thank the gods Khety never found one."

If he had, they never would have survived.

"Indeed."

Mereruka had sent Nofret to Rhacotis, detailing his instructions and the goods she was to commission and escort into Keftu. He couldn't afford to let a single detail go wrong, lest he be on the bad side of two separate kings. Reluctantly, Mereruka also parted ways with Qar, sending him and some trusted soldiers to retrieve the children. Should anything happen to them on their journey, Khety would no doubt use it against him. While he hated not to have Qar near, the shapeshifter couldn't even enter the seasonal palaces, and Mereruka would rather the man be of some use in securing Maat's future allies.

Upon hearing of Mereruka's success with Keftu's king, not even Khety could complain openly. The king's mood was further fouled by the fact that even under duress, not one of Nefertnesu's travelling companions admitted to the murder. Forced to halt his journey, backtrack and still left with nothing but a dead former princess of Maat for his trouble, whispers of Khety's curse were once again rampant. If Mereruka had helped place those same rumours, no one was the wiser. By the time the procession reached the Court of the Inundation, the northernmost palace, every courtier with a lick of sense was tense, waiting for the king to lash out.

Troubled though they were with Nefertnesu's killer on the loose, Mereruka and Taisiya had the next part of their plan to enact. An aurora of magic danced along his fingertips as Mereruka added to the protections Taisiya habitually wore. They had a long night ahead of them and she would need every advantage. There was only a single evening to get hold of Inkaef's cartouche and tamper with the tribute before Khety dedicated it in the morning. With Khety in the darkest of moods, it would merely take one more outrage before he succumbed to his temper.

"Run through the plan with me," Mereruka insisted as Vasilisa put the finishing touches on Taisiya's make-up. Taisiya should, by rights, be tended to by multitudes. In future, he might trust someone else to assist her, but not until she was queen and they had been thoroughly vetted by Nofret. For now, Vasilisa's efforts would have to be enough.

"Again?" Taisiya asked with a scowl.

"Humour me," Mereruka said.

"I invite Itet and Inkaef to drink with me for the evening. Bas remains with me as a cat to assist in keeping them busy, or to act as an early warning for you if I fail. You and Vasilisa infiltrate Inkaef's pocket realm to steal his cartouche. Once that's done, you glamour yourself to look like Inkaef and access the tribute. When you are inside the wards, you and Vasilisa change the seals on the tribute before you leave. Once you're done, you'll come to pick me up, at which point I will be lucky not to be completely inebriated," Taisiya replied.

The newest charms woven into the beads of her necklace would hopefully help with that.

"And what is your excuse as to why I'm not joining you?"

"You are busy planning a proper burial for Nefertnesu."

This, technically, was his responsibility, and what he would be doing before Taisiya lured Inkaef away from his pocket realm. A truth, but only just.

"Are you certain you can keep your secrets to yourself, even when drunk?" Mereruka asked.

Vasilisa snickered.

"Taisiya prefers to sing naughty poems when she's sloshed. She doesn't get chatty."

At Mereruka's raised brow, Taisiya blushed and cleared her throat.

"I'll be there to be a distraction if she starts saying something compromising," Bas said.

"It's not like we'll be drinking something Itet has any experience with, either. The spirits my family makes are exceptionally potent. We're just lucky my sisters thought to send some with me," Taisiya added.

"Are we ready yet? Because I'm ready now," Vasilisa said, all but jumping out of her skin.

Mereruka ignored her impatience to see his wife off.

"Be as moderate as you can."

"I will," she assured him.

Her blithe reply didn't assure him in the least. Itet was skilled in few things, but one of them was holding her liquor, and the other was tempting others into drinking more than they should.

"And if something tastes off—"

"I know, make a big deal of it so Bas knows that magic is in play."

He didn't think either Itet or Inkaef would do anything to her, but their servants or Khety's? It was impossible to be certain. Spies and malefactors multiplied like rabbits at court. Mereruka would know, as several of his were permanent fixtures there.

"And—"

Taisiya placed a finger on his lips.

"Hush. I'm not the one with the dangerous job."

Her look was censorious. Mereruka frowned. Itet wasn't a normal woman, and her alcohol tolerance was unnatural. But he felt better for having Bas accompany her.

"Kiss me for luck?" Mereruka asked.

Taisiya pulled him down to meet her lips. He held her close, slating his lips across hers, teasing her tongue with his own. It was a shame they'd been so busy with their schemes. He wouldn't have minded another chance to get reacquainted with his wife's cries of pleasure.

"We don't have all night. Also, ew, we're right here," Vasilisa complained as she gestured to herself and Bas.

Bas, at least, had the good manners to find something on the floor to be politely enthralled by.

Mereruka nipped Taisiya's lip before he released her, her eyes dark with desire. By the look of her, he was going to have to feed that pocket realm again. If Taisiya's hungry expression was anything to go by, he was going to be making regular use of it.

"Alright. Good luck, Meri. Vasilisa, protect him. Bas, with me," Taisiya said as she collected herself.

Taisiya turned, grabbing a sizeable amphora full of spirits. She left the cabin of the barge with a cat on her heels, on her way to Itet's lodgings in the Court of the Inundation.

Now, the unpleasant part.

Vasilisa gripped Mereruka's arm and gave him a crooked smile. An involuntary shiver ran down his spine.

"When Inkaef leaves his quarters, I'll bring us out of the void. Until then, try not to flail while we wait. It'll attract the hungry things."

Mereruka didn't trust himself to answer in any dignified manner to that statement. He swallowed convulsively and nodded. Without another word, Vasilisa dragged him into profound and total darkness.

Mereruka had not been exaggerating when he'd pronounced his sister's unnatural ability to consume alcohol. Much to her dismay, Taisiya learned this over the course of a liquor-soaked evening.

Taisiya knew she was in trouble when the spirits stopped burning her throat as she swallowed. Still, she soldiered on, pouring more into Itet's and Inkaef's cups. Thank the gods for Mereruka's spell, otherwise she had no doubt she would be passed out on the floor. Inkaef was already halfway asleep, but Itet was gamely chugging, her lime green hand clutching her tankard. The only good sign was that she was swaying unsteadily in her seat.

"These must be the waters of your Cursed Continent's Hapi." Itet swigged from her cup. "Gods, does that burn. So good."

Inkaef laughed merrily until he was snorting. He fell from his seat.

"Oh, hello kitty."

Inkaef had found Bas, seated beneath Taisiya's chair.

"Shit! No!" She heard his cries in her mind.

Bas hissed. Taisiya soon found out why. Inkaef pulled himself up off the floor with Bas in hand, stroking the shifter's fur and mumbling sweet nothings into his twitching ear. Inkaef's long black hair was a mess, tangled in his horns, though he seemed not to notice. Bas looked miserable in the way only a cat can.

"Pretty kitty," Itet cooed as she played with his tail.

"Help," Bas pleaded with Taisiya.

Only she could hear his mind-speak.

"I miss my cat," Inkaef sobbed. "She was so sweet."

"Inky..." Itet cooed as she patted her sobbing brother's shoulders. "You know, I still have all those outfits you made for her... before she got fat."

Inkaef wailed louder.

Damn, he might end this impromptu drinking party in his current state. Mereruka had yet to come to her rescue, which meant he needed more time. Taisiya looked at Bas and mentally apologised. Someone would have to be sacrificed for this plan to work.

"Why don't we dress this cat in those outfits? It would be fun," Taisiya said with a smile.

"Perfect! Inky, wait here." Itet launched out of her seat and fell to the floor with a guffaw. She weaved to and fro, bumping into furniture as she rummaged about in her grand apartment. Inkaef had finally regained a modicum of dignity, though he was still sniffling loudly.

When Itet returned with a haphazard assortment of clothes, Inkaef's face brightened as Bas' took on a murderous quality. Itet rummaged through the clothes and pulled out a studded, black leather harness that appeared much too large for a cat.

"Oops. That one's mine." Itet winked her sparkling blue eyes at Taisiya before tossing it aside.

Inkaef seemed entirely unfazed, his amber eyes content.

When Itet pulled out a particularly garish outfit, Inkaef gasped with delight. It was made of clashing puce and bright red fabric, decorated with too many bells to count. Even in her inebriated state, Taisiya knew the thing needed to be burned.

"I love that one!" Inkaef smiled.

"Taisiya, if you let them put that on me, I won't forgive you," Bas warned as he wriggled in Inkaef's hands.

"Awwwww," Taisiya cooed, shooting a look of censure at Bas and looking very pointedly at the goblet in her hand. If she could sacrifice her liver for the evening, Bas could sacrifice his dignity.

Bas stopped struggling and mewled pitifully.

Chapter 44

When Mereruka was finally brought out of the void, it took him a moment to remember he had limbs of his own. If he never entered that hellish place again, it would be too soon. Alas, the night was young and he was not so lucky. As he got used to the feeling of having hands, Vasilisa slapped him.

"Excuse me, but I think your hand slipped," Mereruka growled.

Vasilisa shrugged.

"Pain helps people situate after travelling through the void."

Mereruka raised a brow.

"And you slap Taisiya after she leaves the void?"

Vasilisa looked away, taking in the opulent room Inkaef lived in while he stayed in the palace, pointedly ignoring Mereruka as she bit back a smile.

"We should get inside that pocket realm," she said.

Mereruka flicked her forehead in retaliation. He let his magic fan out, sensing his way along the walls and furniture for a trace of something that felt uniquely like Inkaef. Before long, he approached the invisible magical barrier that signalled the location of a pocket realm. Anchored to a golden statue of a cat, it was left out in the open. It made the pocket realm easily portable. Smart. But was its obvious location out of carelessness, or an invitation to misery? He supposed he would find out either way. There was nothing to be done but enter it. Inkaef hadn't left his cartouche out in the open.

"Come along, and don't wander off. Some fae are prone to leaving traps inside their pocket realms."

Vasilisa nodded and followed him through the barrier. When they reached the other side, the realm within resembled a bright and airy house, decorated top to bottom with representations of a very fat cat. The scenery outdoors resembled that common to the delta, where Inkaef's nome lay.

"It's like wading through honey walking through that—good gods! Do you think he likes cats?" Vasilisa asked as she marvelled at the obscene quantity of feline depictions.

"No," Mereruka deadpanned.

Vasilisa grinned.

"So, where do we look?"

"In an obvious place." He lifted his chin at a nearby desk, decorated, unsurprisingly, with cat paraphernalia. The cartouche lay atop a mound of papyrus scrolls, carved into the gemstone of an oversized ring. Mereruka perused the litany of scrolls, but nothing caught his eyes save all the broken seals bearing the Vizier's cartouche. Serfka had buried Inkaef in bureaucratic nonsense. Mereruka almost pitied him. He reached for the ring, waiting with bated breath for some kind of spell to attack him. It never came. Was Inkaef really so sloppy as to not trap his realm?

Item in hand, the hard part awaited them.

The piercing sound of shattering pottery stopped Mereruka cold. He looked over his shoulder. Vasilisa swept a number of shards under a dresser.

"I swear, it looks better now." Vasilisa bit her lip.

"Gods below, woman, have you never robbed someone before?" Mereruka hissed.

"I've robbed plenty," she replied, defensive. "The statue was precariously positioned."

Mereruka rolled his eyes and prayed for patience. Inkaef was unlikely to notice a single broken statue, especially when he would be busy having a very bad day tomorrow. Still, it was evidence of an intrusion—one he couldn't even conceal.

"Why don't you just fix it with your magic?"

"It's never wise to use magic in someone else's realm. Even someone as unimaginative as Inkaef is smart enough to ward against such things. Let's go."

Vasilisa shrugged and followed Mereruka out of the pocket realm. He had only a single breath of freedom before Vasilisa pulled him into the void and through its disorienting darkness. The dim light of his rooms on the barge struck him as ungodly bright when he was free once more. Vasilisa raised her hand.

"Don't," Mereruka warned.

She sighed and walked away, returning shortly with a strand of hair. Inkaef's, and a vital component for this charade.

"Tie it around my wrist. The spell will slowly leech the colour from it. When it's turned pure white, our time is up. You remember what to do?" he asked as she tied the strand around his wrist.

Vasilisa hefted a large pot up on her shoulder and nodded.

"Fresh, sticky clay ready and waiting to cover over Khety's cartouches."

Mereruka nodded and pushed the complicated threads of the spell into the strand of hair. He kept the image of Inkaef in his mind's eye as he assumed the glamour.

"You look exactly like him, height and all. Have you actually shrunk, or am I looking at your chest without realizing it?" Vasilisa asked.

"Both," Mereruka answered with Inkaef's voice.

"That doesn't—"

"It's complicated. Take us through the void to the tribute barge as quickly as you can."

"Fine, fine." Vasilisa sighed before doing as he asked.

The end of this task couldn't come soon enough for Mereruka's liking. He closed his eyes as he slipped into the void once more.

Taisiya was undeniably drunk. Thankfully, so were Inkaef and Itet. While Inkaef was snoring into his cup, Itet vainly tried to coax Bas into coming down from the ledge, where he was vindictively swiping at vases and other trinkets from on high.

"Be a good kitty, or Itet will turn you into a pair of shoes," Itet said in a sing-song voice as she failed to catch Bas' latest victim. "Not the skull! Not the skull!" she pleaded as Bas taunted her, his paw slowly tilting the monstrous skull perched on the edge.

Dressed in a frilly pastel vest and decorated with several bows on his tail, Bas' dignity had set sail some time ago and sunk to the bottom of the ocean. Taisiya would've had an equally hard time being merciful in an outfit so hideous. After an hour of dress-up, Bas had given up being docile.

"Leave him be. He'll get bored," Taisiya slurred.

Itet was torn between Taisiya's suggestion and the potential loss of another trophy. She backed away from Bas and took her seat after a few failed attempts to stick the landing. Bas, for his part, seemed to cool down. He began furiously tugging the bows off his tail, shooting them murderous glares the whole while.

Itet poured herself the last of the spirits and drank them down. She looked over at Inkaef affectionately and patted his head. Whatever else she was, Itet was obviously fond of her twin. They were the only royal siblings Taisiya had seen who had any real fondness for one another.

"This was a nice evening. Think we all needed to loosen up. Losing Nefertnesu like that was bad, especially after what those Keftu bastards did to her. If it had been Inky..." Itet trailed off.

"How powerful are the heartless fae?" Taisiya asked.

Itet looked up, thinking, and then thought better of it. Swaying in her seat, she was forced to brace herself on the table.

"I'm not good with complicated magic. Not patient enough." She giggled. "But those creepy bastards? It's like Oblivion is at their fingertips." She snapped her fingers. "Build a palace? Boom! Done. Turn an army into frogs? Bye-bye army, hello plague of frogs!"

Taisiya shivered.

"Exactly!" Itet nodded. "Rather face a feral dragon."

"Feral dragon?" Taisiya asked.

"When they refuse to go two-legged and lose their minds, start eating people. There's a bunch of them mucking up some royal project or something." Itet waved a dismissive hand. "So what about you? Enjoying Maat?"

Taisiya nodded, though it made her head swim. She gripped the table for the support her body lacked.

"Most of it. Some of you are real assholes though."

Itet guffawed.

"I think I know whom you're speaking of." Itet giggled and put her fingers up by her head to mime an extra set of horns, "I'm a red shithead because no one will fuck my scaly ass. Grrrr," she snarled.

Taisiya howled with laughter. Encouraged, Itet grinned and began flapping her arms like wings and making clucking noises. Objectively, Taisiya shouldn't be laughing—the servants were present, after all—but the liquor was colouring her perception.

"*Oh, thank the gods,*" Bas grouched in her mind.

Taisiya turned her head and fell out of her seat to Itet's peals of laughter. Taisiya looked up to see Mereruka. Well, several of him.

"Meri, what are you doing up there?" Taisiya asked.

"I think it's past time I came to collect you, wife," he answered.

Mereruka bent down to lift her, the ascent making her dizzy.

"Boo! The night is young!" Itet complained.

"Goodnight, Itet," Mereruka replied as he turned away with Taisiya in his arms.

"Come by to drink again any time, Princess Consort!" Itet called and waved.

Taisiya woke when Mereruka put her down on their bed. Dizziness overwhelmed her. She squinted up, surprised and pleased to find she now had several more husbands, each as handsome and blurry as the last.

"Didn't the five of you leave here with a pair of earrings?" she asked.

His horrified expression as he reached up to his bare ear was the last thing she saw before sleep took her.

Chapter 45

"Are you repenting your excesses yet, wife?" Mereruka purred in her ear.

"Leisurely," Taisiya hissed.

Maat's sun was brighter today, she was certain. Her head was heavy and pounding, her stomach still roiling from the night before. The jubilant cries of the crowd made her eyes water. Yet there would be no reprieve. She and Mereruka sat dressed in all their finery in the ceremonial procession, their spacious palanquin carried on the backs of radiant summoned beasts. Itet and Inkaef shared the palanquin ahead, and while Inkaef appeared worse for wear, Itet was making jokes and waving excitedly to the crowd. Naturally, Khety and Betrest sat in the front of the procession, their conveyance the most ostentatious of the lot. Servants handed out bread and beer to the gathered throngs while soldiers guarded the tribute and royalty alike.

"Did everything go smoothly last night?" Taisiya asked.

"Mostly. Vasilisa broke a small sculpture, and I seem to have misplaced an earring during the course of the evening," Mereruka replied.

He was one of the very few fae she'd seen who had his pierced. Most wore jewellery that hooked onto the tops of their ears, or none at all, favouring elaborate headdresses instead. Given how sensitive they were, she imagined piercing them was exceedingly painful.

"Why *did* you pierce your ears?"

"The enchantments, of course. Objects made as a pair have a natural resonance with each other. Perfect for surreptitious tracking, if the spell is already embedded. Like when I followed your family to the graveyard after your sister's wedding." He winked.

"You *what?!*"

"Hush, love. It was simple curiosity." He smiled and touched a teal finger to her painted lips.

"I *knew* you seemed too blasé when I brought you there to make your oaths," Taisiya grouched.

"It was all very impressive, I promise."

Taisiya pinched Mereruka below the ribs.

"Cruel," he grunted.

"Sneak-thief," she retorted.

"Drunkard."

The nerve of this man. She would never have been so immoderate had it not been necessary. He'd earned himself another pinch.

"Royal prick."

He chuckled.

"You like my royal prick," he whispered.

"It's alright." Taisiya shrugged.

"That sounds like a challenge, wife."

"If it does, then you'd best rise to meet it." She grinned.

Mereruka howled with laughter.

"Gods below, was that innuendo—from you? Next, it will rain in Maat."

"It... it doesn't rain here?" Taisiya asked, shocked.

She was well aware it was a desert, and she knew about them in theory, but Maat had the first one she'd been intimately acquainted with. Surely it rained here sometimes, even if those times were rare?

Mereruka shook his head.

"Ever?"

"No. Never. Sandstorms, certainly, but not rain."

"That's unnatural."

"Rain would be unnatural," Mereruka snorted. "Well, outside the coastal areas, that is. Even there, it's rare."

Before Taisiya could reply, the procession slowed and everyone was entreated to disembark. They descended from the palanquin and into the searing brightness of the daylight. Thank the gods her charm allowed her the comfort of a familiar temperature. Taisiya suspected she might have embarrassed herself by fainting in the heat of such a day otherwise.

As they crossed the dividing line between the rich black soil and the parched golden sands, they came upon a strangely humble outcropping of monoliths arranged in a circle. It was less impressive than Taisiya had expected, given the pomp of the previous journey. But as she grew closer to it, a strange feeling wormed its way into her. The cries of the crowd grew dim in her ears, replaced by a quiet as heavy as it was expectant. A weighty, ancient magic surrounded her, making her feel as small as a grain of sand and even less significant. The forgotten gods lay here.

The crowds of onlookers were a way off, forbidden from venturing past the stark, fertile boundary, and only nobles and bureaucrats remained to witness the spectacle at a respectful distance. Taisiya was not unfamiliar with the process of praying and giving tribute to the forgotten gods, but she'd never seen it on such a scale, nor been crushed by the elusive presence of the divine.

Inkaef was busy directing broad-shouldered servants to place the tribute before Khety. No one had paid much attention to the new seals. Taisiya began worrying that their little stunt would go entirely unnoticed.

She needn't have.

Menace rolled off Khety in waves as he stormed towards the tribute. If looks could kill, Inkaef would have been torn to bloody pieces by the icy blue of the king's glare. Itet picked up on the threat first, positioning herself to protect her unwary twin.

"Inkaef!" Khety commanded.

Inkaef looked up from his task, shock and terror evident. The courtiers in attendance held their collective breath. Inkaef approached Khety slowly, Itet following closely behind.

With unthinkable speed, Khety grabbed hold of one of Inkaef's horns and dragged him towards the tribute. Tossing him to the hard-packed sand at his avian feet, he pointed an accusing taloned finger at an amphora. Itet protested, but Khety silenced her with a look, his white hair whipping violently as he turned his head.

"What in the hells is this?"

Betrest was closest, and even her perfect mask slipped to reveal her shock, like a golden, green-haired statue captured by a talented sculptor. Serfka and Radjedef approached next. The blue-skinned vizier covered a gasp with a hand while Radjedef blinked owlishly, like he couldn't believe his eyes. Taisiya and Mereruka approached, her hand on his arm and lightning humming beneath her skin. They both gasped at the sight, eyeing Inkaef with practised alarm.

"I-I don't... This can't..." Inkaef stuttered as he trembled.

"What is the meaning of this, Inkaef?" Khety growled.

Itet rushed forward and gasped at the sight of the cartouches.

"This must be a mistake! Inkaef would never—" she began.

"Silence! Inkaef will answer for this himself." Khety cut her off, his glare arctic.

The brown feathers of Khety's wings were slightly raised, like the hackles of a dog, making them appear twice as large. Taisiya noted with some humour that pointed ears twitched with emotion all around. How delightful.

"I don't know how this happened," Inkaef pleaded.

"Is this not the mark of your official cartouche? Yet you plead ignorance and incompetence! Radjedef!"

"Yes, Your Eternal Serenity?" Radjedef appeared at Khety's side in an instant, ever the loyal dog.

And yet Khety had never appeared less serene in the whole time she'd known him. By now, even the crowds had caught the dangerous mood brewing by the ancient circle. Jubilant cries turned to fearful murmurs.

"Confine this fool to quarters. I will deal with him shortly. Serfka!"

Radjedef led a shell-shocked Inkaef off with a few soldiers at his side.

"Yes?" Serfka approached.

"Take over the duties of the overseer of king's tribute and remove the seals. I shall dedicate this in the old way."

Itet went a few shades paler than her usual lime green. She stepped aside as Serfka ordered the servants about, her fists trembling at her side as she watched Inkaef disappear into the crowds. The nobles present wisely kept their whispers and sidelong glances hidden from Khety's furious gaze and sharp ears. Taisiya and Mereruka kept their expressions stony and grim.

The tainted seals were gathered and disposed of with alacrity. Khety approached the tribute once more, failing to hide the fury in his curt, sharp movements. In the light of day, he appeared radiant, dressed in glittering gold and bright blue to set off his bright orange skin and complement the warm brown of his feathers. Now, it only made him stand out all the more, his pique at the insult visible to all.

"To the gods, forgotten by foolish mortals, I beseech you, in the name of King Khety of Maat, to bestow your favour upon me. Grant me this as you granted our ancestors your boundless world, Oblivion, formed from your decaying souls, and rise from obscurity," he pronounced.

The tribute sank into the ground and vanished between breaths, accepted by the gods below. Taisiya, Mereruka and the rest knelt before Khety and raised their hands up towards him.

"May the forgotten gods see fit to remember you," they chanted in unison.

Khety and Betrest were the first to leave in their palanquin. The rest of the royal family left in accordance with their birth order. Itet was shaking, her blue eyes faraway as she was ushered into her conveyance. Mereruka and Taisiya were last.

Khety's world was turning on its head. A formerly servile brother had conspired to publicly embarrass him. Once-adoring crowds whispered warily as he passed. His all-powerful façade was crumbling around his pointed, twitching ears. Basking in the confusion of the fearful, rumbling crowds, Taisiya squeezed Mereruka's hand and suppressed a smile.

"I believe that was a success," she whispered.

"Only time will tell, but I doubt we'll wait long to find out." Mereruka winked.

CHAPTER 46

Mereruka could count on one hand the number of feasts he'd attended that rivalled this awkward, stilted atmosphere. Everyone was simply waiting for Khety to stop stewing on his obvious fury and explode. Hemetre was gamely plying him with wine and whispering sweet nothings into his ears, much to everyone's relief. Not even Betrest seemed to begrudge the woman her valiant attempts at fawning and flattery. Sadly, Her Most Treasured was simply delaying the inevitable.

As Itet eyed the armed guards mutinously, Queen Betrest was doing her level best to have a civilized conversation with Serfka seated nearby, discussing one project or another. But no amount of glamour could hide the strain in their voices, nor the thin veneer of good humour. Hot-headed Radjedef was uncharacteristically quiet, pushing food around on his plate in time to the tune being played by the musicians in the nearby courtyard.

Mereruka, for his part, was readying a few spells of his own under the table while Taisiya kept her lightning humming beneath her skin. If there were to be a fight this night, they planned to win. Mereruka only hoped Itet would be the one to kill Khety and distract the guards. It would make ascending the throne that much easier.

As Khety swallowed his wine, Hemetre whispered something in his ear and petted his arm to soothe him. But it seemed he'd had enough of her cooing. Khety shoved her to the ground as he stood, throwing his silver chalice in a rage, wine splattering the smooth, painted floors and Hemetre's shocked face.

"Radjedef, bring him here! I'm ready to sentence that bastard!" Khety commanded.

Radjedef was gone in an instant, relief plain. Itet clutched the arms of her chair, eyes wide. Betrest and Serfka stopped mid-sentence, waiting with obvious trepidation.

It was a pleasing sight. Mereruka revelled in their discomfort. Let them marinate in their fear and uncertainty. For decades, they'd tolerated Khety's petty indignities towards him with nary a word in his defence. And when Nefertnesu had needed them, they'd turned their backs on her as well as his pleas on her behalf. They deserved to feel as powerless as he had, forced to watch as he terrorized them all. It would soften them towards a change in leadership when the time finally came. Let Khety become a true tyrant in their minds, and not just his.

Radjedef returned with Inkaef in tow. Inkaef immediately went to grovel before the king.

"Please show mercy, brother! I have wronged you, but not out of malice or with intent. I shall swear upon my name that I had no knowledge of what happened to the tribute!" Inkaef pleaded, his amber eyes tearing up.

Khety set upon him, grabbing him by his horn and dragging him from the feasting room and into the nearby courtyard. The musicians scattered.

"Get out!" he snarled, waiting until only the sounds of Inkaef's ragged breaths could be heard in the silence that followed. "Fear not, brother. I will show you all the mercy you deserve for this embarrassment."

"Please, don't hurt him!" Itet rushed to her twin's side and fell to her knees to beg.

Khety turned on her, his furious blue gaze meeting her pleading one.

"You think Maat is governed by council, sister? When have I ever needed your input to rule my realm?" he hissed.

"Please, whatever punishment, I will share it," she said, tears in her eyes. "It was I who goaded him into drinking with me last night. This wouldn't have happened if I hadn't."

"No!" Inkaef gasped. "No, the fault was mine, only mine. Itet had no part in it."

"Radjedef, hold her down." Khety pointed his talon at Itet.

Radjedef hesitated. Khety snarled at his split-second delay, lashing out with a strand of magic and tying Itet tight.

"Useless!" he screamed at Radjedef.

Radjedef flinched, eyes on the floor as his fists clenched.

"What is your sentence, Your Eternal Serenity?" Serfka asked calmly.

"He shall take the mark of disinheritance," Khety said smoothly. He jutted his chin out at Radjedef, who took a proffered blade from one of his soldiers.

Inkaef looked mortified but kept his cries of pain to a minimum as Radjedef carved the mark upon his forehead. The rune ensured the skin scarred and that the scar remained impossible to conceal, even with the best of glamours. Itet wept with relief. But this was not the end. Khety was far too calm given his former fury. Perhaps Khety would make Itet take the mark too, out of spite alone. Rage still visibly boiled within the king. He still needed an outlet. Hopefully, Itet's tears would prevent him from seeking it elsewhere. Taisiya looked to Mereruka, a question in her eyes. He shook his head. Whatever this spectacle was, it wasn't over and it wasn't yet time to strike.

"You will be stripped of your title, lands and responsibilities, Inkaef. From this moment, you are no brother of mine, you are a commoner of Maat."

"Thank you for your mercy, King Khety." Inkaef spoke the words, his voice hollow as bright red blood ran down his green face and dripped onto his dirtied finery.

It was a harsh punishment, but just shy of what Mereruka had hoped for.

"Vizier!" Khety called.

"Yes, King Khety?" Serfka asked, wary.

"What is the official punishment for a commoner who dares to insult the king of Maat?"

Betrest gasped with shock. Itet stilled in her magical bonds, her hollow, unseeing eyes meeting her twin's.

"Be ready," Mereruka whispered to Taisiya in the mage tongue.

She nodded.

"No! No! Please! Please don't, Khety!" Itet lunged forward, throwing herself in front of Inkaef in spite of her bonds.

"Silence!" Khety shouted, another strand of his magic gagging Itet. Her muffled pleas and sobbing continued. "Vizier?" Khety asked, menace in his tone.

Serfka paled, but cleared his throat in preparation to answer. Servile coward. They really were just going to watch as Khety stained his hands with the blood of another sibling. Only Itet had been moved to beg for clemency.

"The punishment is death."

The second the words left the Vizier's lips, Khety unfolded his wings, doubling their length, and struck Inkaef with a spell. Taisiya gripped Mereruka's arm tight as the spell dissolved Inkaef before their eyes. When the gruesome ordeal was done, Inkaef was a bleating, green-haired goat. Khety grabbed hold of Inkaef in his raptor's feet, puncturing flesh and raining blood down as he took off into the sky, soaring high with the powerful thrust of his wings and a potent updraft created by his magic. Itet screamed behind her gag, thrashing in her bonds. Khety circled overhead for a moment, Inkaef flailing in his grasp. He tore one limb from Inkaef, then another, each raining blood and gore down from above as they splattered in the courtyard below. Finally, he released the transformed, bleating fae to the pull of gravity. Itet screamed and screamed as Inkaef fell and fell, until at last he struck the ground.

Betrest stumbled away from the sight, her hand at her mouth as she suppressed a gag. Serfka's shock rooted him to the spot as all four of his hands hung limp at his sides. Itet cried and screamed as she crawled over to Inkaef's bloody, broken form despite her restraints. Radjedef rubbed a shaking, scaly hand over his face, his eyes riveted to the broken corpse. When Khety landed in the courtyard and folded his great brown wings, he looked pleased at last, as if the dark spell of his anger had finally dissipated.

"Radjedef, have Itet escorted out. She's ruining the mood."

Radjedef snapped his fingers and several men dragged Itet away. Servants were already cleaning up what had become of Inkaef. Khety swaggered over to his seat and sat down to his meal. Woodenly, everyone else did the same. Though now it was less a feast than a hostage-taking. Hemetre, the pink petals of her hair quivering, filled Khety's cup once more with wine and whispered sweetly in his ear. Mereruka was almost impressed by her fortitude.

When he was finishing drinking his cup dry and signalling for another, Khety spoke into the silence in the room.

"I think it goes without saying that this year's tribute has left me feeling... unimpressed. Princess Consort Taisiya?"

When Khety turned his wily grin on Taisiya, Mereruka stiffened. Would today be the one he finally killed Khety? Most of the guards had left the room, escorting Itet out. The rest of his siblings were in various states of shock. They would be slow to react. They might not even complain overmuch, given Khety's bloodthirsty display.

"Yes, King Khety?" Taisiya asked. Her voice belied none of her fear or trepidation. Beneath the table, Mereruka could feel her thigh quivering.

"What did you contribute to this year's tribute?"

Taisiya paused. The wary eyes of the royal family turned entirely to Taisiya, as if wondering what manner of death the king would bestow next.

"I left such details up to the first scribe of my nome, Your Eternal Serenity," she answered.

Khety was quiet, but only for a moment.

"Regardless, it was tainted by that criminal's actions. It would please me if you would find something wondrous to replace it."

"And what does the king of Maat find wondrous?" Taisiya asked.

Mereruka waited with his heart in his throat. It was good she hadn't fallen into the trap of agreeing immediately to find such a thing for Khety, for she would have failed no matter the object. Mereruka's hand on her thigh, he ran a soothing thumb along the gauzy gown that covered it.

"Dragon scales," he answered. "The larger and more luminous, the better. Bring me dragon scales, and I will forgive you for not selecting the tribute yourself," Khety said as he sat back in his seat, pleased at his little trap.

"How many would you like, and how large?" Taisiya asked. "I ask because I have never seen a living dragon or its scales for myself."

Khety frowned. Taisiya had defeated his ploy once more.

"Fifty. As big as my head. And not a scratch on them," he answered. "Serfka?"

"Yes?" Serfka asked.

"Where was it that our workmen were having trouble?"

Serfka's eyes filled with pity and dread.

"Along the proposed route of the Ruby Sea canal. A number of feral dragons were reportedly roaming there."

Mereruka kept his face neutral and his lips shut as he called Khety every filthy, vile name he knew in his mind. It was a gods-damned death sentence. It seemed the king felt rather liberal with them this day.

"There should be plenty of scales in the vicinity. Radjedef, you should escort the princess consort on her journey. We wouldn't want her first experience with a dragon to be a tragic one. And Mereruka, you should join your wife. Naturally, a newlywed couple shouldn't be separated."

"Naturally," Mereruka replied.

Khety was under the delusion that Mereruka and Taisiya's lives were joined by the vows of their marriage. Aiming at Taisiya's more fragile life was his blatant attempt to kill them both. Would anyone question his motives when he finally slew that hateful man?

"It would be my honour," Radjedef replied.

Ah, and Radjedef would pay for his moment of conscience. Khety expected Radjedef to return with the good news that both Mereruka and Taisiya were tragically eaten, and going by Radjedef's defeated expression, he well knew it. By the looks of everyone else present, they, too, suspected the purity of the king's motives.

"I shall do my utmost to return with the dragon scales you desire." Taisiya bowed her head.

"Then swear to it, Princess Consort. I have no patience for those who fail me."

Mereruka's heart nearly stopped. He couldn't prevent her from swearing to it and keep up this ruse. Before he could open his mouth to object, Taisiya gripped his hand under the table.

"I so swear, Your Eternal Serenity."

It was as good as a deal. Taisiya must have felt it too, her grip tightening a second later as the magic sank into her bones. Khety looked directly at Mereruka, triumph in his icy blue gaze and a smirk on his face.

"Best of luck."

Chapter 47

"He's going to try to kill us," Taisiya sighed as she slumped into her seat.

Seated on their barge, the soldiers were already hard at work, provisioning them for their lethal voyage. Khety had given them little time to prepare, insisting that they leave immediately. It would take a day or so to reach their destination. Then, it would likely be a wholesale slaughter, conveniently out of sight of the palace and general populace.

She declined the glass of wine Mereruka offered her. Just because she had been able to stand the sight of violence and bloodshed without throwing up didn't mean she could stomach food or drink. The banquet feast, which had started off tense enough to cause indigestion, had become a veritable buffet of horrors. Wine had become blood raining down from the heavens; platters of meat, the gore-strewn courtyard. Even now, the sound of the servants scraping up the remains, the slap of rags on the stone floors erasing the stains, the memories alone made her gorge rise. Inkaef's fall and the silencing of his bleating wouldn't leave her mind. Another nightmare. Taisiya shivered.

Mereruka, face impassive, sat across from her and picked up his wine glass.

"Yes, he will," he answered calmly.

The game had shifted that afternoon. Shadowy, underhanded tactics had been cast aside in favour of unconcealed boldness. There could be no question in anyone's mind now that the king wished them dead. Inkaef's death was a blow. There would be no way to win Itet to their side now, and so his death had stolen two potential allies to their cause. She'd held no ill will towards the calm, amiable Inkaef, nor the bold, ribald Itet. They could have eventually become friends. Now, all that was lost.

"It was good of him to make it so blatant. We need to capitalise on this as best we can. I want everyone whispering that the king has truly been cursed—killing one brother and then demanding another face feral dragons. By the time we return, we'll have people wishing someone would take Khety's head."

"Oh, trust me, I suspect those whispers have already reached the courtiers. The palace servants are notorious for gossip." Mereruka smiled.

"I must say, I'm finding it hard to believe he ever outwitted you. Overpowered, perhaps. But those were not the actions of a shrewd man."

They were the actions of a tyrant who'd lost all sense of subtlety, brandishing unchecked power like a cudgel and solving all their problems with brute force. In fact, Khety was acting much more like Radjedef than the wily opponent Mereruka had made him out to be. Had her husband been overestimating his opponent all this time?

"He's changed..." Mereruka began.

"How?"

He ran a hand through his hair, frowning, as if he too couldn't quite believe what had become of his foe.

"I've never seen him act so rashly. If something foul needed doing, he was the soul of discretion and caution. He never started fights he wasn't absolutely certain he would win. This change of his makes me wonder if he really was cursed in my absence."

"Wouldn't he be protected from such things?"

"Yes." Mereruka sighed, tapping the arm of his chair in contemplation. "We'll need to be ready to kill Radjedef. We can worry about Khety when we get back from this latest death sentence. He sent us out there to die quietly, where all witnesses to the fact could be silenced, but that means the same fate can befall my brother."

"Surely we'll need to prepare for battle? Radjedef will be bringing soldiers along with him, won't he?" Taisiya asked.

"Yes, as will we, though my best is currently on his way to Keftu." Mereruka groaned.

Radjedef wasn't the issue. One man against all their combined might could easily be felled. But the royal guard? That presented some problems. There had to be a better way to deal with Radjedef than a full-frontal assault, one that would prevent him from using those same soldiers.

"Does Radjedef care for anyone?"

Mereruka blinked in surprise.

"Not that anyone is aware of. I can't imagine someone wanting to be in his obnoxious presence long enough to form an attachment, can you?"

"A wealthy prince with the power of the military behind him, and not a single partner? Personality aside, someone out there must be ambitious enough to put up with him," Taisiya mused. "Vasilisa?"

Vasilisa stepped from a nearby shadow.

"Shall I spy on him?" she asked.

Taisiya nodded.

"If he has anyone significant, take them and put them somewhere in the void for safekeeping. It will give us bargaining power."

"Can I do it dramatically?" Vasilisa asked with a sly grin.

"If they scream as you drag them away, I won't complain." Taisiya smiled back. She turned to Mereruka. "Any objections?"

"None." He grinned. "Good hunting, Vasilisa."

As soon as Vasilisa was gone, Mereruka's expression turned grim once more.

"What is it?" Taisiya asked.

"My lost earring...I'm concerned it will come back to bite us. I'm certain now that I lost it while Vasilisa and I were on our little mission. And I can't risk using the magic connecting the two, lest someone notices and then tracks it back to me. Bas?"

"Yes?" Bas asked once he returned to his two-legged form.

"I'm afraid there's no good excuse for a cat to be in the desert. Will you dispose of my earring discreetly and then recover the missing one? We can't afford to have this sort of loose end, and there's no one else I trust enough for this task," Mereruka explained.

Bas scowled.

"You're going up against that bastard *and* his soldiers and you want me to pretend to be a cat here at the palace?! I should be by your side in the desert!"

Mereruka shook his head, unmoved.

"And if Khety finds the earring, he'll have an actual reason to see to it that I share Inkaef's fate. A reason most of Maat would rally behind—tampering with Oblivion's tithe is a threat to the order of the kingdom. I would be fighting him at a political disadvantage."

Bas narrowed his eyes at Mereruka, ears flattened on his head while his tail swayed, agitated.

"You don't need to protect me. I could be useful in the desert."

"But I *want* you here, tying up loose ends and keeping an eye on the goings on of the palace. We can't afford to be blindsided by another of my brother's outrageous demands." Mereruka remained obstinate.

Bas bit his lip. Taisiya could understand not wanting to be left behind, but knew they couldn't afford to return to the palace unaware of Khety's newest schemes. At the rate the two of them were going, though, her husband and son would end up parting ways on bad terms.

"No one else is welcome everywhere in the palace. Without Nofret or Qar, the role of spy falls to you, Bas. It's what you've trained for, and my lightning is faster than any spell, rest assured." Taisiya did her best to smooth Bas' frustration.

"Radjedef is strong and fast. He could easily kill you." Bas' hands fisted at his side as he looked to his feet.

"Which is why Vasilisa is trying to find his weakness," Mereruka replied, his citrine eyes never wavering. "If you want to be more than just my son, you must learn to do as I say, even when you don't want to."

"Fine!" Bas hissed before turning to smoke and, as a cat, leaping from the opened window with a last, backward, baleful glare.

"Did you have to be so harsh?" Taisiya asked.

Mereruka sighed and slumped in his seat.

"Yes. If Radjedef even got a hint that I love Bas, as a young man or a cat, he wouldn't hesitate to gut him just to hurt me. Bas can't hide in the void to avoid my brother, and if anything were to happen to us, I want him away from the danger as much as possible."

Mereruka's eyes were haunted. Taisiya didn't see the danger with Radjedef, even if they were unable to find a weakness, per se. He was an easily riled hothead who would take the first opportunity to strike. Master manipulator and cunning foe, he was not. The second that scaly, red lizard of a man drew a sword or readied a spell, Taisiya would put a bolt of lightning into him and gladly. Personally, she was more concerned about the royal guard and potential dragon attacks.

Taisiya playfully kicked his shin under the table.

"So, you'll keep your son safe from danger, but not your wife?"

Mereruka's eyes widened with shock and guilt. He reached across the table to take hold of her hands.

"I never—"

"Hush!" Taisiya grinned, pressing a finger to his lips. "It was meant in jest."

Mereruka frowned.

"Not funny."

Taisiya shrugged.

"That's just your opinion."

Mereruka's expression turned solemn, focusing on her hand in his, tracing the lines of her palm.

"If I could keep you completely safe, I would."

"Meri?"

"Hm?" He looked up.

"There's nothing safe about what we're doing, or what we want."

"You have a wonderful way of calming my nerves, wife." He scowled.

Taisiya chuckled. Watching as he memorized every line of her hand and every detail of her fingers, she could see that he was lost in his own little world. Sometimes she suspected that he craved the feel of her simply to reassure himself that she was alive. Sometimes, in the night, she did the same. If life had taught her anything, it was that everything could change in an instant and that the people she loved could die far too easily.

"Write a letter for Bas, so that you can return from this on good terms. Then come to bed for a few hours, Meri," she beckoned, rising from her seat to stand before him. His eyes were filled with uncertainty. Running her fingers through his hair, she kissed his head. "Neither of us will get much of a chance to sleep properly for the next couple of days. Radjedef and this little suicide mission can wait for a few hours at least."

"I can think of other things I'd rather do." He pulled her into his lap and wrapped his arms around her.

"And you can do them all," she whispered in his ear, "as a reward for when we return safely. We need to be at our best, and I suspect you'd want to keep me up all night."

Mereruka chuckled and leaned his head against her collarbone, his breaths fanning out across her chest.

"Cruel."

"Effective."

Mereruka laughed in earnest at that. When he looked up at her, he was smiling, the shadows banished for a short time. Success.

"I have no counter to that."

"Then you're losing your touch. You know what would help?"

"Sleep?"

She kissed his forehead.

"Precisely."

Chapter 48

A day into their ill-fated journey, someone sabotaged the barge. As it lay tethered in the night, some malefactor pulverized enough of the floating stones to cause it to fall to its side, irreparably damaging it and wounding several. Mereruka had exited his pocket realm that morning and plummeted into the opposing wall. Thankfully, he'd had the wherewithal to turn around and cushion his wife's inevitable fall using his magic. Forced to go the rest of the way on summoned beasts, and send his wounded back to repair the barge, tensions were riding high.

Fewer than half of the men and women on this suicide mission came from Mereruka's household. While his soldiers were loyal and well-trained, they didn't have access to the very best weapons, armour or spells that Khety could afford to lavish on his military force. Taisiya sat beside Mereruka but was careful not to touch him, lest she need to use her lightning at a moment's notice.

"Our only hope is to isolate him entirely," Taisiya whispered.

Mereruka grunted his agreement. Indeed, Vasilisa had been unable to locate a friend or lover important enough to Radjedef that he might waver in following the king's orders. Vasilisa refused to give up, and was shadowing Radjedef without his knowledge even now. If need be, they could still have him dragged into the void in the dead of night or in the middle of a confrontation with a feral dragon.

Mereruka sat beside Taisiya, both in their travelling clothes and shoes, safely and comfortably ensconced inside a palanquin carried by a summoned beast. It took an effort of willpower not to smirk whenever he saw it, for Taisiya had been the one to insist that the creature resemble Radjedef perfectly in the hue and texture of his red, scaly skin. The resemblance had not been lost on Radjedef or his men, and his brother had summoned a creature with Mereruka's colouring in retaliation. The difference was that Mereruka could take a joke.

As a rule, the convoy travelled quietly. Dragons came in all shapes and sizes, and there was no sense in attracting the attention of a ground-dwelling one with undue noise.

"You see a dragon, you strike Radjedef first, then call Vasilisa. We'll hide in the void until the creature has sated its hunger on his soldiers," Mereruka said.

"And what of our soldiers?" she asked, brow raised.

"They have their orders—protect us first, then retreat. And none of mine are foolish enough to try their luck against a dragon," Mereruka answered.

Mereruka looked out to his men and women atop their beasts in the bright light of morning, their scaled armour glinting and their eyes constantly scanning the horizon. They had travelled through the night, but were unfazed. All around was the hard-packed, reddish gold sand of the desert, for they'd left the rich, verdant black of the inundation zone some time ago. Stark, dry cliffs and parched valleys greeted them as they marched along the proposed route of the canal to the sea far beyond. It wouldn't be long before they stopped for mid-day. No sane person travelled or worked in such heat, but it would also mean they would rest right on the edge of the safe zone.

Taisiya's hand gripped his thigh. Haunted amethyst eyes met his own.

"Do you hear that?"

Mereruka's ears twitched as he concentrated on the sounds around him—the breaths of the beast, the dull thud of its reptilian paws on the path, the clink of weapons against armour, the faint sound of the wind through the empty valleys, the disgruntled whispers of his people. He shook his head, certain none of those things were what his wife was speaking of.

"There must be a graveyard nearby," she whispered. "I can hear their hearts." Her breath hitched and her hands fisted.

Mereruka swore under his breath. No wonder the dragons were so fierce in these parts. Dragon graveyards drew feral and civil dragons alike. That damned canal Betrest was so keen on would never be built. Travelling further into the desert would get everyone killed. Mereruka ordered one of his soldiers over to call a halt to the day's march. He leaned over to Taisiya and whispered in her ear.

"Say nothing of the hearts to anyone. How many do you hear? How close?"

She shook her head.

"There are too many songs for me to count, but we're close, probably on top of a few right now."

His next words were cut off as Radjedef, atop his summoned horse of teal and violet, raced towards him with a scowl on his face.

"What are you doing, calling a halt? Is the heat too much for your fragile wife?" Radjedef sneered.

"I'm certain we can find dragons scales right here," Mereruka replied.

A dragon's graveyard all but guaranteed that the scales, which were nearly impervious to rot, would be found in abundance where they stood. Radjedef was unconvinced.

"Are you a coward, too afraid of venturing deeper into the desert?" he goaded.

"Are you a fool, with no sense of responsibility for the lives of your soldiers?" Taisiya shot back, her voice carrying far.

If Radjedef could flush noticeably, he might have done so at that moment.

"Tell your wife to watch her tongue! I am the overseer of the royal guard, and am here as a courtesy extended to you by King Khety!"

"Then as a courtesy, halt the march. When the heat of midday has gone, we can search the area for scales," Mereruka replied, sounding as reasonable as possible.

This was a game he did so enjoy playing. Winding up the predictable Radjedef and then taking advantage of his outburst to appear the wise and cool-headed younger brother was always a treat. In all his centuries, Radjedef had never succeeded in mastering his own temper or reflecting on his shortcomings.

Radjedef's scowl deepened as he took in the trepidation of his soldiers. They were well-trained and battle-hardened, but they were not ignorant of the dangers of venturing further. While respected for his strength and battle prowess, it would dent his reputation among them if Radjedef ordered them to be more reckless than this, king's orders or not.

"Halt!" he called out as he raced back towards the front of the convoy.

"Well, that was easier than I thought it would be." Taisiya smirked.

"Expect some petty retaliation in the least."

"Such an immature man. One would think that a few centuries would give him time to grow up."

Mereruka laughed.

"I think you will find it greatly disappointing to learn that age and wisdom only rarely go hand-in-hand. Be it a century or a decade, a lost cause will always be a lost cause."

Taisiya's smile was forced and stiff. Her eyes wandered over the landscape, glazing over. Was she as drawn to the hearts of dragons as other dragons were? He placed a hand on hers.

"Don't answer their call, Taisiya."

"I know... it's just... difficult."

The yearning in her eyes chilled him. He was greatly regretting telling Bas to sit this mission out. With his most trusted allies scattered, he would have to rely on his soldiers to keep his wife from harm in the event of a confrontation.

A plaintive, discordant hum rang out across the desert, tormenting Taisiya alone. While the resonance of her family graveyard had been soothing to the marrow, this place was enchanting yet wrong, leaving her heart aching. She could barely remember to eat the food placed before her, so distracted she'd become. No matter how hard she tried to focus, reminding herself of the dangers present, those melodies drew her to drink them in, to simply close her eyes and lie down beside them in a fitful sleep.

The soldiers were by now busy digging in the sands and thankfully finding dragon scales regularly. Radjedef had set his own camp in the distance, his soldiers no more than hazy smudges against the hard-packed sand and rock. Khety's schemes would be thwarted soon enough, she hoped, her soul freed from both the bonds of his magic and the music of this place. It would be best not to be caught out here again.

"Taisiya!"

She jumped. Mereruka's citrine eyes held only concern. He reached out his hand and brushed her cheek.

"You haven't heard anything I've said."

"I'm afraid not."

Mereruka sighed.

"Stay here. I'll leave a few soldiers with you. It seems my brother has decided to confiscate our scales for his soldiers' target practice. I'll return shortly."

"Meri!" Taisiya gasped.

It was likely a trap. She needed to be there with him.

"I'll go with you."

"No, you will not. I can already see your attention drifting."

He was right. She could barely keep her eyes on his face.

"But he might—"

"I'm aware, which is why my soldiers will be there with me."

Taisiya gripped the fabric of her dress as her brows drew together.

"Take Vasilisa with you."

Mereruka nodded.

"Vasilisa?"

"I'll have his back," the darkness mage replied from the shadows.

Taisiya sighed in relief.

"I'm sorry."

So much for being a key player here. She might as well be dead weight, adding complications instead of dealing with them. If anything happened, would she have the wherewithal to defend herself? Mereruka pressed his lips to her cheek and grinned, dragging her back.

"I can handle my brother."

He quickly became an indistinct outline in the distance atop his summoned beast, approaching and then stopping at the enemy camp. Taisiya fought the pull of the melodies to stay focused on him. And yet her eyes and mind wandered. She tightened her fists until her nails bit painfully into her palms. This was nearly as bad as Nefertnesu's spell, robbing her of her ability to think clearly.

Mind drifting once more, an unnatural screech hit her like a gut punch. Taisiya jumped in her seat. The soldiers regarded her with concern.

Had only she heard it? The screech ended in an instant. Taisiya tried to keep her breathing even and her expression placid despite her terror and uncertainty. Something was wrong. What had that awful sound been? Was it connected to the hearts buried in the sand and rock?

Another heart-stopping screech, this one closer and more piercing than the last, had her reeling, her hands on her ears as the ground beneath her rumbled. The soldiers took out their weapons.

"Protect the princess consort!"

"What is—"

"A dragon! Please, escape with your attendant, Princess Consort!"

Taisiya's heart fell into her stomach.

"I can't! She's with Meri!"

"I'll take to the skies with her. Pray this dragon does not fly!"

Taisiya accepted the hand of the soldier closest as he summoned a winged beast. She was barely seated in front of him before they took off on a punishing updraft. Not a moment too soon. The ground below cracked and crumbled. Soldiers took off on their own beasts as the ground gave way to a gaping, rocky cavern. In the black and swirling dust, something caught the light, glittering as it writhed. Whipping winds tossed her hair in her face, causing her to lose sight of the creature. The soldier behind her fought back her lengthy strands and in so doing, detached her necklace. Taisiya lunged for it, only to be dragged back, her hand empty.

"Jewellery can be replaced, Princess Consort!" The soldier castigated her as he hauled her back into position on the beast and flew higher.

Be that as it may, she felt naked now, her protections gone. The creature below moved again, fracturing the surrounding rock. Another horrid screech reached her ears. Taisiya flinched as it, too, was silenced. The creature below let loose a terrible bone-shaking wail and uncoiled, its enormous head breaching the surface.

Glittering gold and black scales sparkled like cursed treasure. Numerous horns like a fan of daggers framed its serpentine face. The dragon glared at the fleeing fae with wicked, cruel cunning. Lunging from its burrow with alarming speed, it grabbed the nearest soldier atop his beast with ease, its fangs thrice as long as the man they pierced. It swallowed with a delighted gleam in its black eyes.

"It's feral!" the soldier at Taisiya's back cried. "Thank the gods," he said under his breath.

Taisiya looked back at the man behind her with bewilderment. How on Oblivion was that a good thing? The soldier smiled. Then the glamour he'd been using fell away. This was not a man she recognised—and he was wearing the armour of the royal guard.

"I have nothing against you, Your Harmoniousness. But Radjedef must survive."

Before she could strike him with her lightning, his magic enveloped her, crushing her, breaking her. A horrid taste, like spoiled milk, made her gag. She lost sight of herself, her whole being unmade. Limbs dissolved and reformed and suddenly nothing was where it should be. Still reeling from the transformation, she heard the soldier's voice.

"I'm a fair man. I've given you a fighting chance."

And then Taisiya, whatever she was, began falling.

Chapter 49

Radjedef's life was hanging by a very thin thread. It was too bad the pest in question didn't know it.

"Should I just drag him to the void? Tell him he can't come out until he agrees to our demands?" Vasilisa asked from the shadow behind Mereruka's ear.

"I'll let you know," Mereruka replied, his voice hushed.

Much as he would have liked to simply send Radjedef to the void and be done with this, it would leave Khety room to accuse Mereruka of foul play. He also hesitated knowing just how loyal the guards were to Radjedef, and how quickly they would retaliate to avenge him. If Radjedef had been anything but the obedient dog that he was, Khety would've done away with him a century ago.

Radjedef's soldiers were serving him food and liquor while others grabbed the scales Mereruka's soldiers had collected and tossed them high. Arrows and enchantments just barely scratched the scales, a testament to the defensive powers wielded by dragons. Mereruka kept his face calm as his blood boiled. His wife needed to be gone from this wretched place as soon as possible, before her condition was noticed. Radjedef's petty games were hampering him.

"Have you eaten something sour, brother?" Radjedef grinned as Mereruka's party approached.

"Simply amazed you wish to spend more time in this gods-forsaken place... and that you allow your soldiers to so blatantly disobey the king's orders." Mereruka watched with some satisfaction as Radjedef's soldiers paused in their games. "Recover our scales," he instructed his own soldiers.

"And yet, these are our scales, brother. Yours have already been used for our amusement." Radjedef stood from his seat and loomed over Mereruka, a sneer on his scaly red face.

"So good of you to admit to your pettiness. Take *his* scales. Fair is fair, after all." Mereruka smiled.

Radjedef raised his hand and his soldiers readied themselves for a brawl. Mereruka's braced for the fight.

"Why must you always reach for things which are not yours?" Radjedef asked, his voice quiet.

Mereruka was caught off guard by the seriousness of Radjedef's gaze and the sincerity in his tone. It was the only time it seemed Radjedef seemed to be asking more than one question at once.

"Wouldn't you agree that they belong to the person most determined to take them?"

"I pity you. Nothing I've done has ever taught you your place." He sighed, resigned.

"I know my place, Radjedef. I am merely teaching the rest of the world where I rightfully belong." Mereruka raised his chin.

"So be it. Soldiers! Att—"

Radjedef's command was cut off by the ominous rumbling of the ground beneath their feet. Mereruka turned, eyes frantically searching for Taisiya, left behind at their camp. A soldier was already taking flight, Taisiya's copper hair whipping about like a flag, announcing her safe retreat. He could breathe again.

"Vasilisa. Take him to the void," Mereruka said quickly.

Radjedef's bewilderment lasted only a moment before panic overwhelmed him. He disappeared into his own shadow like the ground itself had opened up beneath him. The soldiers of the royal guard leapt back in horror.

"As Prince of Maat, I curse you, soldiers of Radjedef, to heed me or remain stuck fast." Mereruka cursed, his magic striking the ground. Angry shouts rang out as legs were dragged under the rocky soil. Oh, the soldiers had every enchantment imaginable woven into their tunics and mail, but few ever bothered to enchant their sandals. "Form rank and protect the princess consort!"

He didn't turn around, despite the quaking of the earth, not until he saw the resigned acceptance on the faces of Radjedef's soldiers. As they obeyed, their limbs were freed.

Mereruka turned around as the dragon lifted its head out from under the sands.

"Gods below," he gasped.

The dragon's head was as large as his barge. It snapped one of his fleeing soldiers from the air, swallowing him. Feral, then. There would be no reasoning with this creature. Mereruka dragged his eyes from the dragon and looked up to where Taisiya should be. Her red hair still tossed to and fro.

Until she was enveloped by foul magic, and her red hair disappeared.

Mereruka watched, helpless, as a red and purple winged creature fell from the soldier's summoned beast and plummeted, straight down towards the hungry gaze of the dragon.

Taisiya managed to turn, facing the quickly approaching dragon's head. As blood coursed through this strange body and the wind nearly deafened her as it whistled past, she reached for her magic. Father, ever the visionary, had prepared her for the event of freefall. A rather notorious teleportation mage had once made it his gruesome habit to drag his victims into the sky and then watch from a distance as they met the ground. Grigori had been determined that his children could survive such a thing.

Taisiya spread out her arms and legs, such that they were, as she felt the crackle of electricity humming through her body. But as her arms snapped wide, her muscles screamed in pain, as though she might be torn apart by the wind. Instead of slowing, her fall was nearly halted. She turned her head on a neck that was far too long to see that she possessed a pair of wings. Not feathered, but leathery, like Uncle Vadik's. Her shock didn't last long. Even from the sky, she heard the rumble of the ground as the dragon below caught sight of her.

Height!

She needed height. Taisiya flapped her arms—wings—desperately. She flew higher, riding the currents Uncle Vadik talked about, but it wouldn't be enough. The dragon tasted the air as a snake might, eying her. She gathered her magic on the tip of her nose. As she felt the air current swirling in advance of the dragon's strike, pushing her up but not fast enough, she turned around and let loose as powerful a lightning strike as she was able. Gaping jaws missed her by a hair.

The gold and black dragon shrieked, falling back to the ground, breaking rock and throwing up sand and dust in an enormous cloud. Taisiya struggled to ascend, gathering her magic to her once again. She thanked the gods that this transformation hadn't stolen her lightning entirely.

The dragon slithered from its burrow, furious black eyes locked on her. It wound its way up to the top of the surrounding cliffs, gaining at least as much height as she in a fraction of the time. Taisiya's heart constricted with terror. The next strike would reach her.

Her pounding heart and the whipping winds almost drowned out a set of thunderous quakes from the ground below. She kept the dragon below in the corner of her eye. Whatever the fae on the ground were doing was distracting the creature. Taisiya wouldn't let those precious seconds go to waste, even as the air in her lungs burned with cold.

A mighty roar drew her attention, and she readied her lightning to strike. Yet the dragon's head was not rearing up, about to strike. Instead, it was subdued, head held still by the tip of a giant spear—one that had failed to pierce its scales. At the end of that spear was Mereruka, looming larger than even the dragon.

The dragon's tail gripped Mereruka's leg. Attempting to destabilize him, it dragged his ankle through the desert floor, creating valleys and hills as he tried to keep his balance. As he struggled, Mereruka shrunk. The dragon must have sensed it as well. It thrashed its long, serpentine body, nearly knocking him off his feet. Heart hammering in her chest, Taisiya turned and sped downward. While the dragon's head was still pinned, she aimed her lightning, praying its eyes would prove more vulnerable than its impenetrable scales.

No one would take her husband from her, not even a feral dragon.

CHAPTER 50

Whatever madness had convinced Mereruka that he could take on a dragon had been extinguished the moment his spear failed to pierce its scales. Fear for his transformed wife had driven sense from him in an instant. As the spell that made him the size of a titan ate through the magical reserves of the soldiers powering it, Mereruka found he was fast running out of options for survival. The beast flailed its long, coiling, muscular body, becoming stronger the more he shrank. He wouldn't be able to pin its head much longer.

If Khety's machinations lead to Mereruka's death, he would lay a death curse, consequences be damned.

The dragon bucked his spear tip's hold on its head. From the corner of his eye, something sped towards him. His heart constricted.

Taisiya.

Mereruka redoubled his efforts to pin the wily dragon, its hateful black eyes focused solely on him. *Yes,* he thought, *I'm the one you want to eat, not her.* The dragon lunged at Mereruka and tore the spear from his grip, crushing it between its teeth with a hiss. Mereruka readied a spell, knowing it would be hopeless. Dragon scales repelled sword and magic alike.

The dragon reared back, ready to strike, when a high-pitched screech from above distracted it. Mereruka launched an immobility spell that only slowed the dragon as it moved its gold and black-scaled head to face Taisiya. Before he could blink, a blinding flash and the crack of thunder dazzled Mereruka, and the sound of the dragon's pained roar nearly left him deaf. Mereruka blinked furiously, trying to regain his vision. The dragon flailed wildly as it roared, sweeping his legs out from under him. He fell with a resounding crash, fracturing rock and sending shock waves across the desert.

When he recovered, Mereruka found he was now only half the size of the serpentine dragon. Despair and terror threatened to overwhelm him when he spotted bright red blood flowing from the destroyed eye of the dragon. Mereruka had been entirely forgotten by the beast as it hissed and searched the skies for Taisiya. Mereruka found her first, beating her wings furiously as she tried to retreat into the skies where the dragon couldn't follow.

The dragon spotted Taisiya soon enough and began to slither up to the highest point in the hills. Mereruka picked himself up and rushed the dragon, determined to keep it from lunging up at her. As it readied to strike, Mereruka threw himself on the dragon, pinning it with his body. The dragon roared and wriggled. It took all Mereruka's strength to grip it behind the skull to spare himself a bite. Even so, its thrashing left deep gashes as the fan of sharp horns slashed across his face and neck. Enraged, it began coiling around his ever-shrinking body.

The pressure of its unyielding scales snapped bones. A dull, reverberating crack accompanied his screams of pain. Yet still he would not release the dragon. If it crushed every bone in his body, he would not yield. Taisiya must survive.

Another screech had the dragon lessening the crushing pressure on Mereruka's battered lungs and redoubling its efforts to throw him off its body instead. It would soon succeed, for he was only a quarter the size of the dragon now, his arms only just encircling its thick throat.

The deep crackle of thunder and the dragon's agonized roars signalled Taisiya's second success against the beast. Panicked, it began rolling, nearly crushing Mereruka beneath it. The last vestiges of his strength left him, and he released the creature. It slithered back into its great, dark hole, fleeing until not even the rumbling of its movement beneath the sand and rock could be felt or heard.

The last thing he saw before he feared himself consigned to the afterlife was the graceless, hard landing of Taisiya in her dragon form, and her awkward, bat-like crawl to his side. He had to admit, she made a beautiful dragoness.

Taisiya watched, hidden under a broken slab of rock, Mereruka tucked under her... wing, as the soldiers picked their way through the torn-up landscape of the battleground of giants. Always, she kept an eye out for the soldier who had transformed her. If that fae bastard came within zapping distance, she planned to shoot first, questions and consequences be damned.

Robbed of her ability to speak or sob, and terrified that this strange body might harm Mereruka, she could do nothing more than look upon him and ache. Deep gashes, swelling, broken bones, a leg twisted at the wrong angle—Mereruka's life was fading. She wanted nothing more than to see him healed, to erase his pain, and then to lock him away somewhere safe and kill any who approached. She had tried to bathe his wounds in her blood, hoping they would heal him, but it was for nought. Taisiya was no true dragon.

The first to find her was, unsurprisingly, Vasilisa. When she emerged from the shadow nearest, her shock was palpable. Vasilisa had once explained that everyone's shadow had a certain feel to it, and that if she familiarized herself with someone's, she could find them again with ease.

Taisiya hoped the darkness mage trusted her magic more than her eyes.

"Taisiya?" Vasilisa asked, hesitant, half-backed into the shadow.

Taisiya did her best to nod her head and lifted her wing to show Mereruka.

Vasilisa approached warily, her eyes flicking down to Mereruka, assessing his condition. She sucked in a sharp breath at the extent of his injuries.

"He needs to see a healer. Will you let me take him to his soldiers?"

Taisiya nodded, but reluctantly. She didn't want to be parted from him, but she wasn't certain she would be able to follow. She'd managed flight, but not the landing, and wasn't confident she would succeed at take-off. In the meantime, she preferred to hide from the fae that had changed her, lest he snare her in his magic once more.

There were worse forms than that of a dragon.

"I'll come back for you once he's healed and surrounded by his soldiers. Will you be... alright?"

Taisiya nodded again. She wished she could warn Vasilisa about the spy in their ranks, but if her friend were there, the bastard wouldn't stand a chance of harming Mereruka. How frustrating not to be able to speak!

"Stay here and remain hidden. Radjedef is tucked away safely, but his soldiers aren't to be fully trusted."

Taisiya snorted. As if she didn't already know.

Vasilisa nodded, her expression grave as she gingerly took Mereruka from under Taisiya's wing and slipped into the void with him.

All that was left was to wait and to remain vigilant... and not let the hearts, both buried and unearthed, tempt her out into the open.

Mereruka woke with a start, surprised by the absence of pain as well as his wife. A quick survey of his formerly broken bones assured him that he'd been properly healed. He only prayed his glamour had held. It was night, and a brazier had been lit near his bed, but he could tell little else from within the tent erected for him, save that it was not made by magic and he was still in the desert. Hushed, angry voices were reaching a crescendo outside.

"You're awake. Good," Vasilisa whispered from the omnipresent shadows.

"Where is Taisiya?"

"Safe for now, but not for long. The soldiers haven't found her yet."

Mereruka stiffened.

"Take me to her if you know where she is. She has been magically altered. If the transformation isn't reversed within the span of a day and night, it may become permanent."

Vasilisa held out an inky, flickering hand, bidding him to grab hold and follow her into the void. Mereruka didn't hesitate this time. When he'd regained his bearings, he was under a slab of rock, facing a dragon not much larger than a horse. Relief coursed through him. Recognition flared in those purple eyes as they spotted him in the dark.

"Don't fight me, Taisiya. I will make this right."

He inspected the magic with his spell-sight, wary lest a trick or trap had been woven into it. Confident no such thing had been done, he overwhelmed the spell and Taisiya's magic with his own, unmaking her. The horror of that alone made his gorge rise, his wife's form melting before his eyes until she was nothing. But the spell was not over, and so he swallowed down bile as he returned her to her natural form one limb at a time. When she finally stood on two legs, she faltered in her step. Mereruka caught her up in his arms and she shook.

"Th-there's a spy, glamoured to look like one of our soldiers. He d-did this to me."

Mereruka squeezed her tight and stroked her hair, burying his face in her neck. He prayed this was not some strange fever dream, that she was truly alive with him now. There would be time for anger and fear later. All that mattered was the soul-deep relief that she was safe right now.

"Give me a moment, love," he murmured against her skin.

She wrapped her arms around him and sighed, relieved, even as tremors still wracked her body.

In the quiet, he could hear the shuffling of Vasilisa's feet as she waited for their moment to end.

"I can hear you rolling your eyes, Vasilisa," Mereruka griped.

"I'm not." Vasilisa choked out the words, her voice cracking.

The darkness mage surprised him by wrapping her arms around them both, fierce and stronger than he thought possible. She let out a sharp breath before gripping them, a shoulder in each hand as she shook them with ire.

"You're both so fucking stupid! You didn't survive because you were smart, you both got lucky! And... and I had to watch you two almost die! I'll never forgive you for that! And neither will Bas!" Vasilisa raged as tears fell in earnest.

Taisiya reached out and pulled Vasilisa's head close to her chest and kissed her frizzy blonde curls until the mage's cheeks were dry. Vasilisa pulled away to take a shaky breath and dry her tears. Fear gone, now only anger remained. Good. Mereruka felt the first embers of rage lick the walls of his gut. He pulled away from his desperate hold of Taisiya so that he could see her face.

"Taisiya, what do you want to do to the man who did this to you?" Mereruka asked.

"I want him to fear for his life and the lives of everyone he holds dear," Taisiya answered. "It's only fair."

"Would you recognize him?"

Taisiya nodded, confident.

"What about Radjedef? I can always just leave him in the void for good," Vasilisa offered.

"I think we can use him," Taisiya said before Mereruka could respond.

He raised his brow.

"He wanted Radjedef to survive. It was the last thing he said before he..." Taisiya swallowed. Mereruka saw the fear in her eyes, one she quickly pushed away. That man would pay dearly for it. "If Radjedef is the bait, we may be able to lure that soldier out."

The idea of his prickly brother as bait for anything aside from snide remarks was just too amusing. His grin was feral as he kissed Taisiya.

"Then let's lay a trap."

CHAPTER 51

The soldiers were mere moments from open conflict when Mereruka threw back the cloth opening of his tent with a flourish, Taisiya at his side. The shock inside the camp was palpable. They strode into the middle of the budding maelstrom under a heavy glamour, one that projected strength, calm, and unimpeachable fashion sense. Beneath the magic, they were weary, ragged and one suspicious movement from attacking the lot of them. Mereruka glared at Radjedef's men.

"You call yourselves soldiers of Maat?" He spat upon the ground. "You were unable to protect me or my wife. Indeed, it was *we* who saved *you* from a hungry, feral dragon today! Who here has the nerve to stand proud before your prince and princess consort, and feel you have the right to bicker amongst each other while we grace you with our presence?!" Mereruka raged, the weight of it nearly palpable in the night air.

The soldiers knelt, their heads bowed.

"My love, if the royal guard of Maat is lacking, doesn't their overseer shoulder the largest portion of the blame? When a child is thoroughly spoiled, is it not the fault of the parents?"

"Dear wife, you are so very wise," he cooed as he stroked her face. Mereruka turned to Vasilisa. "Bring me Radjedef. He should be punished."

Vasilisa reappeared in an instant, tossing him from the void like a sack of garbage. Radjedef lay sprawled and undignified in the dirt as he slowly regained his senses.

"How do you fare, brother? You were lucky indeed that my wife's loyal servant thought to keep you safe from the dragon by hiding you away. It seems, however, that your own soldiers and servants are so inept that it borders on treason." Mereruka let the word linger on his tongue and was heartened to see the panic that stiffened his brother's body. Perhaps the soldier that had attacked Taisiya was the lover they'd been searching for. "If we cannot find the guilty party, I demand that you take the punishment. After all, as overseer of the royal guard, are the soldiers here not your responsibility?" Curious, Mereruka watched his brother's reaction intently. Radjedef seemed to relax.

"My soldiers have failed to keep you and your wife safe. The fault lies with me," Radjedef answered.

Taisiya's grip on Mereruka's arm grew tight. He looked up to see a soldier raise his head and his hands in surrender.

"Prince, Princess Consort, it is I who bear the blame. Prince Radjedef did not know of my schemes. It would be unjust to punish him."

While Taisiya kept her eyes on the soldier, Mereruka enjoyed the sight of Radjedef's panic becoming palpable. Shoulder's tensing, eyes widening and a trickle of unglamoured sweat rolling down his sand-covered face. Excellent.

"Vasilisa."

"Yes, Prince Mereruka," she replied before she dragged the soldier into the void. He went without a struggle and mouthed a few words at Radjedef before he disappeared.

"No!" Radjedef shouted, stricken. "No, Seneb is not to blame! I demand that you bring him back!"

"Demand? What right do you have to demand anything of me, brother? Have you not wronged me? Has your soldier not attacked my wife?"

Radjedef turned pleading eyes on Taisiya. She returned them with a cold glare.

"You have proven yourself to be inadequate to the task given to you by King Khety. Did he not publicly instruct you to provide for my safety as we collected his tribute?" Taisiya added.

"Yes, a thousand times, yes! So please, show mercy to Seneb and lay the blame for everything on me instead." Radjedef grovelled at their feet, his ragged breaths stirring up sand.

Mereruka knelt down and whispered in his ear.

"Then beg me to give you the mark of disinheritance, as you so richly deserve."

Radjedef looked up at him with resignation.

"Promise me Seneb will be safe from you."

"I give you my word not to do him harm."

Radjedef sighed.

"Brother, give me the mark of disinheritance. I welcome it to atone for my failures."

Mereruka took the blade from his side and carved the symbol into Radjedef's forehead. Once it was done, he whispered in his brother's pointed red ear.

"Your lover is safe from me, but my wife made no promises. Come to our tent if you wish to bargain." Mereruka grinned as he stood, revelling in the devastation plain on Radjedef's face.

"That went well." Vasilisa grinned as Taisiya and Mereruka entered their tent.

"Very," Mereruka replied, beaming.

"It's not over yet." Taisiya sighed, flopping into her makeshift throne, exhausted at denying the siren song of the dragon hearts. It had taken everything in her to keep her focus on the soldiers, not to let her steps stray away from camp. The need nearly brought her to tears, like a child denied their favourite treat. Anxious fire rushed through her veins, draining the last of her reserves.

Mereruka sat down beside her and placed a hand on hers.

"No, but it soon will be. I can hear Radjedef coming."

Taisiya readied herself. With the trap sprung, all that was left was to extract her price from Radjedef. As they'd plotted their actions, Taisiya's anger had time to cool. As much as she wished violence upon the soldier, Seneb, he was more useful alive, and now that Vasilisa knew who he was, the man would always be at her mercy. Radjedef's obvious, selfless love for the man would be the chains she used to bind them both to her will. She had restrained her rage at her half-sister for the murder of their father for her family's sake, she could restrain herself again for the benefit of her new family.

Radjedef entered the tent alone, the blood still trickling down his face from the newly-carved mark. He fell to his knees without an ounce of his former swagger. Gone was the brash, haughty prince. In his place—a desperate man who knew he held not a single card in his favour.

"What will it take to secure Seneb's safety from you and yours, Princess Consort?"

Taisiya let him stew for a few minutes as she appeared to consider his question. Her grip tightened on the arms of her seat as another song begged her to listen.

"A favour. Any favour. To be bestowed upon me at a time of my choosing. And your oath to protect me and mine, and to protect us from any under your command."

"You expect me to contradict Khety's orders?" Radjedef asked.

"To kill us? Yes, I'm asking you to fail." Taisiya nodded.

"And yet you've seen what he does to failures," Radjedef hissed.

Taisiya narrowed her eyes. He pursed his lips.

"Yes, and you've experienced first-hand our sense of fairness," Mereruka said.

"*Fairness?!* It's madness! Without my place in the succession before you, you've attached a flaming damn target on your backs! I kept my rights to protect the rest of you!" Radjedef raged, sweeping his arms wide. "I kept Seneb hidden for centuries to protect him from Khety! You think I don't know who Khety will try to kill when I return with the two of you and his bloody scales?! His identity is known now!"

Taisiya almost jumped when Mereruka launched out of his seat in a rage. Her concentration had drifted already. She bit the inside of her cheek.

"You protected no one! What of Nefertnesu? She paid for your cowardice and Khety's with her gods-damned heart! What of Mother?! Hm? Think I've forgotten that when Khety was slaughtering his way through her personal guards, you and the rest of the royal guard were conveniently too far to reach her in time? What of Inkaef? Did you rush to save him from his punishment? What of me, when he sent me to die across the sea, with soldiers of your choosing and orders to kill me if it looked like I might survive? The only one you've ever protected is yourself!"

"I tried, damn you! I sent my least competent people!"

"Forgive me for being unimpressed with your efforts!" Mereruka retorted.

"Enough!" Taisiya stood and placed herself between them. She shoved Radjedef back to his knees and pushed Mereruka back into his chair. "Radjedef, unlike Khety, I consider Seneb too important to kill off on a whim. He is an excellent enticement for your future good behaviour. If you play nicely, Seneb will live, unharmed." He was about to protest. She held a finger to his lips, punctuating her authority with a crackle of electricity along her skin and shushing him, "And until Khety is no longer a threat to him, Seneb will remain hidden in either Rhacotis or Shedet. It is more than you or he deserves, *after what he's done to me.*"

An experience she'd been forced to live through twice. A violation of every fibre of her being, on par with having her soul torn out. At least the latter she'd chosen willingly. Electricity danced across her skin in earnest then. She could no longer conceal it in her current state.

"Fine," Radjedef grumbled.

"Agree to my terms in full, Radjedef," Taisiya said, her words as sharp as a whip.

"I agree to grant you any favour you desire, whenever you wish it, and my oath not to allow you or yours to come to harm from me or those under my command."

"And I agree not to harm Seneb, or order harm to come to him, as well to hide him until it is safe for him to leave our care."

Taisiya felt the weight of their deal between them. Though she was not fae, their magic had bound her and Radjedef.

"I want to see him," Radjedef said.

Taisiya nodded at Vasilisa.

"I have some words for him as well."

Vasilisa threw him out of the nearest shadow. Radjedef rushed over, checking Seneb for injuries. When Seneb recovered his senses, he threw his arms around Radjedef.

"Seneb," Taisiya said.

The fae man looked up at her, swallowing, his wide eyes made starker in the light of her dancing electricity. His fear was nearly tangible as he gripped Radjedef tighter. Good.

"Radjedef has bargained much for your freedom and safety. I have promised not to harm you in addition to hiding you from King Khety. However, if you ever act against me or mine, I will kill Radjedef, slowly, in front of you."

"I understand," Seneb whispered.

Radjedef went still and turned his head slowly to glare at them.

"Did you forget to bargain for your own safety, brother?" Mereruka grinned. "Pity."

"You know all those rumours about what happened to the fae on the boat ride here?" Vasilisa asked with menacing glee, "They're true. All of them."

Seneb released a shuddering breath and buried his head in Radjedef's shoulder.

"Tomorrow morning, all of Maat will know that Princess Consort Taisiya fed you to the void as punishment," Mereruka said. "So, say your goodbyes tonight, and be ready to travel."

CHAPTER 52

Mereruka had been expecting a fight. Insults, sinister insinuations, condemnations, veiled threats and hidden schemes—he'd prepared for these and more when he and Taisiya presented the scales as tribute to Khety. The king sat conspicuously alone on his throne. Betrest was nowhere to be found. Neither was Serfka, nor even Hemetre, his favoured concubine, was to be seen. Instead, Khety looked almost... tired. Mereruka could hardly believe his eyes, so ready he'd been for conflict. He almost wondered if some imposter was sitting on the throne when Khety inspected the scales and broke his silence with a hollow voice.

"Exactly as I requested."

"Is Your Eternal Serenity pleased with the tribute?"

"Yes. You have not failed me, Princess Consort."

The nefarious deal was at an end. Mereruka inwardly sighed with relief.

"I heard there was trouble..."

"A feral dragon attacked, and one of Radjedef's men used the situation to assault Princess Consort Taisiya. The soldier has been dealt with, and Radjedef took the mark of disinheritance to atone," Mereruka answered.

A muscle in Khety's jaw clenched.

"So be it. Then be gone."

Mereruka didn't need to be told twice. Still, what was ailing his brother, and more importantly, was it fatal? Khety was well into his ninth century now. If Mereruka were lucky, the bastard would die of natural causes before his younger brother's schemes did the deed.

Even the halls of the Court of the Innundation were absent their usual cheer and liveliness. The hatya present drank in sombre silence, casting inquisitive looks his way as he and Taisiya passed. Sedate board games and tranquil music were the order of the day. No one dared appear boisterous when their king was so clearly unwell.

"He looks haggard," Taisiya whispered.

Mereruka nodded. Hopefully it was permanent.

"Maybe Bas has some idea why."

When they reached their barge, now fully restored, Vasilisa was there already.

"Kitty left a note." Vasilisa handed Mereruka the small papyrus scroll, tapping her foot impatiently.

Mereruka unrolled the message and read it over.

"He'll be back by nightfall. He's confident he'll have retrieved my earring by then."

Vasilisa frowned.

"I'm going looking for him."

Taisiya nodded.

"Don't scare him if he's in the middle of something." She raised a copper brow at her friend.

Vasilisa smirked.

"If he's at the beginning or end of something its fine then, right?" Vasilisa tweaked Taisiya's nose. "I've been learning my fae-speak like a good little spy." Vasilisa melted into the shadows before Taisiya could reproach her.

Mereruka chuckled.

"She catches on fast," he said.

"Vasilisa has always been fond of mischief. The way the fae speak is just another game for her."

"And you, wife? Are you fond of mischief?"

He tucked a strand of her hair behind her ear. She looked better now that they were far from the graveyard. Gone were her haunted eyes and strange yearnings. Whatever spell those hearts had over her had dissipated. Though the strain of all that had happened was hidden beneath a glamour he'd woven on her—the dark circles beneath her eyes, a brow pinched in anxiety, palms marked by nails. He was worried for her—for them. Sometimes he feared that if he looked away, she would be gone, that her life would slip from his hands like grains of sand. Or she would decide she'd had enough of the peril he'd placed her in and leave, a part of his heart gone with her. After everything they'd just experienced, he feared he would break—that *they* would break, and that what they had would be undone and never recover.

"Stop looking at me like that."

"Like what?"

"Like I might break. I'm fine." She narrowed her eyes, her voice clipped.

Lies. Mereruka furrowed his brow, placed his hands on her shoulders and turned her around, marching in front of a mirror. With barely a thought, he tore the glamour off her.

"What do you see, love?" he hissed.

Taisiya's hands fisted as she looked away. Always so proud. Always the first to hide from her feelings, needing to be coaxed out. He needed her to be with him in this moment, to share it, to know he wasn't alone in the dark, coiled mess of his heart.

"I can't afford to be weak. Not now. We're so close." Her breath hitched.

Her words wounded him. If she were weak, then he was no more than a cowering mess.

"If not now, when it's just us, then when?"

She bit her lip.

"You're not weak. You're afraid. You haven't had a single moment where you could come apart at the seams, like any sane person would after facing a gods-damned feral dragon."

Like he was about to. Didn't she know how terrified he'd been? How that fear was still creeping at the edges of him, fraying him?

"And yet you're perfectly composed," she accused him, hugging her sides.

He grabbed her wrist, leading her into his pocket realm.

"Come."

When they were through to the other side, he dropped his glamour. She blinked in surprise. No doubt she saw the dark circles under his eyes, the lines bracketing his mouth. No doubt she could see the fear that stalked him. All the anxieties he couldn't speak aloud for fear he would make them real.

He was not a good man and she could do better, or at least be safer. And as events had proven, he was a piss-poor protector—and he wanted to be a better one. He'd never imagined feeling so deeply for the co-conspirator he'd planned to choose for a wife. Before Taisiya, a wife had been little more than an abstract concept. He hadn't planned on caring whether she lived or died, whether she was scared or needed comfort—he hadn't planned on needing her so badly he couldn't breathe without her. Now she was part of him—he couldn't let her go any more than he could keep her safe—and he was going mad from helplessness.

"If you think I'm not one hair away from coming undone, from letting heart-stopping terror at losing you overwhelm me, from the need to hold you so tightly I might break you, then you're not looking closely enough."

Taisiya searched Mereruka's eyes, fierce and vulnerable. She reached a shaking hand up to his cheek, her bottom lip trembling. Only in front of her would he ever reveal such an expression. He gave her permission she didn't know she needed to be as vulnerable before him as he was before her. When she spoke, her prickly pride was useless, leaving an ache in her throat as it tightened with emotion.

"I thought I would lose you and I couldn't—"

He interrupted her with a brutal kiss, his arms crushing her tight as his hands fisted her gown and hair.

"You were never supposed to turn around and fight that fucking dragon!" he roared desperately. "You were supposed to be safe!"

Tears stung her eyes, not because of his anger, not at his words, but because she felt the same bone-deep fear as he did. He released her hair and she wrapped her arms around him, petting his back.

"You will never do anything like that again! I will put you in an impregnable fortress, surrounded by every luxury and protection where you—"

"Will die of boredom and be entirely useless. That isn't why you married me," she reminded him.

When she'd seen him broken, bloody and bruised in the desert, she wanted to do the same. It was why her heart fluttered to hear the sentiments on his lips. This feeling in her was mirrored in him—fear and longing. A fierce and terrifying love that would destroy anything that imperilled the other. She supposed if he were a villain, then she was his perfect match.

He held her face in his hands, forcing her to look into his citrine eyes.

"That was before. Before you were necessary to my very existence. I can't live without you, Taisiya. I don't even want to contemplate a world in which you don't exist. I would burn such a hell-scape down to the bedrock. The only thing I want more than the throne is your safety. Except I need the damned throne to keep you safe!"

He was plucking the words right out of her mind.

"If you'd wanted a pet to keep safe and coddle, you chose poorly." She grinned ruefully, knowing it applied equally to her.

Safe would have been marrying an elderly nobilissimus with too much money and too few family members. Safe would have been accepting the first ambitious merchant as a husband and retiring from scheming. Safe would have kept her from making their bargain. Safe would have been convincing him to give up his schemes and ambitions. But she'd chosen him and his mad schemes in the end, safety be damned.

"Damnit, Taisiya—"

She pressed a finger to his teal lips.

"I love you too, Meri."

He looked as though a trap had sprung on him and he'd only just seen the bars slamming down around him. He laughed, a touch hysterically. Was this the first time she'd said it, either of them had said it? Mereruka looked as if it had only now occurred to him what this wild thing in his chest was.

"I have liked you from the start, Taisiya, but I suppose I am well and truly caught now."

"You will never escape me," she agreed.

"I almost wish we *had* been bound by that bloody marriage oath. It would be a comfort now to know I wouldn't have to live in a world without you. I'm a fool."

"Wishing for a tactical disadvantage is rather foolish."

He traced her bottom lip with his finger.

"You're perfect."

She grinned, a shiver cascading down her spine. His eyes darkened with desire and wild intensity.

"I love you, Taisiya. With every fibre of my black heart. Gods help you."

"Gods help our enemies. They'll need it more."

"Vicious woman," he said with a rumble in his chest as he hooked a finger under the strap of her dress.

"Ruthless bastard," she breathed, her hand sliding under his kilt.

His lips crushed hers. Fierce need overpowered her. They tore at each other's clothes, barely pausing for breath. Fabric split between their needy fingers. He grabbed a breast in one hand and pinched her nipple between his fingers. Taisiya all but threw off the scraps of her dress as Mereruka kicked his kilt away, their tongues still tangling. She tackled him onto the bed and they rolled, fighting for the dominant position. She licked the shell on his ear and he nipped her neck. His tongue on her nipple sent tingles down her spine and she rewarded him by taking him in hand and stroking him.

Taisiya nibbled along the edge of Mereruka's ear and he shuddered in submission.

"Fuck! Taisiya!" he warned.

She eyed him mutinously. His earlobe found itself between her teeth as she tugged. Breath caught on a sensual groan, he gripped her thighs. She revelled in her power.

Until he cupped her sex and rubbed his fingers along her most sensitive spot. Her gasp of shocked pleasure was all he needed to turn the tables, flipping her onto her back so he could punish her in the most wonderful way. Hands once again bound by his hair, he swallowed her cries. There was no sweetness left in him. His tongue fought hers, his hand behind her head holding her close, never once allowing her to pull away, to regain her senses, to be anywhere other than there in his arms. The pleasure built until she was bucking against his hand, desperate for release. And yet just as he brought her close, he eased off. She fought his hold on her wrists.

"Meri!" she pleaded. "Please!"

"No. This is your punishment." He nipped her neck, the sweet sting of his teeth making her whimper. "You're never allowed to be in danger again."

His fingers returned, feather light and utterly maddening.

Pleading had failed. Threats were needed.

"Meri, if you don't—"

"You'll what?" He chuckled darkly before his lips found her nipple, tugging it, sending a shiver down her spine.

His fingers continued their ruthless, too-light strokes. Every time her hips sought his touch, he pulled away.

"Ah-ah. Now you're being a bad girl. Finish your threats, Taisiya," he growled, torturing her other nipple with his teeth and tongue.

Lost and needy, she bit her lip, revelling in his cruel mastery of her body. But she soon reached the end of her tether. She needed it so badly she might go mad.

"If you don't give me what I want I will cut off your gods-damned cock."

She was rewarded with the wet slide of his fingers on her, and a pressure that sent her over the edge. Taisiya splintered in his palm, screaming his name.

Mereruka loomed over her, a hunger in his eyes.

"You're so fucking beautiful when you come."

His hand moved up and down his length as he stared down at her naked body. She pushed him away.

"Taisiya?"

"Get on your back."

Crouching over him, she took his cock in hand, gripping him tight but refusing to move until his eyes locked with hers. She ran her tongue up the shaft, her hand following. She teased the tip with her thumb and tongue until his back arched. The moment their eyes lost contact, she stopped. Two could play this game.

"Taisiya," he growled.

"Meri," she replied primly, rewarding him when his eyes found hers.

The head of him sheathed in her lips, she sucked, gradually taking more. His hips bucked and he hissed in pleasure. Taisiya reached up to his nipple and toyed with it. When next his hips demanded more of her, she let a trickle of electricity dance across her fingertips.

"Fuck! Fuck! Taisiya, gods!" he choked.

She came up for air, licking the head again.

"You're not allowed to die until I tell you that you can. Take your punishment like a good boy," she purred.

"I'm... a fucking... *paragon*," he ground out as he nearly shook with the strain to be still, his eyes dark with the promise of retribution.

There was only one sensible thing to do in the face of such bald-faced lies. Another small jolt of electricity flicked across his other nipple as she took him deep. He roared every obscenity she'd ever heard.

"I'm going to make you beg!" he swore.

She was already aching for it. Another snap of lightning rolled down his chest.

"I'm going to fuck you until you can't remember your own name!"

Just what she wanted. Another slow lick from the stem to the tip as she eyed him without remorse. Another light dose of pain as she tweaked his nipples with the bite of her magic.

"I'm going to ruin you forever!"

"What are you waiting for?"

Then Mereruka lost all control—or regained it. Auroras of magic all around her, he put her on her hands and knees, gripped her thighs almost painfully and bucked into her until she saw stars. She thought he might never stop until he bent her head down to the sheets and angled her hips, his next thrust igniting a newer, deeper pleasure. Breath left her on a gasp. The sound sealed her fate.

Mereruka paused, his rumbling chuckle dark and cruel. His frenzy cooled, every thrust was slower than the last, filling her to the hilt before he dragged himself out, rubbing some part of her she couldn't reach but needed to touch. She reached to touch herself, only to have the sheets wind around her wrists.

"Ah, ah. I made you three promises, Taisiya."

She thrust her hips backward, impaling herself on him on a moan.

"Naughty," he hissed.

His hair threaded around her thighs, holding her immobile.

"You'll pay for that," he purred, refusing to move inside her.

Instead, his fingers found her and stroked her in the same maddening, feather-light way. Now over-sensitized, she didn't know if she were trying to lean into his touch or flee it, only that both were impossible. His caress might have been considered reverential, but for the fact that he was slowly bringing her towards release over and over again only to stop, his magic tweaking her nipples, his cock seated inside her, her hips unable to move. She needed it to end as much as she needed him to never stop.

"Beg," he whispered.

"Meri, please," she sobbed.

"Come for me, Taisiya."

When he finally gave her what she needed, she screamed. Mind-numbing pleasure had her arching her back as he thrust himself inside her. Overwhelmed, her hips sought his, bones turning to jelly at the unexpected intensity. Magic gliding over her neck and nipples like a hot tongue, his fingers on her bringing her close to another release, and his cock thrusting hard and hitting her just right—she was undone. Grateful for the magic holding her up, Taisiya surrendered to the ferocity of his lovemaking. Clenching around him as another wave of pleasure hit, his thrusts turned almost brutal as he reached his own release.

"Do you remember your name, wife?"

All she could manage was a whimper.

"And have I ruined you forevermore?"

She nodded. Her heart might explode if he ever used her in such a delicious, pitiless way again.

Every part of her was weak. When his magic gave way, she collapsed on the bed with barely enough energy to turn to her side and face him. Their harsh breaths mingled, cooling their sweat-slicked skin. He shifted, their noses almost touching. Pulling her close, his eyes were as solemn as his voice.

"I love you, Taisiya."

"And I love you, Meri." She grinned.

He tightened his grip and covered her messy copper hair in kisses. She circled her shaking arms around him.

"If I have to drown Maat in blood to keep you safe, I'll do it, and gladly."

She kissed his chest. Dramatic man. Didn't he know she would do the same?

"No need, when a single head on a silver platter will do." She looked up at him, unable to hold back a cruel little smile.

"A gold platter. I don't do half-measures." Mereruka grinned wickedly.

"Inlaid with precious stones, I should hope."

"Only the finest will do." He nodded.

"Braggart."

"Temptress."

"Villain."

"Villainess."

"Every villainess is in need of a villain." She slid her arms up around his head and pulled him down for a soft, slow kiss.

"How fortunate that we found each other," he murmured against her lips.

He hooked her leg around him and made leisurely, achingly tender love to her. They fell asleep in each other's arms, only to be awoken by an intruder in their pocket realm.

Taisiya gasped awake at Mereruka's insistent jostling. She readied her lightning.

"He's been captured! Bas has been captured!"

The electricity died against Taisiya's skin. Vasilisa had tumbled into the realm with tears in her panicked grey eyes.

"Who has him?" Mereruka asked, fear and menace rolling off him in waves.

Vasilisa shook her head and handed him a bloody note as she cradled something in her other palm.

"What does it say?" Taisiya asked.

"'If you want your shifter, then come find me. Alone. Now.'"

"Vasilisa, how did you…" Taisiya began to ask, knowing neither of them could yet read the fae script. She trailed off as Vasilisa held open her shaking palm to reveal a lump of bloody gore and fur.

"They cut off a piece of his tail."

CHAPTER 53

The halls of the palace were dimly lit, throwing sinister shadows across the faces of the many statues and reliefs. Inlaid jewels and golden paints glinted in the light Mereruka had conjured with his magic. In his hand, the piece of Bas guided them to what he desperately hoped was the rest of his son, alive, if mutilated. Helpless rage, guilt and terror galvanized his steps. If Bas were dead...no, best not to think on it. He'd asked him to remain behind for his safety, and now his son had been maimed. *Careless, foolish, reckless.* He never should have encouraged Bas in this endeavour. He should have found someone else to take into the fold of his secrets, to train as his best spy, someone he didn't love. Whatever happened to Bas, it was Mereruka's fault. What kind of father was he to allow his son to live such a dangerous life? Bas should have spent his days chasing skirts and making friends, not slinking into enemy territory and listening for secrets. Instead, the child of his heart was in pain.

Though this was certainly a trap, he couldn't slow his steps. How good of the soon-to-be-dead swine to give Mereruka what he would need to weave a locator spell. The thin, ugly red line stretched out from the chunk of Bas's tail and pointed the way, like the needle of a grim compass.

"Still unable to locate him, Vasilisa?" he asked.

"I can't. It's like he's not anywhere."

The darkness mage's pronouncement sent chills down his spine. He dared not ask if her magic prevented her from locating the dead.

"He must be behind a barrier of some kind. When we find him, your first priority is to get him to safety. Taisiya and I will deal with whatever other resistance there is. Once he's safe, then you can come back for us," Mereruka instructed, praying he was correct.

Taisiya and Vasilisa nodded. Fury, barely contained, fairly crackled beneath the surface of their hard stares. Good. He'd already explained that this was a situation where lethal force was not to be stinted on.

No one hurts my son.

"You taste anything, even a hint of magic, and you unleash hell, Taisiya."

"It will be my pleasure," she replied.

Taisiya was dangerously under-protected in this fight. He'd had just enough time to fashion a bracelet with some rudimentary defences against the worst fae curses, but this was an engagement for which they were woefully underprepared. He'd not had a chance to commission or create a necklace like the one she'd lost in the desert. It should have been his first priority when he'd returned, outside of assuring Bas' safety.

The spell led them into a newer section of the palace—so new, in fact, that few of the reliefs had even been painted, the outlines still visible where the work would soon begin. The air was hot and thick with constructive magics. The structures surrounding them had only just settled permanently into reality after being created using fae spells.

To be walking so blatantly into a trap, it was just what Khety would want. But the piece of Bas he'd been given was at least a day old. There was no telling how dire his situation had become.

They followed a circuitous route down to a chamber below. Only a few, dim torches penetrated the gloom, but it was enough. Lying across the floor, beaten, maimed and bleeding, was Bas. His hands were tied behind his back, his fingers either broken or missing. His back was a tapestry of gore, his face nigh unrecognizable from the swelling, and his ears appeared tattered and chewed. A thick black collar hung around his neck, no doubt preventing him from shifting to repair the damage.

Mereruka saw red and dashed forward.

"Oof!"

"Ow!"

His light went out, casting the room in even greater darkness before numerous torches came alight in its absence. Mereruka whipped his head back. Both Taisiya and Vasilisa were cradling their noses and hissing in pain at stubbed toes. He was about to reprimand their clumsiness when a muffled sound caught his attention.

"Mrph!"

An indignant feminine growl accompanied the sight of a bound woman, squirming along the stone floor, facing away. Another piece of bait in this pit, no doubt. Whoever she was, she could wait.

"Meri? Meri!"

He looked back again at Taisiya. She pounded on air, as if she stood behind a sheet of glass.

"We can't enter!"

He squinted his eyes. Above their heads, a message scrawled across the arch of the doorway.

"Fuck."

"What?" Taisiya asked.

Stupid, stupid, stupid. Mereruka removed Bas' bindings. He went to unlatch the collar with his magic but found himself unable.

"Shit!"

There would be time for regrets later.

He picked up Bas and gently as he could, fighting his rising tide of panic. He'd been caught like a rat in a trap. There must be iron within this room, to affect his magic so. Just when his son needed his healing magic most, he'd failed him. *Helpless, stupid, weak.* This was all his fault.

"Meri? Tell me what is going on!" Taisiya's eyes widened in fear.

Walking to the invisible barrier, he found his way blocked. Just as he'd feared. He couldn't put a single hair of his over that line, but Bas' head lolled across it. Some small measure of relief hit him.

"Vasilisa, take Bas. Go back to the barge and rouse my soldiers. Have them remove the collar he wears and force him awake. If he can shift, he'll be able to repair the damage while he's between forms."

At least, Mereruka hoped as much. Shapeshifters were notoriously hardy, but Bas was young and had never been forced to reform missing pieces of himself. He'd never been injured to such an extent—Mereruka would never have allowed it. But he'd ordered him to spy on vicious foes. Never again. Handing Bas off was a less than graceful affair, as he had to let his son's body tumble from his arms into Vasilisa's while never crossing the wretched barrier.

"I'll be back with the soldiers," Vasilisa replied, bursting into inky flames as she sank into the darkness, Bas cradled in her arms.

"Meri!"

"It seems I'm caught, my love. The spell on this place says 'One in, one out.'"

"How do I undo it?" she asked.

"Mrph! Mrph!"

Taisiya raised her brow and looked around.

"Is someone else in there?"

"A moment, wife," Mereruka replied.

He grabbed the nearest torch and held it high. The bound woman's skin glinted gold, her dark green hair in disarray.

"Betrest?" he asked.

She was tied and gagged, struggling furiously, her violet eyes enraged. Mereruka put the torch down and freed her.

"You gods-damned fool!"

"You're welcome, Your Most Just," Mereruka replied with all due sarcasm.

"You freed some mangy, half-dead shifter servant instead of your sister-in-law! Now we're both trapped here!" she raged as she clutched her bruised wrists.

"Of the two of you, you can hardly argue your situation was more dire than his," Mereruka replied, holding back his ire. Even if he'd known Betrest had been the bound woman, he still wouldn't have chosen her. As if he would choose his relatives over someone he loved.

"Yes, well now we are both trapped here, with your bloodthirsty imp of a sister on the loose," Betrest hissed.

"This was Itet's doing?"

This elaborate scheme was hers? The same Itet whose life revolved around drinking and brawling? The one who smashed all her problems with a mace? The spell on the entrance was exceedingly powerful, and yet managed to function with iron nearby. Had his sister tied the spell to her life?

"It is. I've spent the last day trapped in here, listening to her mad ranting. Why hasn't Khety come? At least tell me he has soldiers searching for me." Betrest pinched the bridge of her nose.

"If Khety knew you were missing, he has not made it public, or shared the information with me," Mereruka replied.

The information was like a body blow to the queen. It was as if her mind refused to accept it, that the king not only held her in such low esteem, but that he thought nothing of her prolonged absence. No doubt stunned by her own utter lack of importance, the light in her eyes dimmed.

"What else can you tell me?" Mereruka snapped his fingers in front of her face to bring Betrest out of her emotional stupor. "Well?"

Betrest slapped his hand away, tears held in check in her glittering eyes.

"She discovered your servant searching Inkaef's quarters and tortured him for information. Itet knows you switched the seals. Now she wants you and all her other brothers dead. She kidnapped me to play the part of bait and left me here with that servant and a scroll."

Mereruka walked back to the threshold he could no longer cross.

"Did you hear all that, Taisiya?"

"Yes."

"I suspect that if Itet dies, the magic holding us here will as well. For now, I want you to remain nearby, but hidden. With only three pieces of bait and four brothers, I suspect she may still be searching for one final thing."

If he had to guess, it would be something of Radjedef's that he valued more than his own safety. Luckily, Mereruka had already located his hot-headed brother's weakness and had it safely stowed out of Itet's grasp.

"You can't overcome the barrier yourself?" Taisiya asked.

"No. My magic has been dampened. There must be iron nearby."

Taisiya cursed.

"Would iron break the barrier?"

It was an excellent question. Mereruka poured as much as he could into his spell-sight, straining to see the hidden strands of the magic that kept him confined.

"Well?"

"Not unless that iron was shoved into Itet's heart. She really did tie this damned spell to her life," Mereruka answered, almost impressed by his sister's tenacity.

"Of course she did," Betrest scoffed. "That she-goat has so little talent with magic, I wouldn't be shocked to find her sire was an actual animal."

Mereruka ignored her. He wanted to put his hand on Taisiya's cheek, to touch her in some way. His son was hurt, and he couldn't even hold him, couldn't heal him, hadn't been able to do anything aside from drop him into the arms of another and hope for the best. Now he couldn't even take comfort in his wife. Would there ever be a day when he had enough power to leave this sickening helplessness behind him?

"Find somewhere to hide. I will shout if Itet shows her face. If you see her before I do—"

"I'll skewer her with a bolt of lightning," she said, her eyes a solemn promise, her palm pressed to the barrier.

"Good. Trust no one, Taisiya."

Taisiya nodded and turned, reluctance in every line of her retreating form.

Mereruka watched her go until her form was swallowed up by the darkness. Ignoring Betrest's further complaints, he located the scroll she'd mentioned. Seeing the broken seal, his heart skipped. It was a monarch's cartouche—but not Khety's. Using what little of his spell-sight remained, he ran hungry, anxious eyes over the object. Every fibre of the scroll had been meticulously spelled to prevent destruction or decay. Opening the scroll, he hoped against hope that this was what he'd suspected. He read the opening lines several times over, just to be sure.

It had always been a mystery to Mereruka why Khety had killed their mother in cold blood, when it was certain she had but a few decades of life left to her. He chuckled darkly. This was, without doubt, the bait meant to lure Khety. It turned out his long-held suspicions about Mother's murder had been correct after all.

But if this was meant for Khety, then what was the queen doing here?

He turned his eyes on Betrest, a wicked sense of triumph curling in his gut.

"Betrest, dear, who—exactly—are you bait for?"

CHAPTER 54

Mereruka heard his brothers before he saw them. Betrest looked relieved not to have to answer his pointed question, and was quick to run to the barrier. Mereruka followed closely behind, conspicuously placing the scroll within eyeshot of the threshold. He would be curious as to how Khety would react when he saw it.

"Betrest!" Serfka's eyes went wide with shock and then relief as he raced forward. "No one has been able to find you for a whole day. None of your servants could tell me where you'd gone."

Ever cautious, as Mereruka should have been, Khety held back Radjedef and Serfka from getting closer. In Serfka's case, the vizier nearly fell back when Khety grabbed his shoulder with his taloned hand to stop him. Of all his brothers, Khety appeared the most fragile, when in reality he was physically the strongest. Khety looked over the magic and sneered.

"Well, I owe you an apology, Serfka. It seems this was not Mereruka's doing after all. Though I am a little disappointed that he fell for it so easily."

Serfka puzzled over the magic now that he'd realised something other than the queen was before him.

"Itet? But-"

"She's shit at magic," Radjedef finished. "Her father was probably one of the shifters Mother kept in her harem."

Serfka pursed his lips in disapproval at the language, and likely the disapproval in Radjedef's tone. Serfka had long entreated Khety to allow shapeshifters back into court and the administration, to no avail.

As Khety looked over the room, he zeroed in on the scroll. Mereruka held onto a placid expression as Khety's bright blue eyes blazed with something akin to panic. It took an effort of will not to smile. Khety looked away, pushed his white hair from his bright orange face and sighed, recovering his composure.

"To leave, one must take another's place," Khety said.

"I'll call a few servants to—" Serfka began.

Mereruka shook his head.

"Only family may enter, Serfka."

"Then, Your Most Just, please allow me to take your place." Serfka stepped through the threshold and bowed to Betrest.

"Do bring the scroll with you when you leave, wife," Khety drawled.

"Scroll?" Serfka asked.

Khety pointed to the very one.

"Itet swore to reveal the kingdom's secrets if I didn't comply with her threats," Khety answered smoothly.

Without even looking at the broken seal, Serfka picked up the scroll and passed it to Betrest with a warm, reassuring smile and a pat on her hand. Damned fool. How had Mereruka missed this before, this affection between them? Betrest walked towards the barrier and passed through, until the scroll caught her. Try as she might to pull it through, the item wouldn't budge. She looked to Khety, confused and pleading. His scowl dripped with scorn.

"Radjedef, the scroll," Khety intoned.

"But—"

"Now," Khety hissed.

Cowed, Radjedef stepped across the threshold, allowing Betrest to pull the scroll through at last. Khety took the item and clutched it in his hand, relief obvious. Betrest forgotten, he surveyed the trap into which all three of his brothers had walked. The calculation that followed was brutal, but expected. He barely spared Radjedef a glance, though his eyes tightened at the sight of his exceedingly competent vizier. But when Mereruka met his stare, only the predator in Khety shone out.

Before he could speak, a small section of the roof of the chamber parted. Khety and Betrest craned their necks to catch a glimpse of the mechanism, while Mereruka and his brothers stared upwards, wary.

Mereruka's heart sank. A thick metal grate made of iron barred the ceiling, outlined by a multitude of torches burning in the chamber above. No need to search the dreaded stuff out then.

Itet glared down into the trap, her blue eyes wild.

"Where is that fucking monster, Khety?!" she shrieked. She prowled along the edges like starving jackal, growling when she surmised he was nowhere to be found. "Three out of four isn't bad. Just need to kill him the old fashioned way," she muttered. Itet spared her three prisoners a hateful glare. "Goodbye, brothers. May you rot in the deepest of hells, where you belong after what you did to Inky," she hissed.

"Itet! Please!"

"You dumb cow, I—"

Itet silenced Serfka and Radjedef with an enraged scream. She spat at Mereruka.

"At least you have the decency not to protest, you slimy bastard! As for the two of you, neither one of you lifted a gods-damned finger to save Inkaef from Khety! You deserve to die as much as he does." Her ominous tone was punctured by the spiked club she hefted over her shoulder.

Now that Mereruka looked closely, she also had a bow and quiver strapped on, and a tangle of protective amulets strung about her neck. She wore her armour, polished to a high sheen. Khety was her prey tonight. Good.

His relief quickly vanished when several holes opened in the remaining roof of the chamber. Torrents of water gushed out, accompanied by the briny scent of the sea.

"Serfka!" Betrest cried.

Mereruka turned his attention to the queen. A slab of rock rose from the ground at her feet, the better to seal the chamber, no doubt. Mereruka cursed. Calculation complete, Khety smiled genially at his panicked brothers.

"Never fear, brothers, I shall deal with this predicament. Come along, Betrest," Khety said as he tugged her nonchalantly from threshold.

"Hurry, brother! We won't have long before the chamber is entirely flooded!" Serfka called as the slab sealed them inside.

Mereruka looked back up at the grate, but Itet was already gone.

"It's fine. Khety will find her and put an end to this madness," Serfka said.

Mereruka wasn't certain if he said it for their benefit or his own. Radjedef rounded on Mereruka and punched him squarely in the jaw, knocking him to the floor.

"This is your damned fault! We're going to die in here because of you!" Radjedef roared.

Serfka held Radjedef back as Mereruka smirked, touching his jaw.

"He doesn't mean that, Meri," Serfka said, ever the peacemaker, his eyes apologetic.

"Oh? But he's entirely correct." Mereruka groaned as he stood. Already his ankles were submerged. Now, in this dire situation, he had nothing left to do but use it for the likely doomed yet potentially golden opportunity it was.

Radjedef shoved out of Serfka's grip and prowled the room like a restless lion. He rested his forehead against a stone wall and pounded the rough-cut rock in hopeless frustration. Serfka, entirely bewildered looked between the two of them.

"What do you mean?"

"I'm certain Khety will deal with Itet, but only after we die, gasping for air with our faces pressed against the iron grate above."

"He wouldn't—"

"He would. He knows I plan to kill him for the throne. Khety has already calculated that my death is worth Radjedef's life and yours."

"You... you—" Serfka stuttered as the truth sank in. He looked as if Mereruka had stuck a knife in his heart. "All this time, I protected you. I defended you!"

"Tonight seems to be one for revelations," Mereruka noted dryly.

"But I'm the *vizier*! I run the whole of Maat! Khety needs only nod his head and use his seal and his job is done!"

Mereruka nodded sagely, enjoying Serfka's rare outburst of temper.

"And yet, you are disposable, as are we all. Though, try not to think too much of your own fortunes, brother. Pity Betrest." Mereruka did his best to hide his grin as he twisted the blade further in Serfka's heart.

Serfka rounded on Mereruka then, grabbing him by the arms with his four grey-blue hands, shaking him violently.

"What about Betrest?"

"Think for a moment. I walked into this trap to free the one meant as bait for me. The scroll was meant for Khety. How long will it take Khety to realise that Betrest was the bait meant for another?"

Serfka's face was a study in devastation. Mereruka pressed his advantage.

"Poor woman. Married to a man who cared not a whit for her, refusing to even give her the comfort of children. But you can absolutely believe that her infidelity will infuriate him. He's not one for sharing. And to think, what Khety has could all have been yours, Serfka."

"How did you know..?"

Mereruka blinked in surprise. The vizier had known that dark secret all along? He couldn't help but laugh.

"The scroll, Serfka. It was Mother's will. It confirmed what I always suspected—that mother died because she was going to ignore tradition and make you king upon her death. So, if you knew this, why didn't you fight?"

A whole kingdom had been on the line. Serfka had already been well-loved and highly competent back then as well, only a step away from being vizier. The crown could easily have been his, with only Khety's anger to deal with.

Serfka glared, hopeless fury burning in his silver eyes.

"Because I wanted to live, damn you! I didn't want to have to kill my own brother just because of Mother's bloody whims!"

Mereruka scowled. Yet another brother proved craven. Serfka's weakness sickened him. He'd been strong enough, politically and magically, to put up a real fight. If he'd just taken the crown, Nefertnesu would still be whole and alive.

"Well, it seems Mother was wrong about you anyway." Mereruka glared back. "Because your cowardice has only benefitted Khety in the end. Nefertnesu sacrificed her heart for his cowardice. Inkaef died because of his cruelty. While you run the whole of Maat, he does as he pleases. And it pleases him that we three shall die."

"If you hadn't coveted the throne of Maat, then—"

Mereruka shoved Serfka away with a snarl.

"When I am King of Maat, you will get to live as you please, Serfka. Betrest will be yours, no more subterfuge. You will never need fear for your life, because *I* understand its value. If you want proof of my fairness, you need only ask Radjedef."

Radjedef scoffed.

"That's one word for it," he muttered darkly, though he didn't contradict him.

Now that Khety had shown his hand, Mereruka might as well be a paragon of sanity and virtue. Hope shone in Serfka's eyes. Victory.

"Then I hope you have the favour of the forgotten gods, Meri," Serfka replied, hope replaced by misery as the water level rose, "You will need it if we stand any hope of surviving this trap."

Mereruka didn't need the gods to favour him, he needed them to favour his wife. The only way he would survive this was if she managed to kill Itet herself. He sent a silent prayer.

CHAPTER 55

Taisiya sat in a dark alcove, feeling like a useless fool as she watched the entrance to the room below. She'd underestimated Itet, and now Bas had paid in blood and flesh. Taisiya only hoped that something could be done for him.

Beneath that worry and fear for Bas, something darker lurked. Father had always warned her that vows made on the dragon's heart were not just words. Now that Bas had been attacked, she wanted vengeance. That was normal. Except she also wanted to tear Itet apart with her teeth, and rip out her bloody viscera with her bare hands. Her heart was not entirely her own as it sang a siren's song of wicked violence in her mind. Her throat clenched as she fought the urge to howl with fury.

Vicious thoughts were interrupted by male voices and the bright light of magic. She breathed as silently as she was able and held herself still as they passed her hiding spot.

"Who would dare to threaten each of us?" Serfka asked, puzzled.

"Are you really so obtuse? This is obviously Mereruka's work. There is no other man so shameless," Khety scoffed.

"I second that opinion. How can you not see his nature, Serfka?" Radjedef growled.

"He has done nothing but your bidding since you sent him to the Cursed Continent. I know the two of you dislike each other, but you're letting that cloud your reasoning." Serfka's tone was all that was rational.

"We shall see about that. But if he is behind this, I will not withhold my displeasure. He will take the mark of disinheritance for it," Khety said.

Radjedef grunted his approval.

"The two of you…" Serfka sighed.

They descended into the rock-cut chamber below, their voices growing indistinct, taking the light with them. As her eyes readjusted to the darkness, the faint clip of hooves had her freezing once more. She strained her ears. If that was Itet, as Taisiya suspected, the woman was walking away. If Taisiya followed, she wouldn't be close at hand if Mereruka needed her aid. Then again, if she could kill Itet, he would be free. Decision made, Taisiya removed her sandals, ready to hunt her prey.

Indistinct shouting halted her. It sounded like Itet, but she couldn't be sure. No one else made a sound she could hear, then there was a rush of water and the grinding of stone against stone. Two sets of footsteps approached her. No hooves. Taisiya ducked back into her hiding spot as the same magical light returned.

"Khety, we must alert the royal guard. They won't have long until they drown," Betrest pleaded, quickening her pace.

Khety caught her by her arm and pulled her back, a sneer on his face.

"We will do no such thing. We will return to our quarters and rouse the guard in the morning. The wards will keep that she-goat out."

"But Serfka—"

"Was a fine vizier and will be sorely missed."

"Khety, please—"

"I will *not* repeat myself. I have waited two centuries to be rid of Mereruka, and if my vizier has to drown, so be it. Another word of protest, and I'll see to it that no one knows I found you, and Hemetre wears your crown. Have I made myself clear?" Khety hissed.

"Yes," Betrest whispered, defeated.

Taisiya's gut sank. As they left, taking their light with them, Taisiya dared to creep out of hiding. If what they'd said was true, she didn't have a moment to lose—Itet had left only moments ago. Fleet of foot and silent as a whisper, Taisiya held her gauzy skirt bunched in both hands, fearful that even the barest swish of fabric would alert the fae woman she stalked. In time, she caught of a glimpse of Itet ahead. But where to confront her? As she crept along the winding corridors in this newly constructed palace, she entered a vast, colonnaded room devoid of the usual colourful decorations. Sketched lines and half-complete reliefs were reflected by the moonlight spelled into the ceiling. Taisiya ducked behind the nearest column, lest Itet catch a glimpse of her.

With so many places to act as cover, the time to strike had come. Taisiya held her breath as she stepped out from behind her column and loosed a bolt of lightning at the fae princess. The bolt inexplicably arced over Itet. Itet flew some distance but swiftly recovered, her movements nimble. She spun to face Taisiya. Hooking a finger through the chain that held a charm on the end, she sneered.

"Deflection charm."

Shit.

Itet had her bow in hand and knocked an arrow with blinding speed.

"Tell your husband I sent you when you meet him in hell."

Taisiya whirled behind her column as Itet's arrow raced past her ear with a keening whistle.

"I suppose I should have gone for you instead. I hear your lives are linked, and without your lightning, you make an easier target."

Taisiya tore her long skirts to avoid getting tangled in their length. She bunched up the fabric and tossed it one way while she ran for the cover of the nearest column in the other direction. Itet's first arrow found her discarded skirts, but her next arrow sliced through the skin on the back of Taisiya's leg. She muffled her scream.

"Didn't I promise to go hunting together? Tell me, witch, did you know then we would be hunting each other?" Itet hissed.

"Honestly? I had hoped to avoid it," Taisiya answered, throwing her voice. "I was convinced you could be made an ally. Even more so after Khety killed your brother."

"You killed my brother as much as Khety did!" Itet screamed.

Itet's hooves heralded her charge. But she had rushed to the spot where Taisiya had thrown her voice, one column over. Taisiya let loose another shot of lightning. While the electricity failed to harm Itet, the force itself had not been negated. Itet's head smashed into the stone column hard enough to fracture a part of it. She switched her bow for a mace, tossing the broken weapon and quiver to the ground with a snarl.

Good.

Much to Taisiya's surprise, Itet leapt from her prone position with alacrity, brushing off the injury as if it were nothing. She hooked her green finger around another chain. She grinned as she circled, the charm dangling.

"Healing charm."

Not good. Taisiya loosed another bolt, tossing Itet further away. Damn, this wouldn't work. She needed to do something even that charm couldn't heal.

Itet threw her broken mace to the ground and palmed a number of daggers on her person.

"Run."

Taisiya obliged, ducking behind another column just in time to save her already bleeding leg from getting skewered. She barely managed to stay one step ahead, always rushing for another column, dodging another dagger. Taisiya needed to think. If Itet couldn't be hurt by the lightning, or by the force of being thrown by it, she had to hit the woman with something else. Sharp pain lashed her foot, making Taisiya gasp. She'd run full circle, into the rubble left behind when Itet had flown into the column. The solution clicked in her mind. Itet's dagger pierced her calf. Taisiya cried out and fell.

Itet approached her slowly, palming her dagger, a grim, cold look in her blue eyes.

"I think it's time you gave up. We both know you're done running, and Khety is getting away."

She loosed a bolt of lightning, flinging Itet across the room into another column. Itet recovered slower this time, fury in her expression.

"We've been over this," she growled. "Healing! Charm!"

Taisiya unleashed a veritable storm at and around Itet. Pinned against the column by Taisiya's onslaught, Itet howled in anger. Chips of rock went flying, scattering about the chamber and cutting Taisiya as they flew past. Still, she didn't stop, not until she'd done what she needed. Nearly spent, Taisiya relented, gasping for breath. She hadn't trained to use so much of her magic at once before, but it had been worth it. Taisiya looked up, almost ignoring Itet as she approached.

"Done?" Itet asked, shaking off rock dust and rubble.

Taisiya didn't answer, just smiled.

"You know, we could have been friends," Itet said, her eyes cold and hollow.

"I know. But then you hurt my son," Taisiya answered.

Just as Itet made to charge, the ceiling above Itet crashed down with a deafening crack. Taisiya shielded herself with a cage of her own lightning as rocks the size of wardrobes splintered and whizzed past, sending up a choking cloud of rocky debris. As if to add final note to the decimation, a column collapsed, cracking with a deep, reverberating boom. The sharp scrape of smaller rocks flowed outward from the devastation.

When the dust had finally cleared, Taisiya pulsed her lightning cage, shrugging off the last of the rubble and then released her magic, utterly spent. A small fragment of Itet's horn lay littered amongst the rubble. Taisiya sighed. It was over now. The magic trapping Mereruka had been undone. Picking herself up, she limped across the rock-strewn floor, not daring to remove the blade in her leg lest she cause more harm. As Taisiya was testing her balance, the rubble shifted. It was all the warning she had before she was struck from behind.

The water level was half an arm's length from the ceiling. In a matter of moments, it would be impossible to avoid pressing one's face against the iron of the grate above. Mereruka found himself staring up at those iron bars as he treaded water, wondering if the agony would be worth the air his lungs would burn for. At least Radjedef would be the first one to taste that particular horror. Already he was struggling to angle himself so that his four scaled horns wouldn't touch it before it was absolutely necessary. Serfka seemed half in shock as he stared above at the fate awaiting him.

"He can't... he can't mean to leave us to die here."

Mereruka was inclined to slap him, but he was still hoping he might survive this and Serfka needed to be on his side. Thankfully, Radjedef had grown sick of the Vizier's desperate denial. Mereruka was only sur-prised it had taken this long for him to scream.

"If we survive, no one will ever call me thick-headed again! Not so long as *you* stand in the same bloody room! Khety is happy to let us drown! Will you be kissing iron before you realise that?" Radjedef snapped. "And you!" He turned his furious yellow gaze on Mereruka.

"Me?" Mereruka asked.

"What in the hells is your wife doing? How long does it take to shoot one gods-damned bolt of lightning into that fucking she-goat?"

As if in answer, Taisiya was thrown against the iron grate above, barely conscious and bleeding profusely from the head. Her fair skin was a tapestry of cuts, her hair a ragged mess. She cried out as Itet knelt atop her, using his wife's body as a barrier against the iron.

"Taisiya!"

Heedlessly, he grabbed the bars above, forcing his arm through in an attempt to shove Itet off her. The acid bite of the iron burned his skin the same moment his glamour guttered out. His siblings gasped in shock. Mereruka seized on their distraction to grab one of Itet's hooves, grating her leg against the iron bars as he pulled her off Taisiya. She bucked against his hold and shrieked, slicing through his wet hand with her hoof. Mereruka's skin was already blistering in contact with the iron, yet, horrifyingly, Itet's flank recovered before his eyes.

"Oh, that's a rich look, coming from tattooed scum! At least I come by my resistance honestly." She proudly hooked a finger through a healing charm. "And I'm as sturdy as an elf with this little beauty, Mereruka. Now, you can watch your bitch wife choke to death in front of you," Itet growled as she repositioned herself on top of Taisiya and wrapped her green fingers around Taisiya's pale throat.

"No! No!" Mereruka roared, desperate as Taisiya choked and struggled weakly before his eyes. The blisters burst on his hand as he grabbed Itet's wrist, desperate to break her hold. Without any real leverage, she shrugged him off with ease. "Damn you, Itet! Kill her, and I'll lay a death curse!"

"You would, wouldn't you?" she growled, her face twisted in a mask of rage. "Too bad Inkaef didn't think to do the same!"

"I won't curse *you*, Itet! I'll curse Inkaef to suffer alongside me for an eternity, in a special hell just for us! I will rip him away from whatever peace he has!" Mereruka threatened. It was no idle threat, and it was so easily done. If you were willing to suffer an eternity of true damnation for a single dark wish, anything you desired could be done. And if Taisiya was lost to him, he didn't give a damn what happened to his soul.

Itet loosened her hold. Taisiya gasped and wheezed, finally breathing, clawing in vain as Itet's hands still held firm.

"You wouldn't!" Itet hissed, though a note of fear threaded through her vehemence.

"If you take my heart, I'll take yours between my teeth and rip it to shreds!" Mereruka snarled, still gripping the iron, careful not to allow his open wound to touch the metal.

She hesitated, measuring her wrath against his. Itet's eyes turned hollow, as if her heart had been encased in ice. Taisiya choked and flailed, her eyes wide with panic as Itet's grip turned lethal.

"So be it."

"No!" Mereruka screamed, gripping both her wrists in his hands in a futile bid to wrench her hands from Taisiya's throat. It was useless. Itet had always been uncommonly strong for a fae, her strength a rival for any shapeshifter. Now he understood why—the cursed bitch was half-shifter, and she'd inherited a relative immunity to iron's poisonous touch.

The water rose higher. They couldn't avoid the iron any longer. Radjedef swore a blue streak and cursed Itet in every language he knew. Serfka screamed, begging Itet for mercy. Itet ignored them all as she slowly squeezed the life from Taisiya.

"What in the hells is *that?!*" Serfka shouted, his eyes wide with a fear entirely separate from drowning.

Itet scowled at him. Dark talons coated in inky flames rose up out of the gloom and circled Itet's neck from behind. Mereruka's heart leapt with joy.

"Her head! Cut off her head!" Mereruka called, breathing in his last few gasps of air.

Vasilisa shrieked as she ripped Itet off Taisiya and held the fae aloft. With brutal strength, Vasilisa sank her talons into Itet's neck as she thrashed, her eyes wide with panic and agony. Dark blood ran in streams down Itet's chest, pouring from her mouth like a font, splashing into the frothing waters below. Mereruka fancied he could hear skin split and bone crack as Vasilisa tore Itet's neck apart, severing her head in a gory shower of blood.

With Itet's death, the spell damning Mereruka and his brothers to death had broken. The water receded swiftly as the barriers below were undone, sending Mereruka plunging below. He kept his eyes on Taisiya as she wheezed and coughed above. Vasilisa, coated in blood, was already tending to her. Though his skin sizzled with heart-stopping pain, Mereruka could finally breathe easy. Saffron tattoos on full display, he reluctantly turned his attention to his now wary brothers.

"We three should have a very serious discussion once we've swum out of here. And don't get any ideas. The wraith above is one of mine."

CHAPTER 56

Vasilisa's soothing voice and gentle hands had lulled Taisiya into unconsciousness, but she woke to Radjedef's grating shouts. Shockingly, Taisiya felt no pain as she sat upright. No cuts, no wounds. She sucked in a panicked breath, hands shaking as she touched her neck. She could still feel Itet's fingers digging into her flesh, torturing her as Mereruka watched. Itet could have killed her in an instant, but had instead brought her to the brink over and over again, her cruel grasp loosening just enough for a single gasp and then tightening like a vise. But something else was around her neck now, and she fumbled to pull it away. Vasilisa's hand touched hers, stilling her.

"She's dead," Vasilisa answered, pulling her hand away to reveal the charm that had caused Taisiya no end of trouble. It was still dark and sticky with blood. Itet's blood.

"And Bas?"

"Safe and whole."

Taisiya sighed, relief nearly deflating her. The angry hum in her heart quieted.

"Feeling better?"

Taisiya nodded, not daring to put words to her newest nightmare. Gods help her, she seemed to be collecting them of late.

"Thanks to you."

Vasilisa wrapped her arms around Taisiya and took a deep breath.

"Stop making this a habit. You're not supposed to go places I can't follow," she said, her harsh, desperate whisper making Taisiya's heart clench.

Taisiya wrapped her arms around her friend, trying to ignore the jolt of panic at the sensation of skin and pressure against her neck.

"I suppose if I do, you'll have to lure me with treats."

"Not. Funny," Vasilisa grunted.

"It is a little."

Vasilisa frowned, pinching Taisiya's side.

Taisiya's surprised exclamation alerted the men to her state. They ceased bickering, all three dripping wet, with horrible blisters on their faces. Mereruka was at her side in an instant, looking her over with concern before he was satisfied. She reached out to touch his hand when he shied away. Her eyes widened in horror at the sight of them—blistered, deeply cut and bleeding. It hurt just to look at them.

"Your hands!"

"Vasilisa, if you would please," Mereruka's grin was forced. "She is awake and well now."

Vasilisa sighed, abandoning her post by Taisiya's side for the nearest shadow. She glared back at both Radjedef and Serfka.

"Run, and when I find you, you'll wish I hadn't."

It was all the warning she gave before she disappeared into the shadows. Radjedef shivered involuntarily. Taisiya held out the charm around her neck for Mereruka. He shook his head.

"She wouldn't leave your side until you woke. I've asked her to fetch us some water of the Hapi to heal our wounds as the charm won't do us any good," Mereruka explained. "In the meantime, I'm trying to persuade my brothers to heed me."

"Why should I? I may have taken the mark of disinheritance, but you... well, look at you! If I'm unfit to rule Maat because of this," Radjedef gestured at his forehead, "you're not fit to rule over a cave in the desert!" He gestured to Mereruka's many tattoos.

Taisiya blinked again, just now realising his tattoos were visible, and the gravity of it. Though the glowing, saffron tattoos were starkly beautiful against the teal of his skin, they were not alone, safely ensconced within his pocket realm. His secret had been revealed, his bitterness and anger evident in the grim line of his mouth, his fear in the tense set of his shoulders. She flicked her eyes to his brothers, mind buzzing.

"Does my sweet husband require his wife's help?"

She touched the part of his face she safely could with gentle fingertips. He leaned into her touch, a flicker of hope in his citrine eyes.

"It couldn't go amiss."

Taisiya nodded and stood. Brushing her matted, filthy hair from her blood-stained brow, she smoothed out what remained of her torn dress before she donned her best cruel sneer. Testing her magic, she felt the hum of lightning beneath her skin. It reared up again inside her like a hungry beast, restored by the magic within the amulet. Sparks danced across her skin.

"Perhaps you should heed my husband and I, my brothers-in-law, seeing as how I am the only one here with access to her magic."

The touch of iron had suppressed their magic the same as it had Mereruka's. Here, her lightning reigned supreme. Radjedef and Serfka were silent at her threat, eyeing her warily.

"Radjedef, you swore not to do harm to me or mine. I consider insubordination and spreading my husband's secrets to be harm. So, you will either keep your mouth shut or our deal is off, and I will take out my anger on a very specific person currently under my guardianship. Understood?"

"But you swore!"

"As did you! Do not test me!" Taisiya shouted back, punctuating her anger with a crackle of lightning.

Radjedef's glare was positively mutinous. The bastard would no doubt look for the first loophole to betray her and Mereruka. Taisiya sighed. She'd hoped to use this for something a little more grand, but it seemed the time had come.

"I'm calling in my favour."

The magic between her and Radjedef pulled at the centre of her. Heavy, invisible chains snapped tight at her words. He grunted and nodded, silent.

"You will swear your ultimate loyalty to me, using your true name, knowing that if you seek to betray me, you will accept whatever punishment I decide to grant, irrespective of any other deals we make or have made."

Serfka choked in surprise.

"That's treason! You couldn't possibly—" Serfka gasped.

"She can and she will. Laws have nothing to do with it," Mereruka interrupted, a satisfied grin lighting up his marred face.

Taisiya stared Radjedef down until he relented. Kneeling, he made his oath. Just like when she stood over the heart of her ancestor, the magic of a promise seeped into her bones. Radjedef was hers to command now.

"Radjedef, you are now my vassal. I will keep your secrets as you are to keep mine. Mereruka's tattoos are never to be spoken of again, and you will not voice a word of objection when we take the throne, understand?"

"I understand," Radjedef grunted.

"But you can't! It's forbidden for a royal to swear an oath of loyalty to another member of the royal bloodline!" Serfka sputtered.

"Then it's a good thing she's a foreign mage," Mereruka retorted.

Taisiya ignored him, focusing solely on Radjedef.

"Also, when we do kill Khety, you and the rest of the guards will stay out of our way."

Radjedef snorted.

"Gladly."

Taisiya shared a triumphant little glance with her husband. Then she set her sights on Serfka.

"And what are your objections, vizier?"

It was probably not the right question to ask, as he looked like he might pull out a lengthy scroll from the pocket of his sopping kilt. Before he could begin on a blustering, self-righteous tirade, Mereruka cut in.

"Before you answer, Serfka, perhaps my wife should hear the latest secret revealed tonight."

Taisiya raised a curious brow at her husband.

"Now, just wait a—"

Ignoring Serfka's protest, Mereruka fairly glowed with unholy glee.

"It seems the vizier and the queen have grown *close* to one another. So close, in fact, that Serfka happily stepped into Itet's trap to secure Betrest's freedom. For now, Khety seems to be unaware of their tender feelings, but..." Mereruka trailed off, turning predatory eyes on his brother.

Taisiya smiled coyly.

"It would be a shame if Khety was told plainly of the relationship between the two of you. Some might even call such a betrayal... treason. Or am I mistaken in that assumption, Vizier? Is it considered treason to fuck the king's wife, or just very bad manners?"

Taisiya watched with great satisfaction as the blue-skinned vizier squirmed under her gaze. When she smiled, she knew he'd seen her fangs. Cheeks heating and eyes locked on his sopping wet feet, the Vizier tightened his fists and released a small, nearly inaudible sigh of defeat. It was a beautiful sound.

"What would you have me do?"

"Swear your ultimate loyalty to me. We will spirit both you and Betrest away before Khety realises your illicit relationship. Meri?"

"My wife will gladly accept your oaths now," Mereruka replied, standing tall and proud once more. It gladdened her to see it.

Serfka choked out his oaths on bended knee.

"Now you just have to kill Khety," Radjedef scoffed. "Good luck with that. When he sees that we've survived, he might just decide to throw caution to the wind and go for your head himself."

"That is an excellent point," Mereruka mused.

Taisiya did her best not to be petty by adding that she was surprised he'd thought so far ahead. Unfortunately, he'd spoken true. Khety had been willing to see the only sibling he had any use for drown just to be rid of Mereruka. Now that even his most loyal sibling had been turned fully against him, all bets were off. But that was only if they played this next game fairly. And playing fair was a fool's game.

"And if he doesn't know we survived?"

Now that they had his brothers' oaths, Mereruka wanted nothing more than to wash his hands of his brothers so that he could hold Taisiya in his arms without reserve, and then immediately find his son and do the same. However, Taisiya's rather bold plan needed to be worked out before he could let his detestable siblings out of his sight. Oaths or not, he trusted them very little. While she argued over logistics with Radjedef and Serfka, Vasilisa returned with the waters of the Hapi. The darkness mage passed the bucket of water to Mereruka first, her grey, predatory eyes watching his brothers with open distrust.

"Are they really more useful alive?"

"Only time will tell," Mereruka replied, sighing with relief as the water healed the burns and blisters covering his arms, upper torso, face and neck. He would need his tattoos re-inked yet again.

"Qar and Nofret returned not long after we went to get Bas. They're with him now."

His eyes met hers, and yet his voice was trapped. She'd briefly said that he was whole and alive, but that didn't mean his son was well by any stretch. A shapeshifter could recover from injuries between forms, but for those who had yet to reach maturity, the task was not so easily done. Guilt and shame and dread stopped him from asking her. Thankfully, she saw right through him.

"I didn't leave Bas' side until I'd seen that he was going to be okay. Qar helped him. But my delay almost cost Taisiya her life."

Mereruka shook his head.

"You got my son to safety, *and* you saved Taisiya's life. You have nothing to be ashamed of."

The only one here who needed to feel shame was him. No matter what he did, the people he loved were hurt. Powerless wretch that he was, Mereruka hadn't been able to do anything. One day he would have everything he needed to keep them safe. All that was left was this final gambit before he could take Khety's head and have what he needed.

Vasilisa eye's slid to Taisiya, her posture stiff with undisguised guilt, eyes swimming with concern.

"If you touch her, be careful of her neck. She tried to hide her panic, and I don't want either of those bastards to see her flinch," she whispered.

Mereruka nodded, subduing the hot flare of guilt in his gut by sheer will. He reached out his hand to touch Vasilisa's.

"Thank you for saving her."

Vasilisa shook her head, her expression grim.

"You never have to thank me for that."

"Yes, I do. I'm blessed to have you as part of my family, Vasilisa."

Vasilisa blinked back tears and bit her lip before she hid her reaction behind a characteristic smirk.

"You have it backwards, Mereruka. You've been blessed to be a part of *my* family."

Mereruka chuckled.

"So I am. If Bas has recovered, bring Nofret here and tell Qar to stand guard until I return."

Vasilisa stepped into a shadow as he again dipped his iron-burned hands into the waters of the Hapi, grateful for the relief. He scooped up handfuls and let the water heal the last of the burns and blisters along his arms, neck, chest and face. Fully rid of the iron's taint, his magic was at his command once more. Reasserting his glamour, he joined Taisiya in her argument with his brothers.

"You really expect me to abandon my duties for this ill-considered prank?" Serfka groused.

"If they think I'm dead, Khety's men in my ranks will scheme their way into my position!" Radjedef argued.

Mereruka clapped Serfka and Radjedef on the back and grinned with a touch of menace. These assholes were preventing him from holding his wife and son. That wouldn't do.

"Neither of you is looking at this as the opportunity it is. Think of it as a way to discover who among your ranks is untrustworthy in your absence." Mereruka looked to Serfka first. "The administrators you've trained can handle Maat for a few days, else you would never have allowed them to remain in their positions. Were I you, I would concern myself with how best to steal Betrest away unnoticed." He then turned his gaze to Radjedef. "And if Khety's men concern you, then let them make themselves known and be rid of them. Cut the rot from Maat's military forces as you see fit. You'll not hear a word of complaint from me. But only after we've dealt with Khety."

While not ecstatic, Radjedef seemed at least mollified. Serfka, however, was adamant in his distaste.

"Pretending to be dead is a foolish idea. He'll be suspicious when he finds Itet dead but fails to find our bodies. After that, you'll have no hope of ever getting near him. No, I won't go along with this."

Mereruka could see a vein in Taisiya's neck throbbing with her barely suppressed anger. She quirked a copper brow at Serfka.

"What if all he finds is rubble? If he is to assume we were all crushed beneath it? I already destroyed the room I fought Itet in."

While Radjedef and Serfka healed their own iron burns, both the vizier and overseer of the royal guard exchanged glances.

"It could work," Radjedef said.

"Except from that point on, he would have only his most trusted soldiers guarding him." Serfka took note of Mereruka's glamour before looking away. "As... *formidable* as your tattoos have let you become, not even you could overcome the combined magics of Khety's royal guard." Serfka sighed.

Unfortunately, he did have a point. Mereruka scowled, but had nothing to retort. If Vasilisa tried to drag him into the void, it might work, but if Khety already had protections against such an attack, as he likely would by now, her life would be in danger. He didn't want to take any more risks with his family's lives. They had all suffered enough for his lack of foresight.

"Prince Mereruka!"

Nofret emerged from the darkness, a genuine smile on her face.

"Nofret, are you well? We're just debating how to use our soon-to-be publicly lamented deaths to get close enough to Khety to kill him."

"Ah, yes, Vasilisa informed me he had left you to die by Itet's trap." Nofret noticed his siblings, taking note of Radjedef's mark, and bowed. "Prince Radjedef, Prince Serfka."

"Why bring your first scribe? What could she possibly add to this mess?" Radjedef frowned.

Serfka's brow pinched in confusion before he gasped.

"You're not… surely you're not mother's late spymaster?"

"There is nothing *late* about me, Prince Serfka. Though you have an excellent memory. I have not gone by that title for nearly two hundred years." Nofret bowed again. "So you plan to fake your own deaths to catch Khety off-guard? How will you account for your missing corpses?"

"Destroying the buildings," Taisiya said.

Nofret nodded with approval.

"If you wish to get close to Khety, then it must be at the funerals he will be forced to host for you. Though his guards will be present, so will a large number of nobles and their servants, to say nothing of the staff or entertainers."

Wouldn't that be a sight, sneaking into his own funeral feast in order to assassinate his brother? At least when Khety died, neither the festivities nor the sarcophagi would be wasted. Mereruka grinned.

"I expect Khety would hire a great many professional mourners for the occasion. It would be obscene not to, with four siblings and a sister-in-law all having perished in a single night."

Nofret caught his meaning and beamed. Radjedef laughed. Serfka was slack-jawed with disgust.

"I'm speechless! Posing as professional mourners at your own funeral? That… I have no words for such a twisted ruse!" Serfka protested.

"On the contrary, you seem capable of producing a great many words for a man struck speechless by horror," Taisiya retorted.

"I would be honoured to take care of the arrangements for you, Prince Mereruka. Will your brothers be joining you in this, or…"

Radjedef shrugged.

"Might as well."

"I—" Serfka hesitated.

"You'll have no better chance to take Betrest out of harm's way," Mereruka interrupted.

Serfka scowled but relented.

"Gods forgive me. Yes, fine."

Mereruka nodded.

"Though I hate to offer shelter to you ingrates, you will require secure lodgings for the foreseeable future." Mereruka grimaced.

It had not escaped his notice that while his brothers excelled at whining, they were terribly short on manners. They hadn't even bothered to thank either Taisiya or Vasilisa for saving their pathetic lives. If they didn't start showing some damned respect, he'd find another iron cage and leave them locked up in it once this was over.

"Yes, we will." Serfka sighed.

Radjedef nodded.

"Vasilisa, would you be so kind as to deliver my brothers to Qar and explain the situation? Taisiya, Nofret and I will see to the destruction of the building in the meantime."

Both his brothers recoiled when Vasilisa clapped her hands on their shoulders, her smile one of unholy glee. Radjedef's nostrils flared in fear. Unlike Serfka, he knew what awaited him.

"Come. The void awaits. Do try not to flail. It will attract the things which hunger."

"Merciful gods—" Serfka gasped, dragged into the void with a sharp, none-too-gentle yank.

When they were gone from sight, Mereruka swept Taisiya up in his arms for a much-delayed kiss, careful not to touch her neck. She wrapped her arms around him and devoured him hungrily, her shaking fingers clenched in his hair.

"Reckless," he growled between kisses. "Damned," he groaned as she tugged on his hair to bring his mouth back on hers. "Woman," he hissed as she nipped his ear.

"You have no ground to stand on! You could have died!" she hissed back.

"I'm a shameless hypocrite. You already know this."

She huffed but buried herself in his embrace.

Nofret politely cleared her throat.

"Perhaps we should turn this building to rubble? I'm sure you would both like to return to the barge and get cleaned up."

Taisiya's amethyst eyes swam with emotion, mirroring his own turmoil. Best get this over with quick. He needed the comfort of her wrapped around him.

"Yes, let's get on with the destruction."

Chapter 57

The barge was tethered near the palace, still and serene. Only the gentle night breeze and the creaking of wood interrupted the quiet. Within its sumptuous walls, where the noise was muffled, serenity was in short supply. Mereruka, Taisiya and Nofret arrived to raised, bitter voices and a distinct lack of calm and decorum. Mereruka stifled a sigh.

"You'll sleep where I tell you, with my soldiers at your doors. You think I'll trust either of you with your own pocket realms?" Qar snorted with derision.

Qar stood a head taller—and half a man broader—than either of Mereruka's siblings. His hippo ears twitched in anger, flicking his black braids. When he punctuated his words with a feral grin, it was to display overlong incisors.

"But a pocket realm is safest for us!" Serfka whined. "If anyone sees us, your master's whole plan will be for naught!"

Radjedef grunted in agreement, keeping a warrior's stance in Qar's presence. Probably the only sign of respect he would ever give someone of a lower rank than himself.

"No one here will fetch you the requisite sacrifice," Qar replied, not budging an inch.

"What seems to be the problem? Are your quarters not to your liking? Is my hospitality lacking?" Mereruka asked, intentionally letting a hard edge colour his words.

"Your servant's certainly is! All we're asking for is to be able to create pocket realms of our own, for safety!" Serfka replied in a huff.

"Qar is not a servant. He is my overseer of the soldiers, and a man I place a great deal of trust in. And I agree with him on this matter. Though we have your oaths of loyalty, you have not yet earned our trust. You will sleep in your assigned rooms, or Vasilisa will find somewhere in the void for you. After all, since only she can access it, you would be safest of all in there."

Vasilisa helpfully waggled her fingers at his brothers with a sly grin on her face. Colour leached from both their faces.

"What will it be?"

Grudgingly, his brothers followed the soldiers to their rooms. When they were out of sight, Mereruka clapped Qar on the back.

"I'm glad you've returned."

"As am I. No troubles on our way. The three little creatures have been safely stowed in Rhacotis. When we heard you'd been sent to collect dragon scales, we rushed here as quickly as we could."

Mereruka nodded. It was only a shame they hadn't arrived sooner.

"And Bas?" he asked, heart in his throat.

Qar's expression was grim.

"He was in bad shape, but I managed to walk him through the shift. He has his fingers and toes back, same with his tail, and his wounds have healed, but he had a harder time with his ears." Qar flicked his own ears, "I suspect he'll tell you himself."

Just then, Bas came around the corner, bracing himself on the wall, skin pallid and expression drawn. Mereruka rushed to him and gathered him up in his arms. Bas wrapped his arms around Mereruka in turn. *Never again. Never again.*

"I'm sorry." Bas choked on the sob in his throat.

"Hush! The fault is mine."

Mereruka's eyes stung as he peered down at his son. Bas' ragged ears were like an arrow to his heart. Mereruka kissed his head. He would make this right somehow. He would protect his son better, give him the carefree, safe life he deserved. Nofret would simply have to train another to fulfil the role of spy. Bas would never place himself in danger like that again.

"I'll never be a proper spymaster. I broke when she…"

Guilt was a feral beast in his gut. He should never have encouraged Bas in this ambition. *My fault. It's my fault.*

"Nonsense," Taisiya said, touching the small of Mereruka's back. She brushed a few strands of hair on Bas' head. Bas turned watery hazel eyes on her. "Failure is only final if you allow it to be. Do you truly want to be a spymaster, Bas?"

Bas nodded, lip trembling.

Mereruka stiffened, ready to protest. Taisiya's censorious glare might as well have cut off his tongue. She turned her eyes back to Bas, eyes softening.

"Then you will learn from this experience and become the greatest of spymasters. Nofret?"

"Yes, Your Harmoniousness?"

"Do you believe Bas has the ability to take on a role like yours?"

Nofret hesitated when she saw Mereruka's glare but straightened her spine and turned away from him.

"Yes."

Damn her. He would have words for his first scribe come morning.

"Then you and Vasilisa both will teach him. And you Bas, will become the best of spymasters."

Vasilisa hugged Bas from behind, her head leaning on his.

"And I will kill anyone who hurts you," Vasilisa assured him. "Just as I did to Itet."

Seeing he wasn't going to win this battle, Mereruka grudgingly relent-ed. There would be other times to change Bas' mind.

"Nofret, if you will see to the preparations and inform Qar of our plans? Qar, I would like your detailed report in the morning. For now, I'll retire to my pocket realm with my family."

Qar and Nofret bowed as Mereruka escorted his little family into the safest place he knew of.

Taisiya woke in the night to find Mereruka's warmth was no longer beside her. Vasilisa slept to her left and Bas was curled up to the right of where her husband should be. She slipped from the overlarge bed, created to accommodate them all, and sought out her husband as he stared out at the scene of Rhacotis that his magic had woven. Sitting on the edge of the room, his legs dangling off the ledge of the illusory cliff, he sipped wine from a silver chalice, his posture stiff with anger. Undeterred, she sat down beside him.

"Do you need another minute to brood alone?"

"Your humour is grating in this moment."

She waited a few heartbeats.

"How about now?"

His glare was impressive, but the depths of his citrine eyes held no fire.

"You should not have encouraged Bas. He is *my* son. I will—"

"*Our* son, Meri. Bas is *our* son. And if you discourage him after this experience, you will only be telling him that you think he is weak and that he doesn't have what it takes to attain his dreams or face his fears."

"Speaking from experience?" he hissed, a finger caressing her neck as his eyes took on a stony cruelty.

Taisiya did her best not to flinch.

"Yes. Even this." She took his hand and placed it around her throat, forcing herself not to squirm, even though her heart thundered in her chest. "I will overcome it, as I have overcome every nightmare. I know my strength. No matter what, I will endure. As will Bas. You must let him discover his own strength and resolve."

Mereruka snatched his hand away, guilt twisting his features.

"I'm sorry, Taisiya, please forgive me. That was a monstrous thing to do." Setting aside his wine, he buried his head in his hands. "I feel like I'm not fit to be either a father or a husband of late. I've only failed in my duty to you both. When you needed it most, I was powerless to save either of you."

"I knew the risks, Meri. We both did. You'll learn and grow from this. It's the best any of us can do," Taisiya said as she stroked his thigh.

His laugh was as bitter as his expression.

"Speaking from your many, accumulated years of wisdom?"

It hadn't taken her long to learn what her husband feared most was not death—indeed, he was uncommonly brash and reckless. No, her wily husband feared he would have to watch another he loved die, powerless to stop it. She understood it, and him. It was why she could shrug off his foul anger. He didn't need someone to scold him, he needed her to be at his side so he could feel her heartbeat, to know she hadn't left him. He needed someone to make him smile, to turn his thoughts away from death and to remember that those he loved were still here, waiting for him.

Taisiya shrugged and tweaked his nose.

"Some of us are faster learners. Try to keep up."

He chuckled and pulled her close. She wrapped her arm around him, savouring the scent and feel of him. Mereruka was alive and whole, and so was she.

"My wise little wife."

"One of us should be."

"Oh?" She could hear the grin in his voice. "Then what does that make me?"

"Hmmm. The pretty one?" She trailed a finger down his chest. "Best keep in shape, husband. You wouldn't want my eyes to wander."

He shook from repressed laughter. Taisiya grinned into his chest and kissed the spot over his heart. When he could finally speak without snorting, he whispered in her ear.

"You're lucky they're sleeping in the bed. If we were alone, you wouldn't get a single moment of rest."

"Promise?" she taunted him.

He dipped his head down and kissed her, a gentle caress of his lips. When he pulled away, his eyes were sombre.

"I will help you overcome your fears, Taisiya. You won't do this alone."

She reached up and cradled his cheek in her palm.

"Neither will Bas. Neither will you, Meri. I will walk through fire by your side."

His lips quirked.

"Even if I'm a cruel, unreasonable bastard?"

"*Because* you're a cruel, unreasonable bastard." She smiled. "If you were anything but the man you are, I would have done away with you on the ship to Maat."

"Was that the plan?"

"One of many."

"Guess I got lucky."

Taisiya nodded. "Very. But then, so did I."

CHAPTER 58

Never before had Taisiya witnessed such an overwrought spectacle made of a funeral. Her family, and much of Lethe, kept their death rituals largely restrained, almost painfully so unless the person in question was royalty. Paid mourners might weep, but most were expected to remain solemn and dry-eyed. Not since her first few days in Maat, getting accustomed to all of the unfamiliar sights, scents and manners, had Taisiya been so jarred by the customs of her new home.

Mournful, cacophonous music preceded enormous, empty stone coffins chiselled and painted in the likenesses of each of the deceased. Commoners and nobles alike stood at a barely respectful distance, weeping and howling with grief, their clothes and appearances carelessly dishevelled. Taisiya had a front-row seat to the theatrics, walking as she was beside her own coffin, disguised as a professional mourner. Thankfully, Mereruka had woven an illusion over Taisiya, the feel of it like a too-thick, itchy blanket. To all who gazed upon her in this macabre parade, the image of a weeping woman pounding on her breasts, hair coated with dirt, her clothes torn, would meet their eyes. Mereruka and Bas were similarly covered, while Vasilisa hid in their shadows, deadly iron at the ready. She tried not to give too much attention to the coffin and the woman it depicted. It gave her chills, and a sense of ill-omen, to gaze upon it.

As the procession wound through the throngs of public mourners, Taisiya glanced up at their intended destination—Khety's palace. It was there that Khety would make a show of his grief for the eyes of the most important hatya and nomarchs within Maat. Had this been a true funeral, Khety would then lead the procession of the coffins across the Hapi and back to the same stone circle to offer up the bodies and attendant grave goods to the embrace of the forgotten gods.

It would never get that far. Khety would fall while he wept false tears over their immortalized stone visages. Vasilisa was to make the first strike, stabbing iron spikes into Khety's bird-like calves from the safety of the man's shadow. Once the king had been weakened, Mereruka and Taisiya would reveal themselves, make their accusations against Khety and deal the final blow. Serfka and Radjedef, similarly disguised, would see to their own business—one spiriting Betrest away, and the other putting a blade into the heart of whichever lackey Khety had installed in his position. Qar, Bas and Vasilisa's jobs were to protect Taisiya and Mereruka from any of Khety's supporters too zealous to understand that their patron's time was up.

Taisiya felt, rather than saw, Mereruka's fingers entwine with hers. She squeezed back.

This was their final gambit for the throne. She had to trust that they were suitably prepared. Qar and his soldiers would be present, ready to hold the bulk of the guards at bay if they betrayed Radjedef en masse. Nofret had given each of them rare and coveted teleportation charms she'd spent the better part of a day creating. The moment they were crushed or broken, the bearer would be whisked away. If they had to retreat, they could.

As they marched up the many steps to the palace, Taisiya tried to calm her racing heart. Instead of her usual dresses, she wore a simple, short tunic and the scaled armour of the fae. Enchanted leather braces protected her forearms and calves, her feet were shod in sturdy leather shoes, and her hair was braided and secured. Beneath it all, she wore another of her necklaces, this one more like golden armour than the delicate beaded creations she was used to, though just as effective in its protective purpose. If they survived, she would have to convince her husband to tattoo her thoroughly.

Despite the glacial pace of the procession, the receiving hall of the palace loomed large before them. Mereruka guided her along with him, a finger of his hooked with one of her own. Sick anticipation roiled her gut as the coffins were arrayed before Khety.

The first problem occurred as the retainers of the deceased attempted to enter the cavernous hall. Fae guards in all their glittering mail armour barred the door to Qar.

"No shapeshifters."

"That is my prince's sarcophagus there. You would bar me from attending his funeral?" Qar's voice was low but full of outrage.

"No. Shapeshifters," the guard replied, his sneer goading.

There was no way for the overseer of the soldiers to enter. They couldn't afford a grand deviation from the plan, nor could they lose the protection of Mereruka's soldiers. Qar took one of his men aside.

"Be sure to pay my respects to Prince Mereruka in my place. I won't be far."

The soldier nodded and was allowed entry by the guards at the door.

Qar stormed off, mourners fleeing in his wake. Taisiya's anxiety reached new heights. One valuable ally had been removed from their side of the playing board. Mereruka tugged her along. Arrayed near the coffins, their illusions continued to wail and scratch at their faces. As the last coffin was placed before the king, the howls of the professional mourners turned to low-pitched moans.

"I'm getting into position," Vasilisa whispered from the shadow at Taisiya's ear.

Khety stepped forward, his long white hair and clothes artfully dishevelled yet still glittering with jewels and gold, his crown still perched on his brow. Taisiya could almost appreciate the skill that went into the artifice. Gold eyeliner followed the line of crocodile tears down his orange skin, his icy blue eyes all the brighter for it. He knelt by the heads of the coffins and pressed his lips to the brows of each. When he spoke, his mournful, emotion-choked voice could be heard throughout the entire hall.

"My beloved family, lost to Maat in a single night. There has never been such a tragedy in all our realm's long history. I shall send my brothers and sisters into the arms of the forgotten gods, and build great monuments to honour their lives. But I shall also seek vengeance!" The bite of malice in that last word caught the assembly by surprise. Rapt, even the mourners fell silent. "For it was no accident, their deaths. It was murder! Our enemies in the witchlands to the north have conspired against Maat, using shapeshifters in their thrall to attack us."

Gasps and frenzied whispers raced through the funeral crowd.

"He's mad," Mereruka hissed.

"Meri?"

"Of all of Maat's nobles, only my household employs a large number of shapeshifters. He's trying to destroy anyone who ever supported me," Mereruka explained in a whisper. "Bas, break your charm. There is more danger to you in this crowd than you'll be able to handle."

"But—"

"No. Go and warn Qar and Nofret. Their lives might already be at risk."

"No. Something smells strange here. I'm not the only shapeshifter in this crowd," Bas replied.

Taisiya hadn't spotted anyone who appeared anything less than fae, though with glamour being what it was, that was no guarantee. Mereruka and Bas whispered heated arguments as Khety continued whipping up the crowd. Betrest stood behind her husband. Where Khety's appearance and grief were all pretence, Betrest's devastation and fear were unvarnished. She stared at Serfka's coffin with the eyes of a broken woman. Lost in her misery, she didn't notice the mourner approach her from behind.

Damn Serfka! He was going for her too soon. Taisiya tugged on Mereruka's hand to gain his attention, but it was too late. Serfka dispelled his glamour. Betrest gasped in shock and threw herself into his two sets of blue arms. Shouts interrupted Khety's speech, and hundreds of fingers pointed to the queen behind him. Serfka glared as Khety turned to face his faithless wife and revenant of a brother, his shock plain. With a sneer befitting a royal of Maat, Serfka snapped his own teleportation charm and vanished along with Betrest.

Radjedef was next, taking advantage of the frenzy and confusion to dispel his glamour. Soldiers cried out with shock and joy in the same moment the scaly, red fae rammed his sword into the gut of the man who'd replaced him. Radjedef whispered something in his victim's pointed ear, a savage grin on his face, the words lost in the chaos of the assembly. The soldiers mostly rallied to the side of their newly-returned prince, while others fled or fought him.

Taisiya was beginning to wonder when Vasilisa was finally going to attack Khety. Already the gathered crowd was fleeing or screaming. Taisiya grabbed hold of Mereruka so as not to lose him as the crowd began surging. Khety's guard were flinging people aside trying to get to their king, and away from Radjedef's soldiers, who had set upon them from behind.

"Vasilisa!" Taisiya cried out, hoping her friend could hear her above the din.

She had.

Khety let out an unearthly shriek. Any who weren't fleeing or fighting looked upon him and gasped.

The king of Maat had every spare patch of skin covered in glowing blue tattoos.

CHAPTER 59

Taisiya felt Mereruka and Bas' stillness beside her. The remnants of the funeral crowd seemed rooted to the spot. In a flash, Mereruka removed his mourner's glamour and hers.

"Khety, your day of reckoning has come!" He turned to the crowd, "For it was not witches or shapeshifters who killed Itet and tried to kill my brothers and me, but King Khety! Though iron and foul curses were used against us, the plot failed due to the bravery and ingenuity of my wife, Princess Consort Taisiya! Before the people of Maat, I demand vengeance, and claim my right to the throne!"

Fae parted as Taisiya and Mereruka stalked forward. Out of the corner of her eye, Bas' glamoured visage slipped into the stunned but retreating crowd. Only the royal guard wished to be nearby when a battle for the throne was imminent.

Khety howled in outrage, turning from Mereruka's smug grin. Why wasn't he convulsing with pain? Mereruka hadn't lasted more than a few seconds before the effects of the iron became apparent. Though Khety was panting, his brow slicked with sweat, he seemed caught in the grip of fury, not agony. He ripped the iron spike from his flesh and tossed it aside.

Mereruka stopped in his tracks. Taisiya took a step from him to ready her lightning. It was important that Mereruka strike Khety down, but not essential. When Khety took a step forward, Vasilisa, her hand reaching out from Khety's shadow, jabbed another spike into his other leg.

With swiftness no one expected, Khety gripped Vasilisa's smoky black arm and dragged her from the void into the light of day, his blue eyes seething. He crushed her wrist in his talons and raked those of his free hand across her throat, spilling bright red blood over the coffins at his bird-like feet.

"Vasilisa!" Taisiya cried, lunging forward.

Mereruka held her back.

Eyes wild, Khety's cruel grin stretched across his tattooed face as he watched Taisiya's panic. It was enough of a distraction.

Launching silently from behind, his glamour gone, Bas cleaved the king's winged arm in two with a long blade, dragging Vasilisa's limp body from his grip as he dove past. Khety shrieked again, the sound piercing Taisiya's ears. Khety collapsed to the floor between two coffins. When Bas landed, Vasilisa's body in his arms, he nodded solemnly. Charm between his fingers, he snapped it in half, transporting them both away.

Khety ripped the second iron spike from his leg and tossed it aside. Taisiya saw red. She wanted to bathe in his damned blood. Lightning crackled across every inch of her skin. The small, rational part of her that remained wondered how he had any strength after being impaled by iron and losing a limb. As crimson flowed from his gory wound, Taisiya smiled, the beast in her heart rising to the fore. Mereruka gathered magic in his hands, ready to strike.

"Tell Mother I sent you," Mereruka growled.

Mereruka unleashed a sharp strand of magic as if throwing a spear. It hurtled towards Khety, aimed for his heart.

Then it crashed into the floor, shattering stone and tossing the coffins aside with the force.

Khety was gone.

"*Where?!*" Taisiya shrieked.

She wanted to tear the monster limb from bloody limb, sink her teeth into his neck, scorch his innards with her lightning. She would pluck out his gods-damned eyes and feed them to the fucking pigs. Eyes darting, she searched for her quarry.

Mereruka shoved Taisiya aside with brutal force. Taisiya skidded across the floor. A sword was raised against her, one of the king's guards, very much worse for the wear, pointing it at her with clear intent. She released a bolt of lightning straight into his heart and leapt to her feet as he flew backwards with the force. Another of the king's guard broke through the melee with Qar and Radjedef's soldiers, a string of magic between her fingers. Taisiya didn't hesitate. Lightning travelled faster than the woman's spell, killing her in an instant. Taisiya's eyes roamed the rest of the hall. The nobles had fled, mourners too, leaving only those armed with spells and blades to fight. As she raced through the hall, dodging soldiers and striking down any of the guards who came within sight, she searched for Mereruka.

A shadow passed overhead.

Instinct propelled Taisiya's gaze to the ceiling. Caught in Khety's grip, the talons of the king's feet pierced Mereruka's arm. Flown about like a ragdoll by an uninjured Khety, Mereruka traded spells and counter-spells in mid-flight, his blood falling like rain.

Trapped on the ground below, lightning surged inside her, seeking an outlet. Taisiya itched to place a bolt of lightning into Khety's heart, yet she stayed her hand. What killed Khety would also kill her husband, so long as the two were touching. The second the king dropped Mereruka, she would have her chance.

"Radjedef!" Taisiya commanded.

Radjedef sliced his way through the thinning throngs, a grin of feral delight on his face.

"How is this possible?" She pointed at Khety.

"He's part shapeshifter!" Radjedef replied, sword cutting through another throat.

"How do I kill him?" she asked, heart clenching.

"Destroy his heart and cut off his head."

After what he'd done, she would relish it.

"Protect me, and be ready to act on my command."

Mereruka concentrated on deflecting his brother's spells and flinging his own. His hair tangled with Khety's talons, the magic thrumming through it no match for Khety's unbreakable grip. It was all he could do as he waited for his arm to be torn apart. Only the echoing thunder of his wife's lightning assured him she still lived.

"Bloody revenant! Just die!"

"You first, shapeshifter!"

If only he'd known Khety's shameful little secret, it never would have come to this. Vasilisa would still be alive. His wife wouldn't be in danger below.

Khety's father had been a shapeshifter.

Nothing else could explain his ability to shrug off the effects of iron poisoning, his new arm, his disappearance into smoke, or his obscene number of tattoos. Khety didn't have nearly as much in the way of innate magics as Mereruka, hence the tattoos, but he made up for it by being twice as hard to kill. No matter how grievous the injury, so long as a shapeshifter's heart still beat and their head remained attached, they could recover by turning to smoke and reforming themselves.

"You'll tire first! When that happens, I'll tear you apart!"

"Will that be before or after Serfka fucks your wife?"

Khety swiped his other foot at Mereruka, missing his eye by a hair. Mereruka's teeth clenched as agony ripped through him. Flesh tore and bone cracked anew in Khety's merciless grip. Mereruka saw stars, his gorge rising, his strength and magic failing. Better to lose an arm than his life. But he had to get Khety angry enough to actually tear his arm off. He had no doubt Taisiya was watching for him, a bolt of lightning at the ready. He needed his brother to drop him.

"At least someone will give the poor woman children! You were too afraid your spawn would come out more shifter than fae and reveal your parentage, weren't you? Pathetic!"

They traded another round of spells. He tried to sever Khety's legs, to free himself, but the king could shift between forms in the blink of an eye. Khety's rage was making him sloppy, but blood loss would kill Mereruka faster. As his head swam, he hurled another round of insults.

"It's why Mother was going to choose Serfka over you! You weren't fae enough to measure up to her standards, or anyone else's! If you were bloodthirsty enough to kill her for it, you shouldn't have stopped until all of Maat was awash in the blood of bigots. But you've always been a coward! *Poor little faeling!* Covering yourself in tattoos, and still you'll never be good enough!"

"Good enough to end you!" Khety shrieked.

Khety's reaching talons would gouge out his eyes this time. Mereruka reached up to protect his head with his free arm. Khety snatched it, his talons piercing muscle and crunching bone. Mereruka howled with pain. Khety's grin was manic. Still in flight, the king gripped his arms tight and began pulling, slowly shredding sinew. Black spots formed at the corners of Mereruka's eyes. Khety seemed content to torture him to death slowly in mid-air.

Fool.

"I've always hated your ugly feet!" Mereruka groaned between gritted teeth.

With the last of his strength, he sent his magic into his hair. The long violet threads struck out like vipers. Made sharper than a blade, the strands cut clean through Khety's ankles, succeeding where his spells had failed.

As Mereruka fell, he watched his brother become smoke and reform, whole again. Khety dove towards him, his talons a mere hairsbreadth from Mereruka's face, blind to anything but his own rage.

Mereruka grinned.

Searing heat sizzled across Mereruka's face and chest. A blinding light flashed before his eyes, and a second later, a deafening crack rent the air. Khety no longer faced him, and his precipitous fall slowed. He wouldn't have his brains dashed across the stone floor today. Another three lightning strikes later, the room quieted. Though his landing was soft, the agony of his ruined arms had him gasping.

"Healer." He winced.

Radjedef stared down at him. A thread of fear constricted his heart. Would Radjedef kill him in his weakened state? Catching the direction of his thoughts, Radjedef grinned. He leaned down and reached over to his arms. Khety's talons still perforated him. Radjedef took his sweet time pulling them out, one by one, as Mereruka bit back screams.

"Luckily for you, I've healed my fair share of battle wounds." Radjedef's yellow eyes were all mischief.

Radjedef's soldiers, standing guard, grimaced in sympathy.

Magic, tasting of vile sewage, made Mereruka gag. By the time his arms were whole, Mereruka's gut roiled. He turned to his side and emptied his stomach. Radjedef laughed, slapping his back. One of the soldiers passed Mereruka a skein of liquid. Mereruka sniffed, surreptitiously using a spell to check for poison. He hadn't come this far just to be brought low by a nameless nobody. Once he was convinced it was safe, he drank greedily. It washed away the taste of Radjedef's magic and sickness, leaving only a fresh flavour in his mouth.

"What are you doing to my husband?" Taisiya asked, her voice like the crack of a whip.

Soldiers parted and bowed. In her hand, she gripped a rope of long, white hair fouled by blood. It was attached to Khety's severed head.

"Fixing him," Radjedef replied.

Taisiya looked Mereruka over, satisfied. Then she raised her prize, presenting it to him.

"A gift, husband."

"You always did know the way to my heart," Mereruka quipped, standing on unsteady feet.

He took her proffered gift, holding it by the hair. Triumph swirled in his gut. Khety was finally dead. Mereruka finally had the power to protect those he loved, to ensure by all the power of Maat that those he claimed as his own would never again suffer at his brother's hands. Turning to Taisiya and seeing the brittleness in her amethyst eyes, he remembered that his success had not come without cost.

"I want a cloak of his fucking feathers. After what he did to Vasilisa, he died too easily."

Mereruka tossed the head aside like so much rotten meat and reached for her. He desperately wished he could hold her, to comfort her, but electricity sparked across every inch of her skin, her grief overwhelming her. She closed her eyes, gritting her teeth as she battled for control of her magic. Sorrow choked him—choked them both. Another loved one he hadn't been able to save.

"Can I have a matching one?" a hoarse feminine voice asked.

Taisiya whirled around. Vasilisa. Her complexion was ashen and a thick, pink line crossed her throat. Mereruka's heart leapt. Bas supported her, a grin on his face. Tears streamed down Taisiya's face and her breath came out on a shaky, pained exhale. She took a step towards Vasilisa, her hand reaching out as if she couldn't quite trust her eyes and yet couldn't contain her hope. Vasilisa's lip trembled and she opened her arms in welcome. The lightning dancing across her skin quelled. Taisiya launched herself at Vasilisa and Bas. The three went down in a heap of hysterical giggles and choked sobs.

"You're not allowed to die!" Taisiya sobbed.

"Don't cry on your coronation day, I didn't bring your makeup." Vasilisa smiled, hugging her close.

"I'm a queen now. I'll cry if I want!" she sniffed, burying her head in Vasilisa's shoulder. Taisiya looked up and pulled Bas' head towards her, planting a kiss on his dark hair. "Thank you," she said, her voice solemn and fierce.

Bas wrapped his arms around them both.

Mereruka was about to join his family, but slowly, nobles came out of hiding and chanced glances into the hall from the rooms beyond, surveying the damage. Khety's body lay headless, a blackened hole burned through his chest where his heart would have been.

Radjedef sighed.

"And so the cycle continues," he muttered, taking a knee.

Radjedef's soldiers followed suit. Vasilisa wiped Taisiya's tears. Bas helped Vasilisa to kneel as Mereruka took his wife by the hand to stand at his side. Their family reunion would need to wait. They had a throne to claim.

"All kneel before your new rulers, King Mereruka and Queen Taisiya! May they bring order and plenty to Maat!" Radjedef called out.

Hatya, nomarchs, scribes, servants and more knelt and repeated after Radjedef. Taisiya squeezed Mereruka's hand, her eyes sparkling with tears of joy. He lifted her fingers to his lips.

"I told you I would make you queen."

She smirked.

"I made myself queen. I'm just allowing you along for the ride."

Mereruka laughed and swept her up in a fierce kiss. Lifting her into his arms, he walked her to the thrones. As he stepped through pools of blood, over the bodies of their enemies, he'd never felt such triumph. Khety was dead. His remaining siblings were bound and leashed. There was no one left to stand in his way, to make him a wretched supplicant or a powerless pawn. He was king. And it was all thanks to the wicked, lovely woman in his arms. Mereruka put her on the queen's seat and sat down in the king's. This was where they belonged—where they'd always belonged. And now, Maat was theirs to mould into whatever they pleased, its riches theirs to dispense with, her rivals theirs to manipulate into ruin. He could hardly wait.

Mereruka surveyed the kneeling crowd and bade them to stand.

"As my first command, I—"

He gasped, hand flying to his chest, his nails biting into his breast as his heart stuttered in agony. Taisiya's head whipped to face him, her eyes wide.

"Meri?"

The taste of wine flooded his mouth. Sinister magic reached into his soul and cracked it in two.

Chapter 60

"Meri? What—"

Mereruka turned to her, hands clenching his chest, eyes panicked.

"Run," he hissed.

Magic, ugly and foul, made her skin crawl, a sensation she'd never before experienced. Taisiya stood and backed away, reluctant to leave him. Pink peach blossoms and pale yellow skin caught her eye. Hiding behind the king's throne, crouched and muttering, was Hemetre. Taisiya rounded on her, a blade of lightning at the ready.

"Ah, ah, ah, little witch," Hemetre taunted, her green eyes sparkling with zeal. "Interrupt this, and he'll die."

The clank of armour and weapons approached the throne.

"Stay back!" Taisiya screamed, fearing the concubine spoke the truth.

Hemetre's hands spun the grains of a dark cloud into a familiar form. When at last the terrible spell was complete, and the feel of repellent magic abated, Hemetre stood. Cradled in her hands was a small, stylized jar with the head of a man. Citrine eyes, teal skin and violet hair—Meri.

"Careful where you point your blade, Your Most Just. If any harm comes to this, then His Eternal Serenity will follow Khety."

"Hemetre!"

The woman smiled and followed Mereruka's voice, turning her back on Taisiya.

"Yes, Your Eternal Serenity?"

Taisiya followed her around the thrones and stuttered to a stop. A stranger sat in her husband's seat, yet used his voice.

"Do I have you to thank for this happy turn of events?" Not-Mereruka asked.

He had her husband's eyes, and yet they weren't his. He used her husband's voice, but none of his affectations. He wore her husband's physique, but all in the wrong colours. Oppressive power radiated from him, along with a terrible beauty.

Radjedef swore and ordered his soldiers back. Despite her protests, Bas pulled Vasilisa behind cover.

"No thanks are necessary. I believe you will give me what Khety could not," Hemetre replied, still cradling the jar.

"And what is that, soul weaver?" he asked, turning predator as he stalked towards her.

Hemetre only smiled while Taisiya flinched, truth dawning on her. Hemetre had torn her husband's soul apart. Was that his feeling heart in her hands? She had to get it back. Had to put it back into her Meri.

"Chaos. You will destroy Maat. Without limitations..." Hemetre wiggled the jar in her hand. "Your greed and ambition will devour Maat. Finally, the Hapi will flow, free of Maat's control. Oblivion's fae will never die of iron poisoning again."

Mereruka laughed, the joyless sound sending a shiver down her spine.

"Utopia," Mereruka's mouth stretched into a cruel grin, "is a tale for children and fools. Was it you who poisoned Khety's mind all this time?"

She nodded her head, smile serene.

"He was ever so fond of his wine. And so easily turned against his scheming siblings."

"And Nefertnesu?"

Hemetre shrugged.

"Would have opened her pretty mouth about her lost soul weaver. She more than earned her death when she refused to give my mother even a drop of the Hapi."

Something almost resembling affection touched his cold eyes. He reached out his hands to cup Hemetre's face.

"If only you could be made to submit. The realms we could burn."

"I knew my fate when I walked into this damned palace. Do it then, King Mereruka. Let my death herald the end of Maat."

His grip turned punishing and tight on Hemetre's head, his eyes wild as the concubine squeezed hers shut.

"Not the end, you ugly little weed, but the beginning of a golden age. Maat will be an empire!"

He snapped her neck and dropped her body to the floor, the jar rolling about near his feet. Staring out at the fae who had dared to remain, his face lit with glee. He swaggered forward to address them. Taisiya kept her eyes on his soul.

"My first order as king of Maat is to raise Oblivion's greatest army!" Power, thick and oppressive, swirled at his fingertips. Dead soldiers and guards shambled to their feet, listing from side to side, weapons in their bloodless hands. Khety's headless corpse shuffled to the front. "Composed of the living and the dead! It seems my dear brother will finally oversee a successful battle. He shall be braver in death than he was in life."

Sensing his distraction, Taisiya dove for Mereruka's jar, snatching it before the thing that had become her husband could stop her.

As she rolled away from him, her chest hurt. She held a piece of his heart, his soul, in her hands, and it did strange things to her own heart as she beheld it. This small, stylized depiction of her teal-skinned husband stared at her with unblinking citrine eyes, and she could feel his love, his joy, his teasing mischievousness, his warm-hearted compassion, wrap around her. And yet it was not wholly him. Because only a few paces from her stood another man, this one with red-brown skin, impossibly glossy black hair and the wicked part of her husband's citrine eyes. There lay his cunning mind, his cruel brilliance, his swaggering overconfidence, his violent whims. No matter which she looked at, both were wrong and incomplete, like a complex tapestry torn asunder.

If she were to make him whole again, she couldn't hesitate, couldn't waver. Mereruka had said he'd hoped to repair Nefertnesu's heart by making her accept it back. She didn't know what that entailed, but she had to try. She must be Taisiya Dragonsblood, vicious and implacable Queen of Maat, not Taisiya, beloved wife of Meri, fragile heart breaking the longer she stared at this stranger. She stood, straightening her spine, holding the jar that contained her husband's feeling heart with a death grip. If the one before her held the whole of her husband's follies, she had to wield them against him like a weapon. He would try to strike her down, and then he would be made to submit.

"I had forgotten about you, my homely little wife."

"Then you have erred, husband."

"Give me the jar, Taisiya."

"No."

He lashed out with his magic, a great, tempestuous blast of blue-green auroras, menacing enough to swallow her whole. It died mere inches from her face. Bewildered, he struck out again. The magic failed to reach her.

"Did you, perhaps, try to kill me?"

"What have you done to me?!" he snarled.

"I have done nothing other than accept your oaths... over the heart of my ancestor."

Something like fear widened his eyes, gone in an instant. Taisiya tasted his magic on her tongue, his face growing more handsome by the second. His eyes dazzled her, like sparkling jewels. She wanted to run her fingers through his thick, silken hair, her tongue along his flawless, dark skin. Stepping forward, her grip on the jar loosened. Taisiya was ready to give him what he desired, her magnetic, handsome husband. She'd fought long and hard enough. Let her sink to her knees to worship him. Never before had her senses beheld such a man. Never before had she been so bewitched by beauty. Didn't she deserve a chance to surrender, to live a life of easy subservience?

"Taisiya! Stop!"

"Don't!"

He turned his face from her and glared into the crowd, who had retreated behind pillars for cover. It broke the spell for only a moment. He gathered magic at his fingertips, his hatred aimed at Vasilisa and Bas. The bodies of the dead turned as one, their weapons raised, an army yoked to his sinister will.

"Run! Now!" Taisiya shouted.

Vasilisa, perceiving the threat before Bas, latched onto him and snapped her teleportation charm just as a lethal blast would have struck them. Taisiya stepped back, shaking her head. Fucking fae magic! When he tried to work his magic on her again, she let a small current flicker over the jar, praying it wouldn't kill him. He seized his chest with a gasp. The taste disappeared from her tongue. His army stilled, as frozen as he.

"If you even twitch your magic in my direction, I'll destroy this." Taisiya's voice was soft but no less menacing.

"No, you won't," he hissed, trying to get to his feet.

"I will."

"Liar!"

"Are you willing to test me?"

"You would die shortly after. No one would accept a lone mage as queen of Maat! Even now my court watches, waiting to strike."

She had no doubt of that. Were she one of the hatya or nomarchs in attendance, this one moment of weakness would be all it would take to seize control. Or so they thought. She grinned then, as cruelly as he, and adjusted her grip on the jar so that she could place a hand on her belly.

"I would not sit on the throne alone." She let her words sink in. "And both the royal guard and vizier are mine, dear husband. They pledged their loyalty to me alone. I have no need of you now."

He launched another failed volley of magic at her and cursed. Lunging, his hands grazed the skin of her throat, ready to choke the life from her where his magic could not. Taisiya narrowed her eyes as she dodged him, letting a stronger current ripple across his jar. He was brought to his knees, gasping from the pain. The moment he tried to stand, she brought him low again.

"You won't kill me," he hissed between his teeth, a shallow-breathed chuckle whisper-soft. "You love me."

Taisiya kicked him over so that he lay sprawled on the floor at her feet. She glared down at him with every ounce of hatred she could muster for the monster before her.

"I am Taisiya Dragonsblood, heir of my line and queen of Maat. The man I love rests in the palm of my hand. You are nothing more than a malevolent shadow possessing his body and wearing his skin. You have broken your oath to me, Mereruka of Maat, and will now accept whatever punishment I deem fit."

He tried to tackle her to the ground, but found himself bound by scaly chains, his movements hampered. The ghoulish soldiers fell to the ground, inert. He howled in outrage and glared at her with utter loathing. Taisiya smiled, burying her heart under a sea of ice, where it might never see the light of day again. Not if she lost this gamble.

"Never let it be said that I am not fair. Repair the damage to your soul, or accept death by my hands."

"Don't you know, wife? Only a kiss of true love can return my heart to me."

Radjedef snorted.

"Liar. He just needs to say he wants it put back," Radjedef offered.

"I will skin you alive, you scaly red freak! I'll cut off your horns and force them down your fucking throat!"

Taisiya slapped Mereruka hard enough that the sound echoed in the throne room.

"Say the words, husband. Death... or life?"

He looked at the jar with revulsion and then up into her pitiless stare. She whispered so that only he could hear.

"As you are, you're useless to me. A rabid dog who has already given me what I need to rule in my own right. With Vasilisa in the shadows, Qar and Nofret by my side and Bas there to watch over the child, I believe my future will be *quite* comfortable. Maybe I'll even start my own harem..."

Mereruka growled low and lunged again, fuming and powerless. He muttered darkly.

"What was that, husband? I couldn't hear you," she goaded, her heart in her throat.

"I want my heart back, you vile harpy! Put that gods-damned *thing* into my fucking—"

He gasped as the jar became rosy golden sand, its grains sinking back into his body. Taisiya didn't dare hope, not yet. She wouldn't let it sneak between the cracks in her heart until he was her Meri again. She returned the pained, shocked look of the man before her with steely determination, fighting the urge to drop to her knees and beg the gods for her husband's return. As the last of the grains of sand left her hands, the moment of truth was upon her.

Between one blink and the next, Mereruka was himself—whole.

Her breath shuddered as her walls cracked. Taisiya's gambit had succeeded. She needed to cry and laugh and scream all at once. Mereruka was back—*her* Meri. There was her husband, his towering ego, his sly cunning, his protective warmth, his love—the love she couldn't breathe without.

He stared at his teal hands in wonder and then up at her, adoration suffusing his features. She'd never known a heart could break from happiness. Or that it would be her own.

"Thank the gods you're a ruthless bitch."

Taisiya threw herself at him. Mereruka caught her as they hit the floor, their lips meeting in a fierce tangle of tongues. Radjedef ordered bodies removed and soldiers out of the hall, giving them a small measure of privacy.

"Don't cry, Taisiya," Mereruka whispered as he wiped a few errant tears. "Else your brother might come for my head with his merry band of hardened killers."

Taisiya choked on a laugh and kissed him again.

"We should tell Vasilisa and Bas that all is well." She pulled away reluctantly, their foreheads touching.

Mereruka nodded.

"And get this funeral business sorted."

"And get Maat in order," Taisiya sighed.

Mereruka's eyes lingered on her waist.

"Are you really pregnant?"

"No. I lied."

Mereruka laughed and helped her stand.

"Well, let's change that, you beautiful liar," he purred.

"Villain," she teased.

"Villainess."

"My beloved."

"Always."

"Promise?" she asked.

His grin was mischievous, but his eyes were sincere.

"For you, my love, always and forever."

Epilogue

It was good to be queen.

With a crown securely on her head and the last grumbles of a few discontented hatya silenced forever, Taisiya was left with only a few loose ends to see to. It was merely unfortunate that such loose ends lay within Lethe. And that these loose ends in particular were proving especially elusive.

That was what she got for trying to find a slippery light mage.

As she scratched out a missive on the papyrus before her, the calls of gulls and music of Rhacotis drifted through her window. Meri had been right. A few months since crowning themselves king and queen of Maat, and Rhacotis felt like, if not home, then more familiar than she'd imagined. Her study was decorated in purple and gold, dragons and images of her ancestors playing out heroic feats along the walls. The light of the enchanted ceiling precluded the need for sconces and oil lamps. She had found she sometimes missed the scent of something smoky and had taken to burning incense when homesickness struck. There'd been less and less of that, especially now that her kingdom was safe enough for family to visit.

Not that she was ever truly alone here in her new home.

"Come, love. It's time to rest."

Mereruka, her king, leaned against the doorway, an affectionate light in his smile. Today he wore a splendid kilt of blinding white with golden thread glinting in the light, along with his customary jeweled collar necklace and golden sandals. But the crown atop his head was new, one they'd fashioned together. Gone were the bird's wings to frame his handsome face. In their place, dragon's wings.

He was altogether too handsome.

"I've important business to tend to first," she said, refusing him.

"More important than the duties of a queen to her king?" he asked suggestively, amused tolerance raising his violet brow.

Taisiya kept her expression admirably neutral. Since they'd taken their thrones, they'd been rather diligent in the pursuit of heirs. Sometimes her husband convinced her to spend whole days dedicated to...her duties. Though he tempted her sorely, she should not leave her current task off much longer.

"Quite."

"Then perhaps we can find a way to do both at the same time." He stalked towards her with a determined look in his eyes and leaned over to whisper in her ear. "I want to hear you scream my name."

"Leave us," Taisiya commanded the servants attending her. One by one they slipped out of the room. An aurora-like tendril of her husband's magic closed the door behind them.

"You're getting rather brazen with your little displays, husband."

"And you're becoming rather proficient at concealing your blush. Pity."

He turned her chair to the side, knelt down at her feet, and slid the fabric of her gauzy gown up and up.

"Go on then. Keep working."

"You expect me to—"

"Didn't you say it was important?" he asked, kissing her inner thighs as he crept higher and higher.

"I couldn't possibly—"

"Oh, but you should." He smiled, citrine eyes glinting merrily. "Tell me what fresh schemes you have in mind, my love."

Meri yanked her hips forward so that she was precariously balanced on the edge of her seat. As he opened her thighs to his hungry gaze, heat rushed up her chest and neck. Mereruka chuckled.

"My wife is the loveliest hypocrite in Maat."

Or perhaps she merely enjoyed this game between them, the indifferent wife in need of a coaxing from her eager husband. Perhaps she should have worn undergarments today though, if the look in his eyes was any indication of his plans. No doubt he would torment her mercilessly for hours. So much for work.

"And you're a cruel tease."

"You wound me."

"I see no injuries."

"Such cheek."

"Says the idler."

He smiled then, wicked and sensual. The violet strands of his hair wrapped around her thighs, forcing her to bare herself to him shamelessly. An aurora of his magic coalesced, taking on an uncommon solidness as it slid along her wet core.

"Go on then. Tell me what is so very important, my love."

"L-loose ends, ah!" she cried out as more of his magic snaked out and rubbed along her nipples.

"Oh? Do go on," he said lightly, replacing his magic with his fingers, sliding one, then two, inside her, stroking her to distraction.

"The ritual," she panted as he brought her close to the edge. But she knew from experience that he would not satisfy her so easily.

"Ah, yes, I recall. What of it?"

"S-someone else, ah, kn-knew about it. Meri!" she whimpered.

His tongue scalded her. Her hands flew to his head, begging for more.

"And? How do you plan to deal with them?" he asked, pausing his tongue-lashing for the space of a few breaths.

"H-hunt her down. O-offer a life of servitude here in Maat or a swift death."

"So ruthless," he mused. "Why offer anything at all?" he asked, bending his head back to his task.

"She's intelligent. Ah! Meri! Please!"

He brought her close to the peak and let her dangle there, no doubt savouring her pleas for mercy. Taisiya might have given him a taste of her lightning, but for the knowledge that the release he would give her would be greater than any torment he inflicted on her in the process.

"She must be quite special to go to the effort," he said, replacing his tongue with his magic on her oversensitive bud.

Maddening.

Her husband was utterly maddening.

Taisiya relinquished herself to his sweet torture, praying to the forgotten gods he would give her what she needed soon.

And yet such release didn't come. Meri heightened her pleasure and then retreated, bringing her close again and again, only to deny her.

"Meri! Meri, please! Please!"

"You didn't tell me about this mage of yours," he replied, seemingly unaffected by her state.

"She created the original ritual. Deciphered it from an ancient language." The words flew from her lips.

"Ah, now I understand. Well, that wasn't so hard, was it? And I got to see you blush. I suppose that deserves a reward."

He bent his head down and took her over the edge with his tongue, stars blinking behind her lids as molten ecstasy hummed through her veins.

By the time the last of the aftershocks had coursed through her and her heart no longer galloped in her chest, Taisiya was left limp.

"You're a cruel bastard," she croaked.

"Is that the thanks I get for demonstrating my devotion?" he asked, though his accusation held no heat.

"You're entirely unaffected by the mess you've made of me." Taisiya glared, though the look held no true anger.

She wanted him to be undone too. And she was far from finished with him.

"Then perhaps I should show you just how wrong you are."

In moments, he swept her out of her chair and bent her over her desk, scattering ink and papyrus across the floor. As he slid his hard length into her, giving them both what they desperately sought, Taisiya's eye caught on the name of her quarry written in still-drying ink as the papyrus floated down to the ground.

Illustra Hypatia Bright.

"How dare you get distracted," he growled, sending a shiver down her spine.

"I suppose you'll have to do a better job of capturing my attention," she goaded him.

"Don't think I won't make you beg," he said, thrusting deeper.

Her breath caught as her own crown tumbled from her head, following the papyrus and ink bottles.

"I dare you to try." She smiled.

"Your wish. My command," he whispered in her ear, nipping at the lobe.

When Mereruka had Taisiya panting and pleading once more, she supposed loose ends could wait. For now, villainy played second fiddle to her husband's loving attentions. From this day until her last, this was the only reason for which she would beg—her husband's touch—and never again for wealth, or status, or power.

When she saw stars once more, Meri followed her into sensual bliss.

"Rest up, my queen. The day is young," he purred in her ear.

Yes, it was *very* good to be queen.

I hope you've enjoyed Taisiya and Mereruka's story, but the adventure is far from over. A villainess' work is never done, and there's a loose end that needs trimming. Find out what happens when a runaway scholar meets a brooding warrior in the next installment of the *Mages of Oblivion* series, *Isles of Corruption!* Get your copy here: https://books2read. com/ioc

Craving a peek at Taisiya's latest scheme? Sign up to my newsletter for a bonus epilogue to find out what happens when she returns to Lethe for a visit: https://twolaurelspress.eo.page/jpchy

To learn more about my books and other series I'm working on, check out my website here: https://www.elysethomson.com/

Thanks so much for reading, and don't forget to leave a review! http s://linktr.ee/elysethomson

Book Links

Afterword

From the bottom of my heart, thank you for coming on this journey with me. As a child, I would watch the same handful of documentaries on ancient Egypt that aired every summer, shunning the sun for the ancient past. As an adult, I had the privilege to study it in university, and the luck to marry into a family of talented scholars who aided in my continuing education. Conspirators' Kingdom felt like a dream come true to write. I hope it has been equally fun to read.

As you may or may not know, reviews are the lifeblood of any author's career, especially those just starting out. I would be honoured if you could leave a few words about your experience reading my book on Goodreads, Amazon or wherever else you purchased my book.

If you're not ready to say goodbye to Taisiya and her scheming quite yet, you can get signed up for my newsletter and read the bonus epilogue for Conspirators' Kingdom! Other newsletter goodies include my prequel novella, *The Firetongue Heir*. The ebook is free for newsletter subscribers and available to purchase in paperback form.

You can also check out the first book in the *Mages of Oblivion* series, *Poisoned Empire*. https://linktr.ee/elysethomson

Book Links

Acknowledgements

No book is made without the love and support of a great many people. Conspirators' Kingdom was no different. I have so many people to thank. Paulina and Sophia, for being the first to love it. Alex, for being my rock through the whole whirlwind journey. My family; Mom, Dad, Sylvia, Ross, Kyle, Garrett and Jen for never doubting me. The book club beta reader ladies Edie, Sharron, Karen, Shelley and Susan for being my cheerleaders. The best writing friends a girl could have (with a group name so lackluster, it doesn't bear repeating) Paulina, Sophia, Rachel, Asha, Rebecca and Shirley. You kept me sane and gave me a place to belong. My life is richer for having known all of you. And finally, my friends in Pitch'n'Bitch, you always make me smile.

Special thanks to my amazing editor, Rachel Le Mesurier, my talented map maker Alec McKinley and my lovely cover designer, Maria Spada.

About the Author

Elyse Thomson is the pen-name of an author, bookbinder and self-proclaimed hermit residing in Canada's capital. She writes escapist fantasy with daring heroines, magical mayhem, swoon-worthy romance and court intrigue. Having graduated from University of Toronto with a Bachelors in History and Classics, she is delighted to bring her love of all things ancient to her work. When not writing, she's restoring antiquarian books for a select group of clients, playing video games, or snuggling up with either her husband or her neurotic terrier, Freya.

Also By

Mages of Oblivion Series

The Firetongue Heir
Poisoned Empire
Conspirators' Kingdom
Isles of Corruption

Cycle of Calamity Series

The Starlight Princess
The Oracle of Dusk
The Midnight King
...and more to come.

Book Links

www.ingramcontent.com/pod-product-compliance
Lightning Source LLC
Chambersburg PA
CBHW061049210726
48294CB00001B/76